The Mooch, the Thief, the Liar & the Manic

Plus Other Collected Words

Brendon Kolodziej

ISBN: 1503213226
ISBN 13: 9781503213227

"Lay not up for yourself treasures upon Earth, where moth and rust doth corrupt, and where thieves break through and steal: But lay up for yourselves treasures in heaven, where neither moth nor rust doth corrupt, and where thieves do not break through nor steal: For where your treasure is, there will your heart be also" (Matthew 6:19-21).

Contents

Thank you to my parents, family, friends (Jake T. and Jeff F.), and Kevin D. for helping me design the front cover.

The Mooch, the Thief, the Liar

& the Manic

I

The Departure

After utilizing my hypothetical beak to penetrate the walls of the hypothetical egg that encased me, I emerged out onto my feet, and suddenly for the first time in my life I found that I had the will to survive. Tirelessly from my third-story window I watched, balancing on the threshold between darkness and dawn, as the cold, lingering night that gaps the days dragged on and on. Then, at the five o'clock hour, moments before the sun was set to rise and cast sweet warmth to the outside, I opened my window ever so gently, so as to not wake the sleeping bodies around me, and proceeded to shimmy my way down the gutter and out onto the dew-soaked lawn. A sharp divide of dark blue and a distant yellow light soon appeared and expanded across the capacious sky, swirling with strange, golden colors and calling me away from my home.

It was the morning of my departure, the departure from the one place where I had resided for so long and all that I ever really knew. The exodus from the dreary and mundane sights I had been so hopelessly bound to cast my vision upon for eighteen years. When I left that morning, the first thing I decided to do was venture to a shady spot kissed by the lips of amorous nature to sit and begin my legacy, to sit and summon all the words of my language and tell a tale reflective of my feelings and as timeless as any great novel from Gatsby to Jane Eyre. I knew I had it in me. I had the mind of a writer, as my peers would say, and it was about time I had put it to use.

It was the start of June, 1965—the summer between my graduating year of high school and my soon-to-be freshman year of college. Destined to be shipped off overseas come the fall, and after having earned myself a prestigious scholarship, just like my brother and father and his father before him, I was to be an Oxford man. Oh, how my paternal side had molded me in his image... and how pitiful it was! Yet, it was safe to say that I was more than grateful to be given the opportunity at hand: the gift of a boundless education and the chance to expand my knowledge to grand new heights. But all this was for the future; right then, that morning, the start of something wonderful had surely begun. The summer was to be mine and mine alone. I wanted to leave this tired town for good, having finally reached the point where my aching mind had sustained all it could bare of the inescapable redundancy and stagnation of a lifeless suburbia. Certainly both by foot and by wheel, I was going to make my way out of the waning south and venture north to where my uncle Sebastian had a quaint little cabin rightfully hidden in the woods of Wisconsin. And since I had finally gotten my own car—a thoroughly used 1955 Chrysler Imperial which was an unexpected gift for my seventeenth birthday—any destination, acceptable or not, seemed to be within reach. All I was bringing with me were the clothes that I packed, the clothes on my back, and a map I picked up at the drug store. And so, on the roads or in the woods, or to wherever my journey happened to take me, it was quite certain that all along the way I was going to be continuously working on my legacy. I had no clue what was in store for me or what arduous obstacles it might have to face. I knew in my mind though, that all is a lot easier said than done.

I had lived my entire life in Athens, Georgia. There the reckless extravagance of youth and Rock & Roll was a thriving energy that pulsed outside my windows and down the streets of my hometown. There houses seemed to beam with vitality instead of sinking into the ground like headstones. It was as good a town as any to try and live a life. Regardless of my prior bitching and depreciation of the place where I had grown up, my childhood was one of ceaseless joy, my family was whole and nurturing, and my friends were closer to me than my own skin. But all of my life I had this unbearable urge for changes, and I was plagued by a sinister boredom that never seemed to dissipate. It followed me everywhere and showed itself through everyone, so much so that I could hardly get through the day without succumbing to its unyielding inflictions. It left me lethargic, and, as much as I hate to say it, suicidal, in a way. During the peak of my high school existence I turned to writing to console this forlorn mental state I had dug myself into. I would write morbid poetry about death and despair, anarchy and alienation. It succeeded in lifting those dejected thoughts from my mind, but never succeeded in being a panacea for those dreadful contemplations. At that low point in my life, I suppose I had aspired to become a mixture between Ernest Hemingway and Thomas Chatterton: to blow my brains out and be cast away from everyone at the ripe young age of seventeen, leaving nothing but my minimal rants and writings behind as a legacy.

Since then I've spent much time alone just thinking. And what I discovered, or at least, what I believed to have discovered, is that surely it was my environment that had been suppressing my happiness all those years. Yes, my environment, as well as my incessantly growing addiction to self-pity and helplessness. I decided a week or so before my departure that morning that the only way I could ever really reignite the flaming glee of my youth was to leave all that I knew behind, to venture out into the grand new world around me and immerse myself in the art that had made me feel so alive and vital. Words would be my only companions now and that was fine. They were the only things I truly understood, and the only things that understood me. As long as I had them by my side, willingly allowing me to manipulate them into whatever grammatical sequence I desired, to say whatever it was I felt needed so desperately to be said, then surely I would be able to rekindle my long-lost bliss and, in doing so, be able to form my legacy in the process.

After scaling down the side of my house and planting both feet firmly on the wet morning lawn, I tore out a piece of paper from my journal and tacked it onto the front door with a message having previously been inscribed on it one evening a few days before, while I sat cross-legged in my bed, thinking, sweating, shivering with the tremors of remorse and the overwhelming desire to break from my captivity and soar like an eagle; but for now I was but a paperweight, an eagle etched in stone.

The letter read:

Dear mom and dad, it's your vagrant son Sean. Early this morning I slipped away under your sleeping noses and am off to Uncle Sebastian's cottage. I know you will most likely weep when you read this, but please know that it is for my own sanity. Here I feel as if I am a prosecutor in my own murder trial. By that I mean that it feels like my mind is working against me. I need something fresh, something new. I am going to start writing a book and by the end of this summer and my travels it will be complete. Then my happiness will be found again and my genius will be held in my own two hands and there for the world to admire. I promise I will be safe. I promise not to do anything stupid; I simply wish to retreat and enjoy these last few months I have before I become my father. Father, I love you! I promise to call every other Sunday at 7:30 p.m. (give or take a few minutes). Keep an eye out for me; I'll be back when August comes.

Those were the words I left them with as I darted across the lawn, yanked at the metallic handle of my Chrysler, dove onto the black leather seat, and swung the car door shut behind me, feeling truly free for the first time in my life. I rolled down all the windows and backed out the gravel driveway of our home, all knowing that I would never step foot in it again as boy. The next time I would be there I'd be a man, a man with a name and a bright new outlook on life. I raced down our block hitting sixty miles per hour within seconds, frantically trying to make my way to the sanctifying, nature-draped creek a mile or so down the road from where we lived before the sun could fully rise, stealing away the inspiration I knew it would spark, inspiration I so desperately needed to capture in order to maintain that my legacy was indeed one worth recalling.

With pen and paper in hand and my back lounged against an old tree by the riverbed surrounded by an endless expanse of eclectic vegetation, I sat and watched the orange glow of the Georgia sun rise over the arc of the world, grinning vigorously as its emissive rays illuminated my face and body. I looked down at the page that sat in my lap filled from top to bottom with my own words. In the literal heat of the moment, with the bright light in my eyes, I could not even recall what I had written. But it didn't matter, I had begun my journey and with that knowledge I was gratified. I sat there under the tree for some time thereafter not writing a single word. I simply sat and listened to the water rush and splash and make its way down stream. I felt what Thoreau had felt some one hundred years before me: to be free and to float thoughtlessly and relaxed upon the waters of Walden, to be miles away from everything in this world that was harsh and punitive and man-made. There was no better feeling; and to this day I can recall no superior sentiment with which our human souls can detect that is more purifying, hopeful, and buoyant than that of being one with the world around you, unrestrained by the chains of modern-day internment: a captivity that strides to crush the unalloyed goodness in us all.

II

The Mooch

Now that you have familiarized yourselves with the details of my prior days abetted by the means of that quick rundown, it is time to move on, and leave the past in the past. It is only now that the story begins... the start of a suburban legend, another tale to be told. And so I watched with an impressionable mind the third night of my excursions closing in on me as I pulled into a seemingly vacant gas station on the outskirts of Harrison County, Kentucky, in the small and antiquated town of Prospero, where but one two-lane road led you on to Cynthiana, or back the other way. It was a land untouched by time and industrialization, and was home to hundreds of flat, empty fields for the use of agriculture, all lined with ancient linden and dogwood trees, and a green winding river that ran through the center of town and got lost as it continued on into a dark forest. I felt welcomed by the landscape; I felt calm in the presence of these fading outbuildings and vacant farm houses, and the little white church beside the gas station where a blue light hung above the doorway and pulsated quietly, refracting the colors of some haunted rainbow off the stained glass window, a scene of Jacob wrestling with the angel. And so I thought it was a pleasant place to rest, for I needed to do so badly. The previous two days had been spent driving. Hopelessly lost for the better portion of that time, and knowingly on track for probably a fraction of my time astray, I was exhausted, but became so soundly content within that I thought I was most certainly deceased. Those three days, arguably, had been the most significantly eye-opening days I had ever lived up until that point. I was mesmerized by nineteen-plus hours of driving through winding highways that ran like concrete veins over the body of the heartland, outwardly revealing grandiose new ideas and sensations that, to me, were previously unbeknownst. A thousand wondrous plays were performed inside my mind, each with their own unique characters, and each within worlds not unlike our own, but at the same time enchantingly distant, like imagining the lives of Golden Age Elizabethan knights, young actors in actual plays directed by Shakespeare himself, and beautiful monarchs lounging on palanquins held up by the arms of loyal servitude or honest devotion, or by the arms of those who feared. Perhaps, but to me that only makes it more of an intriguing thought.

While my brain twirled and wandered, so did my stomach, it stirred with hunger. I had been living on a ration of candy bars and water for the better portion of three days. And with some $250 to my name—a capital I had saved up from a job I once held as a bag boy at the local supermarket—I planned to keep myself fed for the rest of the summer. While hunger tugged at my guts and shuddered my bones, I closed my eyes and envisioned past experiences. This was the first one that came to mind: Once when I was a child, and in a rare and unprecedented period of prolonged starvation, I ate chocolate-covered live ants in the backyard of a small white townhouse with a kooky sort of middle-aged woman whom I can't seem to remember why I knew. She said that she did it all the time and that they were good. I remember I never told my mother because I just couldn't seem to explain why I had done it, or why I had been there in that woman's home in the first place, whoever she may have been. It is a story that sort of freaks me out, as if I had been possessed to go there and eat those things; and whenever I think about it I'm left with the sensation of tiny kicking legs and gnawing pinchers prickling across my tongue. But anyways, a year and a half ago, (now back on the topic of my capital reserves) I had no idea what I was saving it all for, but if you would have come to me then and said that it'd be for gasoline and junk food that would foreseeably be insuring my survival on this conversionary voyage, this Rimbaldian adventure I'd soon undertake, I would have called you a fool, and probably would have stated that I was going to invest the money in my car. An idea that right then and there, as I was sitting in that dark and eerie gas station parking lot watching shadows of unknown castings contort and flash up and down the pavement irradiated by the over-hanging white lights of the establishment behind me, would not have been all that bad of an idea. Truth be told, my old Imperial was dying. Multiple times since the start of my journey and on various deserted highways across several states now, the engine would overheat and the car would rumble and proceed to shut itself down, coming to a stop with a thud as I agitatedly steered the heap of metal towards the shoulder. I would find myself waving a grimy tarp over the open hood of the vehicle trying desperately to dissipate the rapidly rising steam and cool its gears, or whatever it is that's inside an engine giving it its life.

I stepped out onto the cleft and fractured concrete and finally ensued to fill my tank with gas. With the aroma of fossil fuels looming around me, I felt the pulsation of electricity in the air as it moved with the winds, tickled my nose, and caused me to sneeze into my arm. Though, it was a sensation I had most likely fathomed as a result of the neon glow of signs and advertisements hanging in the windows of the gas station, the humming, somewhat effervescent sounds of which buzzed in and up my ear canals and echoed inside my skull. Just then, the lever on the handle of the gas pump dislodged with a sharp snapping sound, signifying that its job was complete, and succeeding in devastating the stillness of the night rather abruptly and quite to my discontent.

I stood there a while longer looking up at the moon. It was gleaming with shocking radiance down on my little world, as if shining for me and me alone. The night sky was black and cloudless. The landscape surrounding me was barren and secretive; I was beginning to slip off into my own thoughts, when behind me in the distance I heard the sound of footsteps approaching. Playing like a metronome—left, right, left, right—coming closer and closer, increasing in loudness until I could sense them creeping up behind me and then come to a stop. The push of hot breath being exhaled into my ear rapidly sent goose bumps to swell and quiver from my arms and legs, up my spine, and across my scalp. I spun around hastily with frenzied anticipation and dread to see a feeble-looking young man with his right hand raised at his side pointing a ringed finger at me, mouth half-open, as if I had stopped him brusquely as he was about to say something the moment before I decided to turn around (perhaps intending to have the first word in introducing himself to his new acquaintance).

"Say there," he said with an attentive expression on his face, "you looks like you've just seen a ghost! Did I frighten you? I hadn't meant to. I just strolled down here to grab me a pack of cigarettes; that's actually what I'm coming over here to ask you 'bout. You see, I just realized I damn well must have left my pocket book at home. Penniless, and frankly, quite ticked off at that fact, I was wondering if ya might have one or two you could bum me... and a light?"

I looked at him, somewhat relieved at knowing that he wasn't here to waste me or steal my car; I said, "Sure." I always kept a pack of Benson & Hedges in the glove box. I was never one to smoke cigarettes, at least not in an addictive/ compulsive manner, but I did in fact enjoy the notion that they were there in my glove box at my disposal for those now-and-then occasions where they seemed to just fit the mood and environment of the time or situation. Such was the case then in that gas station parking lot on the outskirts of Harrison County, Kentucky, roughly thirty miles northeast of Lexington: a place where I had never before been and knew not one soul, but still somehow happened to find myself in conversation with a complete stranger there who acted as if he had known me for his entire life.

Smoking his cigarette and waving it at me between each drag as if we were in the midst of a heated discussion, though we had not yet even introduced ourselves, he said to me, throwing his cigarette butt onto the ground, watching it flash like a miniature explosion upon impact and then stepping on it: "The name's Chris... Christopher

Armsworth. What brings you round these parts? I don't believe I've seen you before, thus leading me to believe that you ain't no local."

"Well, Chris," I said to him, adding that my name was Sean Robinson, "I'm on my way to my uncle's cabin in Wisconsin."

"Wisconsin!" he screeched, "Shit, you lost or something? You're a long way from Wisconsin. Where you from anyhow?"

"Athens, Georgia." I told him, turning my back and wanting now to be on my way after having sensed uncomfortable circumstances approaching. Then he looked at me and from the expression on his face I was almost certain that he was going to say something. Sure enough, this is what he said: "Could I bother you for a ride home? I live right on down the road only about two miles, over on Willmoth Street. It's a straight shot! Seems to me you're headed that direction anyways." A moment later, ever so slowly, he looked down at the ground and said to me while running a comb through his slick black hair, "So what do you say?"

I stood there in between the gas pump and the open door of my Imperial looking straight into Chris's eyes as my mind buzzed with indecisiveness, which made me feel as if there were a hundred thousand parasites inside my skull all fighting for the right to the same host. I was slowed mentally, I suppose, due to the exhaustion of driving endlessly, and for that reason I justify my answer. I told him that I would take him home, and I asked if he was ready to go. He assured me that he was, proceeded to shove his way into the passenger seat, and tossed my backpack of clothes into the rear. He turned on the radio, kicked off his shoes, and lit his second bummed cigarette as we pulled out onto the road.

"I love this song!" he shouted, jamming his knee into the dashboard and then lounging back into the seat.

The song playing was *Crying in the Chapel* by Elvis Presley, a track that was played as the last slow song at my high school prom. I remember sitting there in the gymnasium watching from the stairwell out at the crowded room of fashionable bodies. Girls in large ball gowns dashed past me again and again, some pulling their boyfriends by the hand, running off to wherever, and some holding each other tight, dancing gently and intimately under blue lights. I thought about how strange it was that unwelcome memories seemed to just casually appear to me at random as we flew down the derelict highway with the windows low and the music high. Skyscraping wooden poles cradling the veins of wires that ran for miles to bring life to telephones scuttled on both sides of the road and followed us along the entire way. Chris had his hand out the window with five fingers opened wide as if to try and catch something lingering four feet off the ground, and was singing along soulfully in a deep and somber voice: "You saw me crying in the chapel/ the tears I shed were tears of joy/ I know the meaning of contentment/ now I'm happy with the Lord," he sang, making it seem as if the mood in the car beforehand had been sucked out through the windows and replaced by an easy, restful and reflective temperament. I sat back and let the hot summer airstreams gust hammering winds that blew through my hair and cleansed me of days come to pass, shooting down the paved roadways in my tin can missile while the music heartened my soul.

Musingly, I thought of another memory, too. I was pretty young, I recall, and was with my father and a friend of his whose name was Wallace Cleghorne. He was a burly man with comb-overs of black arm hair and tough, grey skin that met its darkest shade beneath his eyes, which were almost always bloodshot. We were driving in my dad's old pickup truck on the way home from fishing on the Tugaloo River; I sat in that cramped backseat with a cup of worms squirming in my lap and a red transparent-plastic tackle box on my knees, looking both out the window and at the yellow lure that swung from the tip of one of the poles beside me, half tucked beneath the seat. Wallace and my father had talked politics all day and were sick of each other, until *My Bonnie* came on the radio and their moods brightened considerably. As Tony Sheridan sang the opening lines, Wallace looked back at me with wind blowing wildly through his thick head of hair, and asked if I knew what life was. I sat puzzled for a moment, and don't remember what I told him in response. It doesn't matter much; it probably was not the right answer, for he said,—and I'll never forget this—"Life, Sean, is driving down some highway going a hundred miles per hour with your hand out the window!"

I blinked away the memories, and looked at the strange man sitting beside me, smoking, humming, his arm reaching out into the roaring wind, and saw for myself: yes, he was alive.

Thus I drove on in a dream, and after a while we pulled into Chris's neighborhood. It was exceptionally old-looking from what I could make out, and the houses all seemed to be large and made of brick, with their upper floors almost entirely hidden behind thriving, deep-rooted oak trees, giving them the appearance of high towers soaring into the sky. The protruding, ancient roots of these trees veined eerily across the leaf-covered lawns, and left sidewalks hilly and cracking; every few houses, it seemed, had a front porch that was noticeably tilted off its foundation. And then I stopped the car at the house Chris claimed to be his own, and he got out. After shutting his door he walked around to my side and gestured for me to roll down the window. I did, and right when it had lowered enough to where it was at my eye level, he said: "So, Sean, how'd you like to stick around for a little while longer? Awful lonely round here in the summer time; well, in the winter time, too. I guess it's lonely round here most all the time." Feeling sorry, I told him that I would, and I rolled up the window, turned off the car, and took a deep breath.

There I was a moment later watching him as we stood amongst the plant life in his mother's garden. He then put his hands into his pockets and carefully proceeded to stand, with both feet tightly pressed together, upon an insignificant boulder that resided there half covered by the topsoil between an oversized patch of hibiscus flowers and a cherry tree. Three houses down the sounds of a relatively boisterous foreign family get-together expelled colorful language and occasional shrieks of laughter down the road, the protracting sounds of which continuously averted my attention from the dire predicament standing before me. He had on grey dress pants and a tucked-in, black collar shirt. His hair was dark and greasy; his complexion was abrasively pale and overly augmented most likely because of his shocking dualistic eyes, which were a strange mixture of blues, and turned an almost cobalt color in the right light. There was a panicked vibe about him though; he could never just stand still, and was always swaying and trotting or tapping away with his shiny black leather foot. He was a dire predicament indeed, towering in front of me as I tried not to startle myself with the fact that I was in his presence. I thought he was a man about to snap and lunge at me with a knife, or attack me with a bite to the neck like some draconian monster. But instead, he just looked down and said to me with the most serious face: "See here, Sean, contemplate all this God-given life blooming around us, so content and pleased with their roots being where it is they're rooted, while we humans scamper about day and night itching our skins off!—simply chasing desires and acquaintances and burdens that inevitably root us down to where it is we reside. And here we are in our residences bouncing off the walls, laboriously trying to get ourselves to unknown, imaginary or ideal destinations. Why is it that—at least for the time we are here—can't we not be unsatisfied or anxious to experience something new?—because in doing so we never get to experience the present world around us. Can't we be content like the shrubbery and the trees that stand confident and tall through thick and thin?!"

When I looked up at him he stopped, turned his back to me and began facing the yard, gazing out at the still neighborhood with its sleeping houses and whirling yellow streetlights. Subtly swaying tree leaves tapped and shuddered in most every direction. I walked from the mulch of the garden to a stone walkway leading to his front porch, where I proceeded to seat myself on the peeling steps and ponder over the rant I had just heard. I could tell that he was crying. Muffled sniffles of pain and embarrassment echoed from behind the thin barrier of a vine-laced wicker fence. I contemplated as I sat there breathing in the air around me. How humid it was, how still and draped in shadows that night had been. I thought and concluded that yes, indeed, I did agree with what this odd man before me was saying, regardless of how random and uncomfortable our acquaintance had been. I always did think that if a person does not take in the world around them, the one that is just outside their windows and doors, then they truly have no grasp on what it means to be fulfilled or happy or how to acquire knowledge, especially knowledge of one's self! Though I may sound like a hypocrite for saying so, considering my recent actions, I only left my home because I seemed to have over-experienced the town in which I had grown up. I feel that it is quite unhealthy to live in any one place for more than ten years at a time.

But suddenly, as I thought to myself on the steps of this strange man's strange home, we soon heard the sounds of someone rustling about behind the front door; a bright porch light came on and illuminated the scenery. I turned around and observed for the first time the true appearance of the house where Chris resided. It was a massive, dark, ivy-laced brick structure with countless gables and a wrap-around wood porch whose dark green paint job had become chipped and fragmented with age, and was in dire need of some touching up. A moment later the door creaked open ever so slightly and a gentle middle aged woman in a nightgown perched her head through the crack.

"Goddammit, Ma! Why must you pester us?" Chris snapped. "Can't you see we were in the midst of a conversation?"

"Oh, Christopher, you're such a sad song," said the woman, then looking over at me with a motherly smile (you know, the one that comes across the face of a mother when curiosity is sparked in her through the actions of her child). "He gets it from his father," she said. "He was such a hopeless recluse."

"That's enough," Chris protested. "Sean, this is my mother Anna."

"Pleasure to meet you, mam," I told her with a smile, "My name's Sean Robinson."

"Yeah, and he's a writer," Chris remarked in a somewhat insulting tone of voice, although it might have been jealousy, as he sounded quite surprised and more so envious at that fact when I had told him it earlier while we were in the car.

"Oh, how wonderful!" she gasped. "I have been quite deprived of any decent company. Won't you boys come in? I have tea already on the stove." With that, she flung herself around dramatically and gestured to us with her tufting-mitten-hand to follow her through into the home. Chris and I glanced at each other momentarily, and, like a dog follows his master, he led the way inside. Upon entering, the first things to catch my eye were the grand chandeliers that hung lavishly in most every room on the main floor, above what seemed like neatly set tables of ornately crafted china or elegantly embroidered dark purple couches and futons. Each room was an exhibit, each table having been set and ready to seat no one. Chris and his mother were the only residences here. And yet, it felt as if the house were home to a hundred borders that at any moment would come rushing down the staircases from their individual chambers and occupy the empty seats of the multiple sitting and dining rooms on the first floor. However, in a way, and as you shall soon be made aware, there actually may have been close to a hundred borders, though not the typical kinds, at least not typical in such a quantity; and with every second I stood there in the home I had the unsettling fear of eyes watching me: the ghosts of those who once surely dwelt within the walls of this empty Victorian, or something else entirely. It was like sensing the life in a house of wax… but that was only my first impression of the place.

"Oh boys!" Anna called to us from the kitchen, flapping her white handkerchief in the air behind the wall and through the doorway so we could see it, "tea is ready, won't y'all join me?"

III

The Crow in the Willow

A nna was sitting in a large wooden rocking chair when Chris and I walked into the kitchen. She was holding her glass in her frail hands and there were two cups of tea steaming and waiting for us as we sat down awkwardly at their dusty old walnut refectory table. Surrounding me on all sides of the room were crookedly hung fillet picture frames encasing everything from portraits of people in uniform to families gathered together in unison. On the wall facing me in the room across from the one we all sat, I could see through the doorway that it was decorated with elegantly framed paintings as well. Depictions of angels and Virgin Marys, along with other biblical themes, garlanded the wall and shrouded the auburn paint job beneath it.

I sat puzzled and refrained, observing the peculiar situation I had found myself in. Their house, though once lavish and quite appropriate for the residences of high societal standards, was in psychotic disarray. I felt as if I was going to contract the plague from breathing in the air around me, air that was visibly clouded with dust and dandruff most likely attributed to what seemed like over a hundred cats all clustered upon the furniture in every room I had seen thus far. They shot across the floor boards and ran in and through the kitchen cupboards. Looking around in dismay, my fascination was shattered as one cat succeeded in landing on my back after falling from the lighting fixture above, causing me to spill my glass and jump up in fear as it hissed in my face and proceeded to dart off the table and around the corning into another room.

"Oh my, those darn kittens! They're always such a meddling nuisance, but you learn to love them, I suppose," Anna said as she walked herself across the kitchen and placed her mug into the sink, grabbed a rag and began cleaning up the spill. Scratching my arm nervously, I listened as she shot at me with multiple questions. "Where you from?" she asked, following immediately with, "What kind of writer are you? How do you know my son? Do you like poetry?—I once took a creative writing class back when Chris was a toddler; I even got to have some of my pieces showcased in a weekly journal!"

I told her that that was wonderfully impressive, and that I would love to hear some of her poetry. "You would?!" she hollered at me in obvious bewilderment, and then sat back down again in her cherry-red rocking chair.

"Well of course, I'm sure it's quite delightful," I said with a plastic grin.

"Then you must!" she insisted, and threw up her arms.

"No, Ma, come on, it's quite unnecessary," objected Chris.

"Nonsense, you're pal Sean here seems to me like a fellow who can surely appreciate great works of art like the kinds I used to make… I'll just be a moment!" And she climbed out of her seat once again to run upstairs into a room where I suppose she kept her nostalgic creations.

"Don't mind her," Chris said, "she's crazy. What do you say I go grab us a pair of *Arturo Fuentes* fresh from my grandfather's old humidor and we can go converse around the fire pit?"

"Yeah, that sounds like a good time to me," I told him, finally starting to allow my nerves to settle, and gradually becoming more and more comfortable with where I was and the people I had happened to find myself with.

A minute later, Anna ran downstairs and whizzed through the ingress of the kitchen with a theatrical entrance. I was shocked and caught off guard as I suddenly happened to find myself standing before her. She had not only gotten her poetry book (a large black leather-bound volume that was gothic and eye-catching), but I noticed that she had also changed her clothing. Instead of a light pink night-gown she now wore an azure shawl, topped with a laced bodice and a dark veil that came draping down over her head, cloaking her in a haze of eerie reverence. We looked at her wide-eyed and tinged with a feeling that was something like fear, mouths gaping as an uncontrollable silence drifted throughout the room.

"Perhaps I should have gone with the tea gown instead," Anna muttered with a scowl on her face. "Too much?" she asked.

"Yeah, Ma, just a little bit," Chris said, obviously embarrassed.

Although initially she had come across as startling and bizarre, and even though Chris was quite evidently humiliated by her actions, I started to take a profound interest in her. She was so curious to me, so awe-inspiring. I was fascinated with her eccentric mannerisms and ardent need for an over-inflated ambiance, along with her enthralling self-fashioned uniqueness. Frankly, I couldn't wait to hear the "great works of art" she planned to present to me.

She motioned for us to follow her as she made her way down the hall and out onto the front porch. Girdled by the black shroud of night, we stood there on the decaying veranda beneath the waning yellow glow of a wallpack lighting fixture. Hued with obscurities from dangling fabrics, she opened the leather bound book and ran her pointed finger down the page and prepared herself to read. She started with a poem that she claimed to have written twenty-two years ago while feeding bread crumbs to the fledglings of common cardinals whose nest stood fitted onto the lowest branch a large tree that her great grandmother had planted in the backyard of their family home, decades before when she was just a little girl. She asked us for our undivided attention and began to read. The poem, from what I can recall, went like this:

Oh, how the radiant hairs of my Willow tree flutter graciously for me!
I know this to be so, attentive as the winds blow;
I stand there before it shunning the dreadful crow.
High up in her boughs it looms and curses
Upon every branch from which it perches.
Casting omens down on us and with no clemency;

I watch in disdain at its vengeful tendency
To isolate and kill and see it through
To distort the beauty of my Willow,
Penetrating my mind at night
As I lay my head down upon my pillow.
Striking fear in the hearts of its stalked and preyed,
Striking fear in my heart as its egg is laid!
Devouring my youthful fledglings
And chasing away the Northern Cardinals
That have so rightfully made their home here,
But now shall not return,
Forever fearing the wrath of the looming crow
Like the haunting sight of your own burial urn.
Cawing down at me and mimicking with scornful imitation,
"Thou shall not return!"

I had the largest grin on my face at this point; she had certainly struck a chord with my curiosity. We clapped for her once we were certain that she was finished, and she took an appreciative bow, bidding us adieu, and stated further that she was off to bed. "About damn time," Chris remarked, obviously upset over this whole poetic episode. "Come with me, Sean, I'll start up that fire and grab those cigars!" he said, seizing my arm and pulling me into the house. We strutted down the evocative hallways and into the kitchen. He shoved open the back door and we made our way down the stone steps of the patio and out onto the dead grass. The field behind the home was lurking with darkness when suddenly, fifteen feet in front of me in the yard, a large blaze of fire, preceded by three small sparks, erupted out of a circular stone pit and spotlighted the property around me. "Come on, Sean, take a seat!" he shouted from behind the flames. So I walked over and sat down in a raggedy old lawn chair and warmed my hands and face, although it was still quite humid out. As the wood popped and burned away into the air of night, I sank into a reclined and comfortable position and drifted off into a state of mindless exhaustion, sore and enervated from the labor of my travels.

IV

The Forest of Revelations

Half asleep, I was soon kicked awake by Chris's leg. "We've been out here no more than five minutes and you're already sleeping?!" he said to me reproachfully but laughing. I blinked my eyes a few times and in my peripheral vision I could see him across from me stoking the fire. It shot up into the sky like a flaming perdition; I was witnessing hell on earth in the backyard of a decrepit mammoth of a home in Prospero, Kentucky, half-conscious and choking on white smoke that came spurring into my face as the winds decided to change their direction. I sat there coughing, eyes tearing, and slapping my hand on the armrest of the chair.

"Sean, don't you know?" Chris asked as if there was some piece of vital knowledge I lacked. "Whenever the smoke comes-a-tumbling into you like that, alls that yous got to say are the words WHITE RABBIT! It's a little trick my father taught me when I was a kid…back before he died," he revealed, growing silent and melancholy.

"White rabbit!" I coughed… "It's not working."

"You've got to keep saying it!"

"White rabbit! White rabbit!" I called out towards the fire skeptically, but oddly enough the smoke began to dissipate and rotated around the pit to blow into the direction of the woods ahead of us.

"What did I tell ya?" Chris said with a proud smile on his face.

I told him I was convinced; he knew that I wasn't. Then after more than a few minutes of silence, and after having noticed that Chris had done nothing in all that time but stare down at his boots or at the ground or at the dying embers that blew from the fire pit and lost their lives at his feet,—of which of these I am not quite sure—I sensed that there was something wretched in him, something causing him pain deep down inside, and I thought I knew what it was. Breaking the silence and turning in his direction, I said to him, "Chris, my friend, if you don't mind me asking, whatever did happen to your father? I realize that we have only known each other for a little over an hour now, but I can sense that something is troubling you; I thought maybe... well, maybe that was it, and I thought that maybe you'd like to talk about it with someone." Not knowing how he would respond, an underhand feeling of dread began to creep over me.

"Gee, Sean, I do appreciate you being so thoughtful and concerned," he finally said after a long pause. "To tell you the truth, I'm not even all that sure I know what it is that's bothering me. But if you believe that my father is the root of my blights then I suppose we surely can talk about it."

"That's good to hear, Chris," I said, "so what happened to him?"

"Twelve years ago," he told me, "after Progressive Steel, a metal smelting and welding company that he worked for over in Owensboro some fifteen years came upon difficult times and were forced to lay him off, he took to drinking rather hedonistically. He wouldn't get violent or destructive, such is the case for most problem-drinkers, but he would get quite withdrawn and introverted. At the time we thought this wasn't all that bad of a situation, since he would no longer have to be constantly driving across the state and living in a shitty motel room during the week days. We thought that it was about time he turned over a new leaf. Unfortunately, things weren't resolved so smoothly. I remember coming home from school some days to find him in his room with the lights out, sitting ghost-like at his desk by an open window. His skin began to take on a pallor that made one think he was terminal. In fact, he constantly thought that he was going to die at any minute, and he would sit there all day long with his will and read it and read it and read it over and over again to himself, while rocking back and forth in his chair, sweating and obviously in hysterics. He would scratch out words and sentences, and then replace them with different words and sentences, and shout and curse at the paper, but eventually decided to leave everything that he owned, this house here—which his father's father had built up from scratch—and all of his money and possessions, to my mother."

Chris paused and lit his cigar. He reached down beside his chair into a small cloth bag and retrieved one for me. He lit mine and resumed with the story. "So you see, Sean," he said, blowing smoke out of his nostrils and mouth, "I came home from a dentist appointment with my mother one cold Sunday morning in November to find him sprawled out dead on the drawing room floor. Earlier, while we were out, he had taken an apparently lethal dose of the opium painkiller Laudanum. I was told later that it only takes up to three or four tea spoons of that shit to kill a man. Anyways, he left no note… except for that damn will. In fact, he hardly even hinted to us that anything like this was going to happen, at least not on that particular morning. I was devastated, like I'm sure most anyone would have been; but I got to thinking, thinking about that will of his. I found out that he left us behind nearly $75,000! Incredible, considering the fact that Anna and I had no idea he had that sort of cash. But I'm set now, don't you see? I can go out and buy whatever I want, whenever I want. I don't ever have to work! I could go to college if I wanted to and come out on the other end debt free!"

"So why don't you?" I asked. "What's more important than gaining newfound knowledge?—knowledge that you cannot just expect to discover here in your backyard! What else could someone want to do with themselves after having realized all the understandings that are at one's disposal while confined to their homes?"

"See, that's just the thing!" he said. "Ever since meeting you and hearing about this journey you're on, it's made me suspicious of whether or not I have actually discovered all the knowledge at my disposal, as you put it, here in my own backyard. I'm afraid to go off to a fancy college somewhere and learn new things without even knowing for certain that I have learned everything I can from where I am now. I fear that if I don't and if I decide to leave this all behind in the pursuit of new enlightenments, then I might just miss out on the most vital piece of knowledge there is."

"And what would that be?" I asked.

"I don't know, Sean, I don't know. But I have a feeling that you are just the person to help me realize it! You know, these woods back here go on for a few miles, ain't nobody out there. We should go for a little hike or camp out in the forest tomorrow. I figure you could stay here tonight; I don't know where else you'd go."

That was something I hadn't thought about either, and unable to think of any other options or any other place to sleep, I said to him, "alright, Chris, let's do it!"

He nodded his head joyfully in agreement.

"So, do you think you'll be able to have some sort of intellectual revelation out in those woods tomorrow?" I asked.

"I sure hope so, Sean, otherwise I might just come along with you on the rest of your journey, perhaps… if that wouldn't be a problem. Maybe I'll even start writing a book of my own!" was his rejoinder, and then he looked down glowering, after having noticed that the fire was about to die, and flicked into it what remained of his cigar. "Well, it's pushing two," he said, "maybe we should call it a night?"

"Sounds alright with me," I told him as I yawned and swatted away at the mosquitos. Chris then hurled a pail of water onto the mostly deceased fire, and we progressed to make our way back into that foul old mansion. He led me upstairs to a spare room; he turned the lights on as I walked in and then, with a wave of his hand, in which he held the cloth bag, he left, shutting the door behind him, and I soon locked it.

I curiously looked around the chamber: there were broken end tables and old bureaus with drawers hanging out of them, caked in cobwebs and crawling with the arthropod children of the infestation. In the corner of the room hung a dusty and old Russian sable fur coat; I could tell that it was Russian because of the way it glistened in the light, indicating that it certainly was high-end clothing. I tried to ignore it though, it made me feel as if I wasn't alone. It made my mind race with countless different theories as to whom the coat could have belonged to and what kind of person they may have been. Were they successful? Were they greedy? Or maybe they were philosophical and wise. Either way, it was questions like those that filled my head to the brim with uncertainties and wonder. I laid myself down on the bed, it creaked and sank as I rested my weight on it, and I rummaged through my bags to salvage my notepad and pen. There I sat in the dark room, lit only by a flickering candle now, and began adding to my legacy. Building upon it word for word, page by page, until I fell asleep and woke up the next morning covered in sheets of scribbled on, crumpled up, white pieces of paper. Like a scene out of an Ann Radcliffe novel, I was startled to my feet by the fact that I found myself still to be in this Udolpho Castle that Chris called a home.

Brushing away the dust and lead paint fragments that had fallen down from the crumbling ceiling and piled up on my shirt and bed sheets, I walked over to the door and jiggled the knob. It wouldn't open; I was trapped! I began to panic and desperately paced around the room looking for a way out. Then I realized that it was I who had locked it in the first place; but what I couldn't realize was why I had gotten so carried away, so anxious to escape right off the bat.

"Sean, you're losing your damn mind!" I said to myself. I then took hold of the dense metal skeleton key that sat on the end table by the entrance of the room where I had left it the previous night; I made my way to the key hole, unlocked the door, and stepped out into the ghostly hallway serenely illuminated with the early morning light rays that shown through the cracks in the draperies. The air was heavy with the scent of burnt-out candles as I turned the corner and made my way down the poorly rigged staircase and out into the kitchen. There Chris was making a pot of coffee and at the same time reading a book.

"What are you reading?" I asked, accidentally startling him and causing him to step onto the tail of an unfortunate cat that let out the most ungodly sound and then dashed off under a sofa, fearing for its life.

"Good morning, Sean!" he said, putting his arm around me. "What am I reading, you ask? Oh nothing, just a silly old book I found buried away in this shamefully hoary Louis Vuitton luggage trunk down in the cellar. It's called The Woman in White."

"I know that book!" I said to him enthusiastically. "Willkie Collins, right?—the story about the art teacher and the woman in white who was once in an asylum, and the unfortunate switch of identities that leaves poor Laura to find herself in a mental hospital as the person she swapped her identity with (the now-deceased Woman in White). It's a classic!"

"Yes, yes that's the one. But shut up now will ya? I'm only halfway through the damn thing and you're spoiling it," he said jokingly, but on the inside he was probably upset by the fact that I had come rather close to telling the ending, and thus ruining the book for him. I would have felt quite lousy if I had done so, too; I know how important it is to certain people to be able to read a book from cover to cover. It had always brought a kind of triumphant and accomplished feeling upon me when I did so, and I'm sure that Chris felt the same way.

When Anna came down from her room, her long black hair was in tangles, and yet again, to our good fortune, she was wearing a light pink nightgown. She sat down with us at the table and buttered herself some toast. We ate a meager breakfast together, and Chris, perceptibly anxious to begin our voyage into the woods, ordered me to go get ready and meet him in the backyard in fifteen minutes. I went back upstairs to the disintegrating spare room I had slept in and put on my blue jeans and hiking boots. I dug through my bags in search of a flash light, a lighter, and a pocket knife that I had decided to bring along with me just in case. Fifteen minutes later I was waiting in the yard as Chris ran out the back door with a duffle bag slung over his shoulder and a fiery desire for adventure burning in his eyes. "Alfresco!" he shouted, and led the way to a small trail on the outskirts of the property.

"Any place in particular that we're heading to?" I asked as we walked down the dirt track under a canopy of tree leaves and winged insects.

"Yes sir!" Chris said. "There's a neat little delta surrounded by a cluster of caves and hollows about two miles down this here trail and about a half of a mile off trail to the west."

I was satisfied with our choice in destination; and so we strode on, side by side down the way, deeper and deeper into the heart of the forest. But with every step I took I felt the increasing thickness of woods claustrophobically entombing me. I noticed as we moved that the walls of the trail were closing in on us narrower and narrower, compressing on all side until the surrounding woodland became so tight and violent that we had to stop and discuss our whereabouts.

"This is about where the trail ends," Chris announced as he pulled the compass out of his pocket and studied it. "West is this way," he pointed, "that's where we need to be heading." With that knowledge, we changed our direction and broke our way into the undergrowth. As we fought our way through, sharp and swatting branches whipped at our hands and faces like violent fencers. After hours of this painful, seemingly aimless wandering, I looked down at my shirt and saw that it was splattered with blood.

"Chris, hold up!" I said to him, stopping dead in my tracks. "Is my face bleeding? Did I cut myself?" Chris turned around and looked at me smiling, but as soon as he saw my appearance his expression faded quickly.

"Sean! You look like your face has been ripped off! You're bleeding profusely, what the hell happened? You're covered with cuts and scratches!" he shouted.

"It must have been the tree branches and thorns we just passed through. Your arm is bleeding just as well, Chris. Have you got any towels or maybe a first aid kit?" I asked, and in dire need of one.

"Yeah, luckily I do!" he said, "but we should probably stop for the day and find a place to rest. We're about a little less than a mile from the caves and I know a neat little spot about a hundred meters away where we can post-up."

With blood dripping from our flesh, and nats and mosquitos swarming and gorging themselves of our leaking fluids, we continued on, and I hoped to God that where he was taking me really was just a hundred meters away. I had to get out of the undergrowth, and I longed to see a patch of sky, black or blue, or whatever color it may be, I just wanted not to feel so trapped.

The hike through the woods had taken most of the day and a lot more time than Chris and I had initially expected,—though it may not have seemed that way in my hurried description, it was about six hours—and as a result, we were drained of our energy and drive for adventure. Now, I'm not a genius or a geographer, but from the time it took us to get to the point we were at just then, I knew that this coveted location was certainly over two and a half miles away. That day alone we must have walked three or four before reaching the end of the path, and Lord only knows how many more through the undergrowth. I guess Chris had misjudged his knowledge regarding the hike, and in particular, the length of the trail.

We made our way to the temporary spot he had suggested so we could rest. It was a happy little clearing in the dense brush that was protected overhead from rain storms by a tall and blooming Kentucky Yellowwood. I sat on a mossy stump as Chris wrapped his arms in gauze and I applied alcohol wipes to the lacerations on my face. It burned like sulfuric acid as it sank into my wounds and pores, and I was tearing up like a spoiled little child who didn't get what he wanted. After our treatments, we decided to start up a fire and cook some canned pork 'n beans that Chris had brought along with him in his backpack. I searched through the forest a few yards off from our campsite for firewood. I came back with a substantial pile, not enough to last us through the night, but enough for a few guaranteed hours of burning. Chris scraped some dry tinder off of a dead tree and bundled it up into a sort of bird nest shape in his hands. He walked over to the other end of our camp, put it under a tipi of logs I had set up, and proceeded to ignite the fire with a single match. Once alive, it swayed rapidly with the winds, and sizzled and popped and hissed as the ghosts of dying timbers wandered away into the darkening sky. I looked over at Chris and he looked over at me, and as he did so, a mutual sense of satisfaction, like a jolt of electric current, detectably transferred between the two of us, and in the company of the lively fire, made it seem like there was a third.

Above my head, large bands of heat lightning pummeled through the thick clouds and sporadically lit up the black woods around me in flashes of blue light. A summer heat storm was moving in, and with it an air of excitement. So far, my journey had been everything I expected it to be and more. I was having the time of my life, and I wondered why I hadn't done something like this sooner, during solstices already come to pass. I sat there by the fire and felt more human than I had ever felt before, both up until that point and since. In a glorious moment of clairvoyance, I finally acknowledged the fact that we are all a part of the greatest story ever told, the story of mankind. We are indeed the finest chapter in the legacy of the world.

V

The Fountain of Youth & the Eternal Flame

I awoke the next morning to the asphyxiating smell of burning wood. I opened my eyes and was momentarily blinded as a thick cloud of ashes blew into my face, scorching my retinas with heated fumes. While smoke filled my lungs, I thrashed about on the ground trying desperately to liberate myself from the tight cocoon of my entangled blankets, when I heard Chris shouting something distressfully in the distance.

"Move! You've got to move!" he screamed from some place hidden behind the smoke.

I could not see him, but he could obviously see me, and after realizing what it was he was ordering me to do, I knew that more likely than not I was in danger. I fanned away the dense smoke from my face and pulled myself up off the ground. I thought I was out of dodge when I looked over my shoulder to see a roughly sixty-foot-tall pine tree splintering off from its severely charred stump and come falling into my direction. It came down so quickly, and the next thing I knew it had fallen onto me, crushing me down into the soil of pine needles and earthworms, and trapping me on all sides.

Surely I was dead.

"Sean!" I then heard Chris scream from somewhere outside my ossuary. "Sean, where are you?!" he yelled again.

"Over here," I tried to say loud enough so that he could hear me, but a heavy trunk was pressing down on my back and I could not get my voice to be audible. Time slowed down like the feeling that comes over you while watching yourself go head on with another vehicle before either smashing together or swerving to the left. I closed my eyes and prepared myself mentally, I suppose, to die. Suddenly, with welcomed respite, the substantial trunk was lifted from my spine and Chris grabbed me by the collar of my shirt to extract me from my crypt.

"How'd you find me?" I asked, lying on my back next to his feet, hacking and choking on air.

"I saw your shoes sticking out from under the tree. Jesus Christ, I thought you were dead for sure!"

"Me too," I said, "me too."

Apparently we had forgotten and/ or had fallen asleep last night without putting out the fire. Embers must have blown over and ignited the dry and deceased plant life at the base of the tree. Soon the fire grew rapidly, spreading to the tree itself and thus causing the previous scenario. I was so lucky to be alive, I thought; I should have been crushed to death by the tremendous weight of it all and left there in the forest as brunch for the rodents. I stood up and shook the fear out of my clothing, along with the needles and broken branches and sawdust. Standing there in shock, looking helplessly at our campsite and all the surrounding destruction, I almost started to cry.

"Chris, we could have burned the whole damn forest to the ground! This could have been completely devastating!" I shouted.

"You're right, you're right! I know! My God, Sean, we got to get out of here!" Chris answered, screaming, acting on the impulses of paranoia.

As I wandered around trying to catch my breath, Chris was looking at the wreckage with his hands on his head and a churning expression of fear on his face. Our tent was crushed and torn to bits. Luckily, however, when the big tree fell, it put out most of the surrounding ground fires with it. Leaves and mounds of sticks and branches littered the campsite as the smoke of vanishing blazes subtly rose up from the mangled earth. Also to our good fortune (if a term like that could possibly be applied to us in a situation such as this one) we were fortunate for the fact that the sun had just risen moments before, meaning that whatever fire had been burning it was during the night, thus making the smoke that it expelled difficult to see in contrast to the dark sky background. In other words, there was a better chance no one else had noticed, and that hopefully some park ranger or forest fire prevention squad would not come running out into the woods in search of us.

"Listen, Sean," Chris said, drenched in ashes and perspiration, "I'm glad you're still alive and everything, but we should really get the heck out of here."

"Ok, yeah let's… let's go," I hastily replied, "which way do we go?"

"West is this way!" he pointed, leading the hike. "What was it like to almost die?"

"Are you joking?" I asked.

"Uhm… I don't know." he replied dumbfounded. "Never mind, you probably don't want to talk about that, huh?"

"It was a rush of life!" I told him with a smile. "It was just what I needed!"

It was just what Chris needed to hear, too. From there on he was a sudden optimist, and open-minded to everything looking to enter— one of many mood fluctuations that showed itself and then disappeared, like a man with multiple people living within him, throughout the day and the course of our travels. And so we made our way through the brush, deeper and deeper into the Forest of Revelations—as Chris now called it—when we came across some terrain that was even more discouraging than the guillotine of that falling tree. The dense vegetation died off as we approached a large crevasse that went down some eighty to a hundred feet into the earth.

"It's impassable!" I cried. "It'd be a death sentence to even try!"

"Well, we've reached that spot I was talking about, although we entered from a rather awkward position," Chris observed.

"Is there another way down?" I said to him, fearing that we had hit a dead end.

"Oh yeah," he assured with a cunning grin, "we'll be able to get down there, don't you worry. Just look, Sean, look over there!" he said, holding his arm out, "over there, see!—where the flash floods have left a slopping track of post-avalanche debris, so to speak. It can work perfectly as a path for us to use to get down into those ravines!"

He was right; the landslide had made an impeccable little decline for us to go down, though perhaps little isn't the best way to describe it. It was still a seventy-five foot or so downward slope littered with logs and thorn bushes and slick with mud and other decaying organic matter. It was risky, but what is life without risks?

We took to it with utmost valor and confidence. I went first, grabbing hold of a wet and mossy log, and digging the sides of my boots into the mushy earth beneath me; I began to descend. At first all went smoothly. However, Chris was coming down hard from behind, and his movements caused flakes and fragments of dirt and crumpling dead wood to fall onto my face from above, momentarily blinding me. The climb became less and less comfortable as we continued, and it was quickly realized that we had drastically misjudged the difficulty of our route.

"This is getting pretty strenuous," I said to Chris.

"Hang in there, buddy, we've almost reached the bottom," he replied, though we were still at a significant distance from being at the base of the cliff.

About halfway down, as I reached to my side to grab onto a termite-ravished branch of tree that was protruding out of a mound of sticks and leaves, I lost my grip, and began to fall, and soon found myself plunging down the steep precipice head first. I was sure I was going to break my neck. I had narrowly escaped being burned alive or crushed to death in my sleep this morning, and I just knew that there was no way on earth I was going to make it away from this mishap in one piece. It would have been a damn miracle. However, I suppose I got pretty lucky, because right then as my face hit the dirt and I began to shoot down the hillside, I felt a sudden jerk and was stopped from sliding any further as Chris had thankfully grasped my ankle and was holding me from my certain expiration. Straddling there in the wilderness of life, hardly escaping the clutches of demise, I turned my self onto my backside and breathed a sigh of relief. After regaining my balance and surviving a near heart attack, I looked up at Chris, who was just as distressed as I was, and hugged him so tightly that I thought I might have broken a rib.

"You literally have saved my life two separate times today in the last hour!" I said to him, more grateful than I had ever been towards anyone in all my eighteen years.

"The first time, Sean, that was lucky. But this… this was a sure miracle," he stated, breathing heavily and with his face congealed in sweat and mud.

Eventually we reached the base of the gully and I turned around and looked up at our route with conquer and pride. Swirling winds blew past me and in the process strew up a wave of leaves and sandy debris that was flung with considerable force and sting at the side of my face. I flinched and covered my eyes with a filthy, dirt-encrusted hand. As the winds died, I reopened my vision and peered around at the caves and bluffs and felt as if I was inside a large mixing bowl of lumpy, solid stone. The trail and forest above seemed like another world to me, another life. Down in the ravine the view was so drastically contrast that I thought I was in the midst of a hallucination. Perhaps I was still under that collapsed tree, unconscious and suffocating as Chris frantically ran around the scene of destruction looking for my remains. Maybe that was the case; maybe I was knocked out cold, and it was all just my squandering mind producing this illusion before me.

"Sean, follow me! I've got to show you the best spot!" Shouted Chris already twenty or so feet away from where I stood.

I followed quickly, watching my footing as we made our way through the meandering badlands, when something snared my attention. "Chris, stop, take a look at this!" I said as I veered off course and walked into a deep and fascinating, diamond-shaped cove that had been punched into the sidewall of the ravine. I heard Chris's footsteps coming up from behind me as I bent down onto one knee. I reached out and took in my hand some sort of artifact that had caught my eye as I was passing. Opening my fingers and allowing the captured sand and dirt to fall away from my palm, I finally saw what it was I held.

"Holy Jesus!" Chris cried out as he looked over my shoulder in amazement.

There in my hand were two objects. The first was a multicolored Murano glass pendant, it was attached to an aged leather string studded with amethyst stones, and the pendant itself had an image of an eagle imprinted into it. The second item—probably much older than the first—was a tiny amulet stone carving of an ancient inhabitant, perhaps of this very region, pouring water from a clay pot onto a child. I suppose it was a depiction of people bathing, but I could be mistaken, it might have had, at some point in time, a more profound and indepth meaning behind it.

"These must have been some sort of Native American heirlooms or… or some sort of aboriginal wedding dowry," Chris said, just as fascinated by our findings as I was.

"Yeah, maybe," I said back to him, completely captivated, "though, I doubt they were wedding dowries, they're much too simple. But who knows how old these things are or who they had originally belonged to!"

I held them in my hands like a delicate infant.

"Yeah, and who knows how much they're worth!" Chris responded elatedly with dollar signs in his eyes.

After standing there in the opening of the cave gawking at these enthralling finds that I held for quite some time, I finally shoved them into my pocket and we then continued on our merry way. We didn't speak a word for some half an hour thereafter, the intrigue of our findings was all that was on our minds. I knew in my heart—and I'm sure Chris did as well—that what I had found was something special, something of considerable worth.

"Say, Sean," Chris said, breaking the silence, "after we get out of these woods, whenever that may be, we should drive on into town and go get those objects appraised. I'm sure there's some snob relic collector out there who would pay top dollar for recovered items like these."

"I'm sure you're right, Chris; but I don't know if I want to sell them. I think I'd like to keep them. You know, as a memento of this remarkable adventure," I replied, crushing his hopes of being able to coax me into splitting the profits with him, I'm sure.

Wandering up and over boulders and banks of dirt and floral, we made our way further into the ravine. After turning a corner and descending down a slope of earth, we stopped and sat at the base of a large sarsen stone that looked as if it had been pilfered away from Stonehenge or something and abandoned here in this gully. We sat there and rested and rehydrated and scrapped the inches of accumulated mud from off the bottom of our boots. I turned to Chris and asked where that spot was he said he wanted to show me a while ago before we had found the artifacts. He said back to me with a vibrant smile, as if I had just reminded him of some important obligation, that the site of the spot was just a little ways down from where we were, and that we should arrive there in probably twenty minutes.

"What is this place anyways?" I asked.

"Oh, I can't tell you, it's far too majestic to spoil with common language. You'll just have to wait and see for yourself," he said, staring at me wide-eyed and anxious.

A few minutes later, after we had gotten up and started back on track, Chris screamed and grabbed onto me with such force that I was, for the time he was holding me, unable to breathe. His fear frightened me so much so that I nearly took off running in the opposite direction. I thought some sort of life-ending encounter was about to bring us to our unfortunate fates, when a clumsy herd of five or six wild turkeys came trotting around the bend, gobbling wildly. Chris immediately let go of me as his fear dissipated and I started laughing harder than I had for the longest time.

"You…you were afraid of those fucking turkeys weren't you?!" I exclaimed, doubling over and crying out in amusement.

"Yes, yes, laugh away, Sean. I'll have you know that I thought it was something else… like a bear. I didn't see it! I just saw a large shadow and heard the sounds of certain death approaching us."

"Yeah, well those turkeys sure got the best of you!"

"Whatever, you were scared too!" he said in defense. "We could've contracted turkeypox or some kind of virus like that if we would have made any further contact with those things!"

"I'm pretty sure only a turkey can catch turkeypox," I said. "And I would know, Chris, my grandfather used to own a farm."

My grandfather never owned a farm, but the absurdity of Chris's claim made my lie seem quite justifiable in comparison, and I even believed it myself for a few seconds after it was told. Isn't that strange though, someone believing their own lies? I fear it is quite common…

But once our run-in with the turkeys had become nothing more than a humorous memory, Chris and I laughed about it the whole rest of the hike until we finally came upon "the spot." Chris pushed aside a large plant whose veiny leaves were blocking our view, and when he did so and I saw our destination before me, my breath was instantly taken away. Fifty feet in front of us the grey and dreary rock formations of the ravine were all but nonexistent, and in their place was a large delta of clear blue liquid fed by a stunning stream-flow waterfall. The pond – I suppose you could call it – was teaming with fish and other creatures obviously visible from above since the water was so strikingly flawless and uncontaminated.

"Pretty amazing isn't, Sean?" Chris asked as we stood side by side gaping at the finest of Mother Nature's creations I had ever had the privilege to behold.

"My God, this is wonderful!" I said, and I was almost speechless.

The next thing I knew, Chris had flung off his shirt and shoes and was making a running start off of the ledge from which we stood, and soon he was airborne. I watched as he flailed above the water and then came crashing down into it, triggering a large upsurge that splashed back onto shore and soaked me from head to toe.

"Come on in, Sean!"

"Alright, here I come!" I announced as I ran, kicking off my shoes in the process. I jumped off the peak into the mirror-like water, causing Chris to go under from the substantial wave my impact had created; the deep pool was pleasant, cool and revitalizing, and made me want to sleep, floating there as would a lily on its crystal surface.

"I feel so alive!" he said to me, once he had reemerged. "It's like we're swimming in the Fountain of Youth!"

And indeed it was. I had never been so free of any stresses or perplexities (the all too familiar kinds that appear to just come along as a given while growing up) as I was right then while swimming in that water. I was bathing my soul, it seemed. I was a born-again optimist. In the Forest of Revelations I had been baptized into the church of self-realization. I was truly alive, and with no fears of the future weighing down upon my shoulders, I felt I was finally ready to become somebody in this world. I felt as if all my dreams were just soon-to-be realities, and the fact that mere water and stone could bring about such life-changing intuitions made me truly believe in my heart that anything was possible.

We made camp about a hundred feet away from the pond up on top of a cleft of rock that was clear of any obnoxious vegetation, and like before, I ventured out into the forest around us to gather a supply of firewood. When I returned, Chris had created a circular pit, almost identical to the one in his backyard, with multiple heavy and round stones, and he was standing in front of it with his hands on his hips smiling down at his creation. Once we got the fire going, we hung our clothes from a stick above it to dry them out, lazed our backs against surrounding trees, and examined the orange blaze as it fluctuated in size and intensity and pirouetted with the wind. I was exhausted and so was Chris, who I think might have fallen asleep by this point. My body was sore and my face and arms ached from the open wounds. I continuously had to smack and swat away the flies that would mercilessly return to land on my skin and fester with my cuts. It was making me quite paranoid. I thought they were laying eggs inside of me, and I proceeded to wrap myself in a thick blanket, choosing instead to deal with the heat over becoming some sort of larvae incubator.

I checked my watch for the time and noticed that it was only about nine thirty, and Chris was already sleeping. Feeling the need to converse, I tossed a wet sock of mine in his direction and it landed, by chance, onto his face. He woke up immediately, peeled it off his cheek, and hurled it at the ground.

"What the hell!" he irritably shouted.

"Don't go to sleep yet, it's so early and there's a fire going, let's talk about stuff," I said to him in a piteous tone of voice.

"What do you want to talk about?" he asked.

"I don't know, anything," I replied, "how about today for example? It was definitely one of the best I've ever lived. Sometimes people go entire lifetimes without living a day as magical and exciting as today was!"

"Well, I highly doubt that, Sean, but I do agree that this was one of the best days of my life."

"Yeah, me too, and it was almost my last!" I said, reminding myself of this morning's traumas.

"It was a damn miracle that you weren't killed… twice!" Chris admitted loudly.

"Na, I don't think so," I told him.

"Well why the heck not?" he replied.

"I'll answer that question in the words of Oscar Wilde. It was he who said: 'I don't believe in miracles, I have seen too many.'"

"Have you now?" Chris asked skeptically.

"Yeah, I do believe I have," I said.

"What's that good old nineteenth century line of wit from, anyways?" Chris asked, "An Ideal Husband?"

"No", I replied, "Salomé."

"Ah… I never did get around to reading that one, or seeing it performed live for that matter," he said, holding a stick into the fire and watching as it smoldered away into an ember of the same shape.

"You should, Chris—he's one of the most influential minds to have ever existed, and he was such a revolutionary thinker, and undoubtedly on my top-ten list of favorite writers!" I told him, quite passionately. "Have you ever read his short stories?—his fairy tales or A House of Pomegranates? Forget Dorian Gray, his shorter stories are incredible! They are so well crafted and realistic that it seems to me then that they couldn't possibly have been created by the hand of a person, they are just too good, too illuminating. He, Kafka, and Thomas Mann have a special place in my heart when it comes to short stories. And how about Aestheticism for a movement worth belonging to—it's what

I believe in. All art is certainly useless though, don't you think? And what a great motto that is!"

"It is visually, audibly, and imaginatively appealing—that's something! There are not many aspects of human life that people put more effort into acquiring than entertainment. On another note, my favorite writers are probably Sophocles and Euripides, I love the classic tragedies. Although, perhaps it is Victor Hugo…Les Misérables has to be one of the most incredible tales of struggle and redemption I have ever read," said Chris.

"I can agree on that," I said. "And we all grew up reading—or, in most cases, were read to—Notre-Dame de Paris… at least I was."

"Nope, never read it," he replied as I looked over at him in sudden though expected disbelief.

"No kidding?" I asked. "I wouldn't say it's better than Les Misérables, but it's certainly close. Quasimodo is arguably one of the utmost memorable characters ever created."

"Again, I just never got around to reading it," he said, tossing the rest of the stick into the fire and then closing his eyes.

"You know, I'm really in no hurry to get out of these woods and go back home. It's so peaceful out here. How about you? Do you feel the same way? It seems to me you're more clear-headed than ever, just look at how much you've written in that book of yours. It's twice the size it was a couple days ago!"

"It is isn't it," I said. "I don't want to leave either, I'm having way too good of a time."

"So then it's settled. We're going to stay… at least for a while. This will be our campsite. We have enough food for the next few moons, and there's numerous fish in that pond down there." He stood up and put a log onto the fire, but not before waving it above his head like a spear and shouting, "Prometheus, I pray to thee! We'll keep this fire burning for days, and every night after our adventures we'll sit down here like we are now and talk until the sun rises!"

"We'll keep it burning for as long as we're out here," I told him. "Fire fuels conversation, does it not? We can call it the Eternal Flame and as long as it burns our contentment shall never die!"

VI

The Night of Multiple Stories

A few days later, around lunch time, after having put fresh wood on the fire, I walked down to the Fountain of Youth to wash my hair and clothes. When I got there, I saw Chris sitting on a distended rock a few feet above the water with an uncoiled shoelace in his hand. He was dangling it into the pond with a hook on the end that had a piece of last night's leftover dinner attached to it.

"Are you fishing?" I asked. "Good luck trying catching any with that contraption, even a fish knows that that's a trick," I pretentiously stated.

Then I noticed that he wasn't defending himself, he was just laughing. I looked over beside him and saw a pile of some eighteen to twenty fish. My naturally expected skepticism had been stabbed through the heart, and I felt like an ass. "Wow! I can't believe you actually caught some… and so many, too!" I said. And in response Chris yanked the shoelace fishing line from the water with a trifling bluegill hooked on it and flapping in distress. He then proceeded to kill the thing with a rock and yelled for me to help him carry his revenue back to camp. I agreed and made my way over to him. I was amazed at his good fortune, and honestly a little jealous, and I think he knew it. Reluctantly, I walked down the dirt trail through the undergrowth some one hundred feet to our campsite with a cargo of malodorous, sopped and bleeding fish in my arms. As we walked, I was being swarmed upon by ravenous, hungry insects that clustered like clouds of buzzing smoke around my head, and the rancid smell of the dead fish under my nose was making me exceedingly nauseous.

"We'll be eating good tonight!" Chris cheered, when suddenly I could no longer handle my disgust, and giving into my repulsion, I vomited the content of my stomach out onto the heterogeneously herbaceous ground that looked as if it were already covered in vomit. Dizzy and sick, with a burning sensation in my nose and stomach acid in my mouth, I finally made it back to camp and was able to drop my nauseating burden onto a blanket of leaves Chris had made, then immediately ensued to rip my shirt off and over my head, and threw it into the fire that was still burning from last night.

"Why'd you do that?" Chris asked in a confused and startled tone of voice, which made me angry.

"Because it was covered in vomit and fish guts, obviously!" I said back to him.

"Well, don't worry, we'll be eating good tonight," he said again, though this time I didn't throw up.

The effects of my appalling task were starting to fade as I purified my hands and pants with some water and sat down under a slumping tree that I had turned into a shelter by threading myself a flimsy roof of sticks and grasses earlier that morning. Chris was perched across from me and next to the Eternal Flame with his survival knife out, gutting and filleting the fish. I happened to notice that there were a few crawdads (or crayfish) in the catch as well. We certainly were going to be eating "good" tonight, and in addition we had six or seven cans of food that Chris brought from home still left to consume! It seemed to me at the time, and I'm sure it seemed to Chris also, that we were getting along quite adequately out in the wilderness, simply living off the land.

That evening, as the sun was setting, all the fish had been cooked and were resting on a flat portion of stone smoking with heat next to the fire. We each sat down on our individually chosen stumps of tree and ate our stomachs full, and until the fish were all but bones and tails. After our sea food feast, that time of night (the time to tell stories and converse and laugh and discuss being alive) had finally come upon us. Chris didn't hesitate. He got quite serious and, in doing so, significantly changed the healthy mood with which we had previously been in. From across the fire he looked at me and said, "So Sean, tell me about your family or your life before this. You've met all of mine already, and you know me about as well as anybody can. Who are you?" he laughed, "I mean, how was growing up in Athens? What are your parents like?"

"Do you really want to know all that crap?" I asked.

"Hell, of course! I consider you a good friend of mine, Sean," he replied.

"Thanks, Chris," I said. "Okay, well—to dive right in—my father's name is Howard and my mother's name is Lenora. He's a banker and she's a classical music professor and former third grade teacher. They aren't strict, but they aren't careless. They're not rich, but are able to provide a pretty damn comfortable life for themselves. I have a brother named Matthew who's away at Oxford right now. In my family, it's sort of a mandatory rite of passage for a Robinson boy to attend Oxford— they've been doing it for generations! Anyways, it's his senior year and he lives overseas, so he won't be coming home this summer, though he's certainly living life how it's supposed to be lived. He's going to be making money and connections, and he has just as good of a time as I do, all while working his ass off. The only difference between him and I, since I'm going to be attending Oxford as well, is that he can find enjoyment anywhere and with the greatest of ease, while myself, on the other hand, has to abandon everything and everyone and come live out in the woods with a once complete stranger just to feel the rush of life and excitement."

Chris and I both laughed. He then proceeded to use the rib bone of a freshly eaten fish as a toothpick before tossing the remaining skeleton into the fire. "What's your book about, Sean?" he asked. "Will you let me read it when it's finished?"

"Yeah, of course," I told him. "I can tell you what it's going to be about, but not in full since I haven't yet thought the entire plot through."

"Alright, that's fine, give me what you've got," he responded, adamantly but fascinated.

"Okay," I sighed dramatically, making it seem as if telling the story was going to be a chore. "It takes place somewhere in Great Britain during the late 1890s. It's the tale of a convict, or something along those lines. He was caught in the act of killing his promiscuous wife and her secret lover. He shot her dead while the two were having a romantic and clandestine dinner together in the house of an aristocratic friend of his wife's. The residence was that of Mr. Bosemont, a successful judge and philanthropist in London. When the soon-to-be convict, whose name is Chester Love, a notorious critic, journalist, and writer, gets news of his wife's disloyalty and secret banquet with her affair from a local rumor spreader during a late night performance by Claude Debussy to a packed house at Queen's Hall, he is thrown into an indissoluble rage." I paused and then threw my freshly eaten fish's skeleton into the fire, where it smoldered away on top of the others.

"Keep going Sean, this is interesting. You do have more, don't you?" Chris apprehensively enquired.

"Yeah I do, I do." I told him, continuing on with the story—

"So after hearing the news, Chester races to his carriage and orders his driver to go to the residence of Mr. Bosemont. At arrival, he breaks in through a back window and proceeds to load his Lancaster hand gun, while he shrewdly searches the home for the two deceivers. In the midst of all this, Mr. Bosemont has taken notice of Chester's presence, but instead of stopping him, he allows him to follow through with his sinister intentions, remaining unseen and watching from a distance."

"What? Why would he do that?" Chris asked, stopping me before I could explain any further.

"He does this because he's a smart man," I continued, "a little twisted and unsympathetic, but a smart man of reputation and justice. He knows that Chester, in his blinding wrath, is going to kill his wife's lover or perhaps even his wife. He knows that if he does this and catches him afterwards, he'll have a high-profile murder conviction under his belt. Therefore, Mr. Bosemont waits patiently while in the next room where the dinner is being held, Chester enters with his pistol drawn. He shoots his wife to death, unloading all the bullets on her and saving none for her secret lover. Once she is dead, and as the other man his quivering with fear in the corner, Chester takes hold of a heavy silver candelabra that had been resting on the table and repeatedly ensues to crush the man's skull with it!'"

As the plot grew with intrigue and intensity, I looked up at Chris and saw how he was so completely captivated by the story that every time I would pause between sentences, his fascinated expression would shatter and he'd stare up at me blankly and confused, hoping that it would not be the end of the tale, not this soon.

"While these atrocities take place," I resumed, "Mr. Bosemont darts from the other room and alerts the authorities of the crime. Moments later, him along with five other officers rush up stairs just as Chester is walking away from the scene, painted in the blood of his lover. They apprehend him and take him into custody. They renounce his name and he is now referred to as simply *the convict*. At trial he is found guilty of murder, and Mr. Bosemont becomes a hero. But instead of hanging him, they order that he be sent away in exile for life at a work camp in the North African country of Algeria, the most brutal and inhumane place on earth. It is a place where death is welcomed like presents on Christmas morning, but death is an all too desirable luxury to be granted at will to the inmates here. They are forced to labor and suffer for years and years until the immense toll of their punishment causes their bodies to collapse and their damned souls to depart." I took a deep breath and scanned my mind for the rest of what would then happen to poor Chester Love...

"As the ship of human cargo that he is now on while being transported overseas to his incarceration bobs rapidly upon the choppy open waters, the cruel and drunken deckhands presiding over the prisoners aboard select him at random one night to be the unfortunate victim of their twisted humor. They beat him repeatedly and piss in his face. After hours of this torment, they decide to tie bricks to his ankles and neck and throw him overboard, certain that he will die. Miraculously, however, Chester is able to unrestraint himself from the bricks and ropes, narrowly dodging a watery demise. But all is not over yet! He finds himself adrift in the middle of the vast Mediterranean. Collecting all of his strength and determination, he swims. For miles and miles he swims, and when he is too weak to swim, he floats. For days he meanders amongst the waves, until one morning on the horizon he sees land. He swims ashore and discovers that he is now stranded on an island, mostly uninhabited—uninhabited all except for a group of three inmates who met the same fate Chester did at the hands of the drunken sailors, and it is from there that the story continues. That's the end…as of now, until I can think of more," I told Chris, out of breath and sick of talking.

"Damn, that was one hell of a story!" he said, "You're going to sell millions of copies of that book, I guarantee it."

Maybe so, but maybe not; who could know?

The muggy night hauled on endlessly though, as summer nights tend to do, and the bonfire of the Eternal Flame rose high into the sky and, as had been predicted, quite perpetually fueled our conversations. Chris and I discussed everything from how we planned to improve our campsite and shelter in the coming days, to L.B.J's "Great Society" and the escalating tensions in Vietnam, to our love of theater and shared admiration for the life and compositions of Peter Warlock. It seemed we had a lot in common, which was strikingly peculiar to me since I had never met Chris before a few days ago, and had never planned on meeting him in the first place.

Then, quite out of the blue, he asked, "what do you think it's like to be a genius, or to be famous, Sean?"

"I'm sure it depends on the person," I replied; "my guess is that it would either be quite strenuous and overbearing, or delightfully gratifying."

"I think it would be relatively similar to what hell is like," he added. "I couldn't imagine having people recognize me wherever I'd go, or having to see myself on the television or in the papers. God, it's already difficult to look in the mirror, I'd probably end up like my father if I was so unfortunate as to have to see myself everywhere I went!"

"That's a good point," I said, "I wouldn't want to be famous either, now that I consider it. But you know, Chris, that being famous and having a famous legacy are two entirely different things. Being famous is how people see you in life. You can be famous for anything, good or bad. But having a famous legacy, on the other hand, is how you see yourself, and how people will see you after you are already dead—which is a thing one shall never come to know, but should not let that hinder them from striding to polish, like a marble bust of one's own head, the aspects of a life once lived that people shall evoke when that person's name is brought into the conversational light. It is only through living a life of fullness and pride, and wholehearted indulgence into the art of one's choosing that one can create a famous legacy. Yes! To be proud of one's achievements and impacts upon the world and upon one's peers is the only way to achieve any significant sort of remembrance. And once again, to bequest onto the world all of the wonderful and magnificent attributes that one's life has so undeniably created and expelled for the pleasure of all those who still remain upon this earth, that's a true legacy! To impress the people with every ounce of talent and genius allotted to us by God, in the hopes and in the fear that otherwise we would all but be forgotten. There is nothing scarier than that."

"Is that why you left your home and started writing that book?" Chris asked.

"That's exactly why," I sharply replied. "They say that to die without a name is the worst way to die, but I think that to live with a name and to die without a legacy is far more repentant, wouldn't you agree?"

"I agree," he said, "I agree."

So there I was in the last real summer of my life, conversations were sustained and fire consumed the limbs of once living trees. We sat and talked and grew to know each other like I had never before been able to know a person in such a short period of time. Discussions and stories were shared equally among us. I had my sayings and tales, and once I was finished and Chris's commentary on what I had said was over and absorbed, he then continued on with a completely new topic or story. For hours it went on like this, back and forth, word for word around the Eternal Flame. All that we would come to discuss was quite fascinating to me, but one fable that Chris would evidently tell on that night stuck gaudily in my memory above the rest.

"Know any good stories?" I asked, as the previous conversation was beginning to dry up.

"Sure, are you a fan of Greek mythology?" he replied.

"Well, of course, one cannot possibly consider themselves a writer without some sort of appreciation for ancient Greek literature. It is the roots of poetry and comedy and tragedy, and countless other aspects that have so significantly come to shape modern-day writing!"

"Good, then you'll love this one, and I guarantee you've never heard of it before," he said, wide-eyed and standing up unexpectedly with a backdrop of flames and ashes rising into the sky behind him.

"Alright, Chris," I said, "I'm all ears."

He was leaning marginally to the left against a slender but stable stick that he held, overlapping it with his boney hands and fingers and then hesitating for a moment while recollecting the words of a story, before twirling the rod over his shoulder like a Welsh Guardsman and then beginning. This was the story he told me, a story I will remember for as long as I live.

"In the 1700's," he said, "a deposit of preserved ancient papyrus writings were discovered during excavations of the ruins in the ancient city of Herculaneum. Most were severely damaged and undecipher-able… all but one, the very tale I shall tell to you now survived, and was secretly extracted and later translated. However, for some strange and unknown reason, this find was never documented in the arche-ologists' recordings or, as legend has it, mentioned of ever again by any reputable institution—perhaps because of its remarkability, being a curious scroll of Greek text in the ruins of a then Roman city, which was destroyed thousands of years ago by an erupting volcano; people may not have believed them. But mark my words, it was found, and it exists! My grandfather told it to my mother as a child, and as a sort of bedtime story when I was young, my mother would tell it to me. If I remember correctly the name of the story, in Greek, of course, is *γλυκιά θεία,* or in English, *Sweet Divine.* It is surely my favorite tale to be told," Chris began; he stood next to the fire with a statue-like pres-ence. Half of him was orange and smoldering, and the other half was shadowed by the immersing cape of night. I felt now that this is where the story really began…

"Amidst the divine Heights of Mount Olympus, the Gods resided; with the vibrant clear air stirring about its dips and peaks, and the radiant halo glow of sky, so close as to produce a reachable ceiling of fettle blue cloudlessness, ensured that gods were meant to live in heaven and here they surely did. Upon the topmost peak of elevation, shining god Apollo rested with his back against a veridical lip of stone. Sitting there deep in cavernous thought and sagacity, a prophecy soon flashed before his eyes. Amongst the lustrous stone faces of the mountain side, intensely lucid visions of a blood-soaked future, populations cowering behind great barriers, ramparts and walls, and troubled times to come, rendered him quite disturbed. After reminiscing in disgust the unfolded events he experienced first-hand of the Trojan War, Apollo sought out to inform Zeus of these disconcerting premonitions.

"In his regal chamber seated in deific majesty, Zeus averted his attention to what Apollo, in his evident distress, had to say. 'My father,' voiced Apollo, 'I have foresight that troubles me greatly. I have seen a third stage of violent unrest. Through broken treaties I've witnessed a deplorable end to these times of mortal peace. Spartans slaughter Athenians, fathers kill their brothers. Plague, famine, devastation, and surrender will come to rape the soils of Athens, and a declining divide of all of Greece shall soon follow! All of man's prosperities will be lost to the swords and arrows of his enemies. For the sake of Greece herself, something must be done. Some plan of prevention must be summoned!'

"While Apollo explained his troubles boldly before the king of all gods and men, heaven and earth, Zeus sat there, wise as he is, and placed his hands of knowledge and power onto the hands of his child, looked him in the eyes and responded. 'It seems so,' he said plainly, but with a tremendous sense of concern. 'It seems so, and I have seen it through that a hindrance of ferocity amongst men shall be intensely endeavored. I have seen what you have; I have known what you now tell to me to be true for some time, and for the sake of the people of Athens, a warrior among men must be raised to fight for man's peace,'—for the gods had become fairly patriotic of their marble-built country.—'Oh, how appalling it is to witness this careless display of death and destruction,' Zeus cried, 'spending the sacred souls of men like they're some sort of flesh-print and blood-soaked currency! Still, there is no wealth of coinage that can honestly justify the wars of populations. And so, something shall be done… it must be.'"

"Okay," I rather rudely interrupted, trying to get the story straight, "I'm going to assume Zeus is playing the hypocrite and no longer feels the same way about humans as he had once felt—that they had over-populated the globe, were a nuisance."

"Yeah," replied Chris, "in this tale he shows his sympathy… kind of, at least towards the people of Greece, which if you think about it really shouldn't be that unexpected."

"Got it." I said, and he, then leaning closer to the crackling fire, delve back into the dialog.

"'What shall you have me do?' Apollo asked, as across the room a large Dalmatian Pelican flew stridently in through the arched window from the fountain outside and landed onto a table. The flapping of its expanded wings caused a golden bowl of fruits to come flying off the surface of it and onto the ground. A shimmering apple, as green as blooms of hellebore, and as ripe it was prize, rolled across the marble floor and came to a stop at Zeus's foot. He reached down and took hold of it, observed its polished, smooth skin, and then placed it back onto the cold stone surface. He stood up and ordered the servants to shut the window and leave the room at once. They did as told. The pelican lingered however, as they could not get it to leave, and so remained, perched there on the edge of the table.

"'What I want you to do,' Zeus finally pronounced, seating himself and then retrieving the apple from the ground once more, 'is to summon Hermes and Maia and instruct them to come down here, for we have important matters to discuss. After you have done that I want you to go on about your day. All that can be done shall be done. I do not want to see you worrying yourself with troubling visions and the pains of men. You are a god, and need not to bare the burdens of the mortal soul!'

"So Apollo informed Maia, she retrieved Hermes, and they made their way to Zeus, and as they did so, a sense of residual anticipation seemed to follow them down the halls and up to the ornate mullion of gilded stone that stood above the large gold leaf, wood panel door. It swung open unexpectedly by an unknown force, and from the doorway and across the room, mother and son watched as Zeus, sitting gloriously upon his throne, gestured at them with his mighty hand to enter.

"'Come in! Come in! And join my company,' he said. 'Wine? No? Very well then, we have much to talk about. I have a task of immense standing with which I desire to present to the both of you. Greece is in a time forthcoming peril and declination. Events that shall trigger the down fall of peace and normality in Greek life cannot be allowed to occur, thus, leading me to seek the involvement of the two of you.'

'What will happen!?' Maia gasped.

'War,' said Zeus, 'bloody war.'

'The humans?' she asked.

"'Yes,' replied Zeus, as he, in despair, placed his face into his hands and his hands into his lap.

"Candles flickered around the chamber and webbed the celling with dancing lights. The drip-drop-tapings of melted wax falling from their sticks and hitting the marble floor beneath was like a calming trickle that helped keep steady the time.

'I look around and I see no evil, I see no violence!' said Hermes. 'What is this treachery of which you speak, and where is it now!?'

'It is… in the future,' Zeus replied. 'It is in the future, and the only way to change the future is to take action in the present. A task, Hermes, that is what I have for you.'

'And what is this task?' he asked.

'Ah, that is the question I've been waiting for!' said Zeus. 'I need to ensure that a leader among men is alive and able in the world during the times of these foreseen declinations. Now, Maia, I need for you to go and find a pregnant mother of Athenian blood. She will be expecting a boy. Tell her that the gods have come to her seeking the well-being of her child. Tell her everything: the wars to come, the need for a hero especially, and of course, the gods' desire to make her son that hero. Tell her that in seven years' time you shall return, and upon your return you will take the boy to the Styx River, there he will find his strength. Mind you, be sure that he is fully immersed in the water. Now, that is all I have to say to you, Maia… you may leave.'

"As she left, Hermes remained, mingling with the serpent coiled around his neck and arms, and soon a heavy sense of obligation fell upon him. The flashing candles made him feel dizzy, and he slumped down onto his knees in a bed of elegant silks and pillows. Zeus, sitting before him, stirred his expansive eyes in his direction and began to speak.

'Now, as for you,' he said, 'I have to ensure that the boy is raised accordingly. I cannot preside over this child for the next twenty years, and obviously neither can you. However, somebody has to do it. So, I need you to venture out into the oak groves and locate a dryad, a tree nymph, or someone of the sort. Then explain to her the circumstances. Tell her she shall be greatly rewarded for her service to me.'

'These dryads, they are extremely wary and reluctant, I suggest inclining Artemis of this task instead of myself,' said Hermes, 'for Artemis is surely the more suitable one for this assignment, and can communicate to them your wishes better than I ever could.'

'No, no, I have already asked her and she refuses. After Chione she never wants much of anything to do with what she considers to be Apollo's affairs,' Zeus replied. 'So it must be you.'

'Very well,' said Hermes.

"'Good, you shall plant an oak tree next to the home of the boy. I want you to inform the dryad of these rules as well,' he said, handing him a folded piece of paper.

"On the paper were written the guidelines which Zeus had set forth for the dryad to follow in terms of her relationship with the boy. Strictly a presider, she was to be. No verbal or intimate contact with the boy what-so-ever. The future of Greece rested in the boy's hands, and Zeus would not have that tarnished by some vile demi-god to mortal love affair, though he had had a few.

"So Hermes set off for the oak groves, and Maia in search of a mother; Zeus remained atop mount Olympus in his regal chamber and thought. Outside the weather was warm and impeccable; he longed for his conscience to be as clear and as bright as the day time was."

Chris then closed his eyes and the story stopped. I shot back into reality and realized that I was no longer with the gods, but actually just sitting outside in the darkness of the woods of Kentucky. The only light was that of the fire, and it was dimming. But it was alright, we were in no hurry to replenish it. What was there that needed to be seen anyways? We had resourcefulness, after all, and a visual imagination. Besides, while describing the night, what more is there to talk about than shadows? From behind the low fire, which we stoked just enough so that it sustained a gentle glow, Chris cleared his throat and rubbed his eyes with his palm. I asked if he was going to continue, and he said that he was, and then did so.

"Hermes emerged into the oak groves," he said, "and as he walked he was gloriously showered upon by all the pollens and overhanging catkins. Any sense of doubt seemed to dissipate as he felt the surrounding forest welcome him amiably. The trees and bushes danced and pirouetted as he passed by, and all across the woodland a peaceable aura of genuine heavens fell upon every creature within, drawing them out from their nests and burrows and after the magnetic attraction of Hermes. At a great and hulking Persian oak, he stopped and paused, and waited for a response to his presence.

"'Surely someone must dwell here!' he proclaimed in an instigating manner. 'This tree is all too fine a specimen to not be occupied! The leaf, so sweet and whole, and this trunk, so strong and free of any galls, leaves me feeling quite certain that there is someone home. I am here on behalf of Zeus!'

"The branches of the tree shuddered jovially as foliage soared down from them and around Hermes like a flock of birds, yet no wind was blowing. A moment later the tree began to glow with a sort of halo illumination, and a strikingly dazzling young woman in a fox fur skirt and a loose silk cape wrapped around her shoulders appeared before him in a flash of rosy brilliance. Her dark hair ran down her neck and back and resembled a flowing stream of water shadowed by the fall of night. It glimmered and waved and hung so naturally and gracefully that even Hermes, for a fleeting second, was breath-taken by her mystical elegance.

"'I am she who resides here,' said the dryad running her slender hand down the trunk of the tree and basking in the shade that the umbriferous leaves above provided for her below. 'My name is Agonia. You, I presume, are the one they call Hermes?'

'You presumed correctly,' he replied. 'I have been sent here by Zeus, for he seeks the assistance of a woman such as you, and a task is what he has asked of me to be presented.'

"'Very well then, you may present!' said Agonia as she jumped up and clung to a large branch, dangling from it with one hand, and delicately stroking the leaves of the tree with the other.

"Hermes reiterated to her the task and Zeus's wishes. He then handed the woman the paper containing the rules, and the woman, still dangling elegantly from the limb, read it out loud. The paper was address: *To the divine messenger.*

'Thou shalt not reveal yourself to the child,' she began. 'Thou shall ensure that the child is raised decent and accordingly. Thou shall ensure the child achieves their fate and for the time presiding, achieves his expectations. Thou shalt not engage in any relationships with the child, whether it be romantic, friendly, or et cetera, mutual or not. If there is trouble, you are to come to Mount Olympus yourself and alert me as soon as possible. Remember you are but an invisible guardian with a task and responsibility. Do not fail me.'

"Once she read this, all the celestial beauty and natural comfort that her presence alone seemed to expel was gone, and a disconcerting expression of dread came over her face of faultless complexion.

'I do not wish to be a part of this task,' she said.

'But you must!' replied Hermes, 'for if you don't, all hope is lost.'

"'Whose hope?' Agonia asked, dropping down from the branch and onto her feet.

"'Well, all of Greece shall lose hope,' said Hermes, filled with tension and somber sentiments.

'I do not wish to fail,' she said, 'surely I am not the only one who fears him!'

'If you do not partake,' Hermes replied, 'then you have already failed.'

'I have no desire to leave this oak or these groves. I love it here; I am one with everything here. This is my heaven!' Agonia pleaded.

"'If Apollo is correct, and I have no doubt in my mind that he is, then in twenty years' time or maybe less, there will be no more oak groves, there will only be ashes and death,' said Hermes, turning his back and walking away from the tree with his head low in defeat.

'Wait!' cried Agonia, 'is all that true?'

'More true than you could possibly imagine.'

"'Very well, I suppose I shall be of service,' murmured Agonia reluctantly, but trapped and fearing for the sake of her beloved wilderness.

'Excellent, you are not making a mistake, I assure you,' said Hermes. 'Once the seed is planted next to the home of the boy, you may come and carry out this task. Will you need me to inform you?'

"'I will know,' she replied vaguely, and then vanished into a canopy of thick leaves and piercing branches.

"Miles away, in Athens, shrouded in a wool cloak, Maia sat in a seat on the side of a dusty city road populated with hundreds of townspeople trading furs and crops and other goods of the sort. For hours she waited alone for a woman who fit the description. She sat there, with gem-like eyes of the most solid black, and gazed into the faces and souls of all who were around her. They were the exact opposite of the eyes of the drunken Lydian man she had seen wandering around the meat seller's shop with a gold coins held between his sockets; a smile stretched wickedly across his scruffy face, and he poked at little girls and stray animals with his worm-eaten walking stick. But as day drew closer and closer to night, suddenly, passing by holding a jute rope tied to the neck of a young goat walking beside her was, at last, a pregnant woman of Athenian blood! Maia stood up with great anticipation and soon followed quietly behind her.

"After walking a quarter of a mile and leaving the bustle of the town behind them, the woman sat herself down on a green patch of grass under the shade of a tree and ate her mid-day bread. Maia made her attendance known and approached her with a striking internal intrigue and an outer presence of motherly solace and, grinning as she walked, sat down beside the young girl.

'How far along are you?' Maia asked.

"'Just about nine months,' said the woman quietly and respectfully.

"Maia then placed her hands onto the woman's belly. The child within kicked and stirred, but the woman remained motionless. They both looked at each other and smiled, and the mother knew right then that she was in the presence of divinity.

'It will be a boy,' said Maia.

"The woman laughed heartily and then said, 'that's what my father assumed after he felt him kicking, but how do you know?'

'I know everything there is to know, my young daughter. Shall we go for a walk? Then again, perhaps not, you are quite pregnant after all. Too much physical exertion might not be a good thing.'

'Perhaps you are right; on the other hand, my goat does need to drink. There's a stream not too far from here, if I am not mistaken,' said the woman. 'Is there something you wish to speak to me about?'

'Indeed there is. Come, let us be on our way.'

"Maia walked hand in hand with the mother down the grassy separation between the crop fields and the densely forested stream. It was a land of high hopes, at one point in time. Now the only hope left was the reassuring sign of nature still surviving. If it wasn't for the presence of this land of expanding trees and swollen rivers, resilience and contentment, no such hope would exist.

"At the stream, while her goat drank the clean, cool, running water, and rested happily, Maia and the mother sat down together on an embankment by the edge of the brook. Maia then told the woman Zeus's orders and the reason why she was here with her, and the woman sat there in amazement as she listened to these words.

'When he goes down to the river,' asked the mother, after hearing it spoken to her by this seemingly angelic being, 'what will you do to him, you know, to make him stronger, to make him a warrior?'

'Now, now,' said Maia, 'some things are better left untold. The river, she'll do what she does; there is no what or how about it, as far as

you should be concerned. All that is needed of you is your approval…
do I have your approval?'

"The young mother paused and looked down at her sandal-
strapped feet, and at the sand that had found its way between her toes,
and the moisture of the earth and the grass below. She thought carefully for what, to Maia, seemed like forever. She was so frail; she was so
harmless, and Maia had little doubt that she would not agree.

'I presume that I really have no other option but to approve,' said
the mother. 'How I love our county and our gods and our culture! I've
had such high hopes for this child since the beginning, and this prospect of such a magnitude surely could only come around every once
in a life time or two.'

'Wonderful!' exclaimed Maia, 'a beautiful blooming oak tree and
a son of desirably chosen great expectations is the future that awaits
you!'

"The woman went home that evening and rested in her bed,
and slept more soundly and silent than the empty night itself. Maia
returned to mount Olympus, as did Hermes, and Zeus was ever so
pleased to hear of the eventual success of his messengers.

"The next day, just as the sun had risen into the sky, Hermes and
Maia ventured to the home of the young mother, unbeknownst to her,
and planted the seed of an oak not too far from the window of the
room that was to one day be the boy's own. Once the soil had been
entirely brushed across the seed, burying it appropriately, the two of
them turned their backs and began to walk away, on to their next individual and additionally unrelated destinations. Then, as they walked,
not more than a few paces from the home, an earth-quaking rumble
and growl trembled vehemently behind them and beneath their feet.
They turned around and saw that what had just moments before been
an oak seed, had now astonishingly grown into a fifty foot tall, soaring and mature tree. Watching as it continued to strenuously push its
way out of the ground and higher and higher into the boundless sky
above, Hermes knew that it was surely Agonia's doing, and of it, he
was methodically impressed. That night, the mother gave birth to the

child and, for the first time in a long time, an omnipresent feeling of marvelous hope fell across the lives of the land.

"Years passed and the boy was soon approaching his seventh birthday. He had already been taking combat lessons with his father, a local soldier, for a few years by this time, and he proved himself to be quite brave for his young age, and a wonderfully quick learner. Still, the family knew that he would soon be taken down to the river, and the gods were bound to return at any day. Once the boy turned seven, in the coming weeks that followed, he found himself unable to sleep at night and was stricken with bouts of restlessness. When he was able to get his mind to sleep, he was tormented with night terrors and lucid dreams of all sorts, leaving him weak and without the expected energy reserves of a young child. Agonia, taking notice of the boy's distress, decided against the will of Zeus to make herself known to the boy that night in the hopes of being able to soothe his agitations.

"Pale beams of light shone down from the sky window, illuminating a single rectangular section of floor beneath. The boy wanders down the hall of his sleeping home and stands in the patch of light and stares up at the soon-to-be morning sky through the above window. A forcible gust rattles the walls of his dwelling from the outside-in. The creeks and clanks of the structure around him echo throughout the room. Then, sensing swift movements in a distant and darkened corner, the boy's attention is averted as some strange disturbance catches his eye. He retreats back two or three steps in disbelief or fear as he watches the roots of a large tree bulge out from beneath the floor boards and tiles in front of him. The roots venously twist and coil with surrounding objects and furniture, making their way up walls and around corners. Fixated, the boy watched as the dryad appeared to him in a stunning light show of flares and flourishes.

"'Perhaps this is a dream,' thought the boy to himself, 'after all, I have hardly been able to keep to my slumber for a number of days now. How I am ever so exhausted!'

"Then, as if his thoughts had been read, Agonia spoke to the boy as if in response to his thinking, and this subconscious communication turned verbal startled him something awful.

'Empty minds are easily filled, my boy,' said Agonia, 'what is it that detaches you from your sleep night after night? Why art thou so reckless, child?'

"Breath taken, the boy rubbed his eyes forcefully and shook his head as to try and wake himself from whatever unpleasant dream he supposed he had wandered into. When that didn't work, he then reached out his hand and placed it onto the cheek of his visiting deity. He felt her, she was flesh, and he knew then that she was really standing there before him. They existed side by side, and he was sure that this was no delusion. His heart sunk and fear of the unknown coursed throughout his body quicker than his own blood. He jumped back, and jerked his hand away from her porcelain face.

'Who are you that stand before me!' shouted the boy. 'Stay away!'

'Oh, have no fear, child, I mean you no discomfort. My name is Agonia. Now tell me, what is it that so obviously ails you? I may hold a solution of sorts, one that I would be more than willing to offer you if I could only bare the knowledge of your difficulties. I mean you no discomfort.'

"'I suppose I can attribute my restlessness to mere anxiety,' said the child, who was also something of a poet, his hands now held tightly behind his back, swaying uneasily and timid. 'Things were always so bright it used to seem, and I once felt welcome here in this home to dream, but now methinks the tides have turned, as our moral bridges burned, and new ideals soon plant themselves inside my mind. Dreams of the future soon turn to nightmares, and then back into dreams again before becoming my reality. I am fearful of who I might one day become. I just want to do good things for my homeland and for the people I have here to love.'

'My, how you are one spectacularly intelligent young man,' said Agonia. 'Yet, you still do not know it all. The world has big plans for you, my child! You have little need to worry, for the gods are on your side. They are always ensuring your protection.'

'Who are you?' he asked.

"Agonia laughed softly and then said, 'I am the one who guards, and I am the one who can help. Your insomnia, dear boy, will not do you any progress. Won't you allow me to intervene?'

'You may,' he replied.

"So Agonia placed her warm, soft hand of consolation over his tireless eyes, and in no time at all, she had granted welcomed sleep to the boy. Yes, just as Athena—regardless of her meddling—had granted sweet sleep to Penelope during grievance for her lost husband Odysseus, weary from three long years alone in a room in Ithaca, knitting and undoing her cloth-work day and night, fooling the unwelcome suitors and dog-like scum of men who sought to take her hand in matrimonial companionship firmly against her will after the assumption of her great husband's honorable death as a result of his enigmatic disappearance after the Trojan War.

"From then on the boy was fine and slept comfortably and routinely. Agonia felt she had done well and feared not the wrath of Zeus. To her good fortune, his wrath never came; it seemed that he and the other gods were entirely unaware of their interactions. Agonia soon took a liking to the boy, and the boy to her. That next morning, Maia appeared at his home, and after comfortingly conversing with his mother, took the boy by the hand and they made their way down to the river. It would be a Sisyphean journey; it would not be quick and it would not be easy; and there was a chance, of which he was well aware, that he would never see it come to an end. For two days Maia and the boy traveled through woods and villages and knolls and deserts, all on horseback and with little rest. Two days after that, they returned home. The boy, he was entirely unchanged from an outward point of view, but inside his drive for valor and strength grew tenfold. Within weeks he was able to out-muscle his father in whatever physical or combat-related challenge he was confronted with. Word of his godlike strength spread throughout the city, and within a short time the boy had realized his true fate. He strode to conform to his expectations, practicing his fighting and sword handling skills daily and exercising persistently. As his determination grew, so did the increasingly more-frequent interactions between him and Agonia. He would often wake in the morning and peer out his window to see her lounging amongst the limbs of the tree, swinging from them and fencing with their boughs. As years passed, with the burdens of war looming on the brim of the future, the boy would often work himself into a frenzy, and again started to lose sleep at night. When he did so, Agonia would come and soothe him, and they would talk and laugh, and as he entered his teenage years, he soon fell deeply in love with her. When Agonia realized what she had done, she felt ashamed and indecisive. She knew that surely Zeus would find out. And what would he do to her then?! And the boy, how she ever did care for him, and could not bring herself to hurt him, let alone break his heart; but realizing the drastic practicalities of her offense, she, one night, finally proceeded to detach herself from the child she had sworn to protect, as had been instructed to begin with."

Chris now sat down beside me and asked if I were still interested in hearing the rest of the story. Considering the fact that hardly anything shocking or wildly plot-twisting had yet to happen—aside from the beginning flames of passion in a newly found romance—I still had that sense of anticipation within me, just as Chris had had when I was telling him about old Chester Love and all of his unfortunate episodes. I told Chris by all means to continue, and he did, sure enough. But before he got back into the world of the gods, and before he could tell me what was then going to happen to Agonia and the boy, an ear-rupturing crack of thunder exploded above our heads like a car crash on the highway, and a light but icy rain began to fall. I immediately connected this occurrence with a scene in *Sweet Divine* that Chris had just told to me not more than fifteen minutes ago. Before the rain fell, the unnaturally silent wilderness around me was making it seem as if this night we were in and this tale being told had all been my permanent environment for the last two years, or maybe more. In other words, time itself had all but left the building and had, in doing so, cluttered my mind with fragments of reality and illusion. Just as the drip-drop sounds of melted wax falling from the candlesticks onto the marble floor of Zeus's imperial chamber kept steady the time, as did the sound of the cool midnight rain hitting the tops of leaves and branches above my head. Then, before I could drift off into my own thoughts like I had planned on doing while standing alone outside of that vacant gas station on my first night here in Kentucky, Chris splintered that possibility as he once again unexpectedly stood up in front of me with a backdrop of flames and rainfall distractingly warping behind him, and began again with the story where he had left off.

"The dawn that followed the night Agonia had finally made up her mind to distance herself from the boy, fearing for her own safety, the boy strode further to attaching himself to Agonia. He approached the tree that morning with an ornately sewn cloth that he had dyed using the valonia of the tree. He wished to offer it to her, but she, quite to his dissatisfaction, never appeared. He sat there in the shade with the cloth and wept. Through some unpleasant subconscious vibe that lingered in the breeze and in the sounds of the leaves fluttering above his head, he knew that she would not return. *What had I done wrong?* He thought. *Why did she not come? Where did she go?* He was haunted by her absence, and soon this misery took a toll on his training and responsibilities. Although Agonia did not show herself to the boy and, in doing so, had made him think she was gone forever, she still kept a watchful eye on him. Once she had noticed her separation had beckoned quite undesirable outcomes, and ravished with guilt for making him feel so down, she again, fearing for her own wellbeing that Zeus would notice the boy's displeasure and scold her for it, resorted back to her old ways of promiscuously and protectively interacting with the young soon-to-be hero.

"As the forthcoming night darkened the parcels and streets and forests, and as the people of Athens all ventured home and into their beds, the troubled boy did not. He had remained under that tree for two whole days and refused to move—could not move, for that matter—as he was stricken with the most soul-quelling case of heartache that had ever been so unfortunately spread from person to person like the disease that it is. Between streams of warm tears, he shut his eyes and fell asleep. When he awoke the next morning the cloth that he had brought for Agonia, the one that she had never come to receive, had been strewn up by the wind, so he thought, and was wrapped around the high branches of the tree. The boy stared up at it with tired eyes, and then began to ascend the trunk in an effort to retrieve it. He climbed and climbed, but the tree seemed endless in its height. After scaling upwards many feet, he peered around himself and observed how obviously encased he was in the leaves. They blocked all sunlight and view of the ground beneath. Land was non-existent, as was his homestead, for he had now entered into the realm of something unknown. Having forgotten all about the cloth as he climbed, and noticing that he had passed it up by a body's length in his moments of forgetfulness, he shook the disorientation from his head and began to clamber his way back down. As he descended however, he was stopped in his tracks as a gentle hand grasped onto his, and, looking up behind him, saw Agonia in all her inherent beauty and splendor, and it might as well have been Venus. His eyes opened wide and his pupils fluctuated as if a piercing light had been shined into them. In the passion of his love and in awe of her presence, he lost his balance and fell from the tree, soon hitting the cold earth below with a loud and traumatic thud. He had been knocked unconscious, but when he awoke he was not on the ground or in his bed or anywhere of the sort, but, to his surprise, right back up in the branches of the tree, while Agonia dabbed his scathed head with a wet cloth, and ran her delicate fingers through his thick hair.

'How do you feel?' she asked.

'Wonderful, now that I can see you.'

"Then, as if under the control of an undesired affection, Agonia lowered her head ever so slightly and kissed the boy on the lips, and he was happy once again. Night after night they would meet. He would climb the sturdy branches of her tree and make his way to the top, where he knew he would surely find her. They would romance and converse and share in each other's company and bask in the joys of their union. She would sing to him and serenade him with her lyre, and he would listen with great attentiveness and fascination as she graced the days of his life with her spirit alone. Their love for each other was now mutual, and for those months that passed as these relations occurred, Agonia had all but forgotten about Zeus and his orders and the task that was her own. In their blinding love for each other, nothing else mattered, and no civil duty or divine responsibilities seemed of any importance to them. As wars and surges of violence broke out around their country, the boy's calling to protect his homeland fell on deaf ears. With the Athenians fighting a losing battle, Zeus soon took sharp notice and realized the situation at hand, and when he did, for the lack of better words, he was furious.

"He ordered Agonia to Mount Olympus at once. She was consumed with dreadful thoughts as she found herself approaching the ornate mullion of gilded stone that stood above the large gold leaf, wood panel door to Zeus's chamber. This time no divine force politely opened it; she arduously pushed the massive doors apart, using all of her strength, and then entered shamefacedly into the room.

"'Sit!' Zeus ordered, 'and if you have the nerve, look me in the eyes!' and so she did.

"'Now, Agonia…' he said as if there were a bad taste in his mouth, 'tell me, what sick, immoral satisfaction do you arouse through tormenting this boy? Do you not understand the consequences of your foolish actions?! Are you a fool?! Because if so, I should cast you down to Hades at this very second; I'd find great pleasuring doing so, too, I'd have you know.'

'Oh, please, have clemency on me, I beg you,' she pleaded.

'Clemency, you say? Clemency! HA!—Do you honestly feel that you deserve mercy from me, after all that you have done wrong?!'

"Quietly, she wept, and at her sulking fear and pity Zeus found great amusement.

'Yes, cry. Please cry; I love it!' he said 'I should straddle your soul to the depths of the underworld and leave you to the black mercy of Erebus! I should strike you dead where you stand!'

'Please, reconsider! I have served you well, please!' cried Agonia.

'You have served me well?' he replied, 'HA! You really must be the liege of all fools if you imagine that to be true! But I'll tell you what, I will have mercy on your pathetic little life, there is too much death already—on one condition, that is. You are here by terminated from the task I had so irrationally entrusted to you. I do not need you any longer, and the boy shall be sent off to fight immediately. Until then, however, you must have no contact of any kind with him… or else. Do I make myself quite clear?'

'Yes,' she replied with tears flooding down her cheeks, and a blush of hot blood reddened her face.

'Good. Now get out of my sight!'

"Still caught deep within the trappings of love, she could not resist the temptation of seeing her partner for one last time. She knew the risk she was taking. She also knew that it was very likely—more than likely, for that matter—that once he was sent off to war, she would never see him again. Horrified by this thought, she ventured to the home of the boy, crept up into the branches of the oak tree, and awaited his appearance, which she knew would only be a matter of time. After maybe an hour, the boy made his way out from an open window, stood at the base of the tree, and called out her name. A frisson passed through her mind when she realized that he was there, and a moment later she was standing in the grass and holding the boy by his hands. She was crying, half out of sorrow and half with delight to see him once more. He was startled to see her so shook up, unaware of her encounter with Zeus, and he asked her what was the matter. So she told him, and then he cried, too. They embraced each other and sobbed, and allowed the pain to flow from their weary eyes. They truly did love one another, and to the boy, the thought of their inevitable separation was worse than death itself.

"After holding each other close with arms wrapped around shoulders and hands clenched tight, she backed away and looked him in the eyes. Agonia knew that she could not stay much longer and so did the boy. It seemed to them that no casualties or revulsions of war could be any more painful than these final few moments that they knew they were about to share together, quite possibly for the last time. The boy was crying irrepressibly, but Agonia had somehow managed to regain her composure and was trying hard to calm him down. She took his hands and pressed his palms against her heart, and he felt her sympathetic adoration and the love for him that coursed through her veins, and she felt the boy's love for her that flowed through his.

'When I am gone and you are down and it feels like suffering and despair exist for you and you alone, just remember, my love,' she whispered, 'as was said in the choruses of Agamemnon: "be sorrow, sorrow spoken, but still let the good prevail!"'

"They closed their eyes, and for one last time, they kissed. As their lips pressed, the most prolific sensation of comfort and acceptance emanated from within them, and then it was over. Hardly could they bask in the love that they shared, for suddenly, along with the sinister resonance of thunder groaning in the distance, a blinding bolt of lightning came screaming down from the violent black clouds above and struck the tree at its heart, igniting it in an explosion of lights and singeing all its leaves to ashes, leaving nothing but naked boughs of smoldering embers blowing in the frenetic wind. When the boy opened his eyes in sudden trepidation, Agonia was gone, and he stood there motionless and abandoned. She had fled to the farthest reaches of the uninhabited realm and was never seen again. Zeus had succeeded in ridding any existence of the beautiful tree and their communal love with one swift strike of wrath and vengeance. The next day the boy was shipped off to battle with a broken spirit and a bleeding heart. As for what was to become of him, and of Greece, and of his homeland, now only history can tell…

"That's the end," said Chris. "What did you think?"

"It was great!" I replied. "One of the finest tragic love stories I have recently heard. It was like a shorter, somewhat warped version of Achilles, and I guess that explains the outcome of the Peloponnesian War."

"You think so? I may have paraphrased a little. And how did you know that that was the war being discussed?" Chris asked.

"Well, it pretty much told you from the beginning. The first clue I suppose was when Apollo mentioned a third stage of violent unrest. A second was his mention of broken treaties and the fact that Athens surrendered, and then the divide of all Greece that would follow as a result. Anyone with knowledge of Greek history could have told you that."

"You're quite right," he said, "I'm impressed. I thought that surely I was going to have to explain that part to you."

"Not this time, Chris," I said. "Though, I am left now with a heavy sense of remorse for poor Agonia and the boy."

"Why?" Chris asked. "She lured him away from his duties, and as a result destroyed all of Greece. Maybe not single-handedly, but she hardly helped the cause. In my interpretations of the story, I'd say Agonia was evil, a succubus, a damned witch!"

"What!?" I replied in a gasp of disagreement. "That's not what I took away from it at all. It was simply a tale of a love that could never be, and I pity them."

"Well, that may be so. But isn't it curious to you that her name was Agonia? In Spanish that means agony, and through her actions and with every person she interacted with, that's exactly what she brought!"

"Yeah, I see your point," I said, "but I wasn't aware that the Greeks knew Spanish." I laughed under my breath, imagining that at some point in time Chris had been heartbroken by a beautiful Spanish girl. I then cracked the knuckles in my hands, the vulgar, unexpected sounds of which had surely sent a horripilation of uncomfortable shivers to run up Chris's back and dance around on his neck. "You may consider her evil," I continued, "but still, I like to think otherwise. It was such a sweet story, for the most part, like an ancient children's tale, and I can't help but to sympathize with her."

"If that's what you believe, Sean..." he said in a taunting laughter.

"It is," I said, "and that's the way I like it."

Then the rain stopped and silence filled the air once more. Sometime soon thereafter we both fell asleep, and in my REM I dreamt of the wondrous past and all the strange and beautiful things that had happened thousands of years before I ever existed; and with those contemplations, I so painfully longed to have been alive in a time that was not my own.

VII

The Curse of the Pendant & the Stone

The moon still shone bright as I peered into the dim morning sky. I was lying on my back halfway outside my roofed-off lean-to shelter and watching it as it hung there in elevation beyond the clouds through a small gap in the thick canopy of leaves. For a while, I laid gazing up at the occasional flocks of gulls that would come soaring across the opening as they made their way to the sea, and I was sung back to sleep again by the nightingale that nested in the birch tree above my head. The sky was like dark blue watercolor paint on canvas, and the few remaining stars above stood out like glimmering dimples. I loved waking up to the sights and sounds of the outside world, and not to the redundant patterns of tacky wall papers and uncomfortable furnishings. Nothing makes you feel more alive than residing in a place where everything you can touch and perceive, and everything around you, for that matter, is living just as well, seeing and thinking and sensing your presence as you sense theirs. Mutual interaction with nature, from the very dawn of time, has always been our true nature, and I'm made ashamed by the fact that modern-day living consists so little of it.

Around eleven, Chris and I were both up and cooking ourselves a luxury breakfast of jerky and chicken noodle soup. Actually it was disgusting, but it was sure a hell of a lot better than starving. I had probably lost around ten pounds since we first started living out there. Occasionally, I would fall victim to migraines caused by the lack of food

I was taking in, usually in the mornings or after a long day of hiking and exertion with no calorie consumption to restore the large reserves of energy I was so regularly exhausting. I needed glucose! I needed it like a car needs fuel, like a ship needs an engine or a sail. Everything you do when you're out in the forest, from finding food and water, to simply walking a few yards from camp to gather firewood, can take a lot out of you. Aside from that though, I loved being where we were, and living so close to the Fountain of Youth made many of those necessities, oftentimes strenuous in acquiring, fairly easy to obtain.

My twig house, my amateur, makeshift chalet, stood a couple feet away from a large bulge of sandstone that protruded out of a slanting dune of mossy earth and leafy plant life. Each morning ever since we set up camp at that spot, I had carved a tallied line of the days onto the face of it. After engraving today's line—slashing across the four previous ones to make five—I added up the markings. There were twelve. I had left my home in Athens on a Friday, and three days later I met Chris, and that next morning we had left the modern world behind us— so that meant that today was a Sunday... the second Sunday of the month. Right then an odd feeling of accountability crept over me, but I couldn't quite figure out the reason why. I sat down beside the large wall of stone and thought for a while. It was something important, it had to of been. Why else would I have felt that way? Then it came to me!—I knew what it was I was trying to remember. It came to me in a visual image of the note I had left for my parents tacked onto our front door. I realized that today was that "other Sunday," and they were surely sitting at home in the kitchen anxiously expecting my phone call!

"Chris!" I cried out, "We've got to go back."

"Why?" he asked in disappointment; so I told him about the note and that dreaded phone call. I told him about their expecting it, and how I feared that they feared that I was dead.

"No problem, Sean," he said in response to my request, as a good friend should. "But we gotta leave now if you want to get there by seven. It'll probably take us all day to find our way back."

"I agree," I said. "You ready to go?"

"Yep," he said, and then cracked a long, detached tree branch in half over his thigh to make a sizable walking stick. "But will we return?"

"Well of course," I assured, "it would be a sin not to!"

And so we left, and as we departed, I stopped for a moment, took a deep breath of clean wilderness air, and looked back at our campsite. While the sun rose and set as days came to pass, like the turning pages of a book, our site, after much attention, had begun to quite accurately resemble a suitable tribal village for two; and I now felt more comfortable there than I did in any spotless, suburbanized structure I had previously lived in. I simply couldn't wait to return, and as we made our way closer and closer to civilization, I began to miss my leafy hut of a home even more.

The hike back to Chris's house was complicated and demanding. Although there were no falling trees or mishaps resulting in one of us plummeting down a mountain side this time around, it still took us hours to find our way back to the trail we came in from after having distanced ourselves from the campsite and clambered down into the ravines. Everything looked the same and yet, so unfamiliar than it did when we first trekked through it. After miles of wandering, we finally agreed that this one particular slope leading out of the abyss was indeed the one we had used to get into it. Ever so cautiously, we made our way up and back out into the denseness of wood. About an hour or two after that, Chris, with his compass in hand, spotted the dirt trail that would eventually lead us back to his property. We fought our way through the interminable, narrow route and passed the violent fencers of thorny branches and, in one welcomed and relieving moment, we found ourselves standing on the dead grass of Chris's backyard, and staring across at that old, crumbling mansion. I had never been so glad to return to that decaying abode—and not because I had grown to resent the wilderness, but because I was exhausted and hungry, and, in my moment of weakness, had forgotten all about my jungle utopia, and gave into the desire of modern comforts, and as Chris said, "a stocked pantry." God, I was so hungry, and before we did anything, we ate a seemingly five course meal of every category of food we could get our hands on. Anna sat there in her rocking chair and stared at us in amazement; and can you blame her? Here we are, two senseless kids that she hadn't seen for over a week, sitting in her kitchen shoveling all kinds of random foods into our mouths as if we were being held against our will by some cannibalistic witch from a Brothers Grimm fairy tale and forced to do so. We were covered in dirt and blood, and our clothes were torn and soggy; I can't even imagine how badly we smelled.

Once we finished gorging ourselves and diminishing the Armsworth's family food reserves for the next month, Anna insisted that we go into town and buy more, otherwise *she* would be the one starving. The time was only around five thirty, and we had a while before my parents were expecting that dreaded phone call. Chris and I trudged our way to the garage where we had parked my car days before. He then proceeded to stand me up against the exterior wall and spray me over with icy water from the hose. I in return did the same to him; and now officially looking like wet, lunatic hikers, we made the drive into town.

Once we pulled up onto Main Street, Chris said, "We should go to this neat little antique shop that's just around the block after stopping by the grocers, do you still have the artifacts?"

"Yeah I do, they're in my pocket. But just so you know, Chris, you're not going to be able to get me to sell 'em."

"I assumed that," he said, "but it'd still be interesting to see what they're actually worth, don't you think?"

"I suppose so," I said, and then veered into an empty parking space in front of the swarming and crowded supermarket, with its large glass panel walls and excessive amounts of sales flyers taped to the windows that were in fact the walls.

Once inside, we went our separate ways. Chris broke off to locate all the items on the list that Anna had made for him of things to buy, and I wandered thoughtlessly, drawing the eyes of most everyone I passed. I strolled down the breakfast aisle, and then the meats and grains, and then I turned into the produce aisle, where next to a wall of lettuce heads, a beautiful colored girl with lengthy dark hair and a vibrant lapis lazuli stone choker hanging from her slender neck was counting the money in her purse and acting flustered and concerned. A greasy Italian man and his Sicilian wife, both dressed rather fashionably for a simple trip to the market, soon accompanied her. I watched from a distance with a strange and undetermined curiosity. I don't know what it was that made me stare and wonder at them, but they were certainly drawing my attention, of that much I was aware. After a few odd moments of motionless gazing, the woman and the man and his spouse turned a corner and left my scope of vision. A half a second later, Chris crept up behind me and swung his flat hand down upon my shoulder, startling me and causing me to drop a box of cereal I held onto the check-patterned floor.

"Are you ready to go?" he asked as he reached down and picked up the box I had let fall.

"Yes."

So we left. When we got outdoors it was sticky and humid, hotter than it had been on the way over, and it felt like the air was more water than oxygen. As hordes of people passed us by on the sidewalk, a warm scent of sun screen freshly applied to the sopping skins of sweating civilians hung in the thick oven-air above our heads and lingered. The sweltering temperature was causing the glass panels of the storefront to fog up with condensation, for the building was poorly ventilated, and the outside wood frames of the windows were all dampened and rotten. We got back into the car where the temperature was twenty degrees hotter, like a torrid fever, and the steering wheel was almost too heated by the relentless rays of sun to touch with bare hands. Eventually, however, I did so, and we backed out into the street. Chris announced the directions to our next destination with enthusiasm as I came to a halt at a stop sign hidden behind a lopsided tree, and then we were on our way again to the "old curiosity shop," as Chris had called it, perhaps stealing that title from the Charles Dickens novel of the same name.

Around the next corner and about a half a mile further, a small and shabby wood structure that resembled an enduring 1880's western saloon stood prominently on a barren patch of unkempt land. I parked the car on the side street and reluctantly put a few cents into a meter. We got out and walked a couple yards to the store where Chris stopped and stared up at the large porcelain sign above the door. *Kentucky Treasures*, it read, and after producing the two objects from my pocket, we entered the shop.

Inside we were greeted by an overall-strapped fossil of a man standing behind the counter and spitting snuff into a rusted can by the doorway. Cigar smoke seemed to loom around his head and throughout the room, but to my knowledge, he wasn't smoking. There was no lit pipe or cigar in sight, for that matter, and there was no one else in the shop. I remained highly positive on this fact as I looked around the store and noticed that there was not much in it. Worn and rusted tools with splintered wooden handles, along with glass candy vending dispensers, empty cans of pomade, and old oil tins lined the walls and filled the aisles and empty corners. It looked more like an unserviceable general store than an antique shop; the man behind the counter must have been the oldest thing there.

"What can I do for you?" he said with a bulging lower lip of soggy tobacco.

"We've got a couple interesting and recently stumbled upon objects here that we thought you might like to take a look at," Chris replied.

"Well," said the old man, "are you just going to stand there or are you going to show me?"

I took the items and set them out on the counter. The man then produced a strange pair of golden scissor glasses and studied the pieces meticulously, and for quite some time. As I watched him, I noticed the intrigued expression he had on at first soon turn to a worried scowl, and he shoved the objects in a rejecting manner across the counter back towards where I stood. He rose up from the seat he had taken while studying them and said in an intense and insulting tone of voice, "Take your goddamn *artifacts* and get the hell out of my store!"

We stared at him speechless and confused by this sudden outburst of anger and refusal. He threw his arms up and shouted at us again, "You boys deaf?! Get the hell out!"

Chris then walked up to the counter in an intrusive manner, slapped both hands onto it, and asked the man what the problem was in an effort to maybe calm him down and remedy the irrational situation, or perhaps to pick a fight.

"You boys have no clue what it is you got here, do ya?" he then said, spitting again into the can.

"If we did," Chris replied, "then why the heck would be here?"

"Now you listen to me and you listen good," said the old man, "I'll tell you what it is you have, but once I do that, you two need to either get the hell out of my store… or get the hell out of my store! Got it?!"

"Got it," I said.

"Got it," Chris said after me. "Now tell us what's so damn important about these objects that you had to go and throw a big ol' fuss!"

"What you've got here," he finally revealed, "are two evil, and in some cases, even deadly, cursed objects. They're entwined with dark magic and possess a sort of conjure or voodoo spell. I suppose you found them things out in the woods, huh? Well boys, you see, this town used to have a large population of African diaspora voodoo groups and practitioners, they migrated up here from Orleans a long, long time ago. They used to hold sacred rituals out in them hidden caves in the woods not too far from here. In order to protect themselves from lawmen and fearful Christians during the 19th century, they would cast spells onto objects just like these and leave them scattered round their sacred sites and habitations. If some stranger with a curious mind or with a plot to do them harm came down into those caverns, they would surely stumble upon these carefully placed objects,—they're traps! Once removed from their original places of origin, and once in the unfortunate possession of those who had disturbed them, the curse would be unleashed and attach itself to that person like a blood-hungry leach, like a vampire tic. Oh, how it is a dreadful curse, and the most dreadful thing of all is that there is no way of knowing what specific curse has been placed on any one particular object before it is too late, and that person has already fallen victim to its torments!"

I was now scared, but Chris, he wasn't fazed at all, and continued to barter with the old wise man.

"Okay, so there's some neat history here—how about a hundred bucks a piece for these fine heirlooms? That's a deal surely even someone as stubborn as you couldn't pass up!" he said.

"Boy, are you crazy?! Those two things ain't worth more than an heirloom tomato to me! But they're as deadly as bullets!" shouted the old man. "Now go! Get the hell out!"

Chris then left, and stood outside the shop on the sidewalk smoking a cigarette and walking in circles. I remained inside; I had a few questions of my own.

"Sir," I cowardly voiced, "if these things are cursed, and now that I have them, am I cursed?"

"Goddamn right you are! Get out!"

"Well wait, you've got to help us! There's got to be some way to break the curse... isn't there?!"

"Sean, you don't really believe that shit, do you?" Chris yelled, sticking his head in through the opened door from outside. "He's just trying to scare you and mess with your mind. He's a crazy old man!"

"Ignore him," I said, "there has to be a way to undo it. The last thing I need right now is a curse on my head."

"Okay, boy," replied the man in a silent and secretive tone of voice, and then leaning down uncomfortably close to me so that I could see his tired, twitching eyes, and the hairs in his nostrils, he said, "There is a way."

"Well, what is it?!" I shouted back at him, now desperate for an answer.

"The only way to break the curse," he replied, "is to take those things back to where ever it was you found 'em and... destroy 'em with fire! Ten days after that, the curse will have been lifted. For if you don't, your fate is misery and your future is black; I suggest you do as I say, boy, or I shan't be seeing you again. Now get the hell out!"

So I left, and as I strutted out onto the sidewalk, I was stricken with fear and panic. "We've got to go and destroy these things right now!" I yelled to Chris, who obviously couldn't care less. "We're screwed if we don't, I'm telling ya! I can feel it in the air! I can sense that something's not right, and that this curse is already in effect!"

"That was just old Mr. Calente," he said, "and if you haven't noticed, they say he's of the superstitious type. He's a local legend… more like a local nutcase. I personally think he's lost his mind, war trauma can do that to you. He was a general back in World War II, and now he owns an antique shop. If you ask me, I'd say he's way too old to be working a job that requires interaction with the public. Seriously, Sean, don't let him spook you with all that nonsense; he's just stuck in the past."

So taking Chris's advice and calming myself down with a few deep breaths, I put the objects into my backpack and forgot about them. We got into the car and headed out of town. We pulled up to Chris's house ten minutes before seven thirty, and in a nervous rush, I stopped the car but forgot to park it, and as Chris got out, the old mobile started backing down the driveway with no one behind the wheel, and I was already sprinting towards the house. When I noticed what had happened, I watched helplessly from the porch as Chris darted down the pathway and jumped into the driver's seat to yank up the parking brake.

"Sean," he said in a stern voice, as if I was talking to my father, "that was honestly ridiculous, you gotta be more careful. Your car almost wrapped itself around that tree on the other side of the street!"

"My bad," I apologized, "I'm so nervous about having to talk to my parents, I forgot to park it. I just know that they're going to give me hell for this whole thing!"

I waited in the kitchen sitting on a stool next to the cultured marble counter top by the telephone anxiously counting down the minutes until the clock hands came to strike seven thirty. While I waited, however, and while Chris was in the cellar restocking his backpack with supplies for our next trip into the woods, the doorbell rang. Anna got out of her chair and walked across the hall to see who it could be. I stood there secretively and then, in a tactically evasive spy maneuver, learned only after years and years of domestic espionage, I tapped across the room and proceeded to extend my head slightly around the corner of the wall so as to catch a glimpse of who was at the door and what it was they had to say. When she opened it, two exceedingly office-accustomed, gangly white men in black cashmere dress shirts stood there on the porch, and then, as a wave of intrigue fell over me, one of them held out a small badge and said, "Mrs. Armsworth... we're with the IRS."

Anna mumbled something to them that I couldn't understand, and then I heard the man say in a demanding voice, "You owe over forty-five thousand dollars in backed taxes. I don't know what else to tell you, but you have ninety days to come up with the money or this home will be reclaimed by the bank, and your possessions will be auctioned off to help pay for your debts."

Then, after slipping Anna a small card, the men left. She sat down on the dusty, cat-crowded sofa and starting crying. Probably after realizing that I was still in the kitchen, she got up slowly and ascended the staircase into a room and slammed the door behind her.

The next thing I knew it was seven thirty, and without any time to formulate an opinion on the short-lived, random altercation resulting in the unfortunate adjustment of the Armsworth's family finances, my procrastination immediately kicked in. "I'll just call at seven thirty-five," I said to myself, "they won't care; besides, I told them I might not be able to call exactly on time." When seven thirty-five rolled around, I knew I couldn't put it off any longer. I walked back over to the grimy counter top and stared blankly at the rotary dial system of Chris's phone. In my state of anxiety and dismay, a lapse of intelligence hit me like a slap to the face, and I couldn't for the next few moments figure out how to enter my home number. Then, I snapped out of my mindlessness and scrolled in the digits, the dial tone sounded, and then it connected, and when I finally heard my father on the other end of the line, I nearly fainted.

"Sean?!" he gasped as if I had just awaken from a yearlong coma, and he had been there watching helplessly, sitting at my hospital bed the entire time painstakingly waiting for this moment come.

"Hi, dad," I said in a pitiful whisper. "How are you?"

"How am I? How am I? Oh, I'm just fucking dandy!" he shouted with a sharp change in character. "Where the hell are you!?"

"Prospero, Kentucky... dad," I answered.

"What in the world are you doing there? You're supposed to be going to Oxford in less than two months, and you pull some shit like this! You little bastard! Have you no regard for anything?"

"That may be so," I replied. "I had to do this, just for the summer, just this once. Seems to me that you guys are mad because you think that I'm a failure, and maybe I am. But so what! I'm not Matthew, dad; I can never be him, no matter how badly you want me to!"

Then he hung up in a fit of aggravation. A second later I called back, and this time it was my distraught mother on the line. Crying silently in the hopes of disguising her pain from me, she said, "Sean, come home. Please! I've been so worried about you, so scared. Are you okay?"

"I'm just fine," I told her in a comforting manner. "I'm perfectly safe, you don't need to worry."

"Well, thank the Lord!" she said. "You pissed your father off something awful. He's storming round the house right now cursing and punching the walls. He packed all your clothes and books and basically the entire contents of your room into boxes and threw them out on the lawn last week. I had to go out there in the middle of the night and gather it all up and bring it back inside so that it wouldn't be warped by the weather. Jesus, Sean, how did you ever expect to make it anywhere in that immobile car of yours? And to try to drive all the way to Wisconsin!—I assume that's why you're in Kentucky… because that damn thing broke down and refused to take you any further. Now we're gonna have to drive all the way out to where ever the hell you are and bring you back home! And Sean, didn't you know that Sebastian is away right now in Rapa Nui? He's been there with a Chilean film crew working on a moai documentary for the CBC. So even if you did make it there, you wouldn't be able to get into his house, it's locked and barred up; he's been away for months!"

"I was quite unaware of that," I said. "But I'm sure he wouldn't mind if I broke a window or two just to get in, as long as I paid for it. And again, I'm just fine, and so is my car. You don't have to come get me. I met some people here in Kentucky, and they're really great, and I'm having the time of my life. So, you can tell dad what I said in the note: that I love him, but I'm just not ready to become him... not yet."

"Sean, you don't have to become your father for him to be proud of you, or for you to be able to feel like you aren't failing him, or yourself, or whatever it is that's driving you to do all these reckless things. You know we both love you."

"I know," I said sorrowfully. "And I don't want to become him, but to become some snobby, bookworm, office-fuck is just the same. Once you attend Oxford you either come out on the other end as T.S. Eliot or John Fowles. Both of which were successful, but dreadfully over-intelligent and dull."

"I thought you were a fan of Fowles's writing?! You used to love *The Collector*, what happened?!" gasped my mother, as if the very foundation from which she knew me had just crumbled beneath her feet. "Besides, Sean, how can you be so pessimistic about this? That Rhodes scholarship of yours is worth more than some silly youthful indulgence of excess and independence, surely! Hell, it's keeping you out of the draft, ain't it? It's practically a gift from God!"

"I don't dislike Fowles," I said. "I just dislike the flaunting academicism of people with a high intelligence quotient. Even though it is their God-given right to display their genius,—as it is my right to parade mine in whatever manner and through whatever medium I feel appropriate—I just don't believe it is decent to be loved or hated or judged or admired by one's own family and friends because of their scholarly endeavors. Sure, I want to go to Oxford; it is the greatest school in the world, as far as I'm concerned. I just get so upset over the fact that I'm now suddenly expected to live up to this family intelligence standard, and to shine as bright as or brighter than my father and brother, otherwise risk being shunned and reprimanded if I don't. Do you see what I'm trying to say?"

"You're quite the contradiction, Sean. But of course I understand," she spoke softly, "I just didn't realize how much our family's competitiveness and expectations affected you. I am not too jaded to admit the fact that we hold each other to somewhat higher standards than most families."

"Damn right you do!" I barked, partly joking. "That's why I'm in Kentucky with my good friend Chris, whom you have never met, and his family, whom you have also never met. In a way, they are the exact opposite of our family, and I've never truly felt more at home."

"Sean, I hope you don't mean to say that you're replacing us... with strangers!" she cried. "I know your father and I have never been the picture-perfect parents, but we love you and want nothing but the absolute best for you. Please, come home!"

"I will come home," I said, "but not tonight. Not this month, for that matter. I have a book to write and a legacy to form. Don't you understand? I've gone too far to just up and turn around. I've been through too much to say that I haven't learned anything. I've committed too many wrongs to admit that you were right. I love you, and I'll see you in a few weeks."

"I love you too, Sean. God, please be careful, you have so much life ahead of you. Don't waste it! Please, don't waste it!"

Then I hung up the phone and sunk into a pit of spiraling emotions, none of which I could accurately distinguish. I had far too many thoughts and concerns spilling over the brim of my mind to have ever really made anything of them. After a few minutes, the intensity of my mood from having spoken to my parents for the first time in weeks began to dissipate, and I immediately thought of the heinous situations regarding Anna and the IRS. Directly after that thought entered my mind, Chris shot up the collapsing wooden staircase from the cellar, and was standing beside me in the kitchen with an armful of blankets, fishing poles, bags of dry rice, beans and other canned foods.

"How'd that phone call go?" he asked. "And is it just me or did you hear the doorbell ring?"

We gathered all we needed in order to survive like we had before, and, after locking myself in the bathroom and repeatedly splashing my face with water from the sink, I met Chris in the backyard. As we left the house and made our way again to that dirt trail on the outskirts of his property, leading us into the woods, the sun light was visibly getting dimmer, and we assumed that it'd be quite likely that we wouldn't be able to make it to our ideal encampment before nightfall.

With the color of the sky deepening and the forest coming to life, as it often does in the dark, I knew I had to get to the bottom of that troubling scene I had witnessed back at the house.

"Chris," I started, "when you were in the basement and I was up in the kitchen, the doorbell did ring."

"So it did?"

"Yeah, it did," I replied. "And guess who came to the door… two IRS debt collectors. Chris, I thought you guys had loads of money left from your late father? Can you explain to me exactly why Anna owes over forty-five thousand dollars in unpaid taxes? Shit, they're going to take your goddamn house away and auction off all your things!"

Chris bowed his head and fiddled with his thumbs in a nervous fashion before looking over at me with sulking eyes. "Well, Sean," he said, "I suppose it's safe to say that I haven't been completely honest with you. If you really want to know the pitiful truth behind my family's debts… well, I admit you have every right to know."

And that pitiful truth, as it turns out, was that Chris had decided to buy houses with the money, multiple properties across the state of Kentucky, and an old grain farm in Tennessee. I couldn't believe what I was hearing, and I was even more furious when I finally came to hear the more detailed truth.

"Houses?" I asked in a shock of confusion.

"Well," he said hastily, "they're not exactly houses…"

"What are they then?"

"They're parcels… lots… no houses, just land," he revealed.

"You bought land!"

"Yes."

"What exactly did you intend to do with that land, Chris?"

"Well, I reckon I intended to grow stuff on 'em. You know, crops and vegetables and whatnot," he said.

"And…" I replied with obvious agitation.

"And what?"

"And… did you ever grow any crops?!" I shouted.

"No," he said coldly.

"Why?"

"The soil was bad," he stated, and then broke off from the conversation as I pierced at him with eyes of hateful disbelief; he picked up pace and cowardly made away ten feet ahead of me to avoid my rebuking glare. A few minutes passed, and after staring at the ground while walking for a tension-filled while, I looked up and saw him coming towards me threateningly from ahead. We stopped there on the trail and were staring face to face with heated vibes of disgust for each other hanging in the air like the mesh of dark branches above our heads.

"What!" I snapped.

"What!" he shouted back, "I'll tell you what! Why are you always so sure of yourself? Why does everything you say have to be so goddamn intelligent?!"

"I can't believe you did what you did!" I replied. "Why do you feel so entitled to everything?"

"Maybe because I haven't been given everything I wanted, or didn't want, but still got anyways, for my entire life!" he yelled. "I long for entitlement!"

"That money should have been for Anna's retirement, if anything, you asshole! Now you've left her and yourself as good as homeless. I hope you're happy!"

Then he got quiet, and I felt a little ashamed for having been so upfront with him, but I was still immensely pissed off.

"I can get everything that I want, but nothing that I need, so a lot of good that does me," I said under my breath but faintly audible.

"How can you even stand there and say that to me as if it's a misfortune?" Chris howled, clenching his hands together in two tight fists of anger, and breathing heavily. "You have everything that you could ever want, and are about to be given the opportunity to acquire everything that you could ever need. You know nothing of disappointment. My life is but a fucking miscarriage! Failure is the worst kind of pain, Sean. Failure hurts more than anything. You're just another conceited, over-confident, cloned human being working at a high rate of efficiency! I suppose… maybe I was wrong about you."

"Well, maybe I was wrong about you, too!" I retorted with a hateful gasp of abuse. "I thought you were intelligent, a little odd, sure, but intelligent. Now I can see you're just a goddamn mooch! You take advantage of anything and anyone you see that you think you can use to your own selfish advantage! You have zero regard for anything but your own desires. You don't work, you just live off the ended life of your father and all his labor! Well, Chris, we have names for people like that, and it's trash, white fucking trash!"

"I never wanted to dig us into this hole, Sean!" he then cried. "When I bought that land, I thought it was my ticket to success! I thought it was going to be like the plot of *O Pioneers!* or some shit. I thought I could toil the land and make it work for me! I had it all planned out, it was perfect! But nothing ever grew, ever! Everything I planted refused to sprout, or died shortly there-after, or was eaten by rabbits and strays. God, I never intended to make the mess that I've made. Don't you think I feel guilty? Don't you think I know how fucked up this whole thing is?! Sean, I'm so sorry I dragged you into the middle of this."

The tensions dissipated almost immediately, and a trickle of sorrow ran across my mind. I did care about Chris, and I was ashamed at how I had judged him the way that I did. In the end, we're all just people… but some people are really stupid.

"It's alright, Chris," I said. "I'm sorry for being so harsh to you; I was just upset about the situation."

"It's okay, Sean, you were right, and I love you for it! I love you because you're the first person to let me know that I've ruined my life! Why hasn't anyone before had the decency enough to tell me? I really needed to hear it said; it feels almost as good as being told that you're loved, because at least there's some trace of concern and honesty behind it. God, I've ruined my fucking life, and I've always knew it!" he bellowed out with his hands on his head and tears in his eyes as the night fell upon us quickly and with little regard for our well-being. We were now stuck in the woods with no fire, no camp, and no sense of direction; but at least we had forgiven.

We met each other with an apologetic embrace, and I said to him, with the nature of a concerned friend, "There's still time to change, Chris, there's still time to make things right. And if it turns out that you can't, well, doesn't everyone end up ruining their own lives somewhere down the line? So what if you ruined yours from the get-go, at least now you don't have to live the rest of your life in fear of awaiting your inevitable downfall like I have to." I laughed and patted him on the back reassuringly, although my words might have had the opposite effect; but I had tried my best to make a completely horrible situation into a somewhat unpleasant but manageable one, if nothing else.

It was now too dark and dangerous to make our way to any sort of specific location. With the drafty chill of night crawling its way up the openings of my sleeves and pant legs, we hunkered down beside a large tree and covered ourselves with blankets. The whole night we were miserable and freezing. It must have been the coldest summer evening I had ever experienced. The temperature, I estimate, had dropped to an unnatural forty-five degrees. If it wasn't for the sheets and blankets Chris had packed, we'd be dead for sure.

Morning came with a blinding light that pained my eyes even though they were shut. My throat was sore, my head was heavy, and my back was as stiff as the tree we had leaned upon the entire night with the cozy bark as my pillow. Today's mission was to finally make our way back to our original site by the Fountain of Youth, and avoid having to spend another wretched night unsheltered in the woods. We set forth following the western arrow of Chris's compass, as we now had no indication about where it was we could be. Chris told me that he hoped the compass would lead us to the ravines, and once there, we'd be able to follow the channels until we reached "the spot."

We filled our canteens with a minimal trickle of old rain water that was still dribbling down the spine of a large elephant ear leaf. Surprisingly enough, with some well-disciplined patience and persistence, we were able to successfully fill our bottles to their carrying capacity and, handing me a ration of beef jerky, Chris and I started back on the hike in search of our village.

Much to my incredulity, we had managed to reach the ravines in less than two hours, and well before noon. We used the long trunk of a fallen tree as a ladder to get down to the base of the cliff and out of the woods above. Everything seemed to be going in our favor, and I had no doubt that the old man's curse was nothing more than delusional, superstitious bullshit. Besides, as Chris had said, war trauma can do that you. But right when I had acknowledged our good fortune, it seemed to have run its course, and we eventually found ourselves moseying around for hours in a labyrinth of winding ravines and inlets leading to dried-up ponds and swampy pits with no sense of direction—quite like mindless lab rats lost in an intelligence-testing maze for scientific purposes. Then, when all hope seemed to have been lost, we began to hear the faint sounds of running water. As we walked, the noises grew louder and louder, and had excited us so much so that we began to jog, and then sprint, and before we knew it, we were racing through the ravines like elands running for our lives away from a herd of starving lions eager to feed their young.

Darting up and over rocks and fallen trees and mounds of earth and puddles of muddy water (as one might expect), we finally came to a stop when we were confronted with a dead end. We were devastated but undaunted, for the sounds of water continued to tease our minds with the thought of salvation. We scaled the wall in order to reach the top and, with an oscillation of revitalizing joy, we found ourselves staring straight out at our campsite, untouched and undamaged, standing exactly the way we had left it. Oh, how the moment was joyous! But the triumph and delight was momentary, and soon an awful stench and a swell of impending death and decay crept over me and made its way under my skin and wrapped itself around my soul like a strangulating squid. We walked over to the Fountain of Youth to find that it had become a shallow, sludgy, green pool of stagnant water, undrinkable and rotting with dead fish floating on the surface of it and devilish crows teeming overhead; periodically one of them would swarm down and peck out mercilessly their lifeless eyes.

Yes, indeed, they seemed to be casting omens down upon us and with no clemency; to isolate and kill was their vengeful tendency. They had distorted the beauty of our cascade like a bacteria-poisoned well that had made an entire village ill with typhoid and giardia, the cadaver-blue bodies of the townspeople lining the sidewalks like a plague-ravished city of the Middle Ages. The putrefying odor of fresh decay and death that arose from the pool made it so that Chris and

I had to step back some twenty feet in order to simply breathe clean air. The film of green murk and slime hissed and bubbled. It was this image of noxious fluids stirring in a cauldron that made me cringe, as pestilential gases seemed to rise out of the cesspit whenever one of these bubbles would pop, gurgling like a hungry stomach and shooting gastric acid high into the air. We were appalled; surely this was the work of a vengeful and unbreakable curse! A curse who like a demonic stalker had succeeded to extinguish the blaze of the Eternal Flame, to stagnate the crystal waters of the Fountain of Youth, and to lead us down a trail of demise without us even having the slightest clue of it. Surely we were fucked, and destined to suffer the harsh reality we had wrought through naivety and the selfish pursuit of frivolous desires.

"Ch-Ch-Chris," I said in stuttering terror, "I'm starting to believe that this curse was no joke. Why can't you believe what that man said? A person doesn't just say shit like that without themselves at least believing it to be true! And I'm starting to believe that we have fallen victim to a lethal spell of long-forgotten times! And that what old Mr. Calente said had been right all along!"

Chris was standing there with eyes wide in disbelief. His hands were trembling, and he was paler than I had ever seen him before (and that's saying a lot). He then turned around slowly with a haunted expression of dismay mortared to his face and said, "Sean, let's go home."

He couldn't have taken the words out of my mouth more quickly. There was something wrong in the way the air seemed to touch my cheeks, and in the way the plants and leaves seemed to sway from side to side, as if they were laughing at us and taunting us for our unfortunate fates. The sound of the eerie sloshing of stagnant waste water from the distant pond sent goose bumps crawling up my arms, and a shiver of anguish rippled from my head to my balls to my toes, then back up to my balls before finally residing in my stomach: the feeling of the strangulating squid grasping my soul, squeezing tighter and tighter, assuring me of my impending doom.

"WHHHHYYYYY!" I screamed, "WHY ME?!"

Our blood boiling with irrationality, we darted back into the wilderness trying to distance ourselves as much as we could from our former site of comfort and happiness. I felt betrayed by nature, betrayed by my own curiosity, betrayed by my own desire for change and excitement. We ran for what seemed like miles, and we kept on running with no destination or end in sight. We ran and ran and ran, until suddenly Chris stopped and slouched down under a tree with tears welling in his eyes.

"Sean, we're lost!" he cried, as would a scared child separated from his family. "Let's be logical. Let's stop here and make a fire before it gets too dark, and well think of what to do next in the morning. This is all too much for me to handle. God, Sean, this curse is real! I can feel it in my bones; it's latching itself to my soul like a throttling squid!"

"I feel it," I said in response to his unsettling, all too accurate and familiar metaphor. "I feel it, too."

Darkness fell, but sleep didn't come. We stared at the fire with dead eyes the entire night through, and never said a word. And while describing the night, or while describing a thing of the night, what more is there to discuss than shadows and obscurities? And it seemed to me that that was all we were, two scared shadows in the night, running away from nothing and everything all at once. We were stiff with fear and uncertainty. Would we ever get out of these woods alive? Would the curse see it through to slay us before the week was done? Was there any hope at all? When morning came, it was time to find out.

I opened my eyes, it was day time. Finally, there was the sun, but Chris was nowhere in sight. I called out his name once or twice, a swell of panic building within me. The large shrub beside my mess of blankets began to rustle and shake, as if some critter was squirming beneath it. I stood up and walked to the other side of the bush, and there I found Chris. He was crouched over in a ball, and I could hear him faintly moaning, trembling, as if in pain. "Chris," I said, "is everything okay?"

He then rolled over onto his back, and I thought my eyes had deceived me. He was sweating profusely and shaking with fever. He was clutching his forearm tight against his chest, and his contorting facial expressions were wincing with agony. "Cuuuuurse!" he squealed, "Cuuuuursed!"

"What's wrong?!" I shouted, but it was obvious.

As Chris slowly revealed to me his arm, I saw what it was that had been causing him so much discomfort. His entire arm, from wrist to elbow, was swollen and throbbing, thick with inflammation, crimson and veiny, like the exposed muscles of a skinned cow, brisket and shanks hanging from steel hooks in a butcher shop. I let out a shriek of fear and asked, in the most frantic tone of voice, what had happened. He didn't answer me with words; instead, using his other, unscathed hand, he started indicating to me a claw or fang gesture with his index and middle fingers arched and thrashing at his wounded flesh. "You were attacked?" I questioned, and he shook his head no. Then in the shakiest and most sickened vocal sound I had ever heard, he said, "Bite! It was a Bite!"

I dragged his helpless body over to the base of the tree where we had slept. There I laid him out and put my backpack under his head. He then gestured again with his good arm, fingers still coiled in their imitation fang position, to his duffle bag, which I knew contained the first aid kit. I ripped it open and extracted the white plastic box with the large Red Cross symbol on its top. I opened it; he pointed to a small glass vile that read *ANTIVENOM*. The only problem was that there were two bottles, one for snakes, and one for spiders. "What bit you?" I asked, and he uttered, "Spi…" and then trailed off as I watched his eyeballs roll to the back of his head. I read the small fine print on the back of one bottle, and it read *Vipera tab.* "Snakes!" I uttered, taking the other one, knowing that it was surely for the spider, and it read *black widow antivenom.* I stuck the syringe through the cap and filled it. I pressed up on the pusher and let a squirt of liquid shoot from the top of the needle. I felt like a doctor, though I had no clue what to do next. I was surprised that I had gotten this far. But knowing that Chris was on the verge of anaphylactic shock, I slammed the needle down hard into his arm and injected the antidote, hoping for the best.

A moment or two later, Chris's eyes shot open and a gasp of breath was sucked in through his gaping hole of a mouth, and he screamed. Then, looking over at me with fraught eyes, he said, "Thank you, thank you!" He leaned back his head onto the soft ground of dust and orange leaves and stared up at the sky. The rest of the day was insignificant in comparison, and we didn't move from that spot; he was too weak to do so at that point anyways. The next morning, however, he was fine, a little weary, but fine, and ready to get the hell out of the forest. It was surely out to end our lives—it meaning everything and anything; and how *it* hadn't succeeded in doing so that day, God only knows.

VIII

The Thief and the Liar

Chris's arm, once back to its normal size and color, was left with a chilling scar. Two tear drop puncture wounds on the center of his forearm, a few inches above his wrist, stood out prominently and were both the size of pin pricks. I asked him if it hurt, and he told me that he had never felt such pain in his entire life. He told me that he was quite accustomed to being in pain, and that when he was around seven years old he was on a tire swing and the branch from which it had been tied to snapped, and in so doing, sent him hurling through the air; he landed on his shoulder and broke his collar bone. On a separate occasion, he continued, he had fallen onto the spike of a wrought iron fence after attempting to jump from his garage roof onto his neighbor's, and had succeeded in accidentally giving himself a stigmata, leaving him screaming in pain and dangling from it with the spike driven through his palm and protruding out of the top of his left hand. He leaned over and held it out to me, revealing the now-healed skin over a bellybutton-like puncture wound. He told me that this bite had been as bad as those two events combined, it was mind numbing and unbearable. "I awoke that morning," he said, "to the feeling in my arm of being branded like cattle with a red-hot iron. I jerked and saw a black spider, about the size of a dime, crawling off me and onto the ground. I smashed it with my foot and then within minutes I became dizzy and sick, my muscles tightened, and it became so difficult to breathe. Do you know what it's like to feel every organ in your body slowly shutting themselves down at all once? I wish I never had; and I doubled over in agony and grasped my arm; and while holding it to my chest, I tried desperately to make a tourniquet out of my shoe lace to stop the venom from flowing to the rest of my body, but before I knew it, I had lost most of my motor skills, and was unable to do so... that's when you found me, thank God."

"Chris, I can't even begin to say how glad I am that you're alright."

"Sean," he replied, "I can't even begin to say how glad I am that you decided to return the favor."

"What do you mean?" I asked.

"Well," he said, "it was only a matter of outcomes and events before it became your turn, if I should say so; after all, I had saved your life once upon a time."

We both laughed, and I wiped the sweat from my brow with the sleeve of my grimy and once white and fashionable button-up shirt, with its slick collar and frontal pocket that went over my heart. It was safe to say, and from the looks of our now tattered clothing, we'd both be long dead and working fulltime jobs as fertilizer if we hadn't been there for each other. I felt blessed, even though I was surely cursed. But still, I was grateful to have him by my side.

"Come on," he said, "let's get out of here."

I agreed, but then a terrible thought occurred to me. Surely, even if we did manage to get out of the woods, we would continue to be cursed, for the objects were still intact, and, to make matters worse, in our possession.

"Man, I want to get the hell out of here just as much as the next guy," I told Chris, "but you've forgotten that it's not the forest that is cursing us, it's the objects. They have to be destroyed! We can't leave here until they're destroyed; once and for all, Chris, let's end this!"

"You're right," he said with a somber expression, "we need to go back to where it was you found them and... what did that guy say?"

"Destroy 'em with fire!" I added.

"Right! Destroy 'em with fire! But there's only one problem..."

"What's that?" I asked.

"Well, I have no clue how to get back to the spot we found them at. In fact, I hardly even remember what the place looked like, so how would we know even if we did find our way back there?"

"I think," I said, "I think I vaguely recall where it was. It was close by when we had gotten into the ravines for the first time, placed on the sandy topsoil dead center on the ground in this odd, diamond-shaped cove."

The location seemed to us easy enough to find, I must admit, or so we perceived it to be at the time; but we were wrong. We ran the completely opposite direction after fleeing the Fountain of Youth, and we were hopelessly astray somewhere in the heart of the forest. Our luck was nonexistent, but still getting worse and worse, and our sense of direction was even bleaker than our providence.

With no other tools to use in terms of improving our situation, we followed the eastern arrow of Chris's knickknack, fifty cent pocket compass for the next two days. The sweltering summer temperatures combined with the dryness of Kentucky air in late July caused us to diminish our water reserves within the first few hours on the very first day after setting off in search of the cave. On the third day, I awoke to find Chris in hysterics. He was digging a hole into the ground with his bare hands, shoveling and throwing scoop after scoop of soil over his shoulder. He was digging for water; I knew this at first glance. My tongue and lips were like dry sponges left under the kitchen sink, gathering dust balls and flaking. Chris's eyes were wild and red and, still digging his well, he looked over at me with the jowls of a rabid dog, foaming at the mouth and panting. I walked back over to where I had slept; I had decided to give up my last mouthfuls of water to him, water that I had labored to obtain by climbing a large tree to retrieve a plastic bag that got caught high up in the branches and had captured some rain. Once I picked up my canteen, I felt that it was empty. I shook it to make sure, hoping that I had been mistaken, only to hear the sounds of a few grains of sand scratching and sliding at the bottom of the container.

"Chris!" I shouted, "where's all my water?!"

He stopped digging and looked up at me, and then sunk his hands down deep into the mud and flinched. He didn't reply, instead he just stared at me with a blank face.

"Well," I said in a more demanding tone, "did you take it?"

"Yes… but I had to! Sean, I would have collapsed, fallen victim to heat stroke and lack of fluids! I can't take it! I can't take it! I can't take it!" he kept on repeating, again and again until I had to run up on him, grab ahold of his shoulders, and shake him back into rationality.

"You crook, I was going to give that water to you anyways!" I said. "We need to find a stream. Come on, let's get going."

"I'd be content with drinking the sludge from the Fountain of Youth," he said as we started off into the woods. "I'd take amoebas over dehydration at this point. I just want the feeling of saliva in my mouth again; I'm not some resilient desert reptile! I can't take it!"

We kept on walking for what seemed like centuries. We crawled through the forest, and as the hours passed, the temperature rose. I soon noticed as we hiked that the trees had begun to wither and limp. Every leaf on most every tree began to shrivel and turn a sickly yellow color, like nuclear fallout had just occurred the week before, and brought with it a radioactive early autumn. I couldn't believe what I was seeing, and Chris, he saw it, too.

"This has got to be a mirage!" he'd shout out loud, and then reiterate the thought another ten times to himself under his breath.

It seemed to me that this curse was going to strike us dead, even if it had to eradicate everything else alive in the process. We were brought to our breaking point, barred from obtaining any of the vital necessities needed to sustain life. Aside from our lack of water, lack of shelter, and lack of direction, every time we'd sit to stop and eat, swarming crows would swoop down from the heavens like stealthy military jets and snatch the food right out of our hands. Whether it be jerky, bread, canned beans and rice, or anything else, they'd surely manage to get ahold of it. Our deaths would not be quick, they would not be clean, and they would not be violent or abrupt. Our deaths were going to be slow and painful, long-drawn-out and cruel. They were going to sting and stretch, burst and fade, and play on and on until we became but two shriveled and forgotten raisins, the ones you find left behind, dried-up and sticking to the bottom of the box. I wasn't exaggerating when, in between consciousness and recurring phases of delusion, I envisioned our soon-to-be sunburnt cancer patient, fasting hobo, rotted-wood- totem-pole corpses baking out in the ultraviolet rays under dead and drooping trees, untouched by wild animals due to noxious gases of decay rising from our demented bodies like heat haze rippling off the hood of a car in the summer time whose engine has been overworked and running for far too long.

Oh yes, it was safe to say that it was about time we had said our prayers. Hope was as strange and far-off a thing as the relieving gust of a cool breeze to take away the heat, or the comfort of a soft bed with fresh sheets and plump pillows. This curse was more physical than I could have ever imagined. I could see it lingering in the air and following us like a dark rain cloud above our heads; but the rain would never come, it would be all too fortunate. And so I thought; then I felt the pain of dehydration burning in my lungs, and I prayed, I prayed for it to be true, for the rain to come. However, it was true that the strangulating squid throttling my soul had long since died of thirst, but my assured doom was still as promising as ever. I knew that if we didn't break this curse before the end of the day, it would certainly be the final chapter in my book. I might as well have begun to carve *Sean Robinson: 1947-1965* onto a stone and lay it on my chest, and I would have advised Chris, who was just a few years older than me, to do the same.

Two hours passed and we finally found ourselves in somewhat familiar grounds. The hanging rock formations were tall and winding, and caves popped up more and more frequently as we continued, all of which we inspected thoroughly just in case. And then there it was, the diamond-shaped cove! And if we looked closely, we even saw the remnants of our old footprints. I set down the culprits of our demise in the dirt; Chris had a small cup full of gasoline he had siphoned from a disposable lighter, and I set up a rock circle as to sort of attempt to contain any kind of fires… but mostly forest. So I bundled up some sticks, and in my peripheral vision I watched as the world around me glowed green with rotting leaves that hung like throbbing tongues in every direction. Spirals of aberration and exhaustion combined with vengeful magic gusted like the breeze around my head, and whispered the sounds of my own death into my ear. "Do it." I said. And he did it.

Immediately the entire pit of stones burst into an explosion—perhaps a little weaker than a grenade, but it was still an explosion. Blue flames and a screeching noise of evil and hatred erupted. I matted my hands over my ears in order to cope with the deafening pain; I had never heard anything like that in my life. It was comparable to the sound of a speeding train veering off its tracks, or an industrial blender puréeing nails. The fire burned for thirteen straight hours. We sat there the whole day and into the night, when the fire finally died completely around seven in the morning. The trees commenced to bloom again, the curse, it seemed, was at last retreating. As the concluding flicker of flames died out, a subtle rain began to fall, and then grew heavier and heavier as we let it soak our clothes and cleanse our pores. But my relief was short-lived as I suddenly remembered what the old man had said: he said that the curse will only be lifted after ten days have passed. "We haven't even started day one!" I shouted, startling Chris who had no clue of the situation.

"Why are you shouting?" he asked.

"The curse takes ten goddamn days to be completely rid of us! The man said so, I think you were outside."

"Well isn't that just perfect. Now I can live today to literally die tomorrow! That's swell, ain't it? But at least those awful things are gone for good."

"At least they are," I mumbled.

That night we had no choice but to start another contained fire and sleep in the actually cave and on the eight feet of half damp, half dry land in the front of it. The rain persisted. I dreamt that night that I had gone to law school and lived in an apartment somewhere and made happy, comfortable money; I sat there and stared at the contents of my refrigerator. That made me happy, too. I closed the door of it and suddenly found myself in an alleyway, a dark and wet alleyway lined with dumpsters and telephone poles, maybe two a.m., and very urban. I was in rags, and in my hand I held a Dunkin' Donuts cup with four dollars and some change in it. An unseen musician high up in the stories of a soaring apartment complex nearby filled the night with the sounds of a saxophone. I may have had pneumonia. That didn't make me very happy. I saw a man and a woman pass me by on the sidewalk, and I impulsively asked them for money. I said, "Please sir, change? I'm a sick old man, won't you help?" And he did, and lectured me, and then tipped his hat and left. I cursed at myself, and wished that he would have just punched me in the face for having gotten to a point in my life when scenarios like that were frequent and necessary. Then I woke up, and it was still black out, and it was cool, and the winds blew strong, but not too harsh. It wasn't harsh… but it was strong, and prevailing. I drifted off again, but I don't remember what I dreamt that time. Maybe my brain didn't want me to. I'm sure there's a good reason behind it.

For Chris, consciousness came with a kick to the face. A tough young girl with ragged blue jeans on, topped with a white T-shirt and a red bandana wrapped firmly around her sweating brow, stood over him. With her boot, she pressed down hard on his cheek as if she were crushing a bug, moving her foot from side to side. He let out a grunt of pain; I opened my eyes and was greeted with a knife to my throat. A tall, thin man with tan skin was kneeling beside me; a good old country boy, it seemed at first, and then I saw the knife in his hand. His hair was dirty and matted under his Ascot hat. I thought he was Mexican, but then I realized he was a Jew; his skin had been baked by the sun. He crouched there by the entrance of the cave and said with a crazy grin while swaying from side to side, still wielding the knife, "I'll cut ya! Eeeyyyy'll cut you!"

"Oh, well, what have we got here, Jim?—homosexuals, maybe? Or perhaps bounty hunters? Runaways? Hicks? Who are you two?!" said the girl with her fists clenched.

"Homosexuals," Chris laughed, and then spit the blood from his mouth and chipped lip onto the girl's pants. She kicked him in the stomach forcefully, and Chris squirmed in pain on the ground, wincing and holding his gut. She walked over to me and the other man with the knife retreated some. "Who are you? Are you going to tell me or am I going to have to kill you to find out?" she spat.

"I'm Sean, that's Chris. We're lost in the woods; so glad you found us. Who the fuck are you?"

"Should we tell 'em?" said the man with the knife to the girl, and she punched him in the shoulder.

"I suppose that's alright," she said. "After all, we're lost, too."

"Oh, wow, Sean, they're fucking lost, *too*. Isn't that such great news? Awesome." said Chris with apparent sarcasm.

"My name is Billie, after Billie Holiday... self-named," said the girl as she picked the dirt out from under her finger nails with the tip of her bowie knife, of which she had just retrieved from a slit in the leather of her boot.

"Who's he?" Chris asked, unknowingly making himself look stupid.

"Actually her name's Shelby Vaughn," said the other guy.

"It's Billie to all of you. I hardly even want him to call me that, let alone you two sickly-looking fellas," she said.

"My name's Jimmy," said the other guy, then commencing to take my hand and shake it. "Yup, Jimmy English, that's my name. Born James, but, I find it so dull."

Jimmy and Billie then revealed to us that they were a pair of unintentional Bonnie and Clyde enthusiasts who were on the run after a slew of knifepoint robberies across the state of Mississippi. It all started, so I was told, when they met one day after the girl had built a tree house in a large oak on Jimmy's parent's property so she and her friends could go up there at night and get drunk. Jimmy noticed after his irate dad threw a fit about it one evening during supper, and he went out to investigate to find that she had done what she had done. He didn't know her, but had recognized her as a girl from his high school, maybe two years before. Against his father's threats and wishes, Jimmy did not take it down. He became tight-knit friends with Billie, and they soon became a couple. Their real trouble didn't start until Billie convinced Jimmy to tear up his selective service card and commit draft evasion in order to remain together. He did it, willingly, of course. "This ain't my damn war!" he said. And they loved each other, and she lived in the tree house.

I soon discovered that Jimmy was greedy, and Jimmy was as lazy and as winey as a spoiled dog, whoring for attention and longing for anything worth trying to get his hands on (mostly monetary things) was all that was ever on his mind. After tearing up his card, he became paranoid, and he and Billie often fought; but I guess they were still together, so they must've liked each other.

On May 24th, 1965, Jimmy and Billie robbed the Mayersville, Mississippi bank at knifepoint. Billie had disguised herself as an employee. She swept the floors of the lobby, her name tag said Shelby, and she chewed a piece of bubble gum. Once the crowd of twenty bank customers dissipated to around half a dozen, she pulled out her fifteen-inch-long steak knife. Jimmy ran up to the register, punched a bank clerk in the face, and she then led him to the money. The employees didn't even know what hit them, it had all happened so fast. And if they tried to call the police, they're hands would have surely been severed. They got away with $6,500 and a warrant, dead or alive.

Once Chris had heard this story, he was in awe, and kind of upset. He said, "Why did we have to run into this shit?! Bank robbers, great; Sean, did you hear the good news yet?"

"Yeah, well, Mississippi is a whiles away, word might not have spread this far," said Billie. "We're hoping for the best."

"Well you got the best!" Chris yelled, and then stormed off back into the cave.

That night, with no plan or destination, we sat around the transient flame, Chris sitting next to me, and Billie and Jimmy on the other side, cross-legged on the dusty ground. The rain had stopped some time ago, and the night seemed to be a clear one. Talking loudly over the droning songs of the cicadas that clung to the endless stalks of trees, Chris demanded to hear their tale again.

"How is it that you two met?" he asked. "And how is it that you're up round here in Prospero? I don't think I'm grasping this whole story."

"Well," Billie started with a wicked little smile stretched across her pink face, "Jimmy's father, Mr. Frankie English, owns a large patch of land, land with forested areas and trees. My mom's a bitch, says she won't let me and my friends or whoever drink in the house any more. 'No more damn parties!' she'd yell. So I said fine, whatever. I was walking home from class one day over at the community college and I passed by his property on a backroad. I saw a tree as tall as a building with thick, sturdy branches. It was nearly in the heart of his estate, but the guy is like forty-eight years old, so fuck him. No offence to you, Jimmy.

"So, my girlfriend Casey and I got a bunch of wood and nails and tools together, and I paid my brother five dollars to build us a little hut on one of the middle branches about fifteen feet above the ground. It took him the entire day, but that night we opened a handle of Albanian grape brandy and some champagne, and had a good old time!"

"Then they woke my ass up!" said Jimmy.

"Right, so here comes Jimmy storming out there in the middle of the night with a broom stick as if to run us out like cattle; and he was, if I remember correctly, fairly wasted, too," Billie added, singeing the sides of a twenty dollar bill in the flames of the bonfire, and acting as calm as I had seen her be thus far. She had a purple fanny pack strapped around her waist that bulged out awkwardly as if it contained a bowling ball; it was really just stuffed to the brim with money.

"My ex-boyfriend, his name was Calvin, had a father who was as tough as nails, and a real general, both literally and metaphorically speaking. Even before all this tension in Nam, Calvin was destined to be a military man. It's kind of hard to break away from three generations of courage and honorable deaths, after all. Every service member in his family, aside from his pigheaded father, had died in battle. A few weeks before Jimmy came chasing us out of the tree with a broom stick, Calvin was pressured into joining the regular Army by his family. He was shipped off to basic training and then overseas within the span of a month. I haven't seen him since; I'm sure he's quite dead. He's never written to me, anyways."

"At any rate," said Jimmy, continuing on with the story where she left off, "we furnished and lived in that tree house on most days, except when it was raining, then we'd go to my actual home. We lived like that for maybe two or three months, loved every minute of it. It felt like being a kid again, aside from the empty bottles and cigarette boxes, remnants of the previous night that cluttered the plywood floor. Then I got some draft card submission notice in the mail. I didn't think much of it until Billie told me that people my age all across the neighboring states were being sent off to fight, little by little. I still didn't think much of it, but she was really upset. She said that if I didn't destroy it, she was going to leave me. She said she just couldn't handle repeated abandonment—so I tore the damn thing up, and watched the pieces blow away in the breeze. It felt pretty good, until I learned that it was soon to be a federal offence. When my information wasn't mailed in like everyone else's, I began to get harassing phone calls from people urging me to do so "or else." Still, I never did it. I was often paranoid about the whole deal, but persistently was able to shrug it off. Then I began to shrug off a lot of things in my life, mostly responsibilities. For one, I stopped going to class; then I let my shitty job at the laundromat slip through my fingers. I stayed out late with Billie, and we'd go to clubs and bars and concerts, and became quite accustomed to the night life. Everything was a party except for the fact that we were broke, that always seemed put a damper on the good times."

"So in short," said Chris, "you two robbed a bank to get money to party. Did I miss anything?"

"Well hold on, hold on, that's not even the best part!" Jimmy replied. "Once the clerk behind the counter got me my money, Billie and I went out to the lobby where a mass of people were standing and shaking with fear. Billie held out the knife and shouted for everyone to get on the ground, where she would proceed to deprive them of their belongings. 'Wallets, watches, hats, jewelry, throw it all in the bag!' she yelled. Everyone complied until we came upon a fat old man gasping for a breath on the marble floor by the window. He chugged a bottle of Pepto-Bismol, and was dripping with sweat, perhaps overwhelmed with terror due to our presence. I said, 'Okay, fatty, give up your shit.'

He shook his head. He kept saying, 'You can't do this to me! They're gonna get you! You can't do this to me.' 'And who are you?' I asked him, and before handing me his wallet as I held the razor's edge to his neck, he said to me, 'I'm the mayor!'"

Jimmy and Billie busted out laughing, and slapped their hands down on their knees and on each other's shoulders, and they laughed until they were coughing. "We robbed the fucking mayor!" they shouted, and wailed at one another in obvious amusement.

"The mayor of Myersville stripped of his golden watchpiece, his silver pinky ring, and his pocket money, all while inside a bank! Ain't that just one big old irony?!" said Billie, hollering with considerable volume, awakening the sleeping birds, and stirring up the nocturnal critters surely hiding out in the trees and bushes around us.

"I can see how one might find wonderful enjoyment in that," said Chris.

"And I can see where one might find a dead or alive warrant in that," I remarked.

"I can see that the two of you are going to stop interrupting me or I'm going to get wrathful!" Billie made us all aware. "So if I could please continue…"

"Go ahead," said Chris.

"Well, the bottom line—or downfall—of the story began when Jimmy's dumb ass dad got hammered with his work friends one night, and had allowed his anger and resentments to spill over almost as much as the alcohol. He and some stupid fucking fisherman from the river port came charging (more like stumbling) towards us as we slept in the tree house during the middle of the night, each armed with glowing torches and an axe. They threw the torches into the branches of the tree, and soon the roof was on fire and crumbling with us inside. He was swinging the axe head into the front entrance, barring our only exit, and causing dozens of razor-sharp slivers of wood to go flying towards us with every psychotic hack of intoxicated, lethal tough love, strict parenting. We kicked out a panel in the back and leaped down to the earth. Watching the structure burn, we stood holding each other on the lawn with what for a moment I thought was snow fall. It turned out to just be ash; the entire tree withered away in front of us. I was brought to tears; Jimmy was brought to his knees. His dad laughed while we wept, and stumbled back into the house and into bed as if nothing had ever happened."

"I wept, yeah; but I had just woken up, so naturally it scared the shit out of me," said Jimmy, rather defensively. "But of course, it's all in good conversation!"

"That it is!" said Chris, who had just now taken on a whole new positive outlook on life, it seemed. He had a grin across his face like I had never seen, and for the first time in a while. I had no clue what had gotten into him, but it disturbed me almost just as much as the stories of these two strangers. And it was then that I realized that Chris was a rather impressionable person.

"Yep," Billie interrupted, "so we ran out of cash, robbed a few banks, held up a gas station or two… now we ain't necessarily welcomed most anywhere; so we escaped to the woods, trying now to get to the Midwest. Our parents hate us; they want me in jail."

"So forget them," said Jimmy.

"Exactly, forget all of them."

"Yeah!" said Chris, as if under some sort of hypnosis. He stared blankly at nothing. The fire made it look like he was made of marble, a statue in a candle-lit Roman cathedral.

"I know what you're thinking, Sean," he then said shifting his empty gaze in my direction. "You're thinking exactly what I'm thinking, aren't cha!"

"What is it that you're thinking?" I asked.

"Never mind, never mind," he said, "I'll tell you later…"

We let the fire burn, and after a while, Jimmy and Billie drifted off in each other's arms, and Chris and I retreated to the cave. The ground was alive with toads and other creeping things that I wouldn't even know how to mention. We had to shoo them all out with a stick before either of us felt comfortable sleeping within. Once we did so, him and I spread a dusty and dirty, but rather thick blanket across the ground and seated ourselves, hunched over and hidden by black shadows like two trolls under a bridge. Chris stuck the torch he had made into the earth beside him, and looked at me as if he were about to say something, and sure enough, this is what he said: "Is it just me, or does their story sound exactly and eerily similar to that cliché Greek myth I told you way back when? Damn bizarre, isn't it?! That's what I was going to tell you earlier, but I figured it'd be awkward to do so." He stopped and looked over at the blistering torch; then he looked back up at me, this time with tears in his eyes. "Oh, Sean," he cried, "how long 'til this will all be over?"

"Nine days," I said, unhappy and squinting painfully from gazing helplessly into the flame. "Just. Nine. More. Days."

IX

The Monte-Duff Manor

When I used to live in Athens, back when I was quite young, I had this toy that I loved. It was a doll of some sort, for boys though, kind of like an action figure of both cloth and wood. I don't recall what or who the doll was of, but I remember that it looked like a peasant, with knots of short brown hair and ragged green clothing. I remember that I would always look at it and feel sorry for the thing, but then soon thereafter get the urge to mutilate it horribly, to cause it pain. My friends and I would throw it high up into the air, and then let it fall back down and slam onto the sidewalk, watching its bones shatter. We would hammer it into a wooden fence with a nail, and then rip it off and stomp on it in the mud, or burn it with matches and lighter fluid. This toy was the most important object in my life; it was my treasured possession. One day, however, I was throwing it into the air and it got caught up in the top and hidden branches of a tree; I never saw it again. We moved away from that house the next year and across town. A few years later, I rode past the old home on my bike to see that the tree was gone; the new residents had had it pulled, said the roots were coming up through the kitchen floor, or something like that. And no, I never did find that figurine; it was not a favorable ending of all's well that ends well. And now, after waking up next to a weirdo and two bank robbers, I had started to see that in life many things will not end well. Just because something starts out shitty doesn't mean that it will conclude any better. So, there's your wise words of the day.

Where do we go from here? was the main question come sunrise. I was sick; my head was throbbing, and there was a tribal drum circle chanting, pounding inside my skull; and to make matters worse it was raining again, and had been for the last three hours.

"So, Sean," said Jimmy with Billie clinging to his waist and swinging happily as if he were a flag pole, "I suppose we don't really know each other, but... you seem to be leading the way here, so... where do we happen to be going?"

I had been leading the way for some time, ever since we had left the cave and tried to find our way back towards Chris's—but it had become more and more obvious that we were hopelessly lost. "Where do you want to go?" I asked.

"To a house," he said, and then gave me a smile, "but please, lead the way."

He motioned gently with his hand in an onward direction, gesticulating it like a feather in the wind. Billie had her hand in his pockets, and they walked as if they were one creature, not two conjoined; and although they were smiling, it was detectible, from some unknown energy, that what they were feeling the most was fear, we all were. Words can't always sum up the emotional, psychological impacts of firsthand experiences, but everyone knows that. I suppose we were a little bit daunted by each other's presence, which left tensions remaining high. The bottom line was that we had no clue where we were walking to, but we just kept on walking. Chris didn't say a word; he was quite back to normal, and unhappy about it. There was an eerie dementia lingering in the air. The sky was growling with unsettling baritone mirages of sound; we couldn't decide whether the noises were real or imagined, for everything looked to be imagined. The trees seemed to be lined with sheets of wet emerald and red garland, and with trunks of heavy bronze. The soil squirmed beneath our feet and created sloshing noises that tickled the inside of my ear canals. My legs had grown as stiff as concrete, and shots of pain would run up my body with every exhausted step. Every sensation was heightened, the physical world around us seemed to have been intensified, and all we could do was walk.

Eventually the dense undergrowth emptied out into a long field of tall grass and then arched around the bend mimicking the shape of a small stream running beside it. We followed the curve along as the form made a sharp right turn and then led us stumbling out into the backyard of a plantation with a huge stone house at the very front of the property; we ran towards it, arms flailing in the air. As we came closer and closer, I could make out the image of a grill on the back patio, and a doormat inscribed with some hospitable message, and a small picnic table with three chairs and two glasses of wine resting on it, quite untouched. We ran to their back door, an all-glass sliding door, and banged against it with our fists and yelled, "HELP, HELP US, HELP!" but nobody came.

Ultimately we quit our hollering and walked around to the front of the house. A fairly steady rain was falling and the lawn was flooding quickly, accumulating heavily in the dips and inlets of the yard, quite similar to the way my own lawn had looked on the morning of my departure. We sauntered over and stood on the pathway that led up to the front door. The residence felt safe and welcoming with its tan, faded bricks, white wooden shutters, and three chimneys—two that rose out from the roof, and one that shot up the side of the house next to a pile of soggy firewood. We took to the slippery steps of the stained cider porch and were finally sheltered from the rain by a manila awning with half a dozen blooming pots of vibrant flowers hanging down from it, each stem, each petal, glistening with moisture and trickling down rain water like a perfect stream-flow onto our already filthy gym shoes and worn-out hiking boots. Above the doorway an aged stone marker was cemented into the exterior wall of bricks. Inscribed on it were the words: *Monte-Duff Manor Est. 1864, Benvenuto!*

Chris was knocking on the front door furiously when I glanced back at Jimmy, who was staring up at the message on the stone, and looking around the property and in through the windows.

"Monte-Duff," he said under his breath, "Monte-Duff, Monte-Duff. You guys, it's alright, let's go inside. Come on!" he shouted.

"What do you mean?" I said. "We can't just break into these people's home, that's out of the question, man; we're not criminals!"

"No, no, you don't understand! You see, the Monte-Duffs are my cousins! Yes sir, Mr. and Mrs. Monte-Duff, and this is their antiquated manor."

"Wow, ain't this just a blessin' in disguise," said Billie gazing up at him with a proud smile; he lowered his head and winked at her, and pecked her on the cheek.

"So, if you'll just follow me…" he said as he pushed Chris and I aside on the porch and jiggled the knob.

A ghostly cob web had formed in the small rectangular window centered at the top of the door, and catches of pollens and dry, dead winged insects hung trapped to the sticky quilt thread and jostled in the breeze. The door was locked; Jimmy had found that out immediately. He rammed his shoulder into the solid slab as would a linebacker, and succeeded in hurling himself to the ground because of the backlash every time. It was no use; we were not getting into this house. Jimmy said, "Wait here," and he sprinted down the steps and into the yard, leaving us standing there on the porch confused.

He came charging back around the property with a hunk of firewood in his hand and his wild, curly hair soaked and flailing behind him. "I am not going to stand out here and suffer like a fucking dog!" he shouted, and then hurled the blunt object through the narrow rectangular window guarded by the crowded spider's web. It shattered instantly and the log went flying into the corridor and collided with a lamp which then fell to the floor and also shattered. Billie was so delighted, as if she had just witnessed a spirited act of heroism, and smiled like a happy school girl during recess in the rain, where all the children are willingly getting soaked as the teachers decide to allow a rare moment of excitement in their day. Chris and I flinched with the sound of crashing glass, and I slipped, nearly tripping on my own feet, but was able to grab onto the cold steel railing for support. We were about to break into a house, next thing I'd know I'd be down town robbing a bank vault with them too. I was honestly frightened; I'm a coward when it comes to unlawful activities; I've seen the inside of too many prisons on church retreats and lesson-learning charitable functions such as that. I've seen the way they act and are treated, and what it is they are forced to eat and think and see and smell. The entire prison smells like piss. Every other day, it seems, you get some defiant nutcase flooding his cell with backed-up toilet water, and laughing as his feces and contaminated sewage spills out into the hall. People will do anything for attention, and I had a feeling that Jimmy was one of those kinds of people.

He stuck his long arm through the hole he had made and unlocked the door from the inside, and then he opened it; we entered into the manor. I was in fear, fearing that it might be like the time I first walked into Chris's house and was overwhelmed by a wave of dust and the scent of another family's odor, but Chris and the others took it as a sign of frailty.

"And welcome home!" said Jimmy as we passed by a life-size bust of the head of Benito Mussolini resting on a shelf above a four-foot-tall old-timey radio. We then turned to where the broken lamp was lying in pieces on the ground, and seeing its scattered remains sent fey, portentous chills down my spine.

"Great job, friend," said Chris with his arm around Jimmy's shoulder like best buds.

"Had to do it for my own sanity," Jimmy said as they walked, "it's like you guys are cursed or something. But hell, let's see what we can find around this place!"

"You read my mind," said Billie, as I noticed that she had already taken some decretory ornament off a table beside her and was cramming it into her pouch.

"Sean, come on, I'm going upstairs!" Chris shouted over to me. So I went upstairs with Chris, and Jimmy and Billie led the way.

A winding staircase with smooth and icy banisters led us up and out into a sinister-looking, poorly lit hallway of two parallel walls with three intimidating shut doors tempting us on each side. Their brass knobs twinkled subtly in response to the stray beam of light shining out of one of the rooms whose door had been left open ever so slightly, and provided the hall with its only source of illumination. It was the last door on the right; it was the first room we entered.

"Can you be any more of a baby?!" Chris said to me, a comment I had earned as a result of my deliberate slothfulness and timid movements as we walked into the bedroom.

"Excuse me for being cautious," I said, and Billie looked back and gave me a wink.

"Burglary is an all-American past time, Sean, right up there with baseball and racism! Don't worry, I know you'll have fun," she said.

"Yeah," I replied, "I can't wait to share the same prison cell as you guys!"

I stood next to the first of four six-foot-tall maple bedposts in the center of the room, and watched as Chris enthusiastically watched Billie and Jimmy dig through every drawer and dresser in sight, and they even looked under the bed. With no luck of any substantial findings, Billie then crawled her attention across the floor and over to where a sealed closet door was. She grinned wildly, took Jimmy by the wrist, and stormed over to swing it open. Inside it was dark and hard to make out the internal content. However, after Billie noticed that a pull-switch length of thin chain hung down from the ceiling, she pulled it and the light flickered a few times and then came on. They walked into the closet, and dangling noticeably from each side were hangers with lavish fur coats and other types of expensive clothing suspending there in color-coded rows.

I had seen enough, at this point there was no way they were just *looking around*; and if the Monte-Duffs were really Jimmy's cousins, well, burglarizing their house didn't seem to be a thing I could see being justified, or presented to them in a way that they would understand, regardless of the circumstances. So I left the room, and walked down the hall and down the stairs, around the multiple corners, looked through five or six passages, backtracked, and then finally found a bathroom. I went inside, plugged the sink, filled it with water, and then sunk my head in it. I probably stayed there with my eyes shut tight and my breath held for well over a minute; I hardly even perceived that I was underwater. When I emerged, I looked down at the sink and, to my disgust, saw that the water had turned brown with dirt. I hadn't bathed in a week, maybe more. I hadn't even seen my own reflection in twice that amount of time! Did I dare do so now with this tempting mirror hanging before me and laughing at my dripping face? I dried myself off with a hand towel and slowly looked up. I was a person I had never seen before. I was like a burnt-up corpse. My skin was dark, just like Jimmy's, and my hair looked more like a shaggy mop left out in the garage for three years than an actual human head of terminal hair. I was miserable, looking there at myself and then hearing through the vents the shrieks of laughter and wickedness taking place up stairs. I thought, why did I get myself in to this? It wasn't how I pictured I'd set out to form my legacy. And I knew that I may not even have the chance to make a legacy for myself now because of this whole situation. It was too late for crying however, so I drained the sink, shut off the light, and opened the door.

When I got back upstairs and into the hall, the three of them had ventured into the room across from the one I had left. I walked in and prepared myself for whatever sight I was about to see. They turned around and straightened their backs, looking over at me from an interrupted pillage of a jewelry box. Chris was again standing off to the side but smiling, and Jimmy walked over to me wearing a satin opera coat with dress shoes and a cap on, pointing an old cane at my chest and tapping his foot. He then took a leisurely seat on the stiff couch in the corner of the room. I looked over at Billie who was still pillaging the jewelry box and then, after sensing that I was staring at her, I suppose, she turned around and looked at me with exasperated eyes, as if I were intruding on her privacy. I was going to half-sarcastically apologize, when I detected a piece of stolen jewelry hanging from around her neck. It was the large and glowing lapis lazuli stone choker that the attractive black girl in the grocery store had on. I was at a loss, and completely incapable of realizing what it was we had just done.

"Where did you get that?!" I demanded.

"What, this?—the cigar box next to the bedside table, its beautiful isn't it?" she said.

"Yeah, it is." I replied. What else could I say?

Billie sat down next to Jimmy on the couch, and Chris stood next to me with his arms crossed and his chin held high. Standing where I was in front of the bed, and facing out at the room before me with its large and detailed wood and stone fire place, and the multiple mirrors and paintings with meticulously sculpted frames hanging from the off-green-colored walls, I was thrust into a momentary captivation. It was a peculiar scene; they didn't look like wild criminals or filthy runaways, they looked like two respectable people who could very well have owned this home. The scene sort of resembled the Henry Treffry Dunn painting *Rossetti and Theodore Watts-Dunton at 16 Cheyne Walk*; except replace Rossetti with Billie, and seat them together on the same couch, and put a paper in Jimmy's hands, then it would be a near perfect recreation.

"'Nuff of this, I'm sick of this room!" Billie moaned, sitting impatiently on the couch with her legs crossed. "Where else have we yet to explore?"

"The cellar," said Jimmy.

"Ah, yes, the cellar. Let's go, shall we?!" she said as she jumped to her feet and exited the room.

We followed her down to the main floor, and she proceeded to wander the halls, opening every door along the way until we finally came upon the one that led to the basement. It was a small wooden door hidden off in a corner of the hallway that sprouted out from the dusty, candle-lit dining room. A strong scent of cinnamon lingered throughout the home. As we started to descend the steps, my personal, imagined perception of how it was going to look (dungeon-like and corroding) was completely false as I made it to the base of the stairs and peered out at the well-appointed and carpeted basement. My eyes were caught by the gleaming lacquer of a flowered Chinese vase that was wooden and had images of bamboo homes and little girls with flowers in their hair painted on it, resting on a table in the distant right-hand corner of the room by an antique gumball machine; but from the way Billie and Jimmy dashed over suddenly to the left of the decorative scenery, I knew that something else had captured their attention. They stopped in front of a fully stocked bar with dozens of clear shot glasses and beer mugs. An entire two rows of shelving allowed for some fifteen to twenty large handles of hard liquor, and another five or so bottles of red wine, to show their presence off to the guests in the room, twinkling from the yellow bulbs of light wrapped around the mirrored ceiling above. Billie grabbed a bottle of vodka and tossed Jimmy a bottle of Slivovitz brandy.

"Tonight's going to be a great night," she said, unscrewing the cap and then taking a long and exaggerated gulp, jerking the bottle away from her face and then shaking her head from side to side with her tongue out to express the harshness of its taste.

"Switch with me," said Jimmy, "and pour Chris and the other guy a shot or two."

"Right on," said Chris with a smile, and I didn't quite mind either.

One shot turned into three, which turned into four, which turned into six plus a half a bottle of red wine, which turned into six plus half a jug of red wine and another three or four impulsive sips of London gin straight from the bottle. By the end of it, I was spinning like a galaxy, and this cozy, furnished, and enviously desirable living area was the unexplored alien cosmos. Every noise, every word or ruckus was processed in my mind as an imperceptible, morphed and murky skirmish of tones, and their bodies but skewed shadows, oblong and misshapen, nothing more than visible blots of food coloring dye in a bowl of hot water. I couldn't tell you whether or not I was standing up or lying down, casually staggering, or running for my life, jumping off the walls, spinning like a galaxy. I loved the transient painlessness, fearlessness, jolliness of unrestrained intoxication. God, I just knew that one day I was going to become an alcoholic—not then or now, of course, but someday. I always had the thought in the back of my mind, a subtle suspicion that I would give into the bottle. Someday I knew that I was going to oxidize my liver with the Devil's juices and waste away in a trailer park somewhere, immobile and suffering, hopelessly overweight on a bed of flannel sheets and wine-stained pillows. Oh, how I know that day will come!

The basement soon became just the start of a long list of places where we could expand to. Chris—I believe it was Chris, at least—had led us back upstairs, tripping and flailing and laughing hysterically with every step we took. We all spilled out into the hallway, and Billie fell to her face. Whimpering with her chin and lips to the wood floor, and then twisting around to her back like a worm before working her way up and onto her feet, she looked at us and started laughing like a panting hyena, and we had never stopped. The hallway went on forever and ever, with tall doors shooting down the walls as if we were standing in a subway terminal just as a train was passing by; I even felt the breeze coming off of it. In fact, it wasn't my body feeling as much as it was my mind, doing whatever it wanted to. I was as numb as a fucking morphine-drip-trauma-victim lying half-conscious on a table in a lit room surrounded by intruding strangers, not knowing whether or not they were here to save my life... or end it. That's exactly what this was.

We stood around in the kitchen; Jimmy, Billie, and Chris were all sitting on the counters. I was standing alone next to the octagonal table. I eventually laid on it, and then fell asleep on it, too. But before then, as we wobbled around the Monte-Duff's clean kitchen, I gazed out of the window into the night and the pouring rain. I didn't notice what anybody else in the room was doing, but I heard them talking in the background. Out the window the pine trees fought each other violently and smacked against the glass. Then, as I stared out at the night, I specifically remember seeing a man. It fazed me not one bit while completely drunk, but there was no doubt in my mind that I saw a man walking through the tall grass. It was a distinct black shadow, shape and size of a man, and it moved with swiftness, and in the process of doing something... of what I am not quite sure. He looked in at me once through the window, extremely close up with his nose pressed against it purposely making himself look like a pig, and while laughing psychotically with a deranged expressing on his face, drew a heart in the fog his breath had created on the glass with the tip of his finger, before running away into the storm. Now that I think of it, it was honestly a pretty frightening sight. Who was this person? Why was he there, and why had he made such a psychotic first impression? Furthermore, where were the Monte-Duffs?

Questions like these would not enter into my head until late next morning, when I awoke with a migraine comparable to the resulting pain one would expect to feel after consecutive blows to the back of the head by Carlos Ortíz. I thought my brain was going to burst, and then deflate, and just as quickly ooze from my ears and onto the floor.

I feared that every time I looked in the mirror I was going to witness a chilling image of myself with eyes bleeding and blood consistently dripping from my cheeks and down the sides of my body, down my now soiled clothing. I moaned, and around the presently cluttered and discombobulated kitchen I heard the emerging groans of multiple hangovers suddenly realized, and the confusion was mutual. It looked as if a cyclone had torn through the place. What had we done to make such a big goddamn mess? I thought, but I couldn't remember; I just wanted to hide from the bright, intruding sun.

Ten minutes later Billie was up and had made us all a bowl of cereal. She poured us each a glass of orange juice and herself another glass of wine, and then she put an icepack on her head. After last night's inspection of the house, Billie practically knew where everything already was. The sun outside was humongous and overshadowed the rest of the sky; we could see no blue heavens or white clouds, it was just blinding rays of light. For the first time in hours it wasn't raining, but I was sure that it wouldn't last. Chris shut the curtains and then sat down with us at the table.

"I think I saw a man last night," I said with a straight face and in an upset tone. "Bizarre really, I can remember it almost perfectly."

"You did?" the three of them asked at the same time. "Who was it?!"

"Not sure," I said, "he was older, like in his thirties or forties… and completely nuts. He came up to the window, and then he left. It all happened pretty fast."

"What did he do?" Jimmy asked.

"He just pressed his face up against the pane, laughed, and drew a heart in the fog on the glass before running off into the storm," I explained.

"Well," said Jimmy with a spark of investigatory inspiration, "there's only one way to know if it is all true. Let's prove whether or not you saw someone. Do you remember what window you were looking out?"

"Yes," I replied, "the one above the sink in the kitchen."

He abruptly ran over to it, and we all followed; he looked meticulously at each section of the window and then, with a gasp of shock or joy, he found the shape of a heart, drawn small and subtly in the corner. Outside the sun seemed to have shrunk ten times in size since Chris had shut the blinds on it two minutes earlier. Above the image of the heart, dark clouds began to roll in, moving swiftly, furiously in our direction. The winds blew hard, the walls rattled, and the bird feeders twist-tied to the trees in the yard swung back and forth, giving off faint bell sounds and clanking noises as they collided into each other and the branches on which they hung. And while we gazed, trickles of rain water began to pelt themselves quietly onto the window in a shower of tiny droplets.

"Only one way to find out for sure, though," Jimmy said, and then he ran his index finger slowly across the image on the glass made opaque with condensation. It didn't smudge; the heart remained. It was drawn on the outside of the window. "My God," he said, "it's true!" We watched with fixated eyes as water slowly seeped down the pane and washed away the picture.

Billie dropped her wine glass out of disbelief and it shattered on the wood floor. A pool of red liquid flowed across the room and collected beneath our feet. We all stood there in complete astonishment. Who had been here last night? What did he want and where did he go? A moment later, the fire in the fireplace went out as a cold gust of wind and rain flew in through an accidentally opened window and rustled around the room. A high-pitched whine echoed throughout the house: the sound of the breeze, it was in pain. Misery and distress, sickness and insanity to come are what it whispered in my ear; and still, the ghoulish forest, with its striking trees, and casing layers of mud and spikes and slime and poisons, went on and on, while the sky darkened above and the dispiriting rains persisted. I sat myself down at the kitchen table where I had slept and recollected the comfort I had once pretended as if I didn't enjoy every single day of my life: the comfort of innocuous normality.

X

The Downfall

Time passed inside the home. It must have been five in the afternoon when a unanimous decision among us intruders resulted in the locating of an axe and a voyage into the forests around the property in search of dry firewood. We were freezing; no window inside the house would remain closed, as a result of the raging storm. We had to tape them all down with rolls of duct tape just to get them to stay shut. As a result of the amount of time it took us to do so, all the cushions and couches were left wet and cold to the touch—you could not sit on these things without the eventual risk of hypothermia! However, standing in the middle of the room was no better, and no more comfortable than would be sitting on a damp sofa.

Jimmy opened a screen door proceeded by a heavy glass door that led directly into the yard at the left-hand side of the property. When it opened and we stepped outside into the change of environments, it hit us horribly with one direct wave of energy and fury all at once. Pacing out under the portico and onto the grass, the winds blew us down to our knees, and we hurried as best as we could into the forest where the storm would be less severe—at least there we had the shelterbelt of expanding branches, trunks, and leaves providing us with a partially effective shield. Nonetheless, there was still the pouring rain and the winter-like frost in the air… and the threat of falling trees, too. Let us never underestimate the threat of falling trees.

We scampered around, wolves on the hunt, following the heavy aroma of blood, and searched tirelessly for the driest wood. When that goal seemed to dwindle into an obvious improbability, Chris informed us of a change in plans. "It's fucking raining," he said, "nothing's going to be dry... on the outside, at least. We've got to cut a tree down if we want any chance of obtaining burnable timber." And he was right. We changed plans and searched for the best tree to cut. Eventually, we came upon a patch of three trees that were thin and tall and reasonably dry. They were manageable, both in terms of the amount of exertion it would take to chop them down, and in how easy it would be to transport them back to the home. With no time to spare, and as the rain fell relentlessly down on us and our dry wood, we chopped the three trees, formed a line where each of us held an end or a middle section of those three trees, and ran as quickly as we could back into the house. Like a mob of charging mutineers, Jimmy rammed the side door open with the cut-end of the trunks, and it flung back with a loud whooshing sound, and unbolted dramatically, crashing into the wall behind it, and rattled on its hinges as hanging landscape paintings fell to the floor.

Jimmy, Chris, and I stood in the hall next to the trees about to shut the door behind us, when we noticed that Billie wasn't there by our side. Before anyone could ask where she was, we heard an ear piercing shriek of terror that echoed in from outside. Though the first scream was audible, the ones that followed were rather subdued by the sound of the hammering rainstorm. But we still heard them. Jimmy knew it was her immediately and ran into the gale without hesitation. Chris and I both pursued, though with some individual hesitation. I had no doubt that it was the police, or some hell-spawn consequence of our curse, some sort of mutant offspring of a conjured beast slowly tearing Billie apart limb for limb.

We ran back into the forest only to see nothing, nothing human, that is. Then, as whirlwinds of leaves coasted through the air around us, soaring on the fury of the stirring tempest, she let out another cry and yelled, "Where the hell are ya?!" We followed the sounds of her wailing and found her quite soaked, with long wet hair hanging in her face, lips shivering, and long lines of runny eyeliner sagging down her cheeks, making her look rather frightening.

"What's wrong?!" Jimmy screamed, grabbing her by the shoulders.

"What's wrong? Look behind me!" she gasped, furiously stepping to the left.

She no longer blocked our vision, and we looked up ahead to see what it was that had prevented her from departing this spot to accompany us back into the manor. But it was a sight I wish I had never seen. There, unmistakably before our eyes, were the silhouettes of three bodies hanging from the muscular limbs of a tree, dripping with torrent rainfall and swaying considerably in the winds of the storm, thick with strewn up debris. Overhead, with the coiling expanses of descending water and severed leaves, fear emanated on all sides and fell upon us quickly.

"Strange fruits, huh?" she muttered.

"Shit!" Jimmy hollered, outraged at her now disgraceful lackadaisicalness. "Shit! This is no time to be clever, Billie, can't you see how serious this is?!"

Chris stared blankly, most likely out of shock or panic. I, on the other hand, was sort of entranced with the sight, and walked up to get a closer look. Hanging there, I saw, and as far as I'm concerned, the Monte-Duffs. Two white bodies, a man and a woman, and a black body, a woman, all hung from their necks, faces darkened and puffy with postmortem rotting and weather-beaten skin. They were the family I had seen in the grocery store, there was no doubt about it. The man had a causal suit jacket on, leather shoes; the woman was in a purple gown, white sandals. The third victim, also a woman, wore a dark blue uniform with beaded gold stitching around the limbs and collar. Aside from being dead, she was once a pretty girl, and looked more like a valet at a hotel than a house keeper. She was the woman from the market scouring through her purse with that uneasy look in her eyes: panic.

"It's the Monte-Duff's!" I screamed.

"Is it?" cried Billie, and we all looked over at Jim.

"Is it?" she asked again.

"Uh, I don't know," he said with a stupid look of numbness across the face.

"Ain't you ever seen 'em?" Chris yelled.

"Ain't you?!" cried Billie. Lighting flashed, and a staggering tree, two stories high, came crashing down into the woods behind us.

"Okay, stop; I may have fabricated a few things that I told you in the past... things that you may have come to think true of me," Jimmy started, "but this one is kinda low."

"What things, Jimmy?" Billie asked with the most vicious of calm expressions.

"Well, mostly the fact that the Monte-Duffs aren't my cousins. I don't know who the hell these people are," he revealed, causing all our faces to turn pale and our stomachs to sink as dismay and nausea contorted with our insides for a moment before being released from us in the form of tears, especially Billie. But Jim just stared at us; he was at a loss of words, undoubtedly feeling what we felt times ten. And then he found the words; though, I'm not too sure they were the ones we were looking for.

"Yeah, I just wanted to get into the house. I couldn't just leave y'alls standing out there in the rain. In fact," he said, standing up straight before us and laying down the law, "In fact, I think I deserve a thank you for my contributions towards that whole *staying alive* thing. We're alive, ain't we? They're dead, but we're alive; so let's get the heck out of here!"

I suppose he wasn't feeling what we felt. He was an arrogant fella, a fucking asshole. And I was no longer comfortable with having him and his spastic girlfriend come along on what was to be my transcendental journey.

"Jimmy, you bastard!" Billie screamed and stomped noisily across the swamped yard back into the house.

"Okay, Sean, what should we do?" Jimmy asked.

"Me! Why are you asking me?" I said. "How the hell should I know what to do right now...or ten minutes from now, or a year from now! I suggest we go and report what we saw; you and Billie can get out of here and get headin' to where ever it was you originally intended to go to before you met us. Chris and I will report the deaths."

"No, no way. Why would I do that, so you can pin it all on us, and tell the sheriff so he can send out a trigger-happy search party? I don't think so! We're all in this together," he snapped. His emotions changed so quickly, and usually due to verbal assaults, or things he took to be as verbal assaults, though usually they were nothing more than common face to face conversations; but when directed towards him, it would eventually set him off, leading to a rampage like the one to come.

"I don't know where to go," he shouted. "I'm not living in the woods again. Forget that! I'm going *into town* with you; we'll be a completely separate party, Billie and I. We'll never so much as look at ya! I just need to find us a way out of here; hitch a train or a truck ride, perhaps try to get to Mexico in a few months' time, maybe we'll even go all the way up to Canada instead, but not here… not Kentucky. Everybody I've met from here so far has been crazy as all hell, just completely nuts!"

"Aren't we the only people you've met here so far?" Chris and I both asked.

"Yeah," he replied.

"It's because we're cursed!" Chris screamed, and he dragged his hands agonizingly down his face and then up again before running them through his now lengthy black hair.

"Y'all are crazy," he said, and walked back across the yard, tracing over Billie's sunken in footsteps towards the manor.

"Okay then," I said, "We're going into town."

"Right behind ya!" he shouted, now in a suddenly optimistic mood, running into the house through the side door, finding Billie, dragging her out of the door and into the rain and mud by an interlocking of arms, forcefully, with her kicking and screaming the entire time, and then presenting her before us like an award as she struggled uncompromisingly.

"Okay, let's go!" he exclaimed.

Eventually, however, like most ultimately do under immense stress and pressure, Billie gave up her thrashing and went with the flow, following our every move and instruction. Jimmy knew he was about to be making decisions that would either save or end both him and his girlfriend's lives. I suppose I was going to be making decisions like that too, maybe just as soon.

We entered again into the forest. It was seemingly melting with all the leaves and mud and rotting, soggy, dead wood—more like brown, murky sponges crawling with slimy insects. Gleaming spider webs hung across every other tree, illuminated by the scattered rays of sunlight through the dark clouds and branches and captured rain water, revealing to me the shape of the web. They were so thick and frequent, and almost man-made in their length and use and quality. It was the scene of a thousand squirrel clothes lines hanging from trees in a neighborhood, a neighborhood that just could not seem to catch a single day of warmth and recovery from the torrential rains, and neither could we. The only difference was, instead of tiny clothing hanging from the lines, there were entangled, trapped, gutted and cocooned insects, snagged out of life in the blink of an eye. Was this a forewarning? Were we destined for the same fate? Again, all we could do was walk.

"Oh, my God, Jimmy. Oh, my God," Billie whimpered. She said this so frequently too, and for the entire hike. "Oh, my God, Jimmy," she said again.

"What?! Oh, my God, Jimmy, what?!" he eventually shouted, not able to handle the intenseness and distress her words were causing.

"You're a bitch!" she yelled back at him. "You've gotten us killed!"

"What? We're alive, can't you tell? They're the ones who are dead. There, hanging from the tree!" he countered, pleading his innocence to her, but only further solidifying our confidence in his lack of it.

"How could you have lied about something like that? As if we weren't in enough trouble already," she said between sniffles and tears; her eyes must have been producing as much moisture as the billows of dark precipitation in the sky.

Lurking wickedness of some unknown force followed us interminably, gliding on the winds; the sun was hidden behind gloomy clouds, and the twisting storm caused the trees to wobble back and forth in a disorientating way. Every now and then a soaked and prickly branch would be flung at my face in an indefensible and unwarranted moment of startling discomfort. The hours kept getting worse and worse. Every moment was a little more intolerable than the one before. I couldn't quite comprehend the situation we were in. How could things have gone from being so good to so unimaginably shitty in no time at all? As I contemplated my misery, the sound of multiple blasts of buckshot being fired from a rifle resonated throughout the forest, causing birds to flee from their tree nests and scatter. We were left halted in our tracks, fearful of the law man, and indecisive on what to do.

"The hell was that?!" Billie shouted as more and more tears ran down her face.

"Hunters," Chris replied. "I hear 'em all night long when I'm at home tryin' to sleep, or in the early morning; the bastards chase them deer like addicts track down opium."

"You sure?" Jimmy asked. "You sure we shouldn't start running? It's never too late to start running, you know."

"Positive," he said. "To them it's open season, even though it's nowhere close to November."

The shots continued for a matter of minutes, making us extremely uneasy; aside from Chris, however, who was almost certain that the blasts were coming from none other than a group of passionate hunters. I was more worried about being shot dead by a stray bullet while I walked rather than whom it was that was actually firing the weapon. I suppose with our diminutive luck and our ever-present curse still looming, it would not be unlikely for some slightly intoxicated outdoorsman to mistake us for a family of deer trotting happily in the distance. Then again, a quick and unforeseen death might have been the luckiest thing that could have happened to me in weeks; but as I was made aware of before, this would not be the case. Our deaths were not going to be quick and they weren't going to be clean. I was going to have to sit around and wait for the end just like everybody else, though, a bit more miserably, it now appeared.

We kept on at a steady pace, perhaps more like a walk-run. Then we all agreed after a few moments of uneasy silence that we felt the eyes of somebody watching; it was the feeling of someone waiting for us around every corner, behind every tree. We walked a little faster, and a little faster still. Eventually we saw empty bullet casing in the dirt, and old footprints zigzagging alongside us. Billie (who was leading the way at this point) turned past a wall of shrubbery and trees to stop suddenly in front of us; we all fell into each other and she fell to the ground.

"Why, hello," said a man in a camouflage jumpsuit and a head of long red hair who suddenly appeared from behind a bush. He had a shotgun in his left hand, and bending down to reach out with his right, he helped Billie onto her feet. "Scoundrels, I should figure? Hmmm? Well?—I'm only messing. But you've got to be quiet or you're going to scare off my game! And for God's sake, get yourselves some jackets because it's cold as hell out here. Have you ever seen such strange weather?"

"Where's town, sir?" Billie asked in a weak and sickened mumble of pity and shit.

"Straight ahead, mam," he replied, "only about a mile."

"Thanks," she said, and we were on our way again, now completely paranoid. This guy was way too close for comfort to where three hanging bodies and a burglarized house stood only about a half a mile in the opposite direction; but there was nothing we could do now.

"Let's go, let's go!" Jimmy urged, enticing us to walk a little faster.

We followed the sounds of ringing church bells in the distance, slowly getting louder, tantalizing us to continue further in the same direction. Eventually, horizons of trees and woodland rather abruptly ended and spilled us out onto a flat, depressing highway. "I know where we are," Chris announced. "Only a little ways down the road now 'til we get to town!"

"Then let's get going!" Jimmy said again in a pressing voice.

After a miserable side-of-the-road hike in the rain, we reached Maine Street, and hit the sidewalks of the municipality, trotting by the seemingly abandoned city hall, the community justice center, and the brand new army recruitment station. After the more modern block of the town had made its way behind us, it led to a second block of aged brick buildings and century-old barber shops and Ma and Pa stores, darkened with rain water and probably leaking on the patrons within. They all stood parallel, gazing down at the street below. There was no one in sight; the lingering sense of empty, impending doom, the uneasy feeling in the pit of one's stomach, swimming in the air, hiding behind every door and down every alleyway, followed us where ever we went.

"There's no one around, why is that, Chris?" Jimmy asked. "Where do you suppose they all are? Or were they ever even here? You know the fucking answers!" he asserted and got up into Chris's face. "You live in this town! Get us the heck out of this town! Get us out of here; I don't know where to go, and I don't know where anybody or anything is!"

"Okay, okay!" Chris replied, stepping away from him with one hand in his pocket and the other grasping the staff of an iron street light. "Let's go to the diner, maybe we can get you guys cleaned up, and y'all can find yourself a ride."

"The diner?" asked Billie with a dismal expression.

"Yeah!" Chris exclaimed. "That's where all the locals hang out. Well, mostly the guys up at the factories, the owner and the bartenders who are related to the governor; a lot of the town tough guys and business men hang out there, too. Ex-attorney William McDonough, for one, and that warehouse owner whose father once ran the old smelting factory down Paris Pike… Jim Sportane, I think his name is; and usually on a good day, which is most days, you'll run into the Willow sisters, Kelly and Rendell. They're just great, but all they really do is whisper little secrets and insults to each other about everyone else in the room."

"What's so great about that?" Billie demanded.

"Well," he replied, "it's sort of attractive, don't you think? Women with secrets… how beautiful; and those two are just the finest things you'll ever, or, depending on the outcome of occupancy when we go inside, may ever, see!"

"Well," Billie remarked, "I sure don't *see* the beauty in it."

"That's your loss."

"You guys can't say a word to us while we're in there," I interrupted. "In fact, why don't you two wait outside for a few moments and let

Chris and I go in first before going in yourselves. You know, just to make things look a little less conspicuous, to make you guys seem like, as you said earlier, a completely different party."

"Done," said Jimmy.

"Alrighty," Billie mumbled in approval, and Chris and I walking into the restaurant.

Inside, glasses clanked, booths were filled, and the eatery hummed with the sounds of afternoon banter. The scent of fried foods hung in the air and in the greasy corners of the room, loitering around the counters near the teeming kitchen of frantic chefs and employees, all racing to fill the demands of hungry customers.

Chris and I walked straight across the building and into the bathrooms across from the door we came in through. The old wooden access with the word *Men's* written on it opened to the optical illusion of a mirror duplicating a hundredfold the reflection of the corresponding mirror hanging from the wall opposite. It stunned us but for a second; we weren't quite prepared for something so unexpected, even something as harmless as that. He and I both were pretty uneasy, and perhaps scared as hell is a better way to put it. So with a stride of indecisiveness, I stepped into a stall. I grimaced as—now that the toilet which I had finally wiped clear of three weeks' worth of dry piss stains was at last clean, and, with my pants still on—I sat down on the seat. Chris just stared at himself in the hypnotic mirror (and I only know this because it was right next to my stall, and I could see one of his untied shoelaces lying halfway inside the booth as he stood on the other side of the divider gazing into infinity).

The inside of the stall's door was, of course, covered with decades of names and dates and obscenities written by truckers and drunks taking shits after a wild night at the bar, or on a healthy platter of fried foods. They scrawling across the entire panel with mindless scribbles, jokes and cartoons—if not across the rest of the stall too, but I had yet to look. The layers of misspelled words and forgotten dates and names—the newer ones now slightly covering the older ones—began to resemble to me, at least kind of in my panicking mind, the replicating mirrors outside. Now looking around, I saw to my right written in bold black letters the phrase: *The splendor of the golden sun can only come when there is none.* Written on the wall to the left of me were the words: *He comes with the clouds.* What the hell did that mean? I thought for a time, but I didn't know; so I got up and left.

Standing next to Chris as he stared into the mirror, and as I washed my hands beside him, we heard the conversation grumble of the restaurant turn to a disconcerting silence; a contagious sense of upheaval lingered down the hall from the bar stools and booths of the diner and through the cracks in the door. Chris and I prematurely exited the restroom in a lure of confusion and stood in the short hallway that looked out into the eatery. Jimmy and Billie were standing in the center of the room; everyone else in the room was dead silent and staring at them, and most were clutching silverware tightly in their hands. Behind the counter a mean bar tender with biceps of a gorilla, and a faintly noticeable stitches scar across his left eyebrow, bent down and came back up holding a wooden bat. When he was bent over, I saw on the wall behind him were plastered two mug shots: those of Jimmy English and Shelby Vaughn. The reward was $1,500 apiece. And from the looks of it, it seemed that the entire diner was about to have their way with them, as if prepared to fight to the deaths in order to get that money. How scrawny they appeared, how disheveled and spineless; and from the look in their eyes, I could tell that they knew the jig was up; they were practically surrounded. The crowd of coffee drinkers and happy hour devotees each felt confident in their own individual abilities to overpower and eventually detain Jimmy English and Shelby Vaughn. There was nowhere to run, nothing to say. And before they could take the last chance they had to escape—to dash out into the streets, probably only to retreat back into the woods—the steel door of the diner swung open suddenly and smacked hard against the wall beside it.

A man in camouflage, dripping with rain water, and wheezing with the pains of breathlessness, stormed into the room. He had his rifle slung over his shoulder, and a look of perplexed animosity combined with an obvious sense of duty on his perspiring face. He was the red-headed hunter from the woods, the man who is credited with pointing us in the direction of town. The man who, at this point it seemed, can be credited with invoking the downfall of my two reckless acquaintances. Everyone in the room turned their attention towards him, away from Jimmy and Billie, providing them with enough time to make some hasty movements—perhaps the hopeless attempt of fleeing—when the hunter shouted for them to stop, and pointed his long steel barrel in their direction. Point blank in the center of the room, he stared at them with one eye shut and the other looking through the scope of his rifle, aimed at Jimmy's heart. He had changed weapons it seemed. No longer was he wielding a shotgun, instead Jimmy and Billie found themselves face to face with a .30-caliber.

"They've murdered the Monte-Duffs!" he shouted. "If you move, even so much as a twitch of the brow, I'll blow you away!"

By this time, the owner of the restaurant, a fat and tired man in a white shirt and yellow trousers, had emerged from his office in the back, and made his way between Jimmy and the red-headed hunter, arms outstretched, pleading for a cease in hostility. The man lowered his weapon and, as soon as he did so, Jimmy took off running full charge towards the door. The people in the room screamed, and a shot was fired; everyone dropped to their knees and I shut my eyes. When I opened them, the hunter, the owner, and Jimmy were the only ones left standing. Jimmy looked down at himself in distress, swiftly patting at his arms and chest area in search of a wound, but came out unscathed. Dust was filtering down from the ceiling where the bullet had lodged itself, and white powder trickled onto the head and hair of Billie as she cowered, crouched in a fetal position near the center of the room.

"I was out hunting in the woods," said the hunter once the smoke had cleared, "and on my hike back to where I had parked my truck, I must have strayed past the Monte-Duff's property. There I saw in the wooded area around the home their three bodies hanging dead from a tree. Mister and Missus, and their maid, all hung up by the neck! Don't believe me, don't see how I could possibly know it's these folks who done it? Well, I saw 'em firsthand trekking through the forest. There were four of 'em, and they asked me for directions into town. A few minutes later, I came upon the bodies, this scene of brutality and waste! God, you devils! And just look, the shrew's got Missus Duff's choker round her neck! The very one I bought her after the death of her mother!"

A gasp of amazement rustled throughout the room. My face twitched as I felt myself spin, as if in the midst of fainting. Chris was hunkered down behind the radiator as to try and keep from being seen, and the showdown between the townspeople and the accused played out before my very eyes. Moments later, two police officers with batons in hand charged in through the entry and demanded the meaning all of this commotion. While the hunter explained himself with an accusatory finger pointed towards Jimmy and Billie, now looking as guilty and as helpless as never before, a firm hand came down upon my shoulder. I yelped, and immediately thereafter another hand was slapped across my mouth, muzzling me as I jerked my head from side to side, trying to break loose. Chris stood up and tore the man off me. The twisted feeling of his sweaty palms still pressing tight against my face remained even after he had let go and retreated hastily a few steps away. I winced, and then beheld the man who had had his arms around me, and when I did so, I collapsed. Everything went black. That is all.

XI

The Manic

When I came to, I was lying in a contorted position behind the radiator in the hall, the sounds of commotion and disorder roared in nauseously from the main room looming beside my aching head. Hovering over me with long black hair sagging down across his face and occasionally feathering the sides of my mine as the ceiling fan blew streams of gentle air towards his thick, silky braids, was a man who then proceeded to smack my cheek hard with a calloused hand in the efforts of trying to wake me, though I was already awake. I swatted his face away and, in doing so, got a fist full of his hair in the process. Its texture was of silk, yet, not a pleasant kind of silk. It was a silk that made your skin crawl when you touched it, more resembling something along the lines of the rags on a corpse, pulled out after ten years in the hole. It was like the hair of a manikin (for a more accurate example), like those porcelain dolls where the paintbrush-thin hairs stick out in neat little rows, always spaced a bit too far apart, always showing a little too clearly the oddly thick pores at the base of every dark and greasy strand.

These thoughts passed through my mind suddenly as the man let out a cry of pain, grasped his scalp, and then lunged onto his feet as I stood up onto mine. He extended his arms, and like a bat, engulfed us in his black cape, and rushed down the hallway to shove us out a back door into the flooded parking lot behind the building. He stood on the landing in front of the door, now swinging fast on its hinges after our expulsion, with the presence of a man with inestimable power, a man with a mind that was so much larger than his own body, uncontainable.

It was the Devil, it seemed, arms raised in the air, standing on the steps before me; he had on shark tooth earrings, a box of chocolates in one hand, a walking cane in the other; a heavy gold chain wrapped around his neck, and his massive cloak of black fabric swelled all around him in the movement of flexible wings. "Candy?" he asked, as Chris reached out and took one, ate it, and smiled as I watched in appalled disapproval.

"RAAHHHAA! That was fatal, poisonously fatal!" the man yelled with a spray of sputum and madness that fell down onto our faces. Chris spat out the caramel candy on the spot and ran the palm of his hand down the path of his pink tongue.

"I'm only jesting" he then assured, "it's just a little ice breaker I like to use. You can have another piece if you'd like." But there was no way.

"If the two of you would prefer to stay out of a bird cage for the next few years," he said, "you ought to follow me. There's a room full of pigs in there that know now, presumably, that you two were involved in whatever trouble they've decided to accuse a couple boys of doing this time, and they're now racing down that very hallway out to get us. So, come with me; I can get you out of here! I am the Messiah, and I have come! But I cannot save your friends, it is too late for them. God has already decided their fates. We have to go now! I've seen bad weather coming, and with it your emission from this whole situation, this whole struggle that you've been so bravely fighting. The answers to your problems come with the clouds," he said. "Everything you've ever wanted falls from the sky!"

"You don't think we actually killed those people, do you? …Because we didn't!" I informed, ignoring his previous tirade of forewarning religious prophecy.

"Ah, yes sir, yes sir! innocent as can be. I have seen it in the clouds. They've made it quite clear of your intentions—few bad. However, your disobedience troubles me."

"Our disobedience?!" Chis shouted, arms raised in the air as we took off running from the parking lot down a never ending road of backs of houses.

The alleyways narrowed into a gravel trail which soon needled down into nothing, and we found ourselves to be back in the Forest of Revelations. We said little to each other; the man twitched his head and neck while he walked, and we always ensured to remain a safe distance behind him. God, he made me so nervous! His movements were baroque and unrestrained. He would thrash his arms out at his sides sporadically, grunt the loudest noises of nonsense, and spit a river of brown sludge-like liquid from his mouth out onto the shrubbery. "This guy's got Tourette's," Chris whispered in my ear. I gave no reply. He spat another flow of goop from his shivering lips that was taken hostage by the breeze and nearly hit me in the face.

He looked back at us now and again, always to urge us to continue, swiping his hand through the air to indicate our onward direction. And, much the same way we had entered onto the property of the Monte-Duffs, we followed a muddy, rain-eroded trail up to the steps of an expansive mansion of crumbling detailed plaster and blackened wood, in the style of an old French monastery. Dual observatory towers arose to the left and to the right of me, jetting three stories high into the forest, almost overextending some of the older trees. A wide front door with a bronze knob stood centered below rows of peeling, creaking, haunting shutters of deep blue, some opened and some closed, all adjoining the numerous windows that expanded across the home's moldering façade.

What were this man's intentions for leading us away from what probably should have been out fates? This question I pondered until I could no longer. It is not possible to answer a question that has no answer, is it? Was this luck? ... It couldn't be. "Leave your shoes in the yard," he announced upon climbing the steps of his porch, "you shan't need them again!"

With little consideration, we did as instructed, leaving our two combined pairs of shoes neatly placed together on the yard pressed up against the mossy sandstone foundation of the structure. "Welcome to my humble abode!" he said, sporting an ear to ear smile as we walked in with naked feet onto the cool oak wood floors of a spacious corridor. The man removed his cloak slowly and swung it around his forearm to allow it to dangle. He then swatted at the fabric with his free hand to expel any lint and smooth out any wrinkles; he aired it out with two consecutive flails through the air before latching it onto a coat hanger beside the door.

It seems that every time one begins to describe the process of entering into a home and so on, they, after portraying to us the extravagant details of walking through a front door, almost always immediately thereafter, regardless of plot in reference to dialogue, allow the preceding few moments of literary happenings to take place in the location of a hallway. And indeed it seems to have happened once again, just beyond that previously mentioned corridor.

The man, who will soon reveal to us his name, stopped in front of a small table, and with Chris and I cautiously hovering behind him, he emptied the contents of his pockets onto it. A tangled rosary, some half dollar coins, and a pill bottle, rolled suddenly onto the surface, clanking into the ceramic lamp that resided there as well. The hanging bulb-light flickered overhead, and his deep breathing made it seem as if he were a strange creature ready to attack.

"So, who are you? ...If I may ask," Chris said with his arms crossed.

"Who am I!" the man replied in a loud howl of a response, and spun around violently. "Well, I suppose it may be that I am Ernest in the city and Jack in the country. It may be that I am really you, and you are really me. It may also be said that I am the one who obscures, who watches and is hidden quietly behind the mask! Do you follow?"

"Yes," I replied.

"Quite the contrary!" Chris remarked, "I have not the slightest clue as to what you are talking about."

He glared at us with wide and frightening eyes, the kind of eyes that pierce right through to your very soul, like a machete through the head of an attacking boar, or perhaps a wild turkey.

"I'm Viktor Lutheran," he then calmly stated, dropping his previous mindset of austerity, proceeding to reach out and shake my hand.

"This is where y'all be stayin' for a while. I live here, and once upon a time, a long, long time ago, my mother and father, too. Perhaps," he continued, "we can further discuss the background of each other's misfortunes later tonight. But until then, how about we enjoy each other's company around a meal?"

"Okay," I said quietly.

"Brilliant! Come, this way to the waiting room," and we followed him further down the hall to stop and enter through an archway into a stuffy chamber of dark couches. As well, there was a large Knole settee with red tassels and trimmings of fabric hanging down from its sides that I noticed as we entered, veiled in the shadows to my left, hidden beside a fastened and shutter-closed window. I imagined Viktor seated there, lounging, smoking an ivory pipe, robed in embossed velvet like a king, like the royalty he thought he was. From beside me he turned a circular knob on the wall and slowly eased the lights on. "Shouldn't be more than an hour," he said; "I have yet to prepare us a meal, so please, make yourselves at home and occupy yourselves appropriately." He opened the double doors behind him, turned, and disappeared into the other room.

Through the thin walls, we could hear the sounds of pots and tins clanking together, the hissing of gas protruding from a stove, and the bangs of an ice chest being opened and shut, and then opened, and then shut again. Chris looked at me and gave me a strange smile; I gave him one back. As the rain pelted against the shutters of the lone window in the room, I suppose for the first time in a while I felt myself relax and my thoughts begin to slow. "Sorry old fools," Chris said to himself.

"Jimmy and Billie?" I asked. "I suppose the way it all ended, after hearing their tale, shouldn't surprise me much."

"I agree," he said, "they had it coming, should have happened way before it eventually did if you ask me. Still, it is sort of unfortunate. What do I care about some held-up banks, or some quivering bloke of a mayor? Starve the fat cats, I say! They do nothing but spread corruption and hopelessness under the falsified veil of an empty promise campaign poster. I feel bad for them, honestly. I think they did the things they did mostly out of fear, fear and hopelessness. I remember one of the last things Jimmy said to me while we were in the manor. I was picking at his brain, still wondering about how it came to be that they managed to grow into such renegades. He started ranting, as he often did, and what he said left quite the impression on me. 'I just want to keep my life,' he said, and I asked him what he meant. He said that he knew how crazy it was to do the things him and Billie had done. He also said he knew just as well how crazy it would be to stay there at home, waiting to be shipped off to a war that was even more meaningless than, as he put it, his own existence. 'Hey, hey, LBJ, how many kids did you kill today?' he started chanting, louder and louder, until it began to frighten me. 'I've got choices,' he then said, 'and no politician or so-called leader of the free world—spreading his lies and waging his wars—can tell me what to do with my life, let alone how, when or where to end it. I didn't vote for that man! Hell, I wouldn't have even been old enough to vote for him if he were to have been elected president, which he wasn't, mind you! I'm scared, Chris, nothing but scared. And sometimes, fear can lead to irrationality. When that's the case, I suppose you get a sorry tale like ours.' He then shrugged his shoulders, brushing off the previous emotions brought upon by his own words and, turning to rummage through a dresser draw in the room we happened to be in, he accidentally kicked over a trash can that stood beside his twitching leg. A few moments later you came up from downstairs, back from where ever it was you had run off to, and walked through the door."

"Well," I began, "it looks as if the ending of their story didn't exactly turn out like the one in yours."

"On the contrary!" he said, and had recently begun to grow rather fond of saying, "Perhaps they'll ride the lighting!"

"Yes, perhaps they will," I said.

That's what I thought then, but now, as you will understand in due time, I feel that they, more likely than not, escaped... or somehow found themselves to be free once again, having there been nobody left to tell them otherwise. An hour later, our host emerged and said, "You shall be served now." We walked with him into the kitchen, where we sat at the table in front of our individual plates of vegetables, meats and potatoes, and as he informed, "a hot cup of posset on the way."

When it arrived, he seated himself at the head of the table and sipped at his drink. He licked his lips indiscreetly and jumped right into his meal. While we ate, not a word was said. He considered it to be quite informal, so he later told us. Although, his slapping of the lips and the flailing of his tongue as he stuck it out to inspect his upper lip and retrieve any straggling food, as well as the tiny squirming varicose veins that twisted above his nostrils when he chewed that food, and the monstrous sounds he made in doing so, all seemed to him to be rather appropriate. Yet, conversation was a disgrace. Not that I had much to say, anyways. Then again, now that I think about it, I believe I actually had so much to say to him that I hardly knew where to begin, and the lengthy dinner that prevented me from doing so made holding in my thoughts, and holding myself together, that much more difficult.

Then, some twenty minutes in, a timer in his shirt pocket went off with unsettling rattles and raucous chiming noises. He stood up quickly, stopped the timer, and then with startled eyes, stared us down. "You may lower your silverware, the dinner is over," he announced. "Now, with nothing with which to hinder our speech, as food often does, where shall I start?"

"How are you," Chris asked, as Viktor's expression changed from eager to bemused.

"So," I began, "I don't believe we have properly introduced ourselves to you. I'm Sean Robinson, and that there is Chris Armsworth."

"Armsworth, aye?" he said. "I like the sound of that. Would you two mind if we carried this happy little discussion into the sitting room?"

Once there, he lit the fire place, and Chris and I sat down on the divan, comfortable and close to the ground. As emerging flames gave the room some needed light, I had my attention captured by the painting hanging above the mantel. It was amazing—the use of purple and gold leaf, the wonder and creepy aura of the whole piece always led my mind to become overrun with imagined happenings and ghostly premonitions, all of which provided me with a curious sort of thrill. It was the finest recreation of a notable piece of art I had ever seen.

"Ah, yes! *The Ghost of a Flea*! Or as Blake himself would have called it, *Das Gespenst eines Flohs.*"

"It's his best work!" I said.

"That it is," he replied with a grin. "My grandfather had it commissioned by a lovely female artist in Brittany for his personal collection. He, of course, wanted a larger version of the piece; the original is so small, only a few inches all around. Though it is indeed among his greatest works, I always wished he had made it bigger."

"I couldn't agree more," I replied.

No doubt my intellectual guilty pleasure was fed while talking to this man; and just as well, this feast of knowledge was complimented by the presence of the paintings he possessed. He took no interest in our questions or responses, however. He ran the conversation, and seemed to babble ceaselessly about the most intriguing of topics.

We sat and listen to him discuss his whereabouts, his political opinions, religious prophecies and premonitions. The man always thought he was being watched or followed. How could he have truly coped with his surroundings if he was forever and always unsure of what those surroundings may have been? Yet, at the same time he was pious, poised, and extremely, almost arrogantly, self-assured. Though flustered a bit, Chris and I sat and listened to him talk. All was seemingly well inside the house of the Manic. That was until Chris rather pressingly asked, "So, Viktor," whereas victor replied, "Yes, Armsworth?" "What was it that finally made you crack?"

The room went silent all except for the creeping footsteps of a cat, or perhaps even a rat, as it made its way over the keys of a grand piano. A crucifix dangling on the wall in front of me seemed to be drooping down towards the floor, as if the wall was melting away behind it. My vision enclosed around that single object. I screamed, but quickly muffled the sound with a shaky hand across the mouth, and then threw myself back into the seat in a frightful thrashing motion. I shook my brain and, similar to smacking the backside of a remote control when it's not functioning properly, forced my mind to either operate or lose all usefulness, such are the odds while hoping to jolt back to life the stale batteries in one's remote.

"What made me crack," he said, rubbing his chin as if sarcastically pretending to think. "I suppose it was the weather. Yes, just as the relentless winds erode the sandstone walls of the old ravines; just as the skin of a child goes through many phases before aging and shriveling away. That, among other things; I've lived a long time, you know. When I was younger, my sister had me sent to a mental ward. There I received a botched lobotomy in '52, and then again in summer of '59. Subsequently, after having the magical touch of surgical icepicks professionally inserted under the lids of my eyes and up into the frontal lobes of my brain, I've been my pleasant self ever since."

After growing quiet following a momentary pause in conversation, he seemed to become rather agitated. His idle hands began to twitch, picking at the dead skin between scraggly fingernails of the one opposite. His wild pupils rapidly dilated and then receded, his breathing deepened, almost as if he were panting—all this before insisting on a change of topic. My mind soon began to wander, certainly in a way similar to how Viktor's mind must have wandered eternally, but due to some unknown external magic that made up everything around him, and us as well.

While spending some time in his home, it seemed as if doors would open for me, as if blown by a gust of wind, and, like I had intended to do with my hand, unbolted slightly, and allowed for me to easily push it aside and enter. There I stood, tip of nose so close as to almost touch the wood of it, fingers feeling for the knob, and then slightly back did it go; my nose was now farther away than it had been before, though I did not move. And on further inspection I see that the door has opened by itself. But now I am straying from what I know you'll really want to hear. So, on we go.

"Viktor, will you be continuing to familiarize us with the history of your life and whatever you feel has played a significant, worthy of conversation role in it, or is this the end of the night?" Chris asked.

"Ah, surely, how could I not? Oh, and where to begin?—relations I suppose. Shall we climb the branches of the family tree?"

"Let's" said Chris smiling and surrendering his attention.

"And so it had been that my father was a portraitist," he began, "and his papa was a vicar. He (my father) was knighted by the Queen after having commissioned a beautiful group portrait of Edward VII and a few members of his royal family, of whom I'm not quite sure. I have never seen this painting, but the likes of which I am told hangs from the wall in a dark and forgotten chamber of Balmoral Castle. Yet, the most exceptional thing about my father was the fact that this was all just an elaborate lie; he did paint, yes, but his repertoire was all but fabrication. It was an eloquent hoax derived to swindle the minds of the unassuming and naïve, and just because it was fun. My father was nothing but a malicious deceiver, and made his fortunes, as I did, and from time to time still do, through the family business.

"The family business?" I asked.

"Ah, yes," he said, "the sale of indulgences. I've made my weight in gold some five times over in that line of work. It's better than being a preacher, I tell ya!"

I started to laugh; Chris, however, didn't exactly find the humor in it, or maybe he hadn't a clue of what the occupation was, if it can even still be considered an occupation nowadays.

"Don't you find that kind of ironic… and wrong?" I asked.

"Wrong!" he shouted, pounding his fist on the table beside him. "What's wrong about it? I catch the irony, sure. But to combat that, I must confess that my name is not derived from the likings of Martin Luther. In fact, I find him a rather deplorable figure, and tasteless, for he was a suppresser of the arts. Why resent well spent wealth and the beauty of things, and the beauty of others?"

"Yes," I said, "that was indeed the irony. And so, don't you think that it is wrong to take people's money in return for falsity? Besides, what you do does not expel the turpitude in one's eternal soul, or the basis of their sins, or how they will be judged in the eyes of God; only a priest has the power to relinquish sin. Are you a priest?"

"I am a performer of sacred rituals," he replied. "Would you allow me to continue?"

Oh, yes continue, please. How could I have waited to hear more? What could I expect to hear next?

"I consider myself a man of many powers," he then said, "sacred and ever evolving. I am a man of God, you see? I am also one to confess my great appreciation for all things beautiful. Indeed, I consider myself a modern-day Medici, at the very least."

"You don't say? We'll then, take me to the statue of David!" I said.

"Ah, clever boy, but I've yet to have one erected," he replied, directing his attention towards me, "though when I do, I would like to put it in the courtyard; but since I don't have one, I suppose I'll have to settle with the garden, what a pity!—But I feel there is much you two can learn from me. I have already noticed that you speak like a poet—do you have the mind of a writer? You are a man who thrives on intellect, I know that much. In the 19th century,—la belle époque!—having intellect was something to be proud of, and something that earned one the respect and interest of one's peers! Wouldn't you say? Nowadays, intelligence labels one a freak or an outcast. As if having a little more than just muscles and blood in one's own head was something to be ashamed of. Oh, what backwards times we live in!

"Yes, yes, our seemingly simple societies! Seen from space, nothing more than elaborately designed above-ground ant colonies, but peeling back the layers and the lives and the opinions, one can never expect to reach a foundation. The way we mock each other and cling, like remoras on the belly of a whale, to the customs and prejudices of the past, and—as if a white man were any more intelligent than his darker brother!—prevent some children of color from going to the same schools as other children of color, because let's not forget that white is a pigment, too! Our blasphemy and the way we rebel, wars waged for the sake of bloodshed alone! It's amazing how long we've survived."

With a billow of light smoke spurting out from the fire place and across his eyes, he smiled an elongated smile, before shattering the vibes his rantings had created with his now trademark laughter of lunacy. "RAHHHAAAA!" he cried, his eyes dilating uncontrollably. "And don't even get me started on all these countless factions of the same religion that duke it out regularly, every day, and for the last thousand years!" he began again. "And to clear up any confusion I may have caused, I am not a Catholic, nor am I affiliated with some

Separatist spin-off; rather, I am a simple Christian, broadly categorized—I pray, I confess, I refrain, and I give ten percent of my income to the Rockefeller Foundation. With the rest of my time I admire artwork, read the Bible, and keep my third eye open to anyone breathing down the back of my neck. They're always there, breathing subtle little breaths, inconspicuous sighs of air, eyes silently blinking, watching me, looming like spiders in the corners of the room…"

"Who?" Chris asked.

"I can't decide. However, I've narrowed it down to either the government or the Devil."

"What's the difference?" I said jokingly.

"They don't show their faces," he said. "They'd rather view me through the lens of a camera, or in public places disguised as shoppers and business men. As of now, they have remained forever in the shadows. So in the night, that's when I keep my eyes peeled the most. Do you two know what they say about the night?"

"They say: that while describing it, what more is there to mention but shadows…?" Chris timidly replied.

"Who told you that?!" he then shouted, angrily stomping on the wood floor with his leather boot. Chris's eyes beamed with astonishment, and perhaps he was alarmed. I, however, had lost track of my emotions days ago. No man's presence could unnerve me, at least not for the time being; though a demonic crucifix still held the upper hand, and the one on the wall still seemed to haunt me. The copper Jesus spiked onto it laughed sickeningly; it winked at me, and tantalizingly called out my name from across the room. "Enough," Viktor exclaimed, a little softer than before, "it is time to retire. Come, I will show you to your rooms."

Suddenly he was off, strutting quickly down the hallway towards the stairs, his right hand loosely caressing the waist-high, ropework molding of the wall as he passed it, snapping the fingers of his other hand in the air, dancing to the beat of an imaginary tune in his head as he ascended the flight of carpet-swathed steps.

And so with racing minds, we followed.

XII

The Flood

With five days remaining until the lifting of our curse, and upon entering into the third day of being in Viktor's home, we found ourselves up bright and early, standing under an umbrella out back in the garden, watching awkwardly as he hoed some rather dark soil. And then with pleasure, he began to dig multiple shallow holes in the ground so as to plant a row of flowers. His galoshes were slowly sinking into the murky earth as he stood there gazing over his indentations, wobbling a tiny gardener's shovel in his left hand, completely ignoring the unpleasantness of icy early morning rainfall. After turning to retrieve a bag of seeds, all of which might possible grow one day into delicious peppers, and then planting them gently into the holes before burial, he stuck his hoe into the dirt and acknowledged our reluctant presence.

"Ain't it funny," he said, stumbling backwards, accidentally stepping onto one of my bare feet, "that I buried those seeds? I buried those seeds, every last one of 'em. They are not alive now, of course, but I did so in the hope of giving them the gift of life. So ain't it funny, that in the existence of a seed they must first be put into the ground in order to live, and we—mere seeds as well—after having lived and then died, must be put into the ground, too?!"

At this scenario he started laughing uncontrollably, but not his signature laughter, rather, it was a laugh of long, hysterical wails. We, with hesitative quivering noises, joined in, though only for a moment before he stopped suddenly and stared down at us again with those wild, jousting eyes.

For a time we stood out back in the rain, the maniac preaching, Chris smoking, myself just trying to absorb it all in, listening, grasping on tight to my surroundings, fearing a lack of gravity. I could tell that admittance into Viktor's world was rare, that I should feel grateful for having been allowed in at all, even if I was uncomfortable; I believe now that that must have been his intention, to make us feel uncomfortable. And whenever we'd tell him that he was doing so through his excessive shouting, crying, or violent mannerisms, as were often the instances, he'd say with a grin, "Good, I want you to be uncomfortable, it's good!"

And so it was that we were uncomfortable, but the feeling grew. Indeed, it grew so that it wasn't painful anymore, the anxiety, that is. One gets used to it, and its grueling persistence thickens one's skin, allowing one to be able to cope with intensities a bit more dauntlessly than would have been achievable in the past. And without hesitation, he stood before us in the garden and began to reminisce, after Chris had urged him to tell us more about himself, for we were curious, as Viktor had seemingly locked us up in our rooms for two whole days, and fed us only at dusk and dawn.

"Ah, yes," he said, "I was a boisterous little child it seems now, though, always burning with the passion and the life of Christ. As a youth, I recall I had fancied myself a god. It was a cold March day when, with a shivering group of grade school friends huddled nearby, wonderfully watching in immense discomfort, I stripped myself of my clothing, and with the incandescent lake waiting for me behind my home, I attempted to take my first steps on water. Of course, that hadn't been what I told my companions. Simply, as an act of great devotion to the likes of someone or something (as they did not know), they were informed that I would attempt to swim the length of the pond, a good three hundred feet, maybe more, water a deathly forty degrees. I swam only halfway before I, not surprisingly, had to quit and come out; I couldn't stop shivering. My friends were shocked, terrified, and angry after having begged me not to go into the water in the first place. And so, as one animal outsmarts another in the race to determine who will become food and who will exist, I utilized their discomfort and anxiety to the best of my advantage. I ate them alive!"

"Where is this story going?" Chris asked.

"To where it all began, Armsworth," Viktor said, "you should be all ears; do I bore you?"

"No, you don't bore him!" I interrupted, "please, go on."

"I certainly intended to," he said. "So, where was I?—Ah yes, the first steps. Like my father the Deceiver, I myself had caught a case of his wicked ways as a boy. No, I never did walk on that water. How could I? At that time I was but a man, I accept that. But that doesn't mean that I was not one with God. Perhaps, even more so than the common believer; perhaps he is like a causal house guest inside my head, always leaving me with good advice and little clues, ideas and support. So subtle, yet so obvious, and I have no doubt that he is there. Oh, and it makes me feel good!

"Anyways, as to spread the word of my divine being, I rather successfully convinced my friends that I had taken a remarkable six steps across the surface before sinking down normally into the icy water. A true miracle it was! They spread the word far and wide, and I arrived at my high school the next day with my head shaved bare, robed in a white cloth. Everybody was so wonderfully uncomfortable, it was quite pleasing. And how I can never forget the faces of the unassured, the revolted, self-absorbed, judgmental, skinny little bitches of the Devil!"

In the course of uttering this last sentence, he picked up the potentially lethal shovel and jabbed it out in front of him with a shaking hand. This startled Chris and I a great deal, and we were able to successfully motion for him to lower it.

"What others thought of me mattered not," he then said; "I didn't need their approval, nor did I care. I was on a mission, still am, probably will be 'til the end. But what more could I ask for in life than to be on a mission with God, hand in hand forever? And that was the message I brought with me in the depths of my heart. Though, in light of that, I had a much larger plan."

"You don't say?" Chris mumbled.

"But I do!" he replied. "Would you like to be a part of it?"

"Of what?"

"The plan!"

"Uh, no I don't think so," Chris said fearfully.

"Well, what's the plan?" I asked.

"The plan is simply this," he began: "First we cover the globe in breezeblocks, line every square inch with sewage drains and adobe bricks. Drain the Great Lakes, filter them through our pipes and plumbing, and then slowly release the run-off back into the depleted land. But alas!—this has already been done for us, the plot is perfectly underway! So to Jerusalem we go! Breach the walls of Temple Mount; creep slowly through the entrance as the Holy Ghost disarms the guards, and with the structure to ourselves, we shall set up camp under the dome and bask in the Divine Presence. Indeed it is a site of unity, for throughout the course of time, four divided religions have called it their superlative house of prayer. This is certainly one of Israel's holiest places, although outside the walls of the temple the local inhabitants have shed each other's blood for centuries. Still, that is how it is all over the world. In America, you have your suburbs, your places of wealth and refuge from the unclean. Then you have your cities, filled with the likes of colorful characters, criminals, nomads, and unfortunate products of the environment: the discarded parts of a dead host, unsalvageable, of no use to the people who've killed it. But at the same time, epicenters of life and renewal, the heart beat that keeps our exploitative yet sometimes miraculous society running. Yes, life! That's why we go to the Temple, we seek life!

"Once there, I shall proclaim myself as righteous. Indeed, it is what has to be done. Too many generations have come to pass without the likes of a spiritual revolution, a leader, a profit, so to speak. In fact, as wrong as it may seem, perhaps Hitler was the closest we have come. Surely, he had no spiritual, godly reason for doing the things he did; and I do not wish to condemn the innocent, thus, the plan comes into effect. The apocalypse, my friends, has arrived! A novel day shall soon dawn; a new way of life shall soon be welcomed with open arms, one that will be impossible to refuse, for who in their right mind would reject the wishes, the dogmas of Christ himself? And so, with the world watching, gazing into their T.V. screens, gripping anxiously to the cushions of their seats, I will make my announcement."

"Announcement?" I asked.

"*My* announcement," he said, "*the* announcement, a shockwave that unnerves the foundation of mankind! I will ascend in a beam of light and glory, high above Israel, the city of the chosen people, just like Muhamad when he ascended to meet with the prophets in Heaven. There I shall retrieve my commandments. Though I've often wondered, if we are all God's people, and people of God, how can there ever be a chosen people? No. There can only ever be but one chosen person. Yes, it is I. And when I descend with my holy stone tablets, all eyes will be on me; that's when the two of you will make your move! Yes, *the* move, *your* move; when no one is looking, we tell all who truly believe to set fire to the earth! We tie every heathen to a stone and drop them in the ocean! Every last devil shall be cast down to the depths from which they came! We'll burn all that is not green; persecute those who wish to persecute women, steal from their neighbors, lobotomize the sick, and submit their obedience to the likes of a generic society rather than to the undeniable truth! And I am God!

"You are God," Chris said plainly, "the God?"

"Or perhaps I should have said, God is me."

"What's the difference?" we asked.

"The difference is that I cannot *be* God, God is God, and God is whoever he wants to be. This time around, he has simple chosen to be me, to be a man, all of which has occurred in the past. I harness within the mind and soul of the supreme deity, all behind the face and body of a man. Boys, it is simple, I have seen the light. I have read the writings, and with my third eye open, have come upon the solutions to the problems that the existence of every man, from Adam to Armsworth here before me, and as a consequence of our sinful ways, have created. But now there is an answer, there is a cure! All this is possible from the temple, and through destruction we shall cleanse!"

"Why do you want to bring upon the apocalypse?" Chris asked.

"To save!" he replied. "This generation, like so many others before, is weak. We lack blind faith; we can't find assurance in words or promises; we need actions, events, signs! That's what this all is, a sign! Christ asked the same questions: why must you need proof in order to believe? I don't know. It's not necessarily true that without proof we can't be faithful, surely we can! But I'm tired of looking into the faces of the inconstant and unconvinced; they make me ill. So let them burn! And those who are good will stay and see the sign which I have made for them to behold, and then their former beliefs will be strengthened. And those who I've damned shall see the sign as well, hitherto their descent into the unholy inferno. They shall see my glory, the glory of God, and they will know the pain they have caused. They will regret their ways and see the truth, but their punishment is just and irrevocable. For in their lives they had the chance to be saved, to be one with the light above, and still, they rejected and denied. So as they melt away in their deserved abyss, they shall know what it is they have rejected and denied, and they will grieve. Oh, how they will grieve! And I will rejoice, as will you, as will the Lord! I find a somber truth in the words of what Adolf Köberle once said: 'The personal and voluntary relationship between God and man that is taught in the Bible has been utterly betrayed and forgotten.' It's so sad, yet, so exact, and what else am I to do? How could I be expected to let the wicked ways of this generation continue on into the next?"

"Since man's biblical fall from grace," I began, "there's a thing called concupiscence, something even the monks and the priests and the Brahmins have been guilty of at some point in their lives. Have you taken that into consideration, or did you just think with your anger instead of your head? Is this generation truly and wholly evil? And If I'm correct, I'm pretty sure Jesus warns of false messiahs numerous times throughout the Bible. He says that they will perform signs and wonders in order to mislead. How do you know that you are not of those he has so exhaustively mentioned?"

"How would you know," he retorted, "what is misleading and what is the truth? For of those signs and wonders mentioned, they amounted to nothing more than man's imitated attempts at making miracles, of mimicking the ways of the Lord. Does a fiery Armageddon sound like a miracle to you? No, it is a ghastly action, a despicable act, but only to those who cannot see the light. Only to those who are faithless does this *sign*, this *plan*, this *announcement,* make for an unpleasant surprise. For if one truly has the Holy Spirit within, no such death, no such destruction could make one shudder. As for concupiscence, well, you must be a fool to make such an argument! For obviously the carnal forces within us have all but conquered those that are spiritual, and most precious! This is our very objective, don't you see? We must reverse this!"

"Viktor," I said, changing the topic rather significantly, sort of on edge now because of the hysteric preaching, "why did you rescue us from the diner, and how did you know we needed help?"

"I knew the two of you needed help long before I ever saw you in the diner," he started, but then paused, and grew quite pale. "You've been cursed, am I wrong? Smitten with all the torments of hell on earth, lost in the woods, withering away; the Devil fastened himself to you tight, chocked your guardian angels, and left you with the good fortune of a leper. You're like the Kennedys! How did I know all this… that was the real question, right?"

"Right."

"I only know what is revealed to me," he replied. "I saw you through a window; my heart was drawn to you, in a way, and I knew I had to save your souls! But what we are to do now, I do not know. We shall wait, and God will soon reveal to me the answer, your next move. In the meantime, go clothe yourselves with the contents of your room's wardrobe, you're all wet. Then look up to the sky and ask me why!" Whereas we then looked up into the sky, the melting sky of endless rainfall, and step by step across the wet field we trotted hastily back into the house.

We entered through the side door that led into the kitchen facing a staircase with a large grandfather clock at the base of it, and while we followed him as he proceeded to walk into another room, and then another, Chris, reigniting the conversation, boldly asked, "Why? Ask me why, you said earlier; what is it exactly that I want to know?"

"Shut your filthy mouth!" Viktor shouted, running in from the other room, slamming his massive hand hard against the plaster wall, causing it to shake. Chris retreated slowly away from him. "What's the matter?" he whispered. "What's wrong, are you fearful, fearful like a whore in church?! Fact is, boy, I saved you, and if you are actually in search of true salvation, I suggest you listen to me!" whereas he then looked over at me.

"What are you looking at?" I asked.

"That bag of yours, who the fuck gave you the *okay* to bring that in this house?!"

"My bag..." I said. "There's nothing in there but a blanket and my book and some socks."

"Book, you say? That's interesting; I was not expecting you to possess a book. This will most likely have to be confiscated for the night. Shall we find out if it is indeed so?" He then turned away from us with my bag in hand, which I had left on the divan last night; he had just noticed, and with it headed quickly for a room on the left.

We followed slowly, and when we arrived at the doorway, he had already been in the room for a good five seconds. There, at a standstill from the hall, we watched in amazement at his actions. Reciting some nonsense, he crouched on his hands and knees, genuflecting on the floor before a large depiction of the Lamentation hanging from the wall beside yet another standing clock. When it struck the hour and began to chime, he stopped, got up off of his knees, and calmly directed us to a room.

"Get dressed," he said, "wine and cheese will be served in the kitchen at four o' clock. I suggest you be there."

"Wait," I said before we left, "so what did all that tell you?"

"It told me to escort you to your room," he said; "it told me that wine and cheese will be served in the kitchen at four o' clock. I suggest you be there!"

With a sort of spin, he turned around and walked oddly down the hall, pretending to use his cane as if he needed it, and then descended the stairs into the kitchen. With him gone, a dreadful, unnerving sensation began to crawl its way up my back with the legs of a poisonous spider. I was beyond concerned that he had appropriated my book, my legacy. What was I to do if something were to happen to it? That was my life, all I had or wanted. I had come so far, written so many things, things I could never write again or duplicate with the same sort of magic. My story, how it had progressed, and was so close to completion. Page for page a product of my mind, cherished in my heart. I was proud of myself for the first time in a while. I couldn't wait to share it with Chris and hopefully with the world. But what could I have done then, he was already gone. Chris said it would be fine, that he wouldn't do anything to it; so we settled into our room, and I tried hard to cope with the bilious sensation that was fostering in my gut.

After a thorough search of the wardrobe, Chris and I dressed ourselves in the finest clothes the two of us, and certainly Chris, had ever worn. We stood there before two long rectangular mirrors, grinning, feeling like kings. Finally we were clean; finally we were respectable. With a new pair of shining leather shoes on, my hair combed, and my hands gently tucked into the side pockets of my overwhelming, velvet and gold frock coat, I was almost as mighty as Viktor, it seemed. Indeed, up until I realized it was his clothing, and he in fact was still undeniably the mightiest one around. I'm not saying that I looked up to him, because that would be ridiculous, I certainly don't. I am saying, however, that he surely had some quality that made him look as if he were larger than you. Even without hearing him speak or allowing him to make you feel uncomfortable, his appearance alone did the trick. With eyes shiftier than those of an intrusive insect, he saw our every move, and he made sure that we knew it. Chris soon changed back into a more modest pair of clothes, but I chose to remain the way I was. We sat there inside the room, sitting uneasily on the neatly made bed. An hour passed, then two, then three, and soon I was beginning to doze. I laid back into the pillow and began to fall asleep. My eyes slowly cemented themselves shut, my consciousness left its post, and I was out, dreaming, escaping, drifting further into the depths of my own mind.

I don't know how much time had been deflected between then and when Chris woke me up to announce that Viktor was at the door, and would not in fact open the door unless I was the one who answered it. With no regard for the sense of urgency that Viktor's banging and shouting had created, I approached slowly, half-awake, and stood before it for a moment just to listen. He was pressing his palms up against the door on the other side. I could hear the thuds they made every few seconds, corresponding with the rising and falling intensity of his words.

"Now, if you don't open up," he said, "I'm going to starve the two of ya like veal!"

I opened the door; "is wine and cheese ready?" I asked.

"No," he said.

"All these hours and no wine and cheese!" Chris yelled.

"No," he repeated. "I have spent that time thinking, and reading, and planning what will happen in the next few hours. Some other instruction had been revealed to me, and the prior was forgotten. But I've got good news, boys! It's flooding up outside! We got more than six inches of water on the ground, and rising quick! We don't have much time; I must tell you everything you wish to know!"

"About what?" I asked.

"About me, of course!" he exclaimed. "You need to know me in full, there's no way around it. For if you are to be my true disciples, then you must know who I am, and what I believe. Otherwise, what else would you write?"

"Write?" I questioned.

"RAAHHHAA!" he spat, "Right!"

But before I could inform him that we in fact did not want to be his disciples, or that we really just needed to get back to Chris's house so I could flee the state, he sat us down at a table in the room, sitting on his chair with it spun around, the backrest now elevating his veiny arms. We could not prevent him from speaking, and he started to converse with us in a fervent manner, beginning with a story about his mother, which seemed to me to have no possible relevance what-so-ever.

"She was a sweet, lovely, red Cuban woman," he said. "She was not my birth mother of course, but oh, how her beauty and comfort knew no bounds! She gave me everything, cared for me so. My father and she were madly in love; we were a family made perfectly to blend in with the pages of a catalogue. My father, however, not only had a deceiving problem, but was a sporadic alcoholic, too. I remember years of my life where he never drank at all. Months would pass without a drunken episode. But one night, four days before my thirteenth birthday, he came home in a rage.

"My mother and I were in the kitchen, here in this very house. It is because of this story that I no longer wanted to have wine and cheese with you tonight. It is a story that hurts me to this day. But, it must be told! As I said, my mother and I were in the kitchen, she was making dinner, and I was coloring in a book or something. Everything's pleasant, that is until the mighty bread winner came plowing through the side door, a bag of groceries in his hand, hunched up on his shoulder a little. His black shirt was wet with booze; his brown leather jacket had cigarette burns on it. He made his way down the hall and into the kitchen where we sat victim, already shouting and cussing at us before he even entered the room. Swinging the paper bag of groceries onto the table, he turned around and smacked my pencil out of my hand, and gazed at me with fiery eyes, and then decided to teach me a life lesson. 'I had a teacher,' he said, with spit falling from his lips, 'and when she was a kid, she used to draw with colored pencils, just like you. Her favorite color was blue, and she'd sharpen it nice and fine! She was so happy one day, she told me, after her blue pencil had just made some wonderful work of art, and before she could even admire what it was she had created, she had to go sharpen the pencil again. She loved the feeling of it, the shortening, the grinding of brittle wood, paint and led. After sharpening it to a glorious point, she ran around the room with joy, only to slip on her clumsy fucking feet! The pencil went right into her forehead, the tip broke off and it was stuck. Twenty years later she was my first grade teacher, and the tip was still in her head, lodged there like a tooth. It was her little bindi, her birthmark, so to speak. She wasn't careful around sharp objects, you see, now she's got led in her fucking face!' I began to cry; he then went on to assault my mother.

"'Wench!' he said, and would often call her when he was drunk. 'Wench, look at your son and all his pretty pictures! Look at him!'" He then took her by the shoulders and shook her dizzy. She fell down onto the floor and began to weep, her wails blending perfectly in tune with mine. As we sobbed and shook like the helpless creatures we were, he walked across the kitchen to where she had been cooking supper, to where a large metal stock pot was steaming on the fire. He stuck his finger in it; it burned him immediately and this sent him into an even more unrelenting rage. Next thing I knew, my whole life had shattered before me and would be forever changed. With hatred in his eyes, and in the color of his cheeks, he proceeded to thrust a boiling pot of barley seeds onto my mother. When it hit her, she melted away like burning candle wax. She withered in pain on the tile floor, steam rising off her twitching body as would an entree fresh out of the oven. Her lips blistered and her eyelids were sealed shut from the now-liquefied skin that ran down her forehead. Before she finally passed out, however, she turned and smacked my father square in the face with an iron skillet. His glasses shattered and blood flew across the room, tainting the pages of my coloring book. In the end, nobody came out unscathed. My mother survived, only by the grace of God, I'm sure. Though, she was bedridden for the rest of her days, and terribly disfigured. My father, on the other hand, didn't get it much better, for he was blinded by his bifocals—what a pity! His sight made forever black by the tiny shards of glass that lodged themselves in his retinas. An artist, blinded by his own glasses! RAHHAAA! Makes me laugh every time; and after that night I never saw him again. I was told that he took the first plane to East Sussex and threw himself over the edge of Beachy Head. I dreamed, for many, many years, of those final, pitiful moments of his life. I would just imagine it for hours—his sinful eyes gazing up towards the receding wall of endless chalk, seeing nothing, sensing only the wind and the sinking feeling that fills one's gut while in free fall, a head of empty thoughts still empty or perhaps racing with disgust at his own self, persisting on and on until he finally hit his watery grave. He washed up on shore some three to six days later, the death doctors weren't quite sure. The remarkable thing about it, I suppose, was that he had not been fed upon by the carnivorous organisms in the water. Not even a fish would dine on the flesh of someone so foul, so callous.

"Thus, alone I sat, here in this home by the sickbed of my mother as she slowly turned to dust. My poor widowed mother, how she grew so old so quickly! How she lost all hope before she even had any to lose in the first place! It gives me the chills, but I can sleep at night a little better knowing that she is free of all that hell. She is waltzing with God now. Everything is in its place; everything is how it should be... that is until you two came along. I thought I had filtered the well clean; I know now that it has still yet to be unpolluted. It seems that I have walked into a sort of enigma, one that troubles me greatly, and the difficulty of the problem lies with you, Sean, in the septic words of this book!" He then slew my manuscript from behind him and pressed it down menacingly onto the table, his dirty fingernails clawing into the title page, leaving an arrangement of crescent moon shapes on the surface of the now-crumpled piece of paper.

"Clandestine diners, uxoricide, promiscuity, a fortunate criminal!—what garbage, a volume of utter nonsense, the likes of which you have created to corrupt the mind of my unborn child! A vile heap of words, that is all; and I won't have it here in my home!" he shouted.

"Fine, then we'll leave!" I replied in anger.

He stood up quickly, and with two massive, sprawling hands, ensued to flip over the large wooden table around which we sat and kicked his chair back hard against the wall. I watched him with a gapping mouth, and followed as he strode swiftly across the room, out the door, down the stairs, into the sitting room, and tossed my manuscript, my life, my legacy, page by page into the scowling fireplace. Without hesitation I ran to stop him; but when he saw me coming, he quickly threw the remaining sheets into the flames and it was gone forever. Unaware of how I was going to react, Chris straightaway led me out of the room and into the kitchen, holding me back with all his strength as I screamed and thrashed my body back towards where Viktor stood. I wanted his life.

Once removed from the situation, I sat down on the white counter top and began to cry. I had struck my lowest point. In all my days I had never been so pathetic, so weak and useless as I was right then. I no longer had the will to live, and with the light from outside dimming, and the rain on the roof above swelling, getting louder and louder, my hypothetical egg, my carapace of grief and self-pity, began to enclose around me once again. I was left delimited on all sides by an impenetrable shell of depression. It would take more than a beak for me to shed the thick skin of this exoskeleton now, and how I would begin to do so, I did not know. It was the worst hit I had ever taken; I can't stress enough the horror, the total shock and horror I felt when I saw those last few pages slowly charring away in the pit atop spiteful embers.

In the other room he laughed and howled. He danced around the burning pages with rejoice and pleasure. "You will start anew!" he exclaimed to me upon leaping into the kitchen where we sat. "You will start again, boy! You have the words inside of you, they are the cells in your skin, they are always there, always ready to be put to use. You shall pen a new gospel! Come, Sean, don't be so down! It is for the best, you'll soon see that it is! I have no doubt. The gospels of the twentieth century shall be written by lonely woman and schoolboys in spiral notebooks. Yes, admit it! Today's sacred Sanskrit is written in graffiti on the sides of freight trains… Now quit your sulking, it's bringing me down! The world outside is drowning, the sins of all those who have committed sin will begin to dissolve, to wash away with the damned and the unclean! Don't act so afflicted, for you two are the lucky ones. God has sent a flood to wash away your troubles!"

"Or has he?" Chris blatantly tested, not looking for a response.

"Have you looked outside?" he then asked. "For if you have not, please, look now and tell me that it is not so: the streets are waterways, the forest around us is but a murky lake of renewal. Can't you sense the resurrection of virtuous faith swelling in the air?!"

And indeed we could. With the thick curtains resting against the back of our heads from where they hung above us, and where we stood draped within, like children who shroud themselves in a game of hide and seek, we stared out into the storm, and saw as the flood rose around the home, in the garden and on the grass, which was now completely submerged in a visible lake of water.

Regardless of our apparent *gift* from God, I went to bed that night with a spike lodged in my heart. I sobbed; my throat burned and tightened. With my raw-skinned nose running, and Chris asleep in his room across the hall, I rested my head back and tried to close my eyes, tried to get some rest. Outside the blitzkrieg of wind and rain attacked the walls, shook the bay windows, and rumbled the floor boards. While the sounds of carnage continued on, my thoughts soon turned to other unpleasant happenings around the room. Before long, I realized it was like Chinese water torture trying to sleep while lying face-up in that bed. The whole night through the aging roof commenced to leak a steady drop of rainwater down after each second-long pause of accumulation and land, more often than not, square on my obvious target of a forehead. Having finally reached my breaking point sometime before 2 a.m., I got up and made my way to Chris's room.

When I arrived at his door, watched as the magic of the house opened it for me before I could do so myself, stood there baffled for a moment, and then entered into the dark room, I found that he was not inside. I turned the lights on, and in the depths of my ears I began to hear the faintest of footsteps, creeping, lurking, and approaching from behind. I turned around to see Chris standing at the entrance of the room with a candle-lit smile, the look of adventure was on his face, flickering between shadow and light.

"You won't believe the scene in the next room!" he said enthusiastically, but also rather serious.

My eyes beamed, and I followed him as he walked back into the hall. With the candle lighting the way, Chris opened the door of a room that faced out at the very end of the passage, a room I knew to be Viktor's. Clenching the knob, he opened the door gently; the lit room behind it illuminated the hallway, hurting my eyes. Inside, a metal fan stood on top a tall lacquered escritoire, blowing Bible pages and wigs and other lightweight debris around the room. Then I beheld, spread-eagle on the floor, like one of those bearskin carpets that utilize the entire bear, Viktor, knocked out, drunk at the foot of the bed. A bottle lay tipped on its side, trickling its content out onto the carpet and pooling around Viktor's feet. The room reeked of hard liquor, burning candles, and total insanity.

Four walls boxed us in, all of which were papered with an infinite number of photographs, news articles, notes and paintings. To my left was a Degas—*L' Absinthe*, if I'm not mistaken—though it was by no means a genuine copy. The funny thing about it was that the man seated next to the woman in the painting looked a lot like Viktor Lutheran; it was as if the artist had worked his portrait into the picture. Next to that was another painting, Edouard Manet's *The Philosopher*, and Viktor was now undeniably painted into this one; he was in fact The Philosopher. To my right was a section of wall which had tape on it in the shape of a rectangle. Within the rectangle were several pictures, the first two were of young women, both I hadn't recognized. The next few pictures were those of people I did. They were ours, and Jimmy and Billie's. I was startled, but then I looked at the rest of the pictures. Below were the images of no other than Mr. and Mrs. Monte-Duff, and their alluring maid. I collapsed in a way; I fell back into the desk with the blowing fan on top and could not seem to keep my balance until Chris came and steadied me with his arm around my shoulder. He was unsure of my reaction for a moment, looking down at me with an odd face. However, with my eyes wide and fixated at the images on the wall, he soon took notice of what it was that had caused me to collapse.

"I bet," I said, my teeth shivering fearfully, "I bet you anything, Chris, that Viktor killed the Monte-Duffs."

"He did," Chris replied, as if he had it all figured out, "isn't it obvious?"

"I'm scared," I said, "he's probably looking to do the same to us. We should leave right now!"

"Wait," he said, "I have something else to show you. Plus, he wouldn't kill us; he wants us to worship him. Don't you think if he was going to do so he would have done it by now?"

I agreed, and with a swipe of the hand, Chris motioned for me to follow as he stepped over Viktor's melted body and across the paper-cluttered Oriental rug. On his bed between the four posts of dark, elaborately shaped wood, his sheets lay in a flat, well made fashion. Only they didn't quite seem to be bed sheets. Rather, it was but one thin cloth, raggedy and stained, but, purposely stained, it appeared. Yes! Upon careful, momentary inspection, it seemed to be stained with the blood and body of Christ! And yet, as my attentiveness began to suddenly enhance, I looked around the room to find that it was numerous in couches and chairs all draped in Shrouds of Turin. It was amazing to me that I hadn't found myself resting my head on pieces of the Titulus Crucis that night instead of a pillow. "Shit," I said, "how the hell does one sleep like this?" I couldn't tell you. So onward across the room I went, Chris ignoring all that I had found to be so gross. He was determined, in a sense, hurriedly trying to reach a goal.

Towards a jib door he approached; the knob was almost nonexistent but mounted a gaping key hole, the kinds that one could peer through with a focused eye from across the room. He clenched it, bent his wrist—oh, the suspense of opening closed doors! He jerked his hand away, and the section of once white-painted wood that emulated the disorderly walls around it swung back quickly; we both stepped aside, and I bumped into another large clock that towered next to a congested bookshelf. Inside it was completely shadowed, yet, a light at the end of the tunnel, a subtle twinkle of something vibrant, something golden, caught my eye. "Come on," Chris said as he entered. "Something tells me that our luck is about to change!"

"What do you mean?" I asked. He never gave a response, for above his head was a two branched chandelier with a half melted candle of bubbly wax crookedly protruding out from the end of one of the arms. Chris, with a lit match in hand, reached up and ensued to give light to the dark closet space. With the room lit, all of my previous assumptions as to what could be within were instantly proven false. A tear ran down my cheek, a warm drop of happiness, of delightfully exceeded expectations, glistened in my eye.

"Now do you believe in miracles?" he asked.

"I believe in freak occurrences," I replied, downplaying my actual enthusiasm. And so, behind that jib door and inside the closet, we were confronted with a small table draped in a red cloth, all surrounded by seven golden lamp-stands. In the middle, upon the table's fabric surface, and below a hemorrhaging Christ appended to a massive crucifix, was a bowl of rubies, and behind that was a two-foot-tall pyramid structure assembled out of carefully stacked bars of gold. They gave off a sort of incandescence; they made it so my eyes winced and watered, and my sinuses began to open wide, allowing for me to breathe quite effortlessly. I slumped to my knees; Chris stood behind me with his hand upon my shoulder. After a minute or two had passed, we both looked up and noticed that the candle had gone out, yet, the room stayed lit: the natural glow of flawless gold proved to be sufficient enough. However, from behind us the sounds of a groaning monster vibrated the floor boards as it choked and flailed like an awakening guard dog, and provided us a reason to be fearful.

"It's Viktor!" Chris announced, "I think he's rousing; who knows how long he's been asleep!"

I reached my hand out to take a bar before we fled, but as I raised it, Chris smacked it down with his, and pushed me away. "Don't," he said, "do you want him to kill us?"

I stared at him shocked. He, of all people, he was the one who'd turn down the opportunity of seizing obtainable riches! I never would have guessed; he had in my mind for so long fit into the shoes of a man with selfish needs. Needs such as money, acquired by means of leeching, mooching, and not so modestly supplicating, I assumed. Was it a sign of redemption, a hint of self-improvement? Right then I wasn't sure, but I hoped to find out.

At that moment we fled the room, and suddenly I knew how this night was going to end. I would crawl back into bed and pretend as if I hadn't seen anything. I would lie awake between stuffy sheets and wait for the sun. That's always how nights like these seemed to end, always has been. I've come to accept the fact that great triumph and excitement usually leads to great drawbacks, unbearable letdowns, and anticlimaxes that exist solely to haunt you in your dreams... or at least to ensure the prevention of their onset. However, sometime during the night I managed to doze, but I never dreamt, not pleasantly, at least.

I awoke, it seemed, into a world of fantasy; I opened my eyes and stood up out of the bed. My bare feet sank down three or four inches into cold and muddy water before hitting the wood floor. I laughed, chuckled to myself, thought that it was all fake... and I suppose to a degree it was. As I recall, I looked to my side and on the nightstand was a silver meal-dish covered with a silver dome. I approached it with a shaking hand extended in front of me. As I sloshed through the water towards the table, I heard the door open slowly. Turning around only to see Chris, I continued to make my way over to the tray. With a shaking hand, and with two fingers acting as surgical forceps, I removed the covering of the plate, only to drop it immediately thereafter. I fell down into the water, squeezing a fist full of muck in my hand as I did so, and ogled affrightedly at the sight of what the dome had once kept hidden. There on the plate grinning for all to see was a head, severed, purple, and bloody.

"RAAHHHAA!" said a voice from behind, "A nice breakfast for ya, eh? Aren't ya gonna eat it up?" It was Viktor; he was standing in the doorway next to Chris, an arm around his shoulder like best buds. "The most important meal of the day," he said, handing me a knife and a fork. "The very best I could cook up on such short notice: the head of Saint John the Baptist on a silver platter. I do hope you enjoy!"

"Now that's Salome!" Chris said cheerfully.

Yes, Chris, that's Salome… but not quite. Though, eager and smiling, I took a bite of the cheek, and then prodded a little at one of his blue lips with the end of my fork; all this before opening my eyes to discover myself face down on a wet pillow, half off the bed, almost waist-deep in yellow water. I broke into a terrible cough and was thrown into a feeling of tremendous shock, confused at the bizarre nature of my dreams. Around me I heard nothing but static and splashing… and yelling. I got to my feet and ran to the door. Behind it the home lay in ruin. It seemed that the flood waters had penetrated the windows and the locks of the front door, and was now pouring furiously into the lower lever. Viktor ran around downstairs collecting all objects of value, shrieking with joy and thanking the Lord. After seeing me gazing over at him from the railing above, he pointed and shouted, "Stay where you are, you'll drown!"

"What am I to do?" I asked, not quite hearing him the first time.

"Stay where you are, we have no choice but to seek refuge on the upper floors; we stand no chance outside!" he said, struggling as he lugged a massive grandfather clock up the slippery staircase, gradually making his way to our level of safety. When he got there, hand on his hips, profusely dripping with river water, he shoved the clock up against the wall and proceeded to chain himself to the metal cable of the pendulum with a pair of handcuffs, and did so rather joyously, I might add.

"Are you crazy?!" I shouted, "why are you chaining yourself to that clock?!"

"It goes where ever I go," he replied, "it has been counting the seconds of my life since I was born. Yes!—the minute my mother gave birth to me my father set the clock into motion. I can't leave it here, therefore, I don't plan on leaving. Haven't I ever told you that I'm a clock maker? Schooled in it as a young adult, but never mind that! This flood is not for me, boys, this flood is for you! What happens to me matters not. And so, what I chose to do in the time being doesn't concern anybody anymore except for God and those who dwell in Heaven."

"What about your plan?" Chris asked in a rather cruel way considering the circumstances: this man was basically committing suicide right in front of us. However, there was no way of stopping it; as well, there was no way of knowing just what was going to happen next. Viktor, still spiritedly attempting to fasten his wrist to the hanging clock part, gave a simple response to this question.

"Well don't you see?" he said. "In order to determine whether or not I'm a false messiah, like the two of you claim, and if it turns out that I am, I will be rightfully destroyed, but…" he began to laugh with deviancy, quietly under his breath, "but, I am quite certain that things will turn out differently; and I have the righteous feeling that we shall all be in the same room again someday, someday soon. Don't consider this the end, boys, for it has all just begun! Besides, how else would I ascend in a beam of light high above the Holy Land? Do you see wings on me, Armsworth? No—first I must become metaphysical!"

"Why did you kill the Monte-Duffs?" he then asked, now enhancing the cruelty. Viktor just stared back, piercing through him with laser beam eyes. "We both know you did it! Tell us why? What reason did you have for doing such a thing?"

He started laughing, grinning with his chin down so that his large brow began to cast a demonic shadow over his eyes. Upon letting go of the cuffs, now tightly secured around his wrist and to the clock, he ensued to once again make me feel uncomfortable, for what he said next hardly seems to have been reality; I suppose the knowledge of what was revealed to me hasn't fully sunken in, as I'm still unable to see it as fact.

"You two, you two had to ask," he said. "The truth, I'm afraid, may not be a thing you want to hear. Yes, even truths sometimes outweigh lies in regards to shock and pain, brining one into denial and depression, which, I know, are the usual results of something like this. It seems one may even prefer a terrible lie as opposed to the undeniable truth."

"Tell us!" Chris shouted, walking stressfully in a circle across the floor.

"Why don't you tell me!" Viktor replied, standing up, though still chained to the clock. "I had to do it because of what the two of you did! Your damn antics, your senseless rebellion! That's what's brought us to this point! That's what this is! How can two souls cursed by the Devil get into the City of Heaven? I had to stop it.—Have you ever heard of a pharmakós? If not, you'll catch on soon enough. You two had caused so much debauchery and sin that there was no way you would be able to be with me in the Kingdom. No way you could be my disciples, and with me, bring the New Jerusalem to the doorsteps of all Western civilization, so as to cleanse this generation free of its transgressions in the waters of our Lord! Now, boys, a pharmakós is a sort of ritualistic, scapegoat sacrifice of a human. It is of Greek descent. Though quite often conducted using drugs (or pharmaceuticals, from which the word is derived), I took a much more, how should I put this... visceral approach. I drugged them up, nice and susceptible, and then hung them from a tree!

"In the woods as I followed closely on your trail, I knew that sooner or later you would wind up at the steps of that manor. So, with my God-given foresight, I set out to fulfill the job I knew needed to be done, a job to ensure your forgiveness. You see, I spoke to God, alone, in a cave in the woods the night you two disposed of those cursed stones. I asked how it could be that you were my chosen pupils, for I knew in my heart that it was surely so. He said to me, 'Indeed they seem to be, but they are a rotten bunch, not worthy enough to stroll the meadows of my kingdom.' Whereas I then asked him, 'My Lord, what should I do?' He said in order to cleanse them of their sins, I must defile the blood of those who have no business in the affairs of the holy, for their souls would then find themselves stuck with the punishments of another's sins. It is a solemn trade, but a decision I knew I had to make! With the Monte-Duff's paying your dues, you'll be free to join me in the eternal bliss that is our right. I have cleansed your souls to the point where you can call yourselves saints, or, at the very least, have been bestowed with some degree of contrition, a faith in God's eventual forgiveness. The man and the women I killed for the two of you, and the maid I killed for myself… I have my reasons. So that's the truth, Armsworth. Do you wish to hear it again, or can I be quite finished?"

"You're a monster!" Chris screamed, grasping the railing for support.

"Wrong! You're wrong!" he said. "The Lord told me to do so; do you still not believe? For God's sake, Armsworth, look around you! The Monte-Duff's are dead, the criminals are in their cells, and the world outside is crashing through my walls and windows with the promise of a new beginning! All for you, my boy, all for you!"

Viktor jerked his arm and the pendulum of the clock smacked hard against one of the hanging chimes within it, setting off a loud and climactic gong sound, a sort of horn blown before the battle. As the noise rung out, we all became aware of the aggressively rising water. "Get out of here!" Viktor cried. "You must not parish!" Chris and I, it seems, couldn't have agreed more, and I made a dash for the now mostly submerged staircase, but stopped when I saw that Chris hadn't followed. Instead, I caught the faint glimpse of him turning in the opposite direction to run back down the hall. I pursued him, and when I turned the corner I saw no one. Then as I stood there indecisively staring out at the passage of half-open, half-closed doors, Chris leaped out from one of them and quickly resumed his position by my side.

"Where did you go?" I asked.

"To get your bag," he said with an odd smile, and I was left relatively baffled as to why my bag held any importance to him.

We made our way through the knee-deep water over to where Viktor stood, one arm restrained, the other fingering the petite, spherical shell of glass that encased the bronze hands and black numbers of the clock. Once the protracting note rung from the heart of the timepiece slowly died away, the home stood silent, even the sound of the rushing water seemed to disappear. Chris halted, trying to determine what our next move was going to be. While I should have been doing the same, I instead began to take notice at how his baggy russet coat, a lighter shade than my expensive frock, blended in quite nicely with the charcoal-colored wall on which he rested up against.

"You must leave now!" Viktor urged.

"Come with," I said, "we can't just leave you here to drown."

"Drown!" he spat in a derisive way, as if what I said had been completely absurd. "I shan't drown; I have the Lord to protect me, and my faith… and the agents. If *my* god fails me—which he won't—then it is certain that the government will intervene. The spies, they won't let anything happen to me, otherwise their hard work would all be for nothing!"

"How can you be so sure that you're being watched?" Chris asked, and then immediately looked down and noticed that the water level had risen to his knees, and then higher, and higher still.

"The reason they're watching me is because they are aware that I know they're watching," he replied, leaving little room for disagreement.

"What are you, Agent Jesus?" Chris asked jokingly.

"No," he said, looking suddenly mournful, "I'm just the widow's son. If there ever was an Agent Jesus however, I would start to seriously consider the maker of this flood as a possible suspect. It is no act of nature, I can assure you that!"

"I don't know how much longer these walls are gonna hold," Chris then said, as the sound of crashing waves resumed and a noticeably audible reverberation of splintering wood and crumbling stone rumbled all around us. "I think we better leave… NOW!"

"GO!" Viktor cried, "GO! GO!"

So we ran, but soon found ourselves imprisoned, as the staircase was nowhere in sight. In fact, nothing much remained except for the upper floor hallway that led to the staircase which led to the now-submerged lower level. The water was up to our chests at this point. The house began to cringe and sway, imploding from the outside in.

"You must find a window!" Viktor shouted to us from his restrained location across the hall. "The room on the left, it has an awning that you may be able to reach!"

Yet before we switched our attention to the preservation of our own lives, we stood and glanced for one last time at our hospitable benefactor, our lunatic host, squirming, thrashing, fighting in the water, trying to catch a breath. The way he was chained, it meant that in order to stand he needed to stretch out his shackled arm, arch his back, twist his neck and raise his chin, the latter two being of actions made in the effort to try and stay in the realm of breathable air. Once or twice I strained to swim over to him, tried to pry him free. Each time he would resist, and strike at me when I came too close.

"This is the parousia!" he said. "What I have done in this world was for myself, but what I shall do in the next is an endowment to the world I have left behind. Undoubtedly, I am destined to return, destined to recommence! Yes! Recommence, my brothers, recommence in the name of the Lord!"

It turns out, right then, that the good Lord couldn't seem to wait for us to recommence the world quick enough, and so he decided to do it himself, as we stood, not knowing whether or not to idiotically stare at Viktor until he was no longer there to look at, and risk our lives in doing so, or ensue to try and save ourselves from ending up like he was surely about to. The structural tremors enhanced, the sound soon turned to a thunder, and the ceiling of the corridor from which our landing on the top floor looked out at suddenly began to crumble down, then heavier, quicker, louder, in larger portions of wood and plaster, bricks and water, furiously dropping in from above.

The house was soon dissolving before my very eyes. The whole front wall of the structure, some twenty feet high, was stripped away by the currents. There was a noticeable rift, and Chris and I were shot up out of the water. The chandelier overhead crashed down and shattered on the only remaining section of floor, a small ten foot by four foot patch of shag carpet and wooden boards at the start of the multi-chamber hallway in which we had spent our nights, and all of today. The house had splintered in two. For a time we were all in about four feet of water. When the house split, our hallway reemerged and was dry; but Viktor began to quickly sink, for he was not on the elevated half. Then from behind us came a wail, a sonata of grotesque tones and pitiful shrieking. Down the hall, straddling his grandfather clock, his head just six or so inches above the rushing flood waters, under grey and storming skies— as the home was no more, only except for where we were sheltered on the upper level—Viktor was in hysterics. Now, I couldn't tell you if he was happy or sad, crying or overcome with joy, but I can tell you that he wasn't going to go down quietly. Until the very end he flailed and screamed and prophesized, and shouted the name of his lord until his throat bled. And like some manic Titanic scene, he perished with the similarity of a passionate captain descending into the depths with his sinking vessel, abandoning all hope, going down with the ship in an obvious act of madness. All that remained was the glass sphere of numbers at the top of the clock and Viktor's bobbing head, mouth opened wide, eyes red and veiny, capturing the attention of all those capable of having heard him by horrifically screaming these words of gargling, choking desperation until he was no more: "NIRVANA! NIRVANA! … WHO SHALL SAVE THE WIDOW'S SON?!"

XIII

The End

Yes, the end was quite near, and for some it had already arrived, and then come to pass. All around me was a town in ruin, an ocean spilling out from across the land. One could feel the wind that the currents alone seemed to give off. We leaned back against the wall in the hallway; the rest of the house was gone. We leaned back against the wall and prepared to be washed away, to be sucked down into death like water retreating into a drain. It was then that I was at my most contented state. For reasons I can't expound on, my mind seems to dwell on things that matter not, especially things other than what's right in front of me. This can become a dangerous practice, for instead of worrying about the flash flood ripping through the walls of the home I was in, or how we would progress to safely exit that home (or at least what was left of it), I had my thoughts on dissimilar concerns. No, no, those things didn't seem to worry me at all! What did, however, was the still rather wild and improbable idea that I had somehow caused the vile oblation of the Monte-Duffs in exchange for the abdication of our sins, and the thrones from which they sat on, draped in a castle of gold within our hearts, commanding, denying our souls to the Lord; and that I had unwillingly partaken in the abysmal task of robbing the dead; or that there were still three days left until the lifting of our curse! Though, if I hadn't been brought back into reality by Chris at that very instant as those stupid thoughts were passing through my mind, that curse may have been lifted a bit sooner than planned. Or,

I then thought, was that exactly what this was: something completely predetermined and inevitable? Was this going to be my end? ...the end of me? Without Chris it most certainly would have been, I believe.

Eventually, as I soon realized to be the case, we found ourselves moving with the currents now, as opposed to standing against them like before. On a slab of plaster and wood, we, like a raft, strode across the dark and choppy waters of the flood and all its strength and power. From every direction we watched as massive waves and landslides of mud tore through barns and fields, houses and lives. Yet as we flew through time atop the flood, safe on our raft for now, I saw next to me in all this chaos a seemingly familiar sight nodding gracefully in the water. All bedlam ceased around me, and I found myself gazing at *The Ghost of a Flea*, fitted in its gilt frame, quietly dissolving there, delicately stirring with the swells and changing the color of the water around it a shade of dark purple as it bled its life mournfully back to the earth. These sights caged my attention for the next few minutes, I assume, for when they did no longer, the scene was much more unpleasant. Yet, wasn't that to be expected?

In a shit situation, the two things one can expect to find is false hope or an utter derailment of comfort and pleasure. Since at this point in our story I seem to find myself at my most vulnerable, and in complete decline, suffering harshly from the derailment of consciousness and functioning, it is only right, that while I linger in a state of unresponsive carelessness, I shall fill in this unfortunate blank with a tale, one that smoothly allows us to ease into proceeding events, as well as to reveal some insight on an objective of sorts that I try to keep in mind throughout the day, and especially in shit situations. When I was in first or second grade, for example (I can't remember which), my friends and I thought we were chimps, and would climb up, on, and over anything. While doing so, it seems, I fell from a counter top in a class room and hit hard the laminate floor beneath, cracking my head open, and just in time to leave for the buses at the end of the day. After that I knew how melons and coconuts felt when they were so cruelly hacked apart so our hungry mouths could feed on their inners. I had an animistic mindset as a kid, and so after that I refused to eat fruits or anything that needed to be busted open in order to consume. Yet, that wasn't the worst result of my accident. Sadly, a minor case of head trauma, I believe, had been sustained. For years and years after the incident, throughout most of my early youth, I had a rather acute and painful problem with my ears. I remember trying to sleep at night, but being kept awake by the noises both coming from and created by my own ears, deep within their tubes and tunnels. A steady march, a parade of people tramping down the road, all pounding their drums and maracas, played throughout my head. "It's like there's a giant ant colony marching in my ear canals, digging their own rooms and bur-rows!"—is how I tried to convene my agony to my mother with only the vocabulary and knowledge of a six year old. Nevertheless, it was hell. For many years after that I had to have check-ups and surgeries, and I could never go swimming, otherwise risk the highly likely chance of developing another ear infection—which still seemed to happen even when I hadn't been in the water for weeks. All that shit, all that pain and discomfort because of an unfortunate blow to the head. So, what relevance is any of this to the present situation, you're probably won-dering; where's the mentioned objective? We'll, relevance isn't always a game I like to play. But yes, of course, all this has relevance towards mine and Chris's situation; for as we were riding atop the flood, and while I gazed away my fear at the vanishing painting beside me, we struck hard against the brick wall of a building downtown, and I splat-tered my face across the concrete. So there's your relevance! Since I had not been rendered unconscious, the first thoughts in my mind were the events of the tale just previously told. The pain of unrelenting discomfort, the fear of commonly safe objects and activities: the kind of stuff that quickly grasps hold of the primeval terrors that suspend within us all—that, as well as the hope that this time around things wouldn't end so painfully. A swift death would have been fine, a pleas-ant recovery would have been even better; but one had to keep in mind that he was still under the authorities of a curse, a curse whose sole existence was to see him to his grave in the cruelest possible way, and that not considering this fact could lead to false anticipation, false expectations, false hope: a thing more lethal than a flood or a curse or a bullet or a train. To be cheated by false hope one too many times is to be knocking on death's door with the lepers and the condemned; it will eat away your soul! Yet, since occurrences of that kind are most certainly preventable, I pride myself on not letting them get to me. So here's the subtle objective: When in a shit situation, either brought upon by unfortunate circumstances or the deceptions of false hope, keep the mindset of a man with no worries in the world, and try as hard as one can to not let it eat away at the foundations of personal happiness, personal comfort, and personal dreams. We are all our own vessels, and the only ones ever truly in control of its movements, and whether or not it can function and take you to where it is you want to be. Always keep a sound mind, and do not let external affairs stand in the way of internal peace. However, I must admit I am no champion, monk-like pacifier of unpleasant emotions, and the way they easily take control of a person's actions. In fact, I'm terrible at it. Nonetheless, I still try to keep this goal in mind, for I know it is true, and display it as often as I can. Now, at last! it seems I am finally on the verge of returning to coherence, and ready to again confront the battle that rages around me.

Smashed up against the windowless stone wall and the slab of Victor's house we had sailed in on, Chris, now a few feet above me, had succeeded in climbing a thick pipe that went up the side of the building in front of us and onto the roof. Clinging timidly onto a single protruding brick, I, on the other hand, hung for my life above the whooshing waters. Our raft, suddenly struck by a large propane tank gliding on the torrents of the flood, exploded beneath my feet, and was now in a thousand shards, quickly washing away with the rest of the city. For a moment, a gap in time separating the present and when I supposed I would finally find the courage to climb to the roof myself, I turned my concentration inward once again—how foolish of me!—after having only been expelled from my introverted mindset for little over a minute. Am I the only one who in times of high stress is able to fall back comfortably into their own head, fall back softly like a corpse into a cushioned casket? I'd hope not; I'd hate to think that I was somehow abnormal. But as my attention turned to internal matters, I ran my tongue across my smooth teeth. A foul taste of copper sloshed between my gums, my lips, and the roof of my mouth. I was bleeding. Then, abruptly, I shot out from my reclusive hideaway, having been smacked in the face by Chris who was hanging down two shaky, distended arms over the ledge of the building. "Get your stupid ass up here!" he hollered, pleading for me to take hold of his hands. I looked down slowly as thick pellets of blood dabbled down my face and onto the wet, grey bricks of the structure. It ran down the wall, speckled with the falling rain, as would a curious garden snake, thin and intrusive; I felt unnerved, chilled. I felt the same way about the streams of blood that still flowed from my mouth but had yet to fall, how they tickled my chin as they curled underneath and dribbled down my neck, pooling around my collar. Yet, before I could come to terms with my injury, I found myself to be airborne, and then, with a tumble and a thud, found myself lying on my back on a grimy surface of gravel, wet dirt, and spit-out sunflower seeds. Chris, seemingly harnessing the powers of a superhuman, had pulled me out of the surge and up onto the roof. There, as I gazed out over the estuary of what was once Prospero, I noticed that I was somehow able to stick my tongue straight between my front two teeth. Strutting around confused for a second, I came to terms with the now-obvious fact that one was missing.

If I had it my way, I would have stayed on that rooftop and waited out the destruction. Unfortunately, that wasn't going to be a possibility. It was not because of hotheadedness that we eventually left the safety of the rooftop, it was because of the water. We stood up there for half an hour, and all the while the rain continued to fall, and the waves around us continued to rush and rise and plunge. The water level rose, and soon it was spilling in from over the meager ledge of the rooftop, flowing into our safe haven, forcing us to consider yet another plan of escape. By the time the brown liquid had risen to our ankles and made it so that we could no longer see the structure on which we were standing, Chris and I knew that we had to make a move. Another few minutes and we would have been washed away by the flood whether we liked or not.

I couldn't tell, for the sensation was a strange one, but it seemed to me like we were sinking, as opposed to the actuality of the water rising around us. Yet either way, we would have found ourselves quite submerged; the river had come to reclaim its land once again, and not for a second would it have considered the fact that we stood in its way—not willfully, of course, but that didn't change the specifics of our whereabouts. Chris hovered over the invisible edge of the building and out at the great surges of muddy water and debris, raising his hand like a visor over his brow as would a skipper, trying to spot a workable platform for us to jump onto that was heading in our direction. I gawked out at the catastrophic sights all around. When at last that platform had arrived, Chris grabbed me by the wrist, and pointed in the direction of where a significant portion of picket fence was coming forth on the current. I prepared myself to jump.

And then the time came, finally after what seemed like an hour of watching this heap of debris linger towards us. But indeed it was time—the leap of faith, the trust fall, the plunge to end all plunges; we dove forward, arms spread out, hands ready to grasp, focused on the preservation of our own existence, the only opportunity I knew we would ever get to do so—and thus, we took a plunge. I struck the fence first, but as Chris followed, our weight sent us hurling down into the icy depths, which was a substance comprised more of dirt and shards of wood than actual water. But still, under the surface we remained, the current's muffled roar hammering in my ears, my eyes shut tight, praying not to strike another concrete wall. Upon what felt like gliding aloft a steep hill, we shot up from underneath the slimy swamp of hell and back into the troposphere. I felt safe, in a way; I felt as if we had conquered an enemy, though in my mind I knew that the battle was still yet to be won. I tried to stay vigilant however; I tried not to fall back into the senseless thoughts that had flooded my own head, for I knew that if I did this time around I really may just be intentionally lying myself down into a cushioned casket. As to prevent this, I tried to elevate myself atop the planks, and peered out fictitiously courageous at the rapidly approaching town before me. What I saw in the distance gave me a sick sort of awakening, a reluctant revelation. It was the naked presence of the human condition, the human instinct, the kill or be killed, the my-life-over-yours mentality that had damned so many countless nations, extinguished so many beautiful lives, and surely splattered red the pages of our history books forever. Before me was the sight of a hundred citizens all fighting to stay afloat in the water, clinging helplessly to whatever debris they could. Some gathered on the few remaining rooftops that still rose beyond the flood, staring down ghostly expressions, emotionless countenances, and their hands wrapped around waists or tucked deep in coat pockets, frozen in denial. They would not offer any assistance, they could not. It was but lifeboat ethics now, and nothing more could be done.

Unevenly distributed around those who were safe, gazing down from their towers, clusters of men and women fought quite literally to the death for a spot on multiple scattered slabs of wood and other floatable material. While watching these clusters, nothing more than flailing bodies, jabbing fists, and horrible cries of anguish, I do believe I witnessed firsthand the inhumanity that makes us all so frighteningly human. The complete disregard for the health and life of all others often works its way into our mind when it seems that others have disregarded us, when the world seems to have disregarded us. In the moment, we may take it upon ourselves to be just a merciless as the disasters that have caused our pain in the first place. Yet, the truly haunting thing is that if I was out there, and not here, I would have been doing exactly the same thing as the rest of them, savage as it may be. But, as we approached one of these clusters, I began to take guard as I would if I were actually there involved in the quarrel; I dislodged a plank from the fence and held it out as a warning to all those who may attempt a mutiny: I would fight back. This lifeboat was full.

We strode closer to the scene of violence. In astonishment, I dropped my 2x4 of a spear as we came to pass the Raft of the Medusa. I was awestruck, watching as from the mound of squirming bodies a bare-chested black man stood on top of another man, a bearded old sack of wrinkled skin and bulging eyes, so as to elevate himself above the rest, crushing the life out of the other as he did so, and only to wave his fist wildly in the air, shouting for the cowards on the rooftop nearby to throw him a rope or a chord. I pointed forward, but Chris wouldn't look. He knew what he'd see, and so instead just laid there on his back, staring up in despair at the godless heavens, the ruthless billows of cloud that had favorably sanctioned all this horror to unfold. I looked back; the man had gotten his rope, there was people climbing up it and onto the roof. But below, forgotten on the raft, lay a canvas of demented, mangled corpses, left to drift aimlessly throughout the town like the float of a homecoming parade, ostensibly adorned with roses and comatose limbs. The old man, not seriously harmed, it appeared, pulled the drowned body of a young pale boy onto the raft, and sat there with his bruised torso and sorry head in his lap, gazing pitiful eyes at the escapees above as they heartlessly wound up the rope and turned to hide their faces. A tear fell from my eye as we drifted on, passing the town, and soon made our way into the forest, now floating quite calmly down a thin, lazy river that flowed through a narrow channel of mostly submerged trees and obstructed earth. In the forest the winds and rushing currents seemed to be lessened, and the chaos subsided. What could we do now but wait? Nothing, that's what; so we waited. I hunched down next to Chris on the raft as we coasted on slowly, gazing up at the sky as the clouds receded and the birds swarmed past in triangles of three or four hundred strong. It all came across as an unpleasant sight: the world's careless dismissal of all that was so obviously horrible, just a few moments ago. Nature, it seemed, was over it; the sun outstretched from behind the darkness.

"I've concluded," Chris said, "that if we keep on in this direction, we'll come right up past my house. I sure hope Anna is okay. I hope the damage ain't too bad."

"Dido," I said. "I hope my car isn't destroyed."

"I see no reason to be optimistic on the favorable outcome," he said in a flat tone. "I never got to finish the Woman in White."

"That's a shame," I replied, "that's a shame..." But I didn't care. Nobody cared. All anyone was concerned with was their own selves. It was no surprise, though. Chris didn't care about my car, and I didn't care about his unfinished book. Lack of sympathy is a thing our generation seems to be great at. It was all I had ever seen growing up, nothing but selfishness and want, and the stepping on the hands of others in order to attain what it was one so desired. From every little shit of a kid begging for presents, toys and treats, to their parents, so caught up in the stupidity of fitting into a desirable reputation at all costs, never being able to justly raise the lives they brought into this world: all I had ever seen growing up was selfishness and want. And most who wanted out of selfishness got what they wanted. That's what makes it so sad. People, completely useless and egocentric, walking around acting like self-proclaimed kings, dickheads, yet, they see no karma, and they see no consequence for their behavior; but for some reason a whole town can just get wiped off the map, innocent people lost, selfish people unharmed. All my life that's what I saw, that's how I acted, that's how I was taught to act—so for the first half of my life I couldn't really blame myself. But once that specific part of your brain develops to the point where you can wake up in the morning and know what to do that day so as not to be a fucking asshole, then you are old enough to not be a fucking asshole. But if you are, I have no regard for your existence. Anyone who takes into consideration my feelings, I certainly will do the same, and have not a problem in the world with you, wish you nothing but the best. Yet, if you do not, if you are an ass-hole, then I'll waist not a second of my time on you. There are plenty of people out there. Yes, that's how I'm going to do things from now on. I'm sick of the unnecessary disregard for other individuals that is so routinely displayed by the venal and the inconsiderate, emphasized by the posh and sedentary lifestyles of the rich, and in the belittlement of others who are completely equal to you whether you can realize it or not. Open your eyes!

"Sean…Sean! Open your eyes!" Chris screamed. "Look!"

"What?" I asked, wearily moving my arm from off my brow to see him standing up on the fence unbalanced and tottering, pointing overhead to a mud-stained street pole partnered with a once green sign flagging off of it, the words Willmoth Street suspending crookedly before us above the now-calmed but ever expansive waters. We jumped off the raft, for Chris's house was only just around the corner, and luckily we were able to touch the bottom. We plodded towards our destination, though we were nervous to see what we might find when we got there. I couldn't shake the feeling that our troubles had yet to pass. How many days were left anyways… two, three? I couldn't remember; I didn't feel like doing the math. Yet, surviving all we had been through was reason enough to no longer fear this curse, I concluded; it hadn't seen me to my grave yet. Although, the psychological impact of this summer had been enough to fry more than a couple brains into a tasty cuisine, a hale and hearty feast of *cervelle de veau*. Still, I felt assured that I'd be able to recover from it, learn from it, grow from it someday, and I knew that I would never again be naïve. It was all quite the experience, even though I never fully formed my legacy. I did, however, have some damn good memories. Most not good in the sense of being pleasant, but good in the sense that they were unforgettable, unforgeable. Oh, the pathos we've experienced, the acquaintances we've made, lessons learned, virtues forever instilled! Who in their right mind would not appreciate it, even at the end of a shit day? Before I could throw out a guess as to whom, we found ourselves to be treading through Anna's garden, gazing up at the fruitless cherry tree that still stood in the front yard, drooping, as bare as a bone, yet enlivened, standing strong before a background of slate-grey and reflective waters.

The structure was mangled, surviving, but mangled. However, it was built on a hill, a low one, but a hill nonetheless. As we approached the steps of the porch—the veranda now collapsed in on itself and scattered around in sections of moldering wood, blocking the door—I saw how the water did not even reach the foundation of the home. It rippled in like a gentle tide around it, like an abode built on open ocean, it appeared from a far, a house boat. We were lucky… our courage hadn't drowned along with the city, we were still strong, and hopeful for better times ahead. We were lucky… and it still to this day feels weird to say such a thing. Chris's grandfather, it seems, had built their family home atop one of the mountains of Ararat, or at least on top of the highest hill in Kentucky!

As soon as we stepped foot on the porch, Anna, screaming with relief, presumably waiting and watching anxiously for our return, hurriedly made her way out of a shattered window next to the obstructed doorway and ran over, shouting with joy. In a bear hug she embraced us close, and like a family we stood there on the steps of their home and held each other, loved each other. Everything was going to be okay. And with that knowledge mutually accepted, she led us in through the back. Inside, a few inches of silent water overcame the floor; the cats were wailing and crying, trapped upon bookshelves and other high furniture of the sort. "God, you stupid kid!" she then yelled, and smacked Chris hard on the back of the head. "The hell you think you're doing trying to live out in the woods like some retard without a chaperone?! Because that's what you are, seems you've for gotten all about me!"

"I love you, I'm sorry," he said.

"I never thought that God would break his promise with the rainbow. But nevertheless, this house was a damn good arc! Was it not?" Anna replied, no longer absorbed in the sorrow of five seconds ago. "Sorry for the slap. I'm as cheery as a tulip now that you two are okay. Besides, it didn't surprise me much the fact that you didn't want to stay here… living with me. I'm as old as Titian, and no one wants anything to do with a crazy old woman; I probably had y'alls scared from the get-go with that awful poem." Then the sorrow returned, and she gently lowered her head.

"Honest," I said," I enjoyed it!"

"So did I," Chris mumbled.

"Yeah?" she sighed, hatching a proud smile. "Thanks… So what do you suppose we do now? And how did you two survive out there for so long with nothing but that bag and whatever's in it?

Anna and I both looked over at Chris; he had my bag slung across his shoulder the whole time. I hadn't even realized, let alone thought of the fact that he retrieved it since Viktor's house had given way beneath our feet. Chris, standing in the spotlight, stepped back a bit from the circle we had formed in the middle of the kitchen. He had an odd expression on his face, something uneasy. Not fear, not panic, not joy, but more like a combination of the three. Chris smiled, and then he started to cry. He rushed back over to us, and with my bag held above his head, tipped it upside-down over the table… a hundred bars of gold fell to the grimy surface, scattering in an explosion of illustrious color. Anna dropped to her knees, and so did my jaw.

"NOOO!" she began to scream. "You're a bank robber!"

"No, mom!" Chris yelled. "It was given to me, by God himself! I've saved our home, don't you see? We're going to be okay!"

Then, staring face to face perplexedly for a moment, they broke down and hugged each other, sobbing onto each other's shoulders, whimpering on the curvature of each other's necks. It was a nice scene, and just about the first good thing I had witness in days. I was amazed at what Chris had done. To be truthful, and even though it may sound stupid, I hadn't one thought in my mind that morning about those bars of gold after I realized that the flood had commenced to destroy the home. Thank God, though, that some people are a bit more intuitive… or recklessly greedy.

For the evening, Anna said she'd cook. On the upper level it was dry, she said, and she had made a make-shift oven out of metal cans and such, and would allow us into her room. But before that, she led me to my familiar chamber, and left me to change, but not before enlightening me on the fact that the rest of my clothes were still safe in the drawer where I had left them so long ago. I stepped in, she closed the door behind me, and I soon locked it, and then fell to the floor.

There I lay for an hour. I can't move. I'm so distraught, so horribly afflicted with complete and uncontrollable happiness. I can't stop laughing, wallowing, grinning in tears, holding my knees to my chest on the damp floor. And it was there, after finally ensuing to rest myself down on the bed, I recalled balancing on the threshold between darkness and dawn, crying out to the world for answers to things that I could never know. All this pain and mishap, all this in the effort to create a forced legacy, a hoax, like the life of Viktor's father. He was nothing but a man behind a mask, and neither he nor anyone he would ever meet could truly know exactly who he was. It was then that it occurred to me what I had do wrong. A legacy formed for the pleasure of others is no legacy at all, let alone a way to live a life. Individualism and healthy self-expression is the key to potential lasting remembrance, or, at least, if nothing else, a state of personal happiness that persists for as long as one rises in the morning and slumbers in the night. And it is just that achievement of self-realization and joy that should ever matter to anyone, and is the one true attainment worthy of being sought after and obtained by men and women in their daily efforts, in their labor and in their art. It is the one sure achievement that people truly seem to admire. Maybe, I thought, as opposed to any one physical extension of my existence, my life could be my legacy, that my life alone was basis enough for a story, and one not any less interesting than simple fiction, especially after all I had been through. I can't think of anything better to do with a life then to love and explore and to make a living off one's own authenticities. For wages, for a job, an occupation, one should not want to sell their time, but rather their talents. I had always wanted to be a writer of words, and to flaunt genius like my idols once had. Thus, my life is a book if I desire it to be, and it writes itself, as does yours. So what does it all matter? You will never really get to know your full legacy, it's all what you make of it; and either you die and never see as a whole what you have done, or simply just the fact that you can never know exactly what other people are thinking, will be enough to ensure this. But I know that there is a part of me capable of creation. I was brought forth into life in order to create something. And here, staring down at the moist floor boards of dark, spongy wood, I commenced to drag my finger nail across the surface of it to create the image of a cross. Yes, there on the floor boards, a large cross, an etching of faith. A sign of respect for Viktor, for Jimmy and Billie, for the people of Prospero, for myself and my family, Chris and his father, and for everyone in this world in the midst of a struggle, I drew a cross.

Then I sank into the pillows of my dusty bed for a while. My mind was at an unexpected ease. I felt warm; I had my sense of normality gratefully restored. Then a knock sounded at the door, it was Anna. She cracked it open a little; I watched as her long, hooked nose crept into the room before her as would an elephant's tusk, or the fin of a shark above water; the rest of her body followed shortly thereafter and she sat down at the foot of the bed.

"I'm sure your parents are awful worried about you," she said.

"They are, especially after they get word of this whole flood on the news," I groaned.

"It was the Licking River," she said, "after all this rain we had, and then continued to have, unrelentingly, the water level exceeded its banks by some fifteen feet, came hurling out into the towns and counties. It's happened before, it'll happen again. But this time was the worst. If our phone worked, I'd insist you called them. Unfortunately, it doesn't. So let's go to my room, Sean, Chris is already in there waiting, probably eatin' up all the oysters before we can have any ourselves!"

Pulling me up to my feet, we ran from that room and into hers. There, beside her modest bed of black sheets and comforters, between a standing lamp of blue stained glass and a dusty bureau like the ones in mine, Chris sat on the floor next to an array of meals on silver trays: oysters, bread, wine, vegetables, among other things, and no severed heads! My stomach growled; I sat down beside them on a cushion and put a cloth halfway down my shirt to create a bib, modeling Chris who had done the same thing but using a pillow case.

"I just been tellin' her about the time you fell down off a mountain and I saved you," Chris said. "Done told her about gettin' bit by a Widow, too."

"Yeah," I said, "did you tell her how I saved you?"

"Indeed he did," Anna started, "you quick-thinkin' lad! But what I really want to know, Chris, Sean, is how you got this gold."

"Did you ever hear of a man named Viktor Lutheran?" Chris asked.

"Yes," she replied unamused, "although back then he called himself Viktor Luther. Gosh, I can't even remember his real name, he's changed it so many times… his last name, at least. Anyways, he was the nutcase who tried to stab an Arab that owned a grocery store near my stepdad's home in Philadelphia. Don't think he ever did prison time for it; they put a lot of so-called "crazy people" in hospitals back then, as opposed to prisons. I only know this because he grew up here with me in Prospero; I only went to my stepdad's over winter break. He was a strange boy when we was young. In grade school, for the most part, he was completely normal and uninteresting. Then one day, quite literally, he was altered completely. It was as if some entirely alien soul had dropped from the heavens and into his skull to replace the one that we had all come to know. It was as if something suddenly snapped inside his head, and he was from then on somebody else. He used to go through awful phases of certitude, somehow convincing himself that he was some kind of holy man, always shaving his head bare and dressing in robes. Then we wouldn't seem him for a while. Then he'd be right back in class, months gone by in between."

"So why was he in Philly?" I asked.

"Suppose he was stalking me, but I never did get an explanation," she replied. "However, boys, you must understand, I was a rather attractive woman back in the day; I was stared at or stalked quite a few times throughout my twenties, so I didn't really think much of it... should I start?!"

"Well," Chris sighed, "that's whose gold this is. He acquired it, I believe, by selling people the promise of a clean slate in the eyes of God, and supposedly leaving them with an untarnished soul—what a massive scam! But it's ours now, I assure you."

"And where is he?" she asked.

"The flood took him," I said. "He tied himself to a clock and the flood took him."

"Oh," she said, bewildered, itching her aged, filmy skin above her eyes with the tip of a worn finger nail. "How inconvenient; perhaps he left a card?"

"No, mom, there's no card. I took it all, and Viktor drowned."

"Oh," she said again, mouse-like, "how very, very sad. Has anyone said a prayer?"

"Nope," said Chris, looking about the room. "Should we?"

"How about a poem?" Anna asked.

The answers she received were yes and no. However, not wanting to be detested, she said she'd say one to herself in the night, I suppose settling with this alternative so as not to displease her son. Probably a wise decision, if you asked me. And the relief in his eyes was ever so visible when she said she would not, and he slid a mussel down his throat, and flicked the shell onto the plate.

"You won't believe what I saw earlier—not that it can stand in comparison to what you two have probably seen, but for me it was quite the sight!" she said, flapping her dark and curly lashes that sprouted out from eyelids of soft, wrinkly skin, like that of a glabrous, infantile rodent, and of which she continuously rubbed with the palm of her hand, and the tips of her fingers, as if tottering on the verge of sleep. "Cheeky me, I swear I saw a couple clad in striped jumpsuits, handcuffed, sailing past on the road in front of the house, and while the flood was at its worst, on top the hood of a car. I walked to the kitchen, and then came back for a second glance to see the entire police force riding single-file on a log chasing after 'em! Then theys were all swept away."

We shot unsettling expressions towards one another, Chris and I. I wanted to tell her who those people really were, as did he. Yet, there was something holding us from doing so. I knew that if we did it would be frightening to her, an unprecedented shift in reality, and miles away from the seemingly heroic fantasy tales she had heard us tell before. Shock over the death of the Monte-Duffs, the defecation of their home—all this would not have sat well, and I didn't want to ruin the night. Presumably, then, it's safe to say that Chris didn't either, for not a word of the matter was spoken. And if I had it my way, would never be spoken of again. Yet, something inside of me hoped that those two got away.

With the odd silence of the night, the lack of the sound of raindrops exploding on exterior surfaces, I fell to sleep rather quickly to the voice of Chris portraying to Anna another one of our accursed adventures, and after many happy hours of similar conversation, closed my eyes and woke up the next morning on a dusty bed, in a dusty room, staring down with a sigh of exhaustion at the skeleton key that rested like a gleaming sword upon the nightstand. It said, "Let's take on the day! Slay a fucking dragon! Come on!" and I followed.

The sword led me downstairs and into the kitchen. It seemed I was the only one up. The sun had risen, and the morphed outlines of the windows swathed gently across the dark floor. There was no longer a lake of shallow water on the ground. Cats yawned and squirmed throughout the room, their stretched-out bodies dotting the carpet, itching at their backs, all around me—on the table, on the couch, on top of the cupboards—they were damn near everywhere I looked! I was a dog person myself, and always a fan of much smaller quantities.

"Sean," Chris whispered, as I spun around quickly holding out my blade of a key in his direction. At my appearance, my shaking, key-wielding hand, and my wide eyes and missing front tooth, he laughed and sat down in a chair. Feeling stupid, and slightly frightened, I put the key in my pocket. "Seems the sun woke you, too," he said.

"Been wondering about my car," I said. "Hope it still runs, ya know?"

"Let's take a look, why don't we?" he replied, and went to get a pair of shoes.

Once returning, he unlocked the hardly intact door to the backyard. Upon its opening we came face to face with a remarkable orange light, the overwhelming stench of raw sewage, and the eventual witnessing of a drowned and crumbling countryside, the spires of the church down town showing visibly behind the leafless branches of crippled trees, soaring there like an eerie handprint in the sky of better times come to pass. The flood had mysteriously withered away during the night. The previous ocean now resembled a drying lakebed. Across the lawn, cautiously creeping over sharp debris and other diluvian wreckage, we made our way to the door of the garage, separate from the house itself. Chris, using all his muscle, pushed aside the large wheel of a tractor that had been washed up against it during the storm. Chris didn't own a tractor, nor did his neighbors. The door never opened either, instead it fell straight off its hinges onto the ground. A stray cat—presumably one of Chris's—had to suddenly leap out of the way, else risk getting smashed. Inside what we saw was no more encouraging. There were dead fish everywhere, some still flapping helplessly in the shallow puddles that remained, mouths chomping for a breath, eyes bulging, dying. The shed smelled like a septic nightmare. The situation seemed rather bleak to me, and I had no real expectations; I wouldn't have bet money on the chances of getting that car started, especially as I came to approach it and saw more clearly what I knew I'd find all along. Hunkered up against the wall, covered in leaves and mud, decorated with the busted pieces of metal of what was once somebody else's mailbox, wedged there, splintered into the leather of my back seat, was my car. Handing Chris the skeleton key so as not to confuse the two, and pulling out my car key from the opposite pocket, I leaned in through the window, prodded around for the ignition, and with zero confidence, gave it a shot.

"And if it starts…" Chris said.

"And if it starts…" I repeated, now turning the key, successfully starting the car without a hitch. Yet, sadly I had nothing to reply, nothing planned, nothing set in stone. It was early August, we were just about curse free, and I still had time, I figured, for one last sought-after experience, whatever it may be, prior to being shipped off abroad. Chris handed me my bag. "There's some gold in here for you," he said with a grin. "Try not to let it go to your head, Oxford Man."

"I'll put it towards my legacy," I told him, and he slid up the panels of the garage door, revealing the prospect of a dirt road cutting through the density of the forest ahead—one that was narrow, rutted, and swampy, but passable. A bright flower twinkled in a heap of ruins, breaking through the thick veil of destruction, ready to conquer the day like a man with a sword. And right then, shaking Chris's hand on the brink of departure, basking in the splendor of the golden sun, I knew that I had but two options of which I was aware: I could either go to Wisconsin… or go home.

Other Collected Words

Talk of Things Less Morbid

L et's ignore this bone disease for a second, I thought, finally pushing aside the curtains to peer outside, and talk of things less morbid. For alone by this lamp, by this ugly yellow lamp, I've sat for hours and hours, rubbing the chicken-shit muscles of my legs and thighs, trying in vain to soothe a persistent ache, and still, I can't seem to come up with a good enough reason to leave the house—aside from my bone disease, of course.

But let's talk of things less morbid. I've had a weakness in my stomach as of late, and I can't much handle anything more than slightly pessimistic. So with that in mind, I suppose I'll try to continue, keeping our goal of abstaining from doom and gloom assuredly in my prudence. I'll begin with the events of yesterday evening. While rummaging the aisles of a nifty market near my home, I ran into a friend of mine, a friend I hadn't seen in many years.

He said to me, "Wow, don't you look familiar! Have we met?"

"Indeed we have!" I say, "But not for quite some time." And we shook hands, and continued walking.

Lee was his name; we played on a youth hockey team together when I was a kid. We had gotten our first jobs together a few years later—after I was satisfied with a high school diploma, and he went on to put both mind and body forth so as to achieve a scholastic benchmark. He was my polar opposite, but we got along famously. It was by his side that I ran through hot summer streets five miles to get back to my home, bloody, and with a smashed ankle after having jumped off a roof trying to escape my vengeful pursuers: the owners of a gas station I had robbed for gum... or maybe this time around it was the comic book shop. I don't very well remember details; but Lee's thin, crawling skin, and his sunken eyes, crooked jaw, were all details I did in fact recognize, and quite distinctly, too.

So we strolled on down the many aisles, eyeing canned goods, boxes of Wheaties, jello; merely talking as if there hadn't been a nearly twenty year gap between us. We checked out together, paid the clerks, left the store, stopped and faced each other on the sidewalk. "Listen," he said, "I've got to run, kid's got a doctor's appointment; shoved a pebble up his nose last night, says it ain't coming out."

"I see," I said, trying not to sound disappointed.

"Yeah, but why don't you come over next Friday, have dinner with us; would you be up for it?"

"Of course!" I told him, "I'd love to."

With that, we shook hands, he tossed me his card, and we walked in opposite directions down the road. I kicked a rock lying in the street-gravel next to my foot as I turned around, and slowly made my way back home, breathing in happily through my nose the invigorating spirit of the summertime that was so visibly alive that day, coursing through seminal gusts of wind, through crepuscular currents of sweet-scented air, animated by the hot rays of a setting sun and the coruscating faces of the blithe and youthful, dancing all around me like demented circus performers on every street in town. Then it suddenly wasn't so cheery, and my masochistic body soon reclaimed the best of me. With my shuddering hand, aching, I ran my fingers through my coarse hair and across a leather-like scalp. The pain rooted in my joints and knuckles and ankles and bones seemed only to be alleviated on that day by the heat and comfort of standing in direct sunlight, soaking in the vitamin D. I stood there on the curb looking out into the festering street, only I was gazing into spiraling blackness and starting to lose consciousness, for I was in the midst of another spasmodic episode, commonly and always attributed to *my* condition. I stood on the curb, arms outstretched towards the sun in a presumably illuminated Jesus Christ pose, numbing myself with its passion and power right there on Market Street, in the middle of downtown, in front of everyone.

I went home that night and into my sickbed. I woke up the next morning (this morning) with the shakes; took a piss, got dressed, combed my hair, and ate breakfast with the shakes; then spent the rest of that morning sitting by the yellow lamp on the couch across from the closed window with the shakes. They dissipated around noon, and I finally gained the courage to find a reason to go outside. Everybody, sick or healthy, I believe, unless completely incapable, should step outside for at least half-hour a day. Understandable in colder climates, frequent in these Chicago suburbs for many months of the year, but in the summer, one should keep out doors for at least an hour to an hour forty-five minutes each day. Not all at once, if one chooses, but periodically—and this too is understandable. Too much of a good thing can make the very idea of that thing quickly spoil. God, I can name about a hundred off the top of my head!—Food, for example, and music, people, faces, the sky, the cracking, curving, fucking endless miles of roads that sprawl across my town, the droning sounds of civilization, even life itself. With regards to extending our discussion on the topic of overexposure, and how it makes the good soon turn bad: can you believe that just last week, down the street from where I live, in a healthy suburb spotless of eyesores, the city put up a goddamn MCDONALD'S (or MCDANK'S, as my friends and I used to call it) right next to a large elementary school and a brand new preschool on the other side of the road, and directly in the backyards of people in a neighborhood who were paying off the hell of six-figure houses?! If that wasn't bad enough, now they got a dead-cow-cooking, colon-killing, landfill-filling, chubby-fucking, capital entity: a massive growth on the flesh of our community, sucking the marrow of the blithe and youthful, predatorily guarding its claim in their backyards. They were probably haunted by its presence, you know?—staring down at it from their tiny, wavy glass windows that people have in showers on the upper level of a home, or when they sat down to eat a meal or read a book. With that said, I still go there from time to time…

It must also be mentioned that there are many of these kinds of entities, yet it is the custom that they are established on the sides of a main road, not in the heart of a residential area. However, it was built in a mini strip-mall, which those who created it will use as justification for its placement. There was only a Walgreens and a dentist's office there before the entity came. Those, at least, are tolerable, and do no real, noticeable harm to the surrounding populous. I can just imagine the quantities of rats this place is going to bring in! It's a block from miles of long cornfields and paralleled by a railway shrouded in undergrowth and an out-of-use generator building of some sort. That, I suppose, is a bit of an eye sore as well. But what can be done about it? The site is of two massive silos on a thirty-foot-tall concrete platform. Once covered in rust stains and graffiti, but if I'm not mistaken, I'd say it's been removed today. Yet, it's not all bad. As a kid, we, in a group of happy/high/high on life/reckless/ranting/ dirty little friends, would hide in the brush and wait for the traffic on the road nearby to slow. Then, when the time was right, we'd hop the chain-link fence and drop down onto the chalky gravel of the lot. Under the yellow spot-lights we'd sprint by, dancing our shadows across walls and doorways. It was only then that we could feel our way through the darkness to the location of a gigantic ladder, coated in flaking blue paint, and one that jetted all the way to the top. That's where we intended it to take us; and one after another we jumped the four feet to the first step and crawled our way painfully up, up, like a mole ascending its burrow. Once we'd all filed onto the roof,—backs pressed hard against the steel barrier, behind our shoulders a lonely, emanating road of hazy lights, looming fifty feet below—Lee, or anybody really, would crack a joke, or bring up some drama that had happened to them in school that morning, or how so and so is an asshole. From there we'd talk the night away, turn life into a conversation, and linger in the mire of boundless existence, of rebellion, of freedom… continually reminding ourselves to keep looking over the edge now and again for cops. Yet, we'd get home that night, innocent and unseen; we've known it all along. This town was the safest place on earth, ninety percent of the time, and that had been enough for me.

The memory of times like those is what drew me outside today, but where it was I was going I had yet to decide. So I walked down the newly cemented pathways of my block, stopping only under the iron arched pavilion of a small park at the end of it. There, curiously, I peered up at the limbs of a tree to where a squirrel had nested. It stood hunched over and peering right back at me. Its rib cage showing beneath its tight skin, keeping safe its shriveling seed of a heart, of a stomach; starvation had left a crazy look in its eyes, a reckless, desperate sort of expression. On earth, most everything was bound to starve, unless you had a stable, sovereign structure of government to ensure that you didn't, or if you were wealthy. Ah, the sedentary lifestyles of the rich! It was all up to luck in the end (or in the beginning). If you were born on this slab of land, chances are you'd be fine; but on that slab of land, you'd be but a famished squirrel, reckless and desperate! There is a place known as Africa, and from what I've seen thanks to commercials on T.V., much of this entire continent is but a wasteland of starving children and thick jungles riddled with over-poached animals and infectious mosquitos, all carrying a plethora of diseases that cause you to shit blood and excrement and mucus every ten seconds for days on end, until your body is so dehydrated and your insides are so torn up that you simply shrivel apart and die. This wipes out millions of native people every year, taking their lives before the hunger and malnutrition can get to them first, in most cases. It's a place where toddlers sleep on splintered pieces of ply wood, next to an elephant, and drink the water they piss in. A place where pirates still exist and hold hostage the vessels that sail past its shores. A place where, in certain countries, life expectancy is but thirty years on average. And it is said, according to American commercials, that my offering of twenty-something cents a day can help to end all this, help turn the withering squirrels into plump, healthy creatures…but I have my doubts. I can't comprehend how a continent, with its many countries, as old and diverse and rich in resources as Africa, can be home to such poverty. My ignorant, sheltered, American mind can't comprehend how a man accepts the poverty around him and continues to dwell there, regardless of fear, regardless of dictators, regardless of pain. Let's face it, an American slum is a third-world heaven; and I myself hardly have the insight to explain and express ways of improvement towards people and communities of people in those unfortunate situations, and on how one is to cope with such an existence. But, in fact, there are people who do. In The Soul of a Man Under Socialism, in regards to a man's seemingly admissible pauperism, and what it is a person in that situation should really do, or how they should act, I recall Wilde as having said: "Man should not be ready to show that he can live like a badly fed animal. He should decline to live like that, and should either steal or go on the rates, which is considered by many to be a form of stealing. As for begging, it is safer to beg than to take, but it is finer to take than to beg." Of course, this is not London we are talking about, and in many undeveloped countries one cannot simply "go on the rates," and may oftentimes find themselves as thieves, which does nothing but continue to fan the flames. Alas, if there was not such a thing as private property, perhaps those sorry people wouldn't have found themselves becoming an analogy to the starving rodents that I see pouting around my neighborhood. Yes, the extinction of private property—what a grand concept! But never in America, for we love our possessions quite dearly, as if they were alive; and they very well may be in a way, since for most they tend to make up who and what we are. Yet, if America cannot set the example, who will? Shall this idea forever be labeled as rubbish? Shall Africa and all places of the sort never be as whole and as safe as my homeland? And if it were attempted, would our world end up an Orwellian post-apocalyptic nightmare of Ingsoc and Big Brother? I do not know; I don't suppose anybody does. Anyways, let's talk of things less morbid, I say, and continue on down the sidewalk, wiping my slate clean of all gruesome realities and enquiries of the mind that only result in unintelligent, Americanized observations. After all, I had enough to deal with, for I knew that within me I had my own personal Africa, the cells as citizens, gripping to stay alive in a land that has rejected them, was dying all around them.

In addition to the park, my block ends at a four-way intersection. To my left is the veterans' building, and to my right is Marky Malzaro's Pizza Place. It had been there since I was a kid, now going stronger than ever under third generation management. Marky has been dead thirty years or so. His son Cameron runs the place now with his wife Rebecca,—a kind of chunky, kind of curvy Swedish woman with a tattoo of a mouse happily roasting a skewed cat over an open fire, the size of a softball on her upper arm. Although her tattoo suggested otherwise, she was actually a completely normal, lovely, and harmless girl. Cameron, on the other hand, was not so sweet. Of course he had always been kind to me, and I appreciate that; I worked there for quite some time. But to others—to the customers and coworkers alike—he was a brute. He wanted money and money alone. I once saw him backhand an employee who had been caught stealing change out of the register. I can understand outbursts of anger in situation such as that, but this girl had only stolen some seventy-five cents, enough for her to be able to ride the bus home. After I saw that, I had made up my mind: he was a fucker. His dark hair was parted down the middle and usually buttered to excess. It seemed as if it would drip gel if he turned his head too abruptly in any one direction. He had a nose like that of a hedgehog. It was tiny, flat, and at the same time plump; when you looked at him, you wouldn't have even noticed that he had one at all. I wondered if he had ever read that story by Nikolai Gogol and compared himself to Major Kovalyov, the Collegiate Assessor who awoke one morning to find himself without a nose. I'm sure Cameron was teased about it as a boy, and if not, I wish that he had been. As I stood there at the end of the road between the veterans' building and the old pizza parlor, I laughed quietly to myself, thinking of all the times I had spent in that stuffy restaurant.

I didn't go inside, though part of me wanted to; I decided instead to sit down on the bench across the street, facing that old joint at a safe distance so as to reminisce in peace. The building behind me had a peculiar wall of façade, and it was studded with deep orange stones, an almost caramel color, some sort of imitation Baltic amber. It hurt the back of my head when I leaned against it. This made me think of those fossilized ants and other insects of the sort that, as I suspected this wall to be, had been petrified in ancient tree sap and were now sold in baskets at gift shops in Michigan City for two dollars apiece. These preserved ants sparked in me the interest of time, and so I pondered. Where I found myself after having done so was here, in this building, with its fading bricks and sprawling smoke stacks, right across the street, so close as to smell the drifting scent of cooking pizzas in the warm air, thick with memories. Cameron had once made me general manager of Malzaro's; however, it was only for about a month, while he and his wife went abroad to plunder a safety deposit box of his father's, left unclaimed in a bank vault in Holland after his death. He got the box within the first week, so I have heard, and the next three weeks he spent exploring the European countryside and enjoying the indulgences afforded by the €48,700 that the box contained. Yet, the real story is what happened to me here, at Malzaro's, in the twenty-seven days that he was away.

———

What goes through your head when you think of a mystery—Sherlock, the Rue Morgue, a creepy butler with sinister intentions to murder his masters with a candlestick? Perhaps it is the enticing prospect of a grand discovery, the unearthing of a wondrous fortune, and the mystery being whom it had once belonged to, or, in this peculiar case, who it had once been. If that's what came to mind, then perhaps this is a story you will enjoy; if not, I hope you will at least try, for it is the plot now, and you can't change it. If you have in fact taken it upon yourself to continue, keep in mind this question: what defines a mystery? Ask yourself: does it have to be solved in order for it to be categorized as such? Must it be sought willingly and with that intention in mind, or can it be something else entirely?

I had been working for Cameron some eighteen months when he left for Europe, leaving me in responsibility of the establishment, both physically and operationally. At that point, I was merely an employee like the others. I was shift leader, yes, but all that meant was that I got to wear a different name tag, made twenty-five cents more than minimum wage, and got to tell you to stop fucking up, if you happened to be fucking up, or good job… if you happened to be doing a good job.

It was the first week, the first week on our own. I remember I was pretty nervous. The veins on my temples would pop out and throb when I thought of the situation. It sent my knees shaking and caused my armpits to sweat. I figured that I was going to have to be the one to tame the lion, you know? I thought everything down to its worst possible outcomes, and it drove me nuts. Then I realized that it really wasn't going to be that bad. For a day or two I thought everyone was trying to run the place into the ground. It was only after some time had passed that I realized nothing had changed. Cameron usually sat in his office all day, and we workers were always left up front unsupervised and basically in charge. So it wasn't exactly a drastic adjustment, in fact, it was all psychological.

Catfish Mike and the stunning from neck to waist, forty-four year old Linda Waters (who were married, Mike deriving his name tauntingly from the obvious whiskers of hair that Linda seemed to have protruding out of the sides of her mouth and chin—of which he found nothing fish-like or unappealing—and were the result of her going some thirteen years without shaving, ten without having looked in a mirror), and Lee, my good old friend Lee, were the employees over which I now presided. Catfish was notorious for being a piece of shit. We liked him, sure, but he was still a piece of shit. He had gotten two girls pregnant last summer and abandoned them both. He moved from a neighboring, unspecified state, married Linda, and changed his name to Mike. Originally, so he as only quite recently revealed to me—and by that I mean in the last fifteen years—his name was Truman Seer, a fry cook and college student. He was the only one out of all of us with any real culinary experience. By saying that, I don't mean that we, and myself in particular, were bad at our jobs. We didn't take it very seriously up until that point, but we knew what we were doing... pretty much, and for a couple fellas under the age of twenty five (excluding Linda, who never lifted a finger) we managed things quite smoothly. Of course, there was always the occasional thief or freeloader who tried to rob us or leave without paying; there was always the occasional spotting of an employing smoking a *steeze* in the cooler room.

"Why does it smell so danky in here?!" Cameron would ask every now and again. "It's the cheese!" we'd say; and we weren't lying, that place had some stinky cheeses. I recall there was about ten or twelve different kinds, all attributing to the variety of 13,000 possible pizza topping combinations!—but I might be exaggerating. However, the odor was still mostly because of the bud. "If we're going to be a franchise one day," he'd reply, "we've gotta get some better cheeses." Then he'd leave, and we'd all burst out laughing, and, with a smile and in a half sarcastic voice, I'd scorn the stoner not to do it again, at least not without inviting me. These stoners, most of them high school dropouts, were the morning staff, overseen by an entirely different "shift leader"—kids I only got to talk to for ten to fifteen minutes a day before they happily departed, having finished their obligations to this greasy establishment. The morning shift was always much more fun, so I'd heard—who the hell eats pizza in the morning?! The days dragged on though, like work days do, and the hours were nothing but thorns in my side—jabbed into me as I dropped my punch-card into the time box upon arrival, removed and bandaged as I dropped it in once again upon leaving, sulking and itching to hit the streets, feeling like a chicken in a coop who just narrowly avoided the chopping block for the day, and anxious to flee.

Now as I sit here on this bench, I'm beginning to make odd parallels between this story and a particularly unforgettable episode from my childhood. I apologize for the tangential frequency, but with a healthy mind and a handicapped body, I'm left upon a sort of immobile pedestal for many hours of the day, allowing me to wander internally, problematically, and deceptively aimless. These stories have practically nothing in common with each other in terms of setting and events, but what they do have in common is the spiritual awakening the two unrelated happenings bestowed upon me: a lurid glimpse of childhood uninhibitedness. And so it had been that when I wasn't in fierce battle, face to face military combat, blowing away my friends one by one with my plastic assault rifle as we ran and hid behind the large dumpsters in the alley—as many American boys, for some strange reason, tend to do growing up; that is, pretending to live as a fighter and/ or die of a bullet wound—I was also absorbing the unexplored world around me like the words of a book. Fucking magic, don't you think—the sponge-like absorbance of young minds, that is? And so it happened that I became suddenly amazed one day. I was with friends, always with friends. Must've been summer too, but it's funny how I can never exactly tell looking back on things that far gone. I was so happy all the time, and in every memory the seasons hardly made a difference; not even a horrible Midwestern winter could cause me to feel down or to not enjoy life—experiencing all that I could as quickly as I could, whenever I could do so, and isn't doing so always the more exciting with friends? If there's anything I miss in my life, now as it comes to an end, it would be company. Shit, but let's talk of things less morbid.

The event, I suppose I shall continue to say, occurred on a hot day, for I do not recall the sight of jackets—so it must have been summer; that much I can remember. It most likely was a day in July. And let me tell you, Julys in Illinois are damn near heaven, especially if your neighborhood is older, preferably Victorian, and has trees that are huge and soaring, like exploding zeppelins, with expansive lengths of black power lines running through their upper braches, creating a beautiful mixture of natural surroundings and man-made necessity. Such was the street that I lived on; and those trees never failed to keep me cool and protected; and with that in mind I could do whatever it was me and my eight year old cognizance decided to. On this particular day I was sitting on a porch-swing with a friend. Outside it was brilliant, with striking lights, and a humid, green sort of sunshine fell upon the block. But quickly a storm was moving in. We made popcorn; he and I sat there on the swing next to his opened living room window, where inside the TV was on and the house was comfortable; sat there and listened to the clouds roar, eerily moaning overhead as darker and darker ones approached with a suspenseful sort of leisure, like two impending armies on a battlefield in the sky. But to us it was like a climactic movie, like the one playing on the screen inside, and we needed to see what would happen next. If you come to think about it, at that point in my life, how many rainstorms had I come to experience? A hundred, maybe less, maybe more—so let's just say a hundred. Out of that hundred, how many had I actually sat down and got to watch, to examine, to realize every detail, every aspect, every drop that landed on every petal? Let's say ten—and it was probably less, so I took the opportunity in stride. Gradually, the winds picked up, and the greenish hue of our surroundings had turned to a grey shadow; I jumped quickly to my feet, enthralled, restless! The temperature dropped. Grasping the white wooden ball that was fixed atop both ends of the railing of the porch whose steps of wide wooden boards inclined before me, I saw as the rain began to descend, and inspected each and every bead of water as it burst into a splotch of moisture on the sidewalk, accompanied by a million others. I gazed as the white concrete pathways slowly turned dark, drop by drop as the clouds let loose their fluids upon us. The noise of all that falling water was triumphant, incredible, the loudest and the most pleasing thing I had heard in my life. That moment was a treasure, more valuable to me than anything gold, anything gleaming. More valuable to me than what I found in the basement of Marky Malzaro's Pizza Place, over a decade later... but not more interesting, I must confess. That just previously discussed event revealed to me the beauty of our world, of ourselves. This one, still yet to be discussed, is what revealed to me the beauty of twisted luck: a thing not uncommon in later life, an uncanny find or occurrence that is obviously more of a blessing than a curse, but at the same time has an unruly grip upon the mind, torturing it, penetrating it, making it so you can never go more than a minute without thinking of that so aversely grateful, dejectedly ecstatic, twisted fucking luck of yours.

That night, ten years gone since the day on the porch, Lee and I stood behind the counter counting tips as the last customers left, and Catfish shut the door behind them. "What a treat!" Lee exclaimed, "five cents for each of us—how's that for making a living!" He then spat into the sink to show his aggravation. "Mother fuckers come in here, drop twenty bucks on a meal, watch us make it from scratch, and then put but a cent or two in the jar—and only one in every hundred will probably have the decency enough to do that!"

"Welcome to life!" Catfish shouted from across the room, where he was busy rubbing down the once white surface of a table now encrusted with tomato sauce.

"More like welcome to hell!" Lee cried. "This place is going to kill me, I just know it!"

"It's already killed me," he rejoined, stuffing the wet rag into his back pocket and walking away from the last of his repugnant duties for which he was paid.

"Same" I added quietly.

God, the hardest time in a person's life has got to be those few years before you become an *adult*, when you finally do realize that most things really aren't as grand as they once appeared to be, and you have to go on living in "hell" for a while, trying to make the best of it. I suppose as you get older, it gets better, and it starts to kind of make the best of itself, in a way. You're still in hell, yeah, but you're just too numb now to feel the blisters and the fire. Man, why can't I keep our promise? I'm a pretty gloomy person, huh? I can't help it; it's just my nature. Just as some people can't help the fucked up way they laugh, or smoking cigarettes, or continuously piercing an ear—it becomes a comfortable, innately expected part of you. It's like breathing. And just like breathing, sometimes I get pretty sick of doing it, wish it would just stop, and leave me in peace.

"Help me with the trash," Lee said in an aggravated hurry, colliding with a table while he walked and spilling over half a dozen diet Dr. Peppers onto the floor that were left resting on the banister: the remnants of some family's happy supper: the root of all my discomforts throughout the day, the payer of my bills.

I called for Linda to get a mop; Lee told me to "fucking forget it," and to "let that bum piece of shit (Mike) clean it up." I had no problem with that, and as we headed for the back door with two heavy, stretching, ready-to-burst bags of trash in hand, we passed Mike on the way out and I told him, "Hey, there's a mess over there, Cameron called and said he wants you to clean it, you bum piece of shit."

"Cameron!" he exclaimed.

"Yeah," I said, "he's watching the cameras; he can see everything you're doing."

Mike ran to oblige. This was a lie, of course, and Cameron gave not one shit about some spilt drink on the floor of his beloved inherited grease factory; he was a million miles away on an adventure—a thing, at that point in life, I had never known. My greatest adventure so far that day was turning out to be our happy trip to the dumpsters behind the building, in the dark and unoccupied realms of a seemingly endless parking lot. It was endless though, the pavement stopped after running about a hundred feet, you'd hit a rusty fence, and then there was a quarter-mile of freshly cut grass and red wooden benches. Behind the restaurant was a park. The same one I had just recently stopped at an entrance of to peer up at our friend the dying squirrel. However, the view of this park from Malzaro's was from the back, disconnected from the parcel of gardens and rose bushes of which the site most often drew its visitors.

At work my days consisted of standing behind a counter, and walking to a dumpster; taking your money, and stockpiling waste; spending your money, and spreading your waste, spreading it like butter, like a buttery cancer across the face of the planet. Malignant. Carnivorous. Mounting. I had lived that life for so, so long.

As Lee swung up the lid and threw in his bags, I did the same, and felt like I had thrown them into the gapping nostril of Old Mother Earth. "I'm sorry," I said to her, but she gave me cold shoulders—is still giving me the cold shoulders to this day, as she very well should for as long as I continue to produce and disperse of my waste into her nostrils, congesting her airways and mind with the discarded pizza slices of a family's happy supper: the root of all my discomforts throughout the day, the payer of my bills.

I asked Lee if he was feeling shitty as well. "Me, feel shitty?" he said, always the optimist, "only about our wages."

"Okay," I said. "Okay, but there really are a lot of things to feel shitty about, ya know?"

"Quit bitching over the trash," he joked, "the earth can't feel, dummy!"

"That's what caused me to feel down in the beginning, yeah," I said, "but not anymore, my mind has jumped to new piles of shit. I'm feeling down because of something else now; I'm like that sometimes."

And he sure knew it; I was like that a lot of the time. He had always resented that part of me, the part that caused him to acknowledge the negative aspects of things, when all he wanted to do was keep focused on the opposite. We were friends, as close as friends could be while still just being friends, and although he resented me for my morbid outlook, pretended not to see where I was coming from, what made me feel so down, I always knew that he knew exactly what I meant. And he knew what I meant when I said I was sad that we were killing the planet, even though we did it every day together, multiple times a day (as is usually required to run a restaurant), and had never expressed my opinion on this practice to him before. It was obvious to me that he understood, and by the way he would reply, it became even more apparent. He said, "So what? What are we supposed to do with this shit, take it home with us and stuff our mattresses with it?! It's trash! And it'll make some great coal one day for future people to use to make more trash. Perhaps it'll even form a new diamond or two. But not now, not in this millennium, so therefore it's useless. And if it's not valuable to me, then it's not valuable at all."

Of course I, and most everyone, I assume, has this opinion, somewhere locked away in the chasms of our mind. I knew it was the truth, even before we had started this conversation. It is apparent, apparent to all those with eyes and simple understandings. Nothing could be done, not from where we were standing, not with our hands. We could not bring this shit home with us and stuff our mattresses with it; that was out of the question, and in the end it would do no good. It was not the definitive act itself, but rather that unalterable awareness, that persistent desperation, the constant knowledge of my own wrongdoings each and every day, which brought me down. That's what made me feel so shitty; and with my pained eyes pressed tight behind my two sweating hands, I soon made an effort to block those sad thoughts from my sad mind.

Inside Malzaro's, Catfish and Whiskers were finally getting off their shifts. Mike had cleaned up the mess of spilt soft drinks and they were now in the kitchen next to the wall which also doubled as an enormous brick oven. It led up to an even more massive chimney, visible from the street jetting out of the structure's roof and into the sky. Pressed against those hot bricks, Mike was getting to second base quick, and Linda was looking to run it all the way home. Her stained blouse, which was her work-issued kitchen uniform, quietly fell to the floor, and her bare nipples were welcomed favorably into the musty air of the room by Mike's tongue. But before he could fuck her however, she pulled away, and seized him by the wrist with a seductive smile across her lipstick-smeared face. Linda, naked and thirsty for pleasure, with her once perky tits bouncing on her chest as she hopped across the room, was leading him somewhere else.

In the dark parking lot out back, Lee and I were sitting on top the sticky lids of the dumpster, talking, feeling rather down as he tried in vain to cheer us both up. When his look-on-the-bright-side propositions seemed to have failed, we turned to discussing the night, and how there's never anything to discuss, it felt, that didn't concern the actual night itself: physically, tangibly, the way it smelt, the shadows and how they crawled across everything and everyone with a mind of their own, the sounds of people and the happening nightlife of the more active streets nearby. Stars twinkled overhead, insects twinkled in the streetlights, and Lee's eyes twinkled in his own head as he sat across from me with his legs overlapping each other and his arms tucked beneath his white smock: a hopeless tactic to preserve his flesh from guaranteed mosquito bites.

"So how's the U?" I asked him, and by that I meant the University. "Still going to be a scientist?"

"A Chemical Engineer," he said, "and yes, I am. But what the hell have you been up to lately? Heard you haven't gone to classes since last May."

"I have," I replied, now on the offensive, "but they're completely pointless, man. It's sucking up all my time and money when all I want to do is work on being..."

"Being what?" he asked.

"I don't know!" I said. "Being a living being, at the very least!—which is anything that doesn't require me to wither away in a stuffy building all day while outside the sun shines down and my life ticks by. For all I know, I could be down to my last few grains of sand in the dial."

"Just get back in classes," he said, "otherwise you'll be working at a pizza place and marrying a forty year old hostess with more facial hair than that blind homeless guy who's always passed out drunk on his heap of aluminum cans and glass bottles behind the dry cleaners."

"The one on 32nd street?" I asked.

"You know who I'm talking about!"

"I think there's something crawling up my leg," I said, hopping off the lid of the dumpster and onto the tar-tracked asphalt. Lee followed, and put his hand on my shoulder. I saw it in the sides of my vision, glowing yellow because of the streetlight, resting there, friendly and reassuring. His ring finger then curled in on me, and the rest followed; his nails all painfully sunk themselves down into my flesh as a resounding noise shot suddenly through the air, pounding at our skulls. It was an explosion! It had come from inside Malzaro's, of that much I was certain; smoke began to spill out from the back door, the one we had left half-open with a wooden stopper wedged underneath it; and I watched as dark smog rose across the bricks and into the vast blue night.

We both ran into the seemingly burning structure. As we darted into the hallway, Lee was already ahead of me digging through the supply room cabinets; he eventually retrieved a fire extinguisher. I swung a table cloth in the air to ward off the smoke as we made our way into the lobby of the restaurant. It was empty, hazy with fog and burnt air. Seats were left on the floor, lying on their sides, tables coated with a thin white film of plaster-dust and ceiling paint. Something had shaken this building to its foundations. Something uncalled-for had surely just occurred. Lee and I both sensed a feeling of helpless despair as the sprinklers overhead abruptly came to life, dowsing us in icy water. The plumes of dark smoke continued to rise and engulf the room in a deep and asphyxiating cloud.

In Malzaro's squalid, crumbling basement—while we were still out back in the parking lot—Catfish was making a fist-sized hicky on Linda's neck. She was completely naked. Her fake nails were falling off one by one as she clawed at Mike's waist, strenuously and fiercely attempting to remove his belt. He made his way from her neck up to her mouth, down to the wet curvature between her breasts, and back up to her mouth again.

"Malzaro's doesn't have cameras, do they?" he tersely enquired in a silent yet unexpected manner, and in the midst of kissing her rather violently.

"No, Mike," she moaned, still taking tongue.

"Son of a Bitch," he mumbled.

"Yeah," she said, "talk to me like that," unaware that his cursing was directed towards someone else. Conclusively, Mike went in to fuck her—or something of the sort—but for some strange, unknown and manipulative reason (mostly likely), she grabbed him by the dick and forced him away, a look of amused disgust shone across her face. He fell into the wall behind him with an even more obvious expression of disgusted amusement on his own. Heaped up against that wall, in a pile of empty shoe boxes, gardening tools, old chefs implements, and rusty pans, was, and for God knows why, a two-gallon drum of kerosene, resting there happily in a shiny red tin, gleaming, though half covered in dust. It fell from amongst the mound and splattered on the floor, covering it and them in cold, nauseating gas.

Across the room was a water heater. Running between Linda's toes was a stream of kerosene making its way towards a flame no more menacing in size than that of a small candle. The basement was old, and the floor, as a result of an earthquake in the 1930s, was slanted in one direction… the direction of the water heater. Mike and Linda probably had no idea, and were more than likely about to both verbally and physically assault each other, but before any hands could get wrapped around any necks, the candle flame had changed to a stick of dynamite. They would have seen streaking lines of fire suddenly erupt across the floor and travel, like snakes or highbred, fast-growing vines of mutated ivy, up the walls and up their legs, towards the heap of shit in the corner.

But when those snakes reached the red two-gallon tin, it combusted; Mike and Linda were hurled through the opposing wall in a ball of fiery hell, and into the laundry room where reluctant employees were forced to wash grimy table cloths and bibs. There, by the grace of God, they survived, lying half-naked and unconscious under a mess of wet cloths and detergent-soaked water that was spilling out from a row of punctured lime-green containers on the shelf above. Mike was put in a coma for three days; Linda lost the two last fingers on her right hand due to severe burns, and some skin off her nose and cheeks,—but not those once perky tits, no, no, thankfully those were unharmed.

In the now-smoke-filled, table- and chair-cluttered main consumption room reserved for those patronizing woes I commonly refer to as customers (or customers I commonly refer to as woes), Lee and I searched through the distortion and fought through the painfulness of breathing in hot air to the source of this emergency and where it was emitting, as well as what was emitting it. "The kitchen!" Lee shouted. "The smoke coming from the doorway to the kitchen is darker than the smoke coming out of the office over there, or the restrooms behind you. That's gotta be where it's coming from!"

"It would make sense," I told him.

Entering the kitchen, the floor before us was mangled and burning, and we had been fortunate not to take one too many steps. A hole, ten feet all around, was left gaping where the meat coolers once stood, the stainless steel sidewall of which was heavily dented and drooping into the pit. Lee and I both peered down at it and into the basement. Mutually, I'm sure, the thought of Linda and Mike, and where they were, and what they might have done, and if they were even still alive, had immediately come to mind. Until around ten or eleven that next morning I had reason to believe that they were both either dead or dying. The scene was too chaotic on that night, when it all began. Police and medical personnel were way too preoccupied to allow us any adequate information on the wellbeing of our licentious coworkers. The authorities only wanted to interrogate us, to get to the root of some nonexistent crime or conspiracy. The fact was, we hadn't a clue as to what could have happened.

As Linda roused in her hospital bed the next morning, now two fingers short, she, in expected weariness, revealed to an eager officer— who had already been seated in the hallway outside her door in case she awoke during the night—some rather sought after information. He had been there for ten and a half hours, the entire length of Linda's temporary coma: the result of a nasty concussion received during the blast. In short, she told the man that Mike had started the fire, when in a fit of rage and not uncommon sexual frustration, *accidentally* kicked over a poorly placed container of gasoline that caused the flame on the water heater to combust like fission. Old Catfish eventually walked away with a hefty fine, and a court supervision officer after the police and the county threw a fit over the whole situation, calling it a threat to *our* peaceful society and the result of unnecessarily reckless behavior. But with consideration to the grandiosity of what followed thanks to and in part of their "reckless behavior," I'm shocked that they took legal penalties against Mike to that extent, for what followed became the find of the century! *A rare unearthing of a lost pharaoh's tomb in the Valley of the Kings*—it was coined and compared to in all the major newspapers—*The Arc of the Covenant exhumed from amongst the accumulations in a basement catacomb of some gothic cathedral!* But in actuality what followed hailed in comparison, and was to be the treasure of the century, the crown jewel upon the head of our generation's triumphs, and the leading source of influence on the revitalization of miserable, wealth-seeking, legend-trailing, myth-busting adventurers.

When the smoke cleared, and the fire fighters had assured the inspectors and detectives that all was moderately safe and allowed them onto the property, they began searching for the source of the explosion. This was a few hours prior to Linda's incriminating hospital-room testimony, and the scent of foul play was ever-present under the nose of the established order.

"Leave it up to a bunch of jack-offs, none, mind you—'cept that girly in the ambulance—any older than twenty-five, and all about as mentally competent as twelve year olds, to run a fuckin' business,— one involving coal burning brick ovens and raw meat, for that matter.

Ya know, thought this woulda happened sooner," said Detective Marc Lime of the Cook County Police Department's Special Investigations Division to his accompanying deputies and his knee-braced and limping partner Julio.

"Ain't we gon check shit out, Marc? We just gon stand here all clueless and whatnot?" asked Julio, anxious to inspect the scene firsthand, gnawing at the butt of his pen, and cradling a sketch pad under his left shoulder.

"Yes," Detective Lime brazenly replied, eyeing the scene of carnage heaped out before him in what was once the kitchen of the restaurant. Red bricks from the pizza oven chimney and cold white embers swathed the little remaining floor space, a mere circle a few feet wide that ringed around a gaping hole of slowly rising smoke and rippling heat. But along with that, to everybody's awareness, it seemed to produce within a haunting sentience that was the presence of death: the result of the pit's protracting blackness and seemingly endless depths, glowing like an ignis fatuus over the sun-isolated swamp of somebody's heedless destruction.

———

That night, the night my place of employment went up in flames and was left with a gaping hole at its center, Lee and I had been hauled off to the police station, placed in separate rooms, and under bright lights, heavily interrogated. They cuffed me, hunched me over and shoved me into the back of a squad car; I saw them do the same to Lee as I gazed in disbelief through the narrow rearview mirror of the vehicle, to where behind us he had been spread across the hood of another and thoroughly searched, then hunched over as well and thrust forcefully onto the seat. After that, all I can recall was the sound of the drops of sweat falling from my face and softly pelting the leather seat below, and the flashing of strobe lights. For a while, I was considered a terrorist. When they took us to the station, they hadn't a clue that we were employees of the restaurant, oblivious as to what had actually happened, and in short, completely innocent on all counts, including, and most specifically, terroristic actions. The first things they said to me upon entering the cramped, manila-colored room, with its two chairs and bare steel table, cold cinderblock walls, was that I had better get the best damn lawyer in the country, and that I had better cancel all future obligations, as I was looking at 25 years. It was after hearing this that I broke down in tears and whimpered until it was almost too obvious that I was as innocent as a little school girl... and I sure as hell felt like one.

Unfortunately, appearance alone was not enough to win my case. Detective Lime, standing up suddenly from the chair across from where I sat, flexed his back by sticking out his belly, a tough bulge of white button-up dress shirt and glistening buttons, curved his spine, as if about to bring the back of his head to his ankles, and let out a grunt of exhausted annoyance while springing himself forward. He stood up over the table looking at me, hands noticeably squirming in his pockets, while Julio stood scowling by his side, wincing his dark face at me in a menacing episode of prolonged eye-to-eye contact. Then the tension exploded as Lime pushed his chair in, turned around and spoke: "Going to have you tested," he said, now turning his back to me, now facing me again, swirling a pencil between his fingers, while I sat like a helpless egg in a nest stalked by carnivorous hawks and owls. "We'll have to take you into the next room."

"What for?" I asked, nervous out of my skin.

"For the polygraph," he replied, grabbing me by the cuffs, and forcing me to rise to my feet. "Until we get solid confirmation from your parents or the owner that you are in fact an employee of that now-ruined establishment, we'll do what we please with ya."

Julio opened the massive steel door by typing in an access/exit code into a number pad above the handle; it made a hissing sound once it had been unlocked, and Julio pulled open, with obvious difficulty, the heavy door to my concrete cube. He led me across the hall to a room labeled *Polygraphed Room 112,* and once inside I found myself sitting in a chair adjacent to one occupied by Lee. He was already partially hooked up to a machine, and had wires extending from his fingers on his left hand, a large metallic headpiece fastened to his scalp, wires extending from that as well and onto the wooden table in front of him, where a shifty machine with the dimensions of a large microwave and the likeness of an earthquake seismograph was being tinkered with by an older man in a dark hat, smoking a fat stogie, and wielding a flathead screwdriver. He, I presumed, was the one administering the test, our inadvertent judge.

Of course, as innocence can never lie, we passed the test beautifully. With wires snaking from our heads and fingers, question after question they asked us, and received nothing to show for it on the machine but straight lines drawn across the paper. They were shocked, doubtful, and concerned, but mostly extremely angry. Oh yes, the anger hit them hard, like a bullet into body armor, and they acted for a moment as if they were about to pounce. Then to our relief, with a few deep breaths of frustration, they gained the strength to hold it all in, and keep our now acquitted asses untouched and in one piece.

Julio seemed to mimic most every move made by Detective Lime, not in the moment, but about a seconded after Lime had completed whatever gesture or motion deemed worthy enough by Julio to imitate. Such was the situation of momentary anger that had previously befallen. I don't know for certain if Lee could, but I for one saw it in that man's eyes that he wasn't really angry, and that he was just duplicating the expressed emotions of his superior, who was obviously outraged. This was humorous to me, though, after our innocence was no longer in question, a lot of things those officers did began to humor me, as if I were looking down on them, mocking, immune, and untouchable. I was okay, out of a job, but okay. And since none of those misfortunates were blamable to me, I find that I got out of that whole situation (at that time) pleasantly unharmed, and better off than I could have.

After further pleading our case with tearful eyes, Lime kicked us out into the hot night, having somehow received confirmation of our employment at Malzaro's; and so we had passed the test! He slammed the building's door violently behind him, causing a whirlwind of insects huddled around the overhanging light to go scattering in all directions. We were, at first estimate, maybe eight miles from where we both lived, which was a relatively short distance from each other. Luckily, Lee had found a few dollars under one of the booths that day, so he told me as we took off walking down the dark side street. "Just enough money to catch a bus!" he said.

At the stop we waited. Beside us a man sat sleeping, hunched up against the plexy-glass wall beneath the black metal awning, most likely the only shelter he could find, for he looked horribly disheveled and sick.

"He drinks," Lee stated, looking over and observing the man from where we sat a few feet away down the bench. "I don't see a bottle, but I can sure smell it on him. This guy is blacked out."

Then, as the bus pulled up, we both stood and stepped towards the opening doors; while the venting of its greasy engine stirred the motionless night, we made our way inside. From the steps, as the doors shut, I glanced back at that sad life, wasted on the street corner. Gazing despondently out the window, thinking in morbid brain waves, a miasma of forlornness and death creeping over me, I remained standing until the lean bus driver, who was wrinkly and drab, like old coffee stains on a napkin, urged me to sit down. Lee tugged me by my shirt sleeve and lowered me into the sunken in seat, patched with tape of a similar shade of brown to conceal the puncture wounds made by restless children and vandals. The bus sped away down the avenue, leaving the cops and the polygraphs, the drunkards and the night, far behind us. Relief was a sensation almost just as pleasant as liquidity, freedom, or self-realization, it then seemed. The relief we felt on that ride home, in that stinking bus, on that sticky seat, gave us a sort of unexpected drive of confidence, a pulse for adventurous living.

Lee turned to me and said, "Let's go back."

"Where?"

"To Malzaro's," he said, "let's check it out; did you see how wrecked that place was? I'd love to go back and take another look."

"I'm in," I replied, always a fan of impulsiveness. "We can stop at my house and then walk back; I'd like to change, grab some bottled waters and a flash light."

"Good thinking!" he exclaimed, "It's better to be prepared."

We got off at our stop and made the way back to where I lived; and every house we passed on the street as we approached mine, every house had a subtly ringing aureole around it, pulsating, languidly in the humid night, in the swaying blackness and hum of the insects' gentle nocturnes. Façades, windows, eves and awnings loomed outwardly, like watchful gargoyles of the neighborhood, and protected those within, giving off a slightly mournful, encompassing aura. Every house, it seemed, but my own. And so we climbed the five steps slowly for me to reach out expectantly and turn the knob to walk in quickly through the front door. The marvelous onset of home air-conditioning made it easier to breathe, and left my skin feeling thick, cool, and rubber-like.

In the attic (also my bedroom), Lee sat on my cinderblock-raised mattress as I dug through the clutter in my closet across from him, searching for black clothing, flash lights, and durable shoes. Inside the dresser gawked down at me from ahead as I arched my body over to begin rummaging the pile: a heap of forgotten memories, childhood toys, boxes of notes from ex-girlfriends, and a crate of paintball paraphernalia, gun and facemask and pods. I took hold of the rifle, removed it from its black, military-grade casing, dropped a single solid ball of paint into the hopper and, after a quick tinkering with the valve on the compression tank, jumped from out of the closet, aimed the weapon, and shot Lee in the center of the chest.

He sat, eyes slowly widening for a moment trying to realize what was happening, and once he saw me pull the trigger, his eyes shut and he fell from the bed and onto the floor. Face down on the dusty white carpet—the kind that literally is the floor and can't be removed, at least not without laborious actions—he remained, hunched over clutching his stomach, and wheezing. I had probably knocked the wind out of him. I stood laughing to myself in the corner, when he strained himself onto his feet, eyes watery from the pain, glanced at me out of mortification, and ran into the bathroom across the hall. *He'll get over it,* I thought; *he always gets over shit like this.*

Five minutes later he re-entered the room, met fierce visual contact with me, and shook his head in disappointment. "Let's get going," he whispered, sitting down on the bed again. Then I pointed the gun at him suddenly, and he yelped, throwing his arms across his face. Laughing riotously, I lowered the weapon, as there was nothing left in it, and he understood that he was safe once again.

"Fuck you!" he said, and raised up his shirt to reveal a quarter-sized welt on the center of his hairless chest. A thin and subtle trail of blood slowly inched its way down his abdomen.

I apologized, out of shame, I suppose. I shouldn't have been so cruel, but it was pretty funny. Being spontaneous is fun. And after he accepted my plea for forgiveness, we left. As we got back out into the street, the aureoles, the holy lights of individual domestic heavens around the homes of my neighborhood, were there no longer. It was a quiet walk, and a short one. I said little, thought little. Not until we reached the same block as Malzaro's, at the gates of the park, there, where we had seen our friend the dying squirrel. Do you remember?— there we stopped. Lee gulped a mouthful of water from his bottle, and fiddled with the light on top the hardhat I had lent him before taking it off, assuming that it was of no use as of yet. We were about to break into the place we had been arrested just two hours prior, and a place where I usually wanted nothing other than to leave, to escape, and thought nothing but dreadful thoughts about, all my days. This realization left me feeling on edge.

Small wooden fences, yellow caution tape, and police barriers encased the building, cluttering the sidewalk ahead. We crept in through a hole in the gate that wrapped around the parking lot, quite near the dumpsters in the far right-hand corner. And after doing so and standing up straight again beneath the waning streetlight— there it was, the restaurant, tall and sound, as if nothing had happened, and completely unharmed. Since I had been shift leader—for by sunrise I assumed that I would be no longer—I had in my possession a single brass key to the back door, and thus was able to grant us access when we slowly crept through the darkness of the lot and approached it. I cupped the cool, grey knob in my hand, and let my fingers rub the faded steel of the handle, the spherical form of it, forever glazed in a thin layer of cooking oil from the hands of greasy chefs. We entered slowly, not knowing what to expect... but expecting anything, any unimaginable outcome.

Inside the air was searing and heavy with the scent of charred walls, charred floors, charred wood, rubber, and metal. The blackness, however, is what really hit us. It was the most extreme blackness I had ever experienced. And for the longest time I couldn't figure out why since the building had plenty of windows. I discovered though, while Lee and I wandered slowly across the hallway leading to the kitchen, that the reason the windows did not avert the blackness by letting in the outside light was because they couldn't: they were covered in a thick sheet of ash and residue. In fact, everything was. I looked down at my clothes, once Lee had switched on the light atop his head, and saw that I was covered in it too, from head to toe completely; Lee and I had literally turned the color of the room around us, and it made it seem as though we were invisible, like we were camouflaged in a jungle of coal. But as we continued, walking only in the meager patch of light that in front of us was casted, I saw ahead the entrance to the kitchen, its once white door now hanging crooked on its hinges, and beyond it a gaping hole, or possibly the depths of hell.

Lee stopped. I turned to look at him and winced when I did so. His head was nonexistent; instead there was a singular beam of light shooting out from where it had once been. He appeared as an illuminated spirit, shinning, or a lighthouse on a distant shore in the night, guiding. But the glow was extreme; my eyes shut and contracted, and pain throbbed from within the center of my skull. Then I looked away, and he said, "Are you ready?"

I reached out my hand, and holding my breath, pushed open the door. I was as ready as I was ever going to be. In that room and down that pit lay nothing but curiosity, nothing but the accomplishment of a cutthroat, risky and spontaneous plan. And with little regard for my wellbeing, I stepped into the room, and immediately slipped on a shard of metal caught beneath my foot. While plummeting to the floor, I gashed open my hand on a jagged, protruding spike of fragmented wood extending from the remnants of a table. Cursing and kicking, jumping to my feet and stomping chaotically in the darkness out of agony and frustration, Lee grabbed ahold of me, and with his blaring light of a face shinning directly into mine, shouted in anger: "Quit thrashing around, moron! You're going to fall into that hole and die! Or worse, get the cops called on us!"

I appeased, took off my over-shirt, turned it inside-out because the grime had built up on it thanks to the condition of the building, and wrapped it taut around my bleeding hand. I felt like Rambo; and if only I had a machine gun slung across my back, and I blade the size of a violin hanging from my leg, I would have had the courage, perhaps, to go down into the hole first.

Like a tosher descending into the earth, into a dark and dangerous London sewer system, Lee lowered himself and dropped, landing in the basement with a crash and a billow of dust rising around him, flooding the beam of light now directed upward towards me. I followed his exact route, placing both hands firmly on the crumbling tiles, and let myself dangle halfway into the pit. Then I let go, and fell rapidly into the void beneath. Once there, I took the flashlight out from where it had been looped around my belt, wondering why I hadn't done so earlier, turned it on, and held it out before me. It shone on the wall across from where I stood, across from where the water heater now rested in a demented and embarrassing mess on the rutted ground in between. The concrete that formerly made up the floor had been pulverized, blown into a million pieces and was now heaped up in random piles of gravel around the room. But the wall that my light revealed was more unnerving still. It was wholly intact, I suppose, except for two long openings centered on it in the haphazard shapes of the human body. On one of the gaps, it was easy to distinguish two flailing limbs below a twisted neck and crooked head. The other was similar in appearance, with the exception of it being slightly larger, and slightly lopsided, with two legs extending out in opposite directions forming an upside-down V shape. Lee stood before it, astonished, gazing with a curious grin.

"This one's Mike," he said, holding out his pointer finger towards the hole on the left, "because it's fatter. That's Linda over there."

I agreed; "You certainly have an eye for recognition," I joked. He smacked me on the back rowdily and peeked his head through one of the gaps, the one made by Catfish, and into the laundry room beyond. There they had found the two quarreling lovers unconscious in a throng of moldy towels and plastic hampers. There they had found the only witnesses to this indefinable occurrence. And there, nearby, as we squeezed our bodies through the fatter of the two openings, we would soon come across the greatest treasure one could possibly imagine... or at least it seemed, then in my juvenile mind.

The washing machine and dryer were mangled, dented and tossed over on their sides, doors swung open, as if gasping for air. Beside one, I caught the sight of something glistening in the dirt. I walked towards it, shone my beam of light down to my feet, and there, between my two shoes, was a golden tooth. Surprised, but figuring that it belonged to either Linda or Mike, and that they might want to have it back, I tossed it into a pocket hanging from my hip, and walked over to Lee who was examining something in the corner.

In the nook of the room, right beside the broken washer, was a small closet. It led into another room used for housing the pipes that ran throughout the building, as well as an old heavy metal furnace. The door to this hidden chamber was about three feet tall, two feet wide. This is what Lee was staring at. It had always reminded me of that door in Alice and Wonderland, where she has to eat the cake in order to shrink down to size to be able to squeeze through it. But the door was there no longer, it had been blown out. Yet, since I suppose my mind has a tendency to only see what it wants to, what is familiar, when I looked down beside the washing machine I saw the door intact. Its light blue paint still glistening with a glaze of spilt detergent; its handle, small and protruding like a wart on an old man's cheek, still poking out, calling, and begging to be gripped by human hands. But my ideal vision was jumbled and kicked away as I watched Lee get down on all fours and begin crawling through the opening and into the next room.

"Jesus!" Lee cried once he had fully made his way across the threshold into what seemed to me to be an entirely different world, a darker one. I stood wide-eyed on the other side of the wall; the intrigue shot through me so intensely upon hearing his gasp that I practically dropped to my knees and dove through the tiny door within a second of him having made it.

There, with our lights streaming phantasmagoric scenes across the crumbling bricks and disfigured piping, Lee appeared before me, crouching, arms stretched out in a state of frozen amazement, of utter disbelief. We were in a sort of crater. There had been an explosion here, too. The floor was destroyed and sunken in a good three feet. Lee knelt there in the center of it, and I watched as he began to shudder; the indentations of his spine quivered beneath his sweat-soaked T-shirt.

"They're dead!" he cried. "They've been incinerated, man! Flesh and body stripped away, nothing left but lanky bones!"

"What are you talking about?" I asked, confused as to why he would make such an announcement. "They were taken away in stretchers, and put into the back of an ambulance; we both saw it!"

"Then explain this!" he shouted, while I hesitatively inched my way to his side and looked down, down to where his light flooded the smoldering earth beneath in a pool of yellow luminance. There, matted in the black dirt of a menacing and crumbling basement room, was the outline of a human body, saturated into the exposed soil once concealed beneath a layer of century-old concrete.

"Who else could it be but one of them?" Lee said, a crazed and pale look on his face, his hands trembling at his sides.

I bent down to study the body with a closer, more scrutinizing eye. I shined my flashlight directly on its face. It was void of any hint of flesh, its sockets were empty, filled in with dirt. This led me to narrow things down to but two conclusions: either this man had been incinerated, as Lee previously assumed, or—which I considered to be the more likely explanation—this was a person who had been dead for many, many years, and had been exposed when the blast tore up the floor and whatever lay beneath it; though, if that was the case, I wondered how it had not been found until now.

And as we stared at this seemingly lifeless creature, and as Lee began to brush the dust and grime away from its subtle outline, a quite peculiar thing happened… it began to glow, the body, that is. It sort of twinkled when we flashed our lights upon it, like a cave of shimmering crystals floodlit in the burn of gas lanterns. Then, as realization hit me, I lost my sense of balance; we turned and faced each other, mouths ajar, eyes wide in staggering disbelief. This was no ordinary person, no typical rotted corpse. No, before us was something never before seen, something remarkable! I traced the spinal column and ribcage slowly with my hand. The bones were slick and icy, as hard as steel, and certainly not what I expected. There before us—in the cellar of a rundown pizza parlor, reflecting spectacularly in the pupils of my eyes—were skeletal remains, those of a man made of solid gold. Lee fell back into the dirt, staring up unresponsively at the leaking web of pipes that scuttled across the ceiling, lifeless like the dead skeleton of a common man, and not like those of divine origin. It was the sheer fact that we knew this was something much, much more than a mere pile of bones that caused him and I to go completely limp, to collapse onto our backs as pacified and still as the somber night itself.

The bones were radiant, like the Buddha in his hour of enlightenment; and with that shinning treasure of a skeleton seeming to cast a comforting spell upon us, Lee and I sunk into the chalky soil, and after a time, quite simply fell asleep. There I dreamt of vast oceans, and of the wreckage of rampant storms. I dreamt of sailing ships on choppy waters, and the black stillness, the expansive emptiness of the unconscious, knowing that that is where we must all go to when we die… it had to be. And I thought of that man, the Being.

Sometime in the middle of the night I roused from my seemingly endless reel of dreams. I was face-down in the asphyxiating dust and gravel that was my bed. I sat up and wiped the dirt from off of my face, spitting it from my mouth and lips. Though in a considerable stupor, I did happen to notice the fact that we were still in the basement of Malzaro's; and Lee just happened to be sprawled out asleep next to me, cradling the golden chest of a dead man, and resting his head across a pair of glistening shoulders. I saw all this, stared into the seemingly lifeless eyes of that beaming skull, and was transfixed. Like the houses on my street, the man's bones began to hum, and then a circle of energy, a green halo of subtle light, began to swell around him. As it spun, my mind began to bubble, to tremble as if with a seizure; I felt the muscles of my brain fizz and pop, like I was having an aneurysm or something, like I was being cooked in a tub of hot oil. Then I found myself asleep. I was no longer in pain or mind-churning discomfort. I was asleep, floating in the afterlife, temporarily visiting my future home; and then a thought came to me. I thought—*yes, here I am in my afterlife... how extraordinary! But that man, that man of gold, who could he have been? And if that question is enough to boggle, just think what this man's afterlife must be like!*

Morning settled in gradually; the sun peaked through the cracks in the ceiling, and a blue glow creeped in wearily through the door from Alice and Wonderland. Beside me Lee was still wrapped tight around the Being. That heavenly sleepiness began to weigh itself down upon me once again, but before it succeeding in doing so, my ears began to buzz with the audible sounds of chatter, of human vocalization. I fought myself back into alertness, turned over and shook Lee until he woke, swatting at me furiously with open hands once he had, and shouting gibberish.

Then, as I clasped my hand across his mouth, the sounds of voices grew louder, and closer, and closer still. They continued until I saw through the opening of the tiny door shadows moving across the debris-heavy surface and blackened walls of the distant room. "In here," I heard one of the voices call to another much lower voice mumbling to himself from somewhere off nearby.

What I knew would happen next caused a piece of me to fracture, and passionately long for the preservation of not just ourselves, but of this metalized man as well. I knew it was the cops. I didn't know what cops exactly, but I knew it was at least someone with the power to take us away, to lock us up. I pounced over Lee, who was staring at the door frightened from the approaching inevitable, and took hold of the man's skull. In my palms it stimulated my entire existence, it reverberated and communicated with me through its intense releasing of self-energy and imposing greatness. My mind began to simmer and bubble once again, but still I held it firm; and hearing the intrusions of the law starting up behind me, broke free the smooth, golden jaw bone of the skeleton's head, tucked it quickly into a pocket, and then zippered it shut.

In the tiny doorway, a gangly man in a dark green suit, now caked in ashes and dirt, grinned at us hauntingly from the other side. It was one of Lime's boys, and he was a twisted fella. He stared us down from that picture-framed image of his head in the doorway, cheeks smeared black with soot, eyes as pale blue as those of the blind. "Come e're," he said, inching his finger in our direction, smiling ghoulishly as spittle oozed down his lower lip and ripples of smoke like that of a woman with long white hair blowing in the wind slowly rose up around his body.

Lee kicked away and clawed towards the Being, lying within arm's reach in the filth beside him. That's when the fella in the doorway entered the room. He snuck in, gun drawn, knees bent and heels lifted off the ground, standing lightly on his toes, twirling his flashlight loosely in the air, and acting completely demented. *He's going to kill me,* I thought. *This guy is going to shoot us down right here, right now, and probably get away with it!*

But somewhere inside me I knew that Lime wouldn't let that happen. By no means did I believe he liked us, or cared for our wellbeing even in the slightest. I did believe, however, that he couldn't possibly let us die, it would be too big a blow to his reputation; he wants us for himself, and I had a feeling he knew we would perhaps return to the scene of the crime. I had known from the start that he wanted to put us away. I could feel it, sensed it when he spoke to me. Now, I can't be sure if that was just because it's true, or if I for some reason just feel that way about all people in a position to legally fuck me and my life into something not worth living. Yes, that's the true fear, the true emotion I feel when I think about getting arrested, or meeting with the police, the idea that they can make my life no longer worth living. That is my all-time greatest fear. And it is for that reason I suppose I'll never know why I sensed those spiteful feelings.

Out of options, all I could do was hope that this time around my life would be spared, and I watched as the rouge officer stepped his way towards me, comically, tauntingly. He ran his cold hands up my shirt and across my shoulders, down my back and then grasped my hands and wrists, which he had instructed me to release to his control. My bloody rag of a shirt fell to the ground, painfully exposing my damp wound to the desiccated air. He cuffed me, kissed me on the cheek, and then rammed the butt of his industrial-grade flashlight into my stomach. I dropped to the floor and smacked my head on the large pelvis bone of the golden man. I was engulfed in darkness and thrown into immediate afterlife, and by that I mean that I had been knocked out.

I awoke in a hospital bed, my hands cuffed to the railing, a pale blue blanket covered my body. I tore the sheets off and jumped to my feet. I was robed in hospital white and barefoot, bandages wrapped snug around my head and various other wounds throughout my body. Hunched over due to the restraints put on my hands, I studied the room for a way out. With little to see, I focused in on a lone window, its shutters were on the inside and they were pulled back to let the sun in; the glass was thick and old, and the wood around it was overly detailed, indicative with the markings of a previous century. But I couldn't get to it; I couldn't get anywhere for as long as I was chained to this bed. Then I heard the door open, and for a while it was almost impossible for me to get myself to look at who was there, who was stepping closer and closer to me from across the room. Each footstep touching the surface of the cold hospital floors, over the lozenges and triangles shaped into the icy vinyl, sent me to further and further retreat from the situation mentally. I stood there over the bed, face pressed against the headboard, making an obvious effort to not acknowledge the man at all. I must have looked like a cowardly fool—I sure acted like one! But really, who can keep a calm front in a situation such as mine? The thing that really had me though, was the fact that I had no idea where the hospital staff put my clothes, and therefore no idea as to where my golden jaw bone might be. I still hoped that it was mine; in fact, I prayed for it. I prayed to God Almighty for it to once again be mine. And at that point, as this intruding presence rested his gloved-hand upon my trembling shoulder, it seems that that was all I could really do.

"Trouble found you once, my boy," the lurking man said cheerfully in my ear, "but now it's up and come back for seconds!" I shrunk my neck so that my chin was about resting on my shoulders; his words played horrendous tricks on me inside my mind. "Look at me dammit!" he shouted and stamped his foot on the ground; I could feel his hatred burning on his sour breath. He grabbed my face, forcefully cocking my head in his direction, and yelled for me to open my eyes. "Open your eyes! Open your eyes and see me!" he said. But I held them shut.

"I'd rather you kill me where I stand" I screamed. "I'd rather you kill me a thousand times over than have to look at you now!"

But I did. Though God knows I didn't want to, I opened my eyes. And who do you think I saw? ...Who else but Detective Lime, that vengeful bastard. He was in his secretly casual office attire and dress shoes, gun on the hip, and bullet proof vest strapped across his upper body beneath a red button-down shirt, as if he was at any minute about to step into a raging battle. He retreated his arms and studied me calmly, searched me down with dark eyes, and smiled a crooked grin. His mustache was the only indicator to what his expression may have conveyed. He had practically no eye brows and no lips; they were thin and pink and about a centimeter thick in visible appearance. But the stache was easy to read. It made the smirks and smiles and frowns and sneers as completely, if not more, distinguishable than those of his own mouth.

Identifying this peculiar feature in him led me to think of Cameron, and his undersized nose; and I began to feel rather sorry. I had let him down, I thought. I had let his restaurant fall to pieces. Then I wondered whether or not he had even been contacted yet. He was on another continent, after all; and even when he was on the same continent, he was still difficult to get ahold of. He didn't even leave me with a cell phone number to call him on; and it wasn't until now that I thought about that fact as being something to consider suspicious or irresponsible. There, staring at the white hospital floor, while Lime stared at me from beside the bed, I wondered whether or not I would ever see him again, or his kindly wife and her boisterous tattoo. God, I sure hoped that I didn't. Can you imagine how intense the confrontation would be? But until the day I did, I knew I'd always be consumed with recurring waves of anxiety, a fear skin-deep persisting on until our eventual and seemingly inevitable exchange of contact.

Lime backed away from me and made off across the room. First he went and closed the door, then he turned around and closed the shutter of my lone window, my one access of escape. He seemed to have known it, too. He smiled large in my direction once he had done so, took off his gloves, and told me to have a seat on the bed. I did, and asked if he was here to arrest me. He told me he wasn't. His wristwatch shimmered in the florescent lights of my sterile room as he reached out and took hold of one of my chained hands.

"Look," he said, "I'm going to take the cuffs off you now, but I don't want you to go thinkin' it's cuz I like you, or believe you're innocent. I can see through you like a screen door, don't think I can't! But it seems like there is more to this whole fiasco than we had originally thought."

"You're right," I exclaimed. "You're absolutely right!"

Suddenly I was ecstatic, suddenly all my troubles were swept away and I was left triumphant.

"So, Mr. Lime," I said with optimism coursing through my veins, "what happens from here?"

"Detective," he replied, clearly asserting his desire to be address by his profession. "And what happens from here, well, that's up to you. But I can tell you this much—in about five minutes' time you'll go out there, onto those steps, and talk to the people. Go out there and answer any questions for the media, tell them what you've seen. The city's going nuts right now, completely captivated by the occurrences of last night and this morning. Seems you and your friend found something of extensive value down in that basement. So live it up, boy, cuz I know it's all fake! It's only a matter of time before you're exposed as the fraud you are. It's only a matter of time…"

As he unchained me from the bed, I got up, and in a high and uncharacteristically prideful gesture, reached out my hand for it to be shaken. He ignored it, put his hand on his hip instead, and slowly moved it over to the nozzle of a can of mace clipped onto his belt. He watched my eyes follow as he softly rested his fingers upon it, and made damn sure that I saw what he was doing. Then he stopped, stood up quickly, kicked the bed back against the wall in a violent convulsion of defeated rage, and left the room without looking back. A few moments later (though less dramatically) I did the same, and made my way down the lengthy, pastel hallways of the medical center outside onto the spacious landing of the medical office building before the descending flight of stairs, in the adhesive balminess of summertime air, and at the attention of a crowd of people some ten thousand strong. Their presence alone vibrated the earth; their voices swarmed the world in crescendos of atonal harmonies and scattering banter. The bleached sunlight crashed down upon the out of doors and everything there for me to behold. It shot across the hoods of parked cars, the bald scalps of men in the crowd, and the jewelry of their wives, of their daughters. Nearby a podium was set up for me, resting on a brown square of carpet on the ledge at the top of the steps. The building was timeworn and dreary, having been converted from an old public library; and beneath the portico of this modern fabrication of a classical structure—like the courthouses and government buildings of Washington, or Jefferson's Monticello—I leaned up against one of the massive ionic columns and prepared myself for what was to come. The multitudes quieted as I approached the carpeted platform and the awaiting lectern, microphone-equipped, ready for me to man it like a pilot does a plane, or a captain to a sailing ship, masts trembling overhead, waves crashing all around for miles and miles into uncharted distances.

Finally, as I stood there before it, thinking of questions that might possibly be asked, a thousand mouths began to shout, and I hadn't a clue as to whose I should answer first. Then to my rescue came a man, running up the steps from the crowd of reporters and news anchors below, and with a wide smile, stopped beside me at the podium.

"Just hold on, son," he said, his blue flannel shirt rustling at its collar, gazing down at me from what appeared to be a six-and-a-half-foot stature. "I've got a microphone here, ya see? I'll give it to these reporters down there to pass round themselves. If things get heated or out-of-hand, I'll step right in; don't you worry!"

He then took off down the steps, and handed the microphone to a stunning girl in the first row with long blonde hair, ears pierced with vibrant gems, holding a pad of written questions loosely in her delicate hand. It dangled at her side, hovering by her thighs and the grey fabrics of her skirt, causing waves of lustful, trance-like temptations to take hold of me. She asked a question, maybe two, but I never heard any of it. When she quieted to wait for my response, and when it never came, the humiliation drove me back into my right mind, and I had to ask her to repeat herself. People laughed; shame blushed red across my cheeks; and then I looked down to see that I was still in a hospital gown, and that I looked like a mental patient.

"What did you find in that basement room?" the woman repeated with a slight tone of annoyance.

"A body made of solid gold," I replied, as grand visions of our discovery played out unconsciously before my eyes.

"And just how did you manage to come across this *body of solid gold?*"

"As we entered the connecting room in the laundry," I explained, "the man was simply lying in the rubble. There had been an explosion, as you all know, and he had been thrown up from underneath the floor during the blast—but we thought it was a co-worker at first!"

"*He,*" she said, with an attitude of resentment slowly creeping towards the surface, perhaps in the effort to entice sexist beliefs from me, thus gathering a juicier story.

"Or *she*, whatever," I replied, and the crowd made a low grumble, as if pondering my response—either in a positive or negative way, but as to which I'm not quite sure. Either way, it caused me no harm. I answered a few more questions of a similar nature, by reporters of a similar character, and then was ushered off the landing and back into the hospital by the man who had passed around the microphone. He had his large hand spread across my back in a guiding presence as we walked inside and down the hall into a tidy office. From there, sitting in a reclining chair at his desk, I was told what had happened to us after I was so unjustly knocked unconscious by the brutalizing actions of Detective Lime, and his crooked officers in particular.

Mr. Frankford—or Mr. Frank, for short—was the name of the man in whose office I now sat. He offered me a glass bowl of pink mints; I accepted, and was allowed to cradle the bowl in my lap, to eat as many as I wished. "So," he said, "I'm sure you're beyond curious as to what has happened, huh?"

"Frankly, Mr. Frank," I said smiling, chewing mints rather carelessly, and noticing as wet pieces of them fell down from my mouth and onto my shirt, "I really would like to know where my clothing from last night has been taken. I sure would hate to lose whatever was left in my pockets."

At this statement, Mr. Frankford gave me a curious look, a look similar to that of a puppy watching humans eat food.

"And what would be in your pockets, son?" he asked, raising a slender eyebrow of inquisitiveness. "Could it have been, perhaps, a golden jaw bone?"

"Yes!" I shouted, rising from the chair suddenly, allowing the bowl of candies to splatter across the floor. "Yes, where is it?!" I begged; I clawed at his clothing, and pleaded like a dying man into his wavering arms.

"Sit! Sit down for Christ's sake! You're making a scene," he said, clamping his hand down upon mine and onto the cold wooden desk. "You are sane, aren't you now?"

"I am!" I insisted. "Believe me, sir, I am!"

"Good, then sit down, and let us talk. You must know, kid, that what you found, it doesn't belong to you. Those remains you so carelessly shoved into your pockets aren't the possessions of any one man; this thing you found—this person—it belongs to the world, you see? It is for the museums, for the eyes and enjoyment of families and kids on fieldtrips, for nosy professors to study, and historians, and archeologists, and theologians. This man, this golden man! God, can you just imagine it!—who he was, who he could have been?"

"I found him," I said coldly, my body stiffening with passion and entitled desires. "I want to be with him. He's a part of me now, I can feel it; I felt it in that basement, when I held his bones, and I feel it now. He is calling for me, and I need to be there!"

"What on earth do you plan to do with him, sit him up in an armchair in your living room as a conversation piece? Listen, you won't be thrown to the side," he said, "I assure you. You'll be the face of this whole thing if you want… the living face, at least. We'll get you in touch with the governor; I know he's dying to speak to you. They'll put you on the talk show circuit, kid! You'll be a sensation!"

"No," I said, "it won't do. Those bones, that's what I need now more than anything, it's what I've always needed." I didn't want fame, I told him, I wanted gold.

—⁓—

As I sat in Mr. Frank's office, pleading for what I most desired, Lee was standing on the steps of the medical office building, behind the microphone-equipped podium, relishing the attention, and answering questions with the zeal of a passionate preacher.

"Why were you two in the basement that night?" he was asked by the same blonde-haired woman in the front row.

"Because we knew it would be a rush!" Lee exclaimed. "We couldn't help but to indulge in a spontaneous plan of immense curiosity. We hadn't a clue what we would find, but surely knew that we'd find something!"

"How is that?" she asked.

"Ever heard of something called intuition?" Lee remarked.

"Are you aware that your companion desecrated these miraculous remains by snatching the jaw bone from its skull and putting it in his pocket?" she asked.

"No," Lee said, only now hearing of this event, having not noticed the occurrence while it unfolded due to immense fear, or an emotion of a similar sort.

"Do you think it was thievery?" another reporter asked.

"No, no way," he said, and was soon thereafter escorted off into the building.

"Well, look who it is!" exclaimed Mr. Frankford as Lee, directed by hospital staff, sluggishly made his way into the office, rubbing his eyes, pained due to the flashes of a thousand cameras exploding from the crowd outside as he stood before them.

"Have a seat next to your friend, why don't ya? We've got some matters to discuss. First off," he said, "I want to begin by telling you how lucky you are." I understood that he was talking to me now, and me only. He stared at me in a very stern, very serious way. "You're lucky that the city isn't pressing charges on you for a long list of offences—trespassing, for one, and tampering with a secured scene of a potentially criminal investigation, for two! Don't you know how fucked you guys could have been?"

"That's good," I said, not caring in the slightest, only thinking of those shimmering bones and that gilt skull. All I wanted was to get back my clothing from the night before. I realized that even though they had surely been searched, and the jaw bone had been found, there was yet to be mention of a golden tooth, and I wondered if it still remained, still lying undetected for me to once again possess. Oh, how strange, the things we covet! I would have walked barefoot through expansive lakes of fire, and meadows shrouded in sheets of broken glass, to once again clench what I so desired. After we found the Being, I knew that the tooth wasn't from one of my co-workers' mouths, it was the man's; I sensed it in my bones and in my blood; and I was enthralled to know that now it was mine. It was the only potentially lasting connection I had between myself and this enchanted soul. Every time I thought of the glowing image of that skull, and the dim radiance of its empty sockets, its pointed zygomatic bones, I yearned to be lying there in that basement, lounging on a cleft of rubble, cradling those bones in my arms like a mother does a sleeping child, forever and always. It was sickness in motion, if I had ever seen it: an intruding virus of greed and longing, immense yearning, unbreakable only until reunited again with what it was I so fervently sought; an ailment that lingered still even through the most rapid, distracting courses of movement and motions.

Around that fake wooden desk, Mr. Frankford (whom we shall now simply refer to as Mr. Frank, for reasons of indolence) began to reveal to us his secrets, the secrets of our night:

"Lime and his gang were cruising around in an unmarked van," he said, "stocked with computers and assault rifles, and cabinets stuffed with thick files of information on wanted people. At around two o'clock in the morning, the posse drove past the smoldering scene of the crime to perhaps snoop around. They've got no clue you guys are inside, at this point. Anyway, of course the first place they're going to go upon entering is the kitchen, and then down into the basement. It's probable that they had the same atrocious curiosity as the two of you."

Mr. Frank then sat up in his chair, after beginning his history lesson; but as to why he stopped speaking escapes me. He seemed to have been trying to search for something on his person or in his desk. He patted himself down and opened the single draw in front of him, threw aside a handful of paperclips and erasers, then apologized for his actions; he was urged pressingly by the two of us to continue speaking.

"Alright" he said; "I suppose I was still going to, just had to stop for a second to… never mind. So, you see," he started, "as that fella Briggs—the guy who knocked you out—stepped into the laundry room, he hears mumblings and whispers, and shit that probably scared the hell out of him, though he won't admit it. He stepped into the attached room and, so he stated, saw you two trembling in the dirt, grasping to something lying on the ground in between. Once you had been cuffed and then assaulted, he found the sight of Lee's frantic eyes staring up at him. He had looped his arm into the man's golden ribcage and was in hysterics, so he stated. Mr. Briggs believed Lee was insane, and was actually trying to cram his entire body into the tiny, hollow shell created by the skeleton's ribcage and breast plate, as if he could escape the terror of intrusion and separation from this cherished framework of shimmering bones by simply jumping right into them, and thus becoming them.

"It gets me to thinking, all this commotion here. I thought, is not the man who first struck gold responsible for the original miasma of our societies, of our very lives? Was this Being a plague, or was he a gift from God?" he said, standing up and slowly walking his way around the room with his hands in his pockets. "Is it not expected to cling to a treasure so great, once in a person's grasps, and try to never let go? Is it really so strange for fortunes to have such an overwhelming impact on the mind as it did in this situation? I think not, and seemingly, too, neither does the city. This, my friends, is quite good news for you; and I think you know why.

"I'll explain to you now the reason for our city and our people's open acceptance and tolerance of your actions. They—the people, especially the eccentric ones—are praising you guys as great explorers, great discoverers. It's really something, I must say. It started early this morning, about five thirty. The state archeologist had been called out to the site, and when he stepped down into that crater to examine the scene, he was fucking baffled! I saw him myself; he was a stocky man with a black briefcase, acting annoyed, as if he had had his time wasted by coming here!"

Mr. Frank broke into a tremendous laughter at this and his cheeks began to redden. "The guy's face," he said, "when I finally saw him leaving the site—oh, God! It was as pale as a cloud! He was so indecisive and stunned by what he had seen down there, he didn't know what he should begin to do next. He ran to a partner, a man more composed at the moment than himself, and had him on the phone with another research team within a minute. About an hour later, a gang of scientists, wrapped head to toe in lime-green biohazard suits, carrying between them a stretcher and a chest of high-tech implements and archeological necessities like brushes and shovels, arrived in front of Malzaro's. But this was to be no dusting off of a trilobite, no! Nor some digging up of a forgotten mammoth's tusk. This was *it*—what this man and his team of researchers had been waiting for their entire lives!

"It seems to me—by your reactions and by the reactions and unbinding enthusiasm of those scientists—that whomever comes into contact with this man, this woman, this god, whatever *it* may be, an instant love and attachment to this creature is almost guaranteed. Do you think so?"

Lee said yes, but I was still locked up inside a prison of yearning and desire too great to portray, let alone be set free of, or answer a simple question while still stuck inside. I stated again to Mr. Frank my immense need to see the man again, as well as reviving the topic of regaining my clothing.

"Surely," he said, though in a somewhat worried fashion. "You can have your clothes, and I will make an appointment for the two of you to speak with the researchers, see the specimen, and, sadly, to speak to some lawyers, too. There is, I don't doubt, much profitability, as well as risk, still yet to undertake in your lives now that this event has unfolded, claiming you two as its main culprits."

"Then let us go," I said, "I've heard enough."

"So you have…" Mr. Frank sighed. "I'll make some calls and come get you guys in an hour. Go back to your room down the hall, you're clothes are there in a box under the bed. In fact, they've been there the whole time, I believe. You do remember where your room is, don't you?"

But before I could assure him that I did, I was out the door and on my way to the rescue of my precious golden tooth. Lee followed quickly behind me. It seems I may have been running, and thus making it hard for him to keep up, as well as frightening a number of nurses and patients alike while sprinting wildly to my destination.

Upon entering, the small rectangular box was lying there on the ground before me, uncovered now by the bed that Lime had earlier kicked across the room. I dropped to my knees and placed my hands on the sides of the lid. I felt it for a moment, the content within. Through the cardboard I felt the ubiquitous magic of the Being; a gentle flow of current was surely emitting from within, and I knew that it still remained! I tore off the lid and dug down to my pants; I opened the zippered pocket and in the next instant pulled out the golden molar, the Holy Grail as far as I was concerned; and I never imagined that I would one day experience such good fortune, such undeniable luck. Lee was astounded, completely speechless at what he saw, and ran up to put his face right in front of it, so as to examine it with flawless accuracy.

"It's the man's, isn't it?" he said.

"It is," I told him, and then I put it away quickly into the pocket, and got up to get dressed.

Lee, who had already clothed himself in something other than unflattering hospital attire, left the room. I felt humiliated that I had been led out onto a stage in these clothes, and not what I had worn last night, or anything decent, for that matter! If Lime would have only told me that my things were there under the bed, it sure would have saved me a lot of embarrassment and distress. But how could I have expected such curtsey from a man like that? It would have been almost just as big a miracle as having discovered those consecrated bones in the rubble of that stinking basement, I suppose, if he had opened his mouth to speak anything but hostile words to me. Now that I had my tooth however, I would be the one on the power trip, I would have the last laugh. Oh, I couldn't wait for what the future held now! Then an idea came to me, one whose purpose was to keep me as close to that golden man as one could possibly become. Letting my flimsy white gown fall to the floor, I stood there naked in the room, laughing sickly to myself. By the end of the week, I thought, I'd be just as golden as He is.

In an hour's time, when Mr. Frank came back to get us, I seemed to have been fairly contented, and no longer the panicking madman I was while sitting in his office. Next to him in the doorway was a man who introduced himself as Prof. Schwartz, instructor of geological sciences, and instructor of theologies at Chicago State, and an adroit conservative as well as restorative archeologist of ancient sites. He was a normal-looking man, not a wiz professor sort of character like one might have expected. He was cool and straightforward. But from the looks of him—from his tennis shoes and khaki shorts, up to his leather belt and the five thousand dollar Rolex that latched around his wrist—I'd say he was a man not entirely sure of how to present himself. On the one hand, he was an intelligent, well-off educator at a renowned university; on the other, he was probably just a normal guy like the rest, and enjoyed watching television, going swimming, drinking beer, and being lethargic, as many people, myself included, surely do. He had thin white hair that came down over his cheeks like sideburns that met in the middle to form a mustache and short beard, similar to the hair styles of nineteenth century southern gentlemen.

"No time to waste," he said pressingly, stepping into the room with an air of urgent business and, walking over and lowering the railings, sat us down on the bed. "So what do you want to do first—see the body, or know the facts?"

"Facts," we told him.

It was at this moment in between that I sensed the shiver of anticipation that obviously had begun affecting Lee. He couldn't sit still—in front of these mem, in this sort of atmosphere—without squirming and shifting his eyebrows, and making impulsive tightening motions of the face; wrinkling the skin on his forehead into fleshy rows, one on top of the other, rising like a pyramid until reaching his hairline and then dispersing.

"Lee, calm down," I said.

"Okay! Okay!" he shouted, and the professor looked deeply concerned.

"Perhaps this isn't a good time?" he asked.

"No!" I averred, and stood up from my seat on the bed. "No, he's fine; aren't you?"

"Yeah, I'm fine," he mumbled, reaching out his hand as Mr. Frank made his way over with a glass of water.

"Alright," said Prof. Schwartz, "But you'd better sit on back down, kid; at least, I would if I were you."

———

So on the bed we sat, and Mr. Frank dragged two folding metal chairs into the room, and they seated themselves across from us. And as they did so, my mind had progressively arose, shifting between the obviously intriguing confrontation unfolding before me and the screams of dying patients, and sprinting, panicking nurses dashing by down the hall, just over my shoulder. There was an odious chill coming from the open door and into the room. It made the hair on the right side of my body stand up and quiver. Then something in my mind told me to snap out of it, and I turned my head back towards Prof. Schwartz, who had already begun talking, and revealing to us "the facts."

"The facts," he said as he rose from the chair, "are few but greatly definitive." He stepped around the room a bit and stood with his back to us, dreamily gazing at a hovering June bug out the now-reopened window with its green foliage delineating it beautifully from the plant outside.

"What we know is this," he started again, walking back over to where we sat by the bed. "Early this morning, one of our scientists received the detached jaw bone of the skeleton—the one I hear you apparently stole. Upon studying the specimen, he discovered that the bones were that of a male. We can tell this thanks to the width of his pelvic girdle, as well as the formations of the man's teeth. This could have been detected with the teeth attached to the maxilla, but this particular scientist didn't have access, at that very moment, or before-hand, to examine the bones as a whole. Another team of research-ers, with a different agenda, had been working on the remains at that time—me and my colleagues, that is.

"What we found, I must say, is quite amazing. You see, these bones weren't molded or smelted into what they are now, they were formed, grown! Just as a diamond grows in the earth, or a baby inside a mother's womb; these bones grew! It's—he's—uh—real; what I'm trying to say is—uh—this may have been a living thing. And if that's the case, could you just imagine? If *he* was an ordinary guy like you or me, could you imagine? There'd probably be hundreds of golden skeletons lying in cemeteries all across the country, across the globe! Forever secreted from our eyes in their rotting caskets! Our knowl-edge of what is few and far between has expanded, and the scarce seem not to be so depleted after all; and it sort of makes you think: what price must I pay—must we all pay—for our own existence? What does it mean to be human; and who are we to idolize now? Is this God, or a god? Was this man a revolutionary force in our world's his-tory? Or, perhaps he hadn't a clue as to who he was, and worked in a factory or a restaurant, had a wife and kids, an address, a name. What are we to make of this then? Would it still be so special, so divine? Or would it just be an outrageous, yet wondrous occurrence? Will our society hold him to the standard of an immortal, a sacred vessel, or will they treat him as they did, say, the Elephant Man, and put his bones on display in a museum, and parade them around like some sort of freak show?"

"Let's not take this too far, boys," Mr. Frank interjected, addressing all, but mainly Lee and I. "Divine? Come on now; I don't want you going off the rails here thinking you've found an angel, or something like that. As of now it's but golden bones, metal! Let's not slew reality here with animism and stupidity."

"Can't you see, mister," said Prof. Schwartz in a firm and matter-of-fact way, "what we got here is like nothing else anyone has ever seen. And unless we all decide to start digging up graveyards, we'll probably never see anything like this again. It's not man-made, it is earth-made, just like a man! It's some kind of magic, it's… it's like bullion, but better!"

We all sat silent for a while, and so did the professor, who had stood back up and returned to his view by the window. Standing there, with his hands in his pockets, he said, "That's about all the facts we have; want to come see for yourselves?"

You can be sure that we did. After a short ride in a black, window-tinted van, Schwartz took us to a facility a few miles away, where they were storing the Being. We got to see those bones lying anatomically correct on a steel table, the kinds of tables they use to prop up corpses in a morgue for autopsies and embalming. There I studied him, gazed at those limbs one by one. Every finger, every rib bone, examined, just like the raindrops on my street when I was young. I looked into his face, and saw that a single tooth was indeed missing from the Being's otherwise unbroken smile. It was the only one, too. The skull was shining with the glow of a million fires; and a shimmer of white light, like that off the tip of a piercing sword, flickered in its sockets; and I knew that he had seen me, had gazed upon me with his own eyes, though they were not there. But I was sure that he had, and with that knowledge I felt triumphant, special, and chosen. I felt as would a mother the first time she gets to hold her newborn child; I felt immortal. So let us always trust in what our instinctual senses tell us we feel, for it is the most accurate choice, although not necessarily the safest, the wisest, or the boldest. But still, despite all the nots, it is the truest, most genuine, in all its capacities. Besides, it is royally unsafe to be safe all the time. In the moment, your instincts are right, even if the resulted actions come back to haunt you in the future. Yes, even if it kills you, your instincts are always right.

Before I could enjoy our spell together, he was ushered off into another lab for tests, and our time was up. The Professor shook our hands, and we walked out to where a driver was waiting to take us back to the hospital. As we departed, the Professor looked at Lee and I, stopped us, and said, "Guys, I really can't explain to you what it is you've found, let alone how important it is; but I think you two know that about as well as I do. Don't let *Him* go to your head, you understand? I've seen many men strike their fortunes, only for it to sink them down to the depths like a concrete shoe. Be smart; listen to what I, an old, ignorant professor, tells you. Okay?

God only knew if we would.

I stayed at the hospital for another few hours after returning, signing release papers, and filling out information statements for Detective Lime. Around nine o'clock at night, my parents, yet to be addressed, and worried semi-sick, picked me up and took me home.

After a long and unpleasant drive, we arrived at my house. Once our car had driven into the garage, causing the light to darken, and making it feel like the room was closing in on me, I closed my eyes and felt the ravages of utter exhaustion ripping at my mind, and the embarrassment of my parents' presence. The tension between us was more than just uncomfortably noticeably, it was practically unbearable. My dad, fuming, and with cheeks reddened by riled nerves and diminishing patience, left the car and slammed the door behind him; my mother did the same, but more gently. They weren't necessarily mad at me, they were, however, in awe of me, I think. It was hard for them to believe what they were hearing, so they expelled those emotions by acting upset. That morning they had watched the unfolding events of our discovery play out on the cable news channel, and had no idea that their son was involved. The frustration came from the fact that the restaurant I worked at had had an explosion, a damn near lethal one, and that I hadn't been thoughtful enough to come home and assure them that I was indeed safe; and also because we had snuck back into the building— a stunt my dad called "recklessly and irresponsibly jeopardizing to my otherwise hopeful future."

I got out of the car last, once everyone had made their way inside; and at the scent of gasoline and musty surroundings, grass clippings in paper lawn bags, and old cigar smoke that subtly filled the air around me, I sighed, and it felt like home: the stenches, the tensions, the remorse. It filled my soul with familiarities that were easy to grasp, and oddly comforting, though not necessarily preferable.

That next morning I was summoned to the breakfast table. There I had a lengthy discussion with my parents, one that was basically the same summary of events as had been revealed to you. Around cups of ripe orange juice, the tartly-sweet taste of citrus, and the feeling of its acidity whirling in my gut, my mother and father sat astonished across from me while I spoke. Our relationship—though never a rocky one—hasn't been quite the same since, I have to admit. They started acting differently towards me. They got quiet when I walked into the room. They tended to refrain from conversation when I was around; and I could sense that I made my mother uncomfortable. As the young man I was then, it was difficult for me to understand why. I couldn't come to terms with their hastiness, their apparent resentment, or something of the sort. Nowadays, however, I've learned to be more open-minded about it; if I were in their shoes, it would have been a slightly life-altering occurrence, too. And perhaps it was I who had changed the most, and that that modification in me is what brought about and strengthened the change in them. All in all, we grew apart. They had another child, anyway. I have a sister, and at the time she would have been about five; I was twenty-two. They had a whole future ahead of them that didn't involve me. But I knew I had to make something of myself, just like we all must try to do when we are young, but grown. I took their change in behavior towards me with the utmost compassion and tolerance, and still do; though, I feel badly about it sometimes.

Now that's enough about my parents, it is too morbid. They are dear to me, but hardly do they play a role in this tale. So of them we will depart, but shall give to them our prayers, wherever they may be.

———

In better days, way back when I was a cool kid, and everyone I knew was still alive, I had found my first love in a girl. We would play childish games together, and lay, and hold each other in our arms, snug in a hammock beneath a drooping tree in my backyard. We'd lay there, watching all the lights in the night sky, and try to decide: is it a star or is it a man… or is it both? A game like that, in relation to the story here being told, is almost a parallel example of what my life became. After finding the Being, everyone I saw, and passed on the street, suddenly was a lot more interesting than they had ever been before, especially strangers. I'd walk down whole city blocks and gaze into the faces of a thousand souls, all making their way to some destination, all strangers. I would contemplate their immortality. I would attempt to see what was beneath the flesh, to where, perhaps, another golden man stood, undetected before me. It turned into a childish game—life, and every day interaction, that is. Lee and I, we'd play it whenever we'd find ourselves walking around together in public or in town. He'd say, "Him, over there, he's real funny-looking; I bet he's an alien, I bet he's got golden bones!" But never knowing for sure if our predictions were accurate or futile quickly brought the game into retirement; with no satisfaction from our wonderings, we soon lost interest. All things completely unknown, despite their alluringness, would never be as fantastic to me as things newly discovered but still not understood.

After all was said and done, as I had suspected, my life was forever altered, forever improved. I finally landed a career. The discovery had granted me fame, and I latched to it, clung to it, like moths around a spotlight. I took on the talk show circuit and the local news channels. I eventually molded myself into a public speaker, and throughout my late-twenties and into my mid-thirties, and even early-forties, until my tale had been fully exhausted, I was paid handsomely to travel around the globe to colleges and auditoriums, lecture halls and theaters. I'd give long talks on life, and happiness, and despair, and the Being. I'd tell of wondrous worlds hidden within our own, yet to be discovered, but accessible to all. Then I'd reach my point, a point which was the talk of all those afterwards who had come to see my discussions. I told the people about that thing, that thing that is more of a blessing than a curse, but still tends to take hold of the mind and grip it until it restricts its circulation and leaves it enslaved, that thing that is sometimes quite common later in life. Yes, I'm talking about twisted fucking luck. And that the real ticket to being successful, from what I've seen, is just that. Simple, personal, mediocre happiness can please many, but I know as well as you do that in the back of our minds we long to be admired, acknowledged, praised, and until that time, most of us will never be truly satisfied, truly happy. You can study and study, and work all you want, but just like billions of others, you are likely to go to your graves with the world not even knowing that you were ever out of them. Even the most brilliant of doctors, of scientists, of explorers, often die without widespread recognition; and it's not because they don't deserve it, but more because of a lack of luck, heavily influenced by the sway of a massive, omnipresent society. In a world that allows skinny models and television actors to be praised as royalty and remembered forever, and leaves the struggling writers, and the determined scholars, and the break-back laborers, builders of great cities, to be perpetually lost to the dusts of time, is it all that shocking that such a thing as a worthy legacy is often left ungiven to those in what would seem to be the right shoes, and presented instead to those who are barefoot? No, sigh not, people, for it is the luck of the world, the chance we all take when we set out to explore this forest of life. We shouldn't envy each other or those with better fortune than ours; and this notion of random selection or societal influence should not be a crutch for those in their youth to use when times are hard, and say that they cannot become what it is they want to. Surely, you can do that! We can all be what we want, don't doubt it for a second. The question is, what do you want to be? For me, I wanted anything that granted independence, fulfillment, and at least meager recognition. And Lord, I sure did get what I wanted. And it wasn't for a lack of trying that it had been seemingly left up to luck—my success, that is. But who knows what I would have become if not for the Being. And so, I say to you, people, set out and discover your own Beings, your own luck, your own fortunes! It all lies there for you to hold, for you to take, somewhere in the out of doors. If luck can find you, then dammit, you can find *it* too! It is out there, waiting like a beautiful bird's egg beneath the hedges, or a glowing conch in the sea. We all must do what we can to dive out into the depths of unrestricted consciousness and retrieve those treasures that lay in wait, left for us by the gods.

Happiness is ephemeral, and that's if you ever find it. As I asked of you earlier, in regards to the random selectivity of winners and losers in this life, do not let the following confessions of an old, broken man detour you from your own personal hearts of gold, worlds of gold, dreams of gold, that can only come true if you have the courage enough to chase them. For although it was a great fortune to find the Being, its presence, its actuality, after many years, began to twist, and become twisted, and defiled my existence to the point of reducing my life to a state of stagnant degeneration, and abandoned me in a defected body with nothing but the nostalgic memories of long-departed joys to keep me company throughout what remained of my time alive. Unlike Lee, who aside from relishing in the light of our discovery during earlier years, eventually did still go on to become a chemical engineer, and with his scholarly success, landed himself an ideal spot in the labs of some high-end manufacturing facility operated by the government, a facility that produced vaccines and held new medicine-testing research aimed toward finding cures for diseases—all things in the division of the field that Lee excelled. So, once the hype over our story had calmed, and then was all but forgotten completely, and though I still had made my wealth on the whole deal, I suddenly found myself an old man, alone, with no more appointments scheduled, no offers left on the table to speak at some school or university. My supportive "fans," they didn't care about me, they cared about the Being, and I was the most direct link. One day my well dried up, and I had less than it was possible to imagine, to collect and call my world, left around me. While riding the wave of success, one that lasted many years, I had ignored all those who were genuine in my life, and instead chased those who were fabrications, and nothing more than a walking paycheck, a walking publicity stunt, and a stepping stone to the next leap of successful ventures, all with what seemed to be human faces. They stared up at me smiling as I hopped across their mouths and eyelids, across to the other side, to where my supposed happiness lay. Those golden bones led me to covet and stride to attain all things of luxury and worth, and forget about what it is that most makes a person human. I disregarded the simplicities of life and indulged like a glut into the gourmet tastes and sensations of this world's forbidden fruits. The fact is, the Being left me financially secure, but mentally corroded and chewed down to the bone, a valetudinarian. I'm ill, and lonesome, and prophetic! Oh, how I cannot seem to stop my fanciful prophecies. They've started again, those subtle paranoid flashes of emotion and mistrust, all stemming from a growing suspicion that someone around me is strutting through life with golden bones. The spiritual wonder it evokes in me is quotidian and beyond words. But its existence, soon combined with the sensing of my own mortality seeping through my bones, in the swelling of my sour blood, soon makes my head spin with deliriums and torments of a grotesque nature, invisible, yet performed before my very eyes. For one half of the day I'll be sane, for the other I'll be in horrible agony, and cursing in a feverish mindset. The only thing I can do with myself, in the space of those few precious hours granted to me before my body declines again, is to go outside, go outside and take a walk. No matter how badly it hurts my muscles and stiffens my joints, as long as I'm still alive, and still a person, if nothing else, I am going to walk outside!

With these misfortunes in mind—my envy of my own past, over lost loves, and forbidden happiness—I sometimes start to wonder, nowadays as I can sense the time beginning to slow, and the end nearing its way, I wonder, is it this mysterious sickness, or lack of a satisfactory explanation, let alone a cure, for this sickness, and not so much my long-lost past, that has caused me to be so morbid? From it I have discovered that the Being is a maestro of death, and my body was a canvas for his masterpiece. His work is almost complete; I should know better than anyone. But oh, this mysterious disease!—and though you need not worry, for I am already long dead, the roots of which I shall soon reveal.

———

Here I am now resting on this bench and looking beside myself to where a festering anthill is still in its early stages of creation. The sidewalk is partially engulfed in working insects, and they fester upon it as if it were made of candy. In the crack, where the concrete meets the grass, that's where they are building, that's where the entrance to the colony will be constructed. Inside, one day, a fat queen will birth the next generation of mindless providers, all of whom shall set out scavenging the earth to feed the mouth of a corpulent mother, the sole creator and consumer of their entire world. This is what separates the lawn from the pavement. We can only appreciate it if we can find the decency in ourselves to not step on them or spit a mouthful of water in their direction, thus ravaging the efforts of a futile existence. Yet, as a child I take credit for single-handedly killing the most ants in the country. I fucking massacred ants. Not because I disliked them or feared them, but simply because I was over-bored. Yes, bored to the point of genocidal lunacy, it seems. I don't think I'm demented though. Most kids, from what I've seen and saw growing up, especially boys, kill the shit out of anything they can. It's usually just a phase, and I cannot remember killing anything larger than perhaps a toad— and that was more often than not an accident involving pellet guns or the wheels of a car. If your kids start killing cats and dogs however... they might have quite a future ahead of them, and you might not! This time, while the scurrying masses worked on, I turned a cheek to the creatures below me and let them be in peace to continue to mound the soil into a city and, like we all must try to do, forge the dirt into a home.

Above me I noticed the streetlights flash on one by one. The side door of Malzaro's opened, and I looked ahead to see who it would be that came outside. An old rough arm, followed by the body of an old rough man, soon made his way through the door. It was Cameron, a sorry, bald, aged Cameron. He had ten years on me; I sure hadn't aged well, and he was always keen on drinking and smoking menthol cigarettes, as well as tanning regularly in one of those heated light beds—so I wasn't too surprised when I saw his ghastly figure standing there under the streetlight across the way. He never got to see me there, though I doubt he would have recognized who I was; and he never looked ahead, he just tossed a bag into the *nostril*, shut the gate, and hurried back inside. I caught a few good glimpses of him as he passed. Although squinting my eyes so as to be able to more clearly see from where I sat across the road, my sight was caught on the sudden appearance of the skin on his forearms. It was a color that stood out on the flesh of anyone; it was like worn-out, hardened leather, and the color of a rotten hide once belonging to an animal with formerly white skin and hair, but now defecated and deformed, and reduced to a shade of brown-green—thus was the leper flesh of my old boss, that sorry bastard.

Years ago we finally did make contact with each other, after all had happened and the restaurant was reopened. I saw him once or twice in the court room, after he sued me, along with Mike and Linda, for damages, in which he lost, and was left not far from well-off, after insurance took up most of the costs. I was passing on the street one day to get to the bus stop, and when I got there, I saw beside me, next to the sleeping drunkard who hardly ever left, none other than Cameron and his hoyden wife.

He resented me, so he explained, for capitalizing on what he claimed to be his misfortunes. "Misfortunes!" I said. "How much business has your joint gotten since all this hysteria, since all this discovery has occurred? Tons, I bet! You don't need to tell me; I already know. I can see it through the windows, in the lights of those new flat screen televisions that hang from the walls, and the new chandelier that hangs like a terrific pendulum above the entry. You're doing better than ever!"

"Well, I can thank you for that, I suppose," he said. "You're a little crook though, don't think I'm stupid. As far as I'm concerned, you got damn lucky. And that luck should last you a while, unless you ever find it a good idea to step inside my business again late at night, or anytime, to be sure!"

To be sure! And since I had been fired less than a week after the explosion, when the authorities were finally able to get ahold of Cameron, the night we found the Being was the last time I had ever been back. It's been years since I stepped foot inside Malzaro's; and frankly, I never wanted to return, if only because of the company, and all the memories that would certainly hit me like a riptide to the face as soon as I walked through the door.

My association with Cameron ended that day at the bus stop. Up until now—as I watch him slip through the entry and close the door—I hadn't seen him since. I'll probably never see him again. That's fine. Farewell!

The day had fled like the rabbits and the birds. I had been sitting on that bench for hours, and didn't even notice. Though my body always seems to ache, it is much less severe while motionless, and so I often find myself—even when I'm not sitting on a bench—settling down some place, or in a chair, and there remaining for extended periods of time. As I said, I have hardly a capacity for functional mobility, and once I become comfortable and in one spot, time seems to no longer exist, for I cannot move regardless, and the hours pass as would a marshaling of dry and dusty tumbleweeds in a storm that blows in from across the fields of wheat and vacant dirt roads of the country, all burgeoning towards the rising steps of my home. All I thought about any more was myself, my past, my treasures, and my pain. As the sky darkened overhead, and shadows began to linger around me on the sidewalk and on the walls of the nearby building, I made my way to my feet, and set off back towards my lonely dwelling.

Lying in my bed that night I couldn't sleep, for I was suddenly pondering the arrival of the day that awaited me. Tomorrow was Friday, and I was supposed to have dinner with Lee. My before-bedtime medication had left me numb and contented, and as I rested there in my room—the walls of which were clustered with framed newspaper clippings about me and the Being, and boxes of scarcely worn clothing lining the floor—I could do nothing but watch the red numbers illuminating from my alarm clock tick by, each minute slower than the last.

When morning came, so did the proceedings of my pre-noon rituals. The shakes, the nausea, the racing thoughts and sweat-soaked flesh, the fever and the pain, all came and went within a three to four hour period. Though it was misery, it hardly was out of the ordinary, or even unbearable, for I did it every day, and had been for the last few years since the onset of this mysterious ailment. Nevertheless, I consider myself a strong person, and am able to fight through it all, only because I know that by noon, or around then, my symptoms will go into remission, and not return until that night. In the morning and in the night, that's when it's at its worst; but the space in between, still far from being at a hundred percent, I'm functional, and optimistic about each new day—though my demeanor usually doesn't show it.

When my malady had started to pass, I found myself sitting by the opened window in the front room, anticipating the moment when the remaining spasms and shakes would be fully subsided, and I could be able to more easily continue on with my day. It was then, as I sat there on the couch, that my phone rang, and on the other end it was Lee, wondering if we were still getting together that evening. "Of course!" I exclaimed, and he said he'd pick me up at six. Until he arrived on my driveway in his slick, black Jaguar, I had remained on the couch with bags of ice resting on my knee caps and elbows, my shoulders and my neck. It was the only way to relieve the inflammation in my joints; and without it, on this day of not so unusually worsened symptoms, I'd be bedridden for sure. It was all that would work: my prescribed medication only made me vomit, and at one point in time had left me weighing under a hundred and twenty pounds for the first time in my life since I was probably thirteen. It came down to either draping myself in ice, or allowing myself to wither away into a skeletal, bulimic creature. I prefer the frozen sting over the gradual and excruciating ebbing away of my body, of my fat and muscle, and will to live.

Once Lee had arrived and I climbed my way into his passenger seat, we hit it off immediately, telling old tales of good times we shared when we were young, and about all that had happened since. In our absence of contact, while he worked and raised a family, and while I traveled to various multi-date speaking tours across the country, and garnered a cult following as large as, if not larger, than that of the Manson family, Frida Kahlo, and those great but short-lived bands like The Smiths and Joy Division—Lee had been in a world of his own creation, secluded from the lives of his friends, and thus utterly caught off guard when learning of the severity of my illness. He knew I wasn't well, he knew it right when he saw me that day in the grocery store, but without explaining to him the truths of the matter, he had had no idea the extent of my sufferings.

We drove up to his home after a short ride across town. The house was brand new—they had had it built from scratch according to his wife's designs and sense of decorative fashion. It had a long and wrapping veranda, and above the first awning and between the few spanning gables at the very top, the home was surfaced in suntanned wooden shingles that bordered large windows with lush draperies to be seen hanging from their frames on the inside. I was suddenly quite proud of my friend, after seeing the way he lived and all he had come to achieve, and I felt humbled to be a guest in his home.

His wife swung the door open as we climbed the steps, and put out her gentle hand with a grin. As I shook it, I couldn't help recognizing the body that the hand was attached to. It was the blonde woman in the front row that day we gave a press conference for the media on the landing of the hospital office building. Lee had married the reporter who had labeled me a thief, and incriminatingly questioned my every move! I couldn't believe it, but I didn't want to say anything, or ask outright if she was indeed the woman with the microphone that day, as I was not a hundred percent certain, but pretty damn sure!

"Yeah, she is," said Lee from behind, and after realizing I had a peculiar expression on my face. "You recognize her, don't you?"

Now I knew it was safe to ask, and so I did. She put on a great smile once I had, and shook her head joyfully in assurance. "Yes, that was me, all those years ago pestering you two during the public interview. I was a young-gun reporter back then, just trying to get a good piece of journalism. Never meant you guys any disrespect."

All was forgiven, I told her. And Lee, putting a hand upon each of our shoulders, kindly directed us into the house. There, beyond a spotless living room and a corridor with marble flooring, an already-set meal, one of fine taste and quality, was left cooling on the large oak table; the chairs were neatly pushed in but anxiously waiting our arrival.

"Where's the kids today?" I asked.

"Neighbor's house;" Lee said, "I didn't want them running around spoiling our time, especially because it's been so long since we last talked!"

"Well that was a nice gesture," I said. "It really is great being able to catch up."

"Bet you're a little surprised to find me married to your old best friend, huh?" asked Lee's wife, whose name, she thereafter informed, was Vanessa, and that Lee and her had started dating some five years after that day of the hospital press conference. They met again in a bar, she said, like most young people do. She had recognized him immediately—and not just because of the interview, but because him and I had become rather recognizable faces for a time, thanks in part to magazine covers, internet articles, and the occasional T.V. appearance, more often than not a late night talk show or Smithsonian documentary film, of which there were a couple, though from different networks and institutions. They had dated for two years, and decided to tie the knot one day after learning she was pregnant. In Marseille, they got married in a church by the ocean, and the minister had arranged a beautiful ceremony, where they each took up a handful of red sand from a vase, and together tossed it into the sea, which represented their everlasting union, for there is nothing more eternal than the sea. All through the dinner I was entertained with stories of their honeymoon in France, as well as the nightmare of staying in a hostel for a week, and the excitement of visiting all the historical landmarks. After the meal, Vanessa left to pick up the kids, and Lee asked if I were interested in seeing his home laboratory. Immediately intrigued, I said yes, and we took off across the long hallway attached to the dining room in which we had previously sat. I followed him to a white door that stood at the end of the hall. It led down to the basement, and as he opened it, a blue light filled my eyes, and the sounds of ticking scientific implements and working software buzzed up the staircase, coiling like a snake of sound in between the banisters and up the railing on which I had placed my hand.

"Got some pretty important stuff here," he said, "I'd warn you not to touch anything." Then with a smile, he made off down the steps, and we entered a room with motion sensor lights that kicked on as soon as we had reached the threshold of the large metal door that was the entrance. Inside a wall of computers was parallel a wall of thick books, human skulls, abacuses, and other bibelots; in between lay a long steel table with a stove built into it, and a dozen beakers and liquid-filled glass tubes rested like a tiny city of flawlessly crafted crystals upon its metallic surface. As I made my way further into the lab, an alarm of sorts went off, as if in response to my presence. It emitted from a tall black box in the corner with a small glass bulb at its top and a row of blinking lights beneath it. I glanced over at Lee who had stopped in his tracks, and had turned a rather pale shade of grey. His face was cast in an expression of absolute seriousness. And before I could ask what the problem was, he took me by the arm and dragged me over to the stairs, where he ordered me to quickly leave the room. He leaped back across the lab to a computer, and with dexterous hand movements, quickly typed something into the keyboard. Then another alarm sounded, and he rushed over to a drawer by a desk that was near the black box, whose siren still rung with relentless volume. Inside the draw he retrieved what looked to me like an old Victorian medical bag often used by doctors traveling from door to door, one that was leather and had two thin handles at the top, and a small silver buckle on it locking the two halves of the pouch together. With this in hand, and after silencing the blaring noise by pressing a mysterious button, he took me by the arm and we hurried back upstairs and into a nearly empty room across the hall.

In the room there were two things: a chair and a vertical file cabinet. Lee placed his leather doctor's bag on top of it, and motioned for me to seat myself, which I quickly did. He had my nerves stirring tremulously, and I was as confused as I had been that night in the parking lot, under the pulsating streetlight with Lee's hand grasping my shoulder, motionless as the sounds of an explosion filled the air and shook the ground beneath our feet. With the bag he did nothing but glance at it occasionally as he stood before me. At this I felt like a child being scolded by their father, and stared blankly at his two legs, his two tall, blue jean legs.

"Sorry if I frightened you," he said, "that thing in there is a machine that is made to detect harmful levels of radiation, so I had to get us out of there quick. Normally it's safe, this kind of thing doesn't happen often. I suppose something I got stewing down there is becoming fairly radioactive. This is pretty bad, believe it or not; and I can't for the life of me think of what it could be. This home is too new, and too well protected for us to be harmed by radon in the earth, which is an actual occurrence, I might add—getting radon poisoning from an old, poorly insulated basement, that is. But nonetheless, there is a hazardous amount of radiation in that lab, that's why I got us out quick."

"So what's in that bag?" I asked.

"Oh, that!" he said, as if trying to deny the fact that it rested there on the cabinet, and had undoubtedly been retrieved for a reason, but as to what that reason could be, I did not know. And he said, after swallowing a lump in his throat: "Radiation, you see, can be a particle or a wave, and those particles and waves all emit from a source. After mentally inventorying the number of current experiments being performed, as well as the byproducts of previous ones, it's highly implausible that something in my lab suddenly became radioactive right as we walked in, for if there was something emitting radiation, it would have been detected by myself already. No, I think there is something else afoot."

"What!" I yelled, "what's wrong, Lee? What's in the bag?"

"In the bag," he said softly, and not looking at me but rather at his feet, "is a Geiger counter, a more mobile device to detect radiating particles. I want to ask you a questing…"

"Go ahead," I told him.

"What did you ever do with that tooth? I read some pretty odd things about what you may have done with it in a local paper once, after it was eventually discovered to be in your possession—and God only knows who started such rumors!"

Then Lee removed the apparatus from the bag, turned it on, and pointed it at my flesh. It hummed and ticked and tocked, and sized me up with its probing antenna, all while a needle began to flicker on a screen near Lee's hand, and then a loud, rapid click began, and rang as urgently as the alarm that had voiced its opinion earlier, downstairs in the lab. "Jesus, you're cooking like a turkey!" he shouted. "You're giving off so much radiation I wouldn't be surprised if I could fry a fucking egg in the palm of your hand! It's telling me that your body is producing, or giving off, measurable levels of ionizing radiation, like something expelled from an X-ray; in fact, pretty damn close to the normal levels emitting from an X-ray used in hospitals. However, exposed as you are to this for God only knows how long, the radiation on and around you is not good at all. Not only is it dangerous to others, but it is going to kill you, no doubt, for it has built up over time through unrelenting emissions, and is now abundant throughout your body!

"Why I brought up the tooth is because of some not so recent information I've discovered on the Being, and I've garnered some suspicions. Do you recall that headline about those dinosaur bones found in Colorado last year that turned out to be radioactive? Well it's the same case with the golden bones; and before they were put on display for the first time, they had been coated in a clear lead-based varnish in order to protect the public from their harmful emanations. The scientists went back to the restaurant shortly after the Being's removal and—due mostly in part to the large amount of feldspar found at the site—used a process known as potassium-argon dating, as well as other isotopic methods, on the rocks around where he was found to try and estimate the age of the location of the grave, and get a better estimate on how long he had been there. But while doing so, they discovered that not only the soil, but the golden man himself, were all highly radioactive. They discovered far greater levels than would be expected, levels much more harmful than those of natural radioactive isotopes. So I'm asking you now, as a friend, and not as your father, or as a bully, what on earth did you do with that tooth?"

Ah, the golden tooth! And yet again we find ourselves approaching an expedient linkage: one that will take us from this side of the river to the other: the recurrent onset of an additional story within a story, all making up what in itself is *the* story… but, sadly enough, one that is to be my last. And so, let us now hear the tale of the golden tooth.

About a year and a half after the discovery of the Being, and after having snatched myself a gleaming souvenir, I woke up one morning, drank a glass of cold water, and found myself suddenly crying out in what was some of the most grueling sensations I had ever felt. My nerves exploded, and the pain wreathed around my skull. It was a cavity: it was microscopic bacteria slowly eating away the tiny bones that sprouted from my jaw, gluttonously feeding on the enamel of my teeth.

I put in a time to see my dentist, a man who, either being in love with his work or slightly psychotic, jovially cleaned my teeth once every six months. His name was Dr. Louis Verger, and when I walked into his office the day of my appointment, he took one look at my mouth and discovered the source of my affliction, as well as the route to correcting it. My molar, the second to last on my upper right side, was being digested by microbial monsters. "We can fill it," he said, grinning as he so often did, "or we can pull it. The choice is really up to you."

"Can we swap it?" I asked.

"Surely, seeing as if you got something to swap it with."

"How about this?" I said and handed him the glowing tooth.

"Well, now that'll do; it is a perfect fit! A golden tooth for the gold seeking boy, coming right up!"

"It's not what it looks like though!" I abruptly said, fearing that since he knew of my tribulations with the Being, might put two and two together and see that this tooth, in all its supernatural perfection and shine, was in fact the one missing from the head of the gilt man, and had just that last weekend abetted to the forming of a mob-like search party of off-duty cops and overzealous citizens of the surrounding community to demand and eventually force entrance into Malzaro's in order to scour the basement for evidence of the missing tooth. Then I saw that Dr. Verger wasn't quite grasping why I suddenly turned so off-character at his utterances, and I realized he hadn't a clue of the unfolded events of the prior week's scavenger hunt. With this knowledge, and trying my hardest now to be normal so as not to ruin my chances of receiving the procedure by raising either vague or possibly harmful suspicions, I filled my face with a reassuring smile, and said that I was just a little dehydrated from the hot weather. He was convinced! and soon again began discussing the specifics of my upcoming dental work.

"It is real gold, yes?" asked Dr. Verger.

"It is."

"Good, real gold is best. But I must inform: the procedure will be a serious one, for this tooth is foreign and inorganic, and cannot grow in your mouth like a normal tooth; and since typically when one has a cavity we only break off a portion of the tooth, and it is there that the gold or silver filling is placed, this is a completely different set of circumstances. It is quite infrequent to have a patient requesting a full-scale tooth transplant! Nevertheless, I am a doctor, after all; it is quite doable, I promise. You'll be one expensive skeleton, that's for sure. This tooth must be solid gold!"

"It is indeed!" I assured. "I can't wait for it to be a part of me, it is a prized possession."

"And I can see why," he said, holding the tooth between his two fingers, and peering over it with his spectacled eyes, twitching with curiosity and enthusiasm at the object behind two dusty lenses.

We scheduled the operation for that next weekend, and it was carried out with the finest of precision and the best of quality. I was beyond pleased; and all that month I was gifted with a feverish excitement raging within me, like the feeling one gets while at the start of an extravagant journey or a life-defining adventure. Sure enough that sweet tickling sensation returned, and hummed in my brain day and night: the touch of the gods: a sign that told me the Being was by my side. I was with him and he was with me. In fact, we were one. It was this tale that I told Lee that day in his home, and afterwards I departed feeling rather guilty, and knowing that I would never see him again. And it wasn't without relief that I had willingly spared him the horrible details of my eventual downfall as a result of the whole procedure. A story that went like this:

Within a year, I saw that my health had suddenly turned. At first, and for quite a long time, I wasn't ill or immobile, like someone with a sickness, but I was certainly weak. I had the aches and pains of an elderly person, and what seemed like the onset of osteoporosis. And just as well, I had the morbidity of a man on his deathbed who had not consoled his heart's troubles, or of a cynic with a warped perception of the way things were, and a longing for the way he thought things should be. In the summers and in the daytime I found myself content. But in the nights, and in the winter, on the other hand, is when I all but fell apart. For the last twenty years this is how I lived: dodging the pains and abnormalities of my body with tricks of the mind and naïve skepticism, always brushing it off as something unreal, imagined, or exaggerated, when really it was slowly killing me. For twenty years this is how I lived: speaking lies to crowds of students, and men and women in various fields of study that tie into the story of the Being, and to the innocent public as a whole; making my living off of a whim, a fluke, a freak occurrence that had happened to me once long ago, and now continued on by being the means through which I put food on the table, and gas in my tank, and fed a dangerous obsession. For twenty years this is how I lived: fantasizing about that man, that life that should have never been. Daydreaming of his eyes and his skin, and of their color and whether or not they too were gold. I dreamt for hours about his life, his home, his world! It enthralled me, jailed me in a mystical captivation, and has held me there ever since; and with the help of my overwhelming desires, had quickly ensued to devour me, to eat me alive like the cavity in my tooth.

I have been to doctors and bone specialist, and it only took one, and a handful of appointments, to assure me of my demise. After a slew of X-rays, amounting to a full body print-out of my structural interior, the diagnosis was a peculiar mixture of bone cancer, of multiple malignant tumors and areas of lytic lesion, as well as an out-of-control, advanced-stage case of arthritis, and the severe forming of crystalline structures in my joints, abundant mostly around my knees and shoulder blades; in fact, one of my deltoids, so said the doctor, was almost entirely encased in a layer of not only arthritic crystals but metalloid solids too, as if it were wrapped in tin foil, but with the textural likeness of sandpaper, and as unheard-of as someone with a foot growing out their ass. I was given heavy sedatives and a pat on the back for good luck, and for good riddance; I was expected to have only months to live. It's been a few years since that doctor appointment, but I've felt recently as if the prognosis was only now about to be proven true. Ah, this moribund existence, this sick journey! It was like sailing on a bullet-riddled boat, taking on heavy water, trying desperately to get to land before drowning, only to reach the shore and realize that you've been shot through the gut, and will die regardless, soon thereafter. I had accepted this fate, however, long before the boat was ever fired upon, and so at least in that sense I was fortunate. It's made living easier, but quite obviously more solemn. I hadn't to wait around hoping for a recovery, I simply came to terms with my reality, my existence, my price to pay, and continued through the days like everybody else. I knew it was the Being that was killing me all along, but I never acknowledged it, not to myself and not to the public. It was a secret, an unspoken fact; and it was as if the golden man himself wanted it to remain that way, and was forcibly preventing me from speaking out and taking action against what was in fact my own fault, and against the radioactive, fatal tooth that, like a ticking bomb, or a septic tank leaking poison, dwelt within me and called my host its home, slowly but surely destroying me with its continuous flow of pollution and disease, and vitrifying my bones! It sucked the life right out of me. But I still loved it, and never regretted it, or wished it never happened. I got what I wanted, after all. Now, I suppose, it's only fair that he—either God or the Being—shall be able to get what he wants in return, and that seems to be my life. So why should I stop him? He never stopped me. I came to him first, if I recall, and I wrapped myself around those bones like a newborn does his mother's breast. I've been ravished, broken, and depleted by this man, this Being. I've been reduced to nothing but aches and pains, and am a walking image of embodied misery. Yet, when I think back on all that I had, and all that had been brought to me as a result of that discovery, the discovery of those blessed bones, and all the wonder and comfort and spirit I found in the likeness of a man made of treasure, I can't say I'm ashamed or unsatisfied. Still, I do wish I could live to see the sunrise, or the sprightly faces of my niece and nephew, Lee and his wife and child, and that lustrous phiz of gold, which I have not since forgotten, in its every detail, down to the last dimple below glistening cheek bones and riveting sockets, mesmerizing those who dare to see where immortal eyes once saw, and blinked, and gazed upon the world with a sage unobtainable to any man, and more glorious than could possibly be imagined within our scope of comprehension, unless one commits their very life and sanity to the pursuit of its meaning, the meaning of its existence, and what it says about our own. Though as much as I admire the gift of those bones and the spectacle they have evoked in me, a single lesson is the eventual reward which I have been granted in return for all my pain and self-sacrifice, and it is one not to be readily forgotten; it begins with a question, and is as follows:

It is unalterably so that to the people of this earth gold is forever sacred, and still, gold is accursed; and when a man is golden, or when golden is a man, of which will he become—sacred or accursed? Nevertheless, exhausted repetitions of history and of our own practical experiences tell us that they are one in the same. Thus, leading those with good sense to adopt the proposition that gold, wealth, and power, just like any other pleasantry of life, must be consumed in moderation. One too many struggles may leave you in the gutter, but one too many delectations will leave you as cold and lifeless as the yearning miner's forgotten pickaxe in the depths of an abandoned burrow. Though wealth had made me happy, it has yet to make it so I talk of things less morbid. And now, alone, contently in bed, warm beneath my quilts and covers, I shall die, after drifting peacefully into an endless sleep.

Margaret

The morning Margaret was born, her father took her home from the hospital, brought her to the stable, and laid her on a bed of hay. She was a beautiful baby girl with full brown eyes; her face was a precocious one, and always filled with the look of curiosity. In the stable she would now be with her "siblings," three Arabian horses by the names of Leroy, Motley, and Nebraska. They were all males, but each as protective as would be a mother. To be with what was now her kind, she was left in their care for the night. At dawn, Margaret's father, with her blind mother at his side, entered the dusty barn-house. Inside Margaret was still lying on the bed of hay. She was naked and gleaming; the other horses had bathed her, and cleansed her over with their hot tongues. Margaret's mother, though sightless, miraculously seemed to know where she was going, and felt her way over to where her daughter was. She sat her up on her knee and fed her a handful of wet oats from the tin can once strapped to Leroy's face; and within a few months Margaret, like the others (though not quite), was situated enough to wear over her mouth a feeder bucket of her own; and her father, buried away in the cellar where he had his so-called "atelier," dreamt of the day where he could find himself busy at work on a what would become a pair of the girl's first shoes.

Inside the home, Margaret's parents, Mr. and Mrs. Joyner, were sitting up in their room, preparing for bed. Mrs. Joyner sat beneath a quilt, reading braille, softly running her finger down and across the dotted pages. The loyal husband stood by the desk, blowing out the last of the lit candles, thinking solemnly about his child lying naked in the stable, and those other children of his, children of old, who had once stood where she now slept. To him, all creatures on the ranch, people and farm animals alike, were his children. With their memory in mind, he walks over and lies himself in bed next to his wife, and there together they'll sleep. But each night he enters an unseen world of monstrous dreams, where animals occupy the dining room, and he serves them, and was the mule on which the horses sat to get from here to there. In his dreams his wife would breast feed the foals and piglets, and lay eggs for the hens to eat, while all day long they hunched together miserably in a feather-strewn coop. These unconscious delusions filled Mr. Joyner with unnatural excitements and satisfactions, and he often woke during the night in fits of laughter.

The Joyners, even with all their unconventionalities, where people with but two desires in life: simplicity and raising horses. They had raised dozens of them in their day, and their life was a thriving revelry of animalistic happiness. Once, not long ago, the Joyner's ranch was blissfully cramped with over thirty-five horses, all of which were treated as precious children. But one year, when the frigid winter came, a horrendous accident was set to run chaos and torture around the property, and a horrible toll of death was to be paid out of the pockets and hearts of Margaret's mother and father.

It was a night in late December, when the frost in the air felt like steel wool on one's cheeks and everything was so frozen still—the trees and the sheds—that even the slightest knock would seem to shatter them to pieces. The sky was freezer-burnt; the subtle blackness above, the skeleton branches of deciduous trees, the pale light of the snow covered ground, and the setting sun, had somehow caused the color of the visible world in between to turn a hazy red, and a somnolent alpenglow swathed across the fields of the ranch. The silos and barn-houses were but little protrusions in the earth, blanketed in deep snow. Only an eve or a door latch could be made out on the structures from afar;

aside from that, everything was but nonexistent, everything except the red tint of the sky.

Just before sundown, Mr. Joyner had lit a large fire in the tin oven of one of the horse stables, where twenty-something horses stood freezing in the drafty room. Mr. Joyner, in the hopes of saving them some suffering, lit the oven well, packing it with logs and newspapers. He did so to the three remaining hovels on the property, and went off to bed. That night, as he was about to lay his head to his bolster and end the day as planned, an orange glow soon shone on the walls of his bedroom. Looking up, he saw what appeared to be hot red embers flickering down on the pane of his window. "It's only the snow" he thought, his mind wilting and filled with on-setting weariness; in such a state, how could he have known any better? The cold had taken all the life from his bones, and he ached, and was consumed with exhaustion. His wife tugged at his shoulder, and lowered him down into sleep.

The next morning, upon waking to the sounds of bells and whistles and banging fists on the front door, Mr. Joyner pulled back the heavy curtains and gazed out at the devastation that was now his ranch. Some thirty horses lay dead and burning in the rubble of his sheds and stables. Their putrid bodies smoking on the frozen ground, their tongues hanging limp from ghastly mouths, from between rows of white teeth, their eyes bulging outward and seeing all! Mrs. Joyner screamed when she heard the news, and collapsed back onto the bed. Mr. Joyner threw on his robe and rushed downstairs into hell.

The ovens had set fire to the hay, which set fire to the sleeping horses, who in effect set fire to the wooden structures and everything else. When all was over, three horses survived: Leroy, Motely, and Nebraska; and Margaret's father, along with his brother, and various folks from town, all helped to rebuild the ranch in the hopes of living life favorably once again. In time, their buildings were rebuilt, and their three horses saved, shipped off to another rancher's metal shed to wait out the winter. When the spring came, they were returned, and were the Joyner's pride and joy, those three horses. They would become real members of the family, which also included a stock of hogs and poultry. However, a lingering sense of unfulfilled desires, and a wish for new stallions still held a firm place in their minds. Though things improved, and guilt about the mass death of their animals had subsided, their finances had been strained, and they found it difficult to satisfy their love for domesticated creatures. Then, when the fall came, after a warm and pleasant summer, and when once again the massive harvest moon hung above their home, Mrs. Joyner found that within her there was growing another. She was going to have a baby. The family was in good spirits, and that next week Mr. Joyner went out and bought a new white leather saddle, and expanded the horse shed with a larger, additional stall, a room that was to be Margaret's, along with the saddle and the hay, the feeder bucket and the metal shoes.

At noon one spring day, shortly after Margaret's birth, two friends of the Joyner's, Mr. Dominic Wimble, a carpenter, and his wife, a lady by the name of Trisha, dressed in their Sunday finery, made their way happily up the path and onto the front porch of the Joyner's home; they were here for lunch, and to congratulate them on the new baby and all the *joy* that comes along with it. Mr. Joyner, with his wife in hand, welcomed them to the residence, and led them inside. Mrs. Joyner's face beamed with felicity. The home was often a lonely one, and the presence of company had risen her spirits quite a bit. They sat around a table and were all treated by Mr. Joyner to a glass of his wife's well-regarded lemonade.

The Wimbles were as ordinary as could be, especially when compared to the Joyners. They lived the nine-to-five life, and stayed in a small condo next to a boggy retention pond across the street from the most popular steak house in town. Trisha was a hostess there, and made more tips than anyone would think possible in a single night. They were content, but Mrs. Wimble was often in a sour mood. Unfortunately, she had become sterile, and would never be able to make babies and raise a family with her husband Dominic. For years this dilemma haunted her, but recently, within the course of a few months, she had been able to grow past it, and the pain of futile motherhood slowly began to ease itself from her mind. When the news of the Joyner's newborn had come, she was cheerier than she had been in years.

"So where is she?" Trisha asked.

"Oh," replied Mrs. Joyner, "she's out in the stable. You see, she really likes it there. Lou and I, we think it's important for her to spend time with her brothers. Siblings have to learn to love each other, you know…"

"In the stable!" exclaimed Mr. Wimble. "Why, are the ranch-hands with her, or the cleaning woman? You don't mean to say you've left her out there alone, and with those horses!"

"Those horses," said Mr. Joyner, a rigid expression on his face, "would never harm her. They'd never hurt her! I trust them with the life of my child over your rotten hands, Dominic!"

"Christ!" shouted Mr. Wimble, and he stood up quickly from the table and took off running for the back door, out into the yard and down towards the stables.

Trisha sat numbed with unexpected fear, with dreadful uncertainty, and her glass shook in her hand, and clanked with the rapping of her plastic nails. They had been in the home less than twenty minutes, and all normality had just now seemed to have slipped through the cracks in the floor, and drifted away like the warm springtime breezes. These were not the people the Wimbles had used to know. They had changed, or rather, something had changed them. Her husband was in a frantic hurry to the barn, and she, distraught, sat still at the table, while the two Joyners stared down at her with glossy, demonic eyes and elastic grins, like those of a horse, with all their pink gums and massive teeth displayed proudly before her.

"You know why I let my little foal be out there?" asked Mrs. Joyner to Trisha, who was beginning to tremble. "It's because Margaret was no ordinary little girl, no. She stayed in my belly, in my womb, for eleven months. Now, Lou doesn't half believe me, thinks that I lost count; but really it's the truth, I swear it."

"So what does that mean?!" cried Mrs. Wimble.

"It means she's one of them!—Eleven months: the amount of time a pregnant horse carries her baby. Margaret was born exactly eleven months and sixteen days after she was conceived. And it's only fitting, don't you think? Lou and I, we have such a love for those creatures! They make us so happy. Lord, it is only fitting."

At this Trisha gave no reply, but in a fluster of emotions, got up and followed after her husband. Mr. Joyner sighed, whispered something into his wife's ear, put on his hat, and stepped out after them.

In the stable, Margaret had been lifted from her bed and was in Dominic's arms. Mr. Joyner came in through the door just as Trisha did, and as Dominic was about to leave.

"Now, Mr. Wimble, what could you possibly want to come in here and wake her up for?" said Lou Joyner from the doorway.

"Christ!" shouted Mr. Wimble, "Lou, it's absolutely ridiculous for you to leave a newborn baby out here, naked in the barn on a pile of hay!"

"Then you'd better leave," he replied, resting his hand on the end of a pitchfork sticking out of the ground beside him.

Mr. Wimble, hesitatively, and with a wave of sudden fearful disbelief, set Margaret back down on her bed, and stepped away. Mr. Joyner was now firmly grasping the staff, and with wild eyes, made his presence a clear threat to those around him. The Wimbles left the home that day not ever expecting to return.

———

A handful of similar situations, involving different friends and family members of Mr. and Mrs. Joyner transpired soon thereafter. And each time, upon hearing of Margaret and how she was being "bred" (as the Joyners called it), they would get all excited, jump up and try to rescue the poor child. Each time they would be ushered off the property by the subtle threats of what it was Mr. Joyner happened to place his hands on. And within the course of a year, the Joyners were all but shunned by their families and from those whom they had once called friends.

Three years pass. The Joyners are still happily reclusive and bizarre. Margaret has just turned three, and is now able to walk. She moves on all fours, bent over like a horse so that her spine is horizontal, and scuffles around like a hermit crab on the beach. She allows her tongue to hang freely, and breaths with a heaviness similar to that of her brothers'. But what she can't do is talk, or read, or write, or stand up straight like a person, like the human being she is! No—her parents had different plans for her. Selfish, neurotic plans.

On a night in early September of that third year, Mr. Joyner could have been found toiling away in his basement workshop. Coming from a long line of farriers and zoo keepers, ranchers and cowboys, Lou was busy crafting for his daughter a shining new pair of steel shoes. Until now she had only ever worn cotton-lined sacks around her feet in the winter; in the summer she let her toes breathe free. But since the day she was born, Lou Joyner had dreamt of the moment where he finally got to fit her with a homemade pair of metal soles. He had done so for all the others, and Lord, it was only fitting that he'd do so for her! After many weeks of crafting and design, there came an evening in September when they were at last completed. Lou, in tears of joy, ran them upstairs and presented them before his wife. There, softly and gently in her nightgown, she felt the steel shoes over with her thin hands. Eyes closed, she touched them with a smile on her face, and a sense of enthusiasm arose from within her.

"Oh, Margaret will love them!" she said.

"I know, dear," he replied, "but I fear her tiny feet might not be able to bare it. She's so much more delicate than the others. The nails might just go in and right out the other side!"

"Give it a try, at least," said his wife, placing the gleaming metal shoes back into his hands.

"For you, love, I will give it a try."

When morning shone, Mr. Joyner, with the shoes in one hand, and a porcelain tray with a small hammer and an assortment of nails resting upon it in the other, made his way to the stable where within her room Margaret lay, still sound asleep. He crept in through a lose plank in the wall, not wanting to use any doors so as to prevent waking the others. He crawled his way inside and rolled behind a lofty mound of straw, where across from him his daughter slept in peace. With the hazy lights of morning shuffling gently in from the makeshift walls and missing boards, Lou Joyner set down his implements and watched his child for a while as she rested innocently before him. In his mind, he knew what pain was, he knew what horses were and what horses weren't; but sometime in the last five years of his life the line between sensible and psychotic, right and wrong, had been blurred, smudged and smeared into unrecognizable designs. Mr. Joyner, though still in a state of outlandish thought, had his first humane idea since the start of this whole project. An idea, as we shall see, that appears to be pre-meditated. In the barn room, as pollens whirled around in the yellow air above them, from his pocket Mr. Joyner removed a bottle of Chloral betaine tablets and fed them down the throat of his daughter as she began to arise. She stirred with mild discomfort and confusion, and strutted around the barn-house neighing loudly; but after a few minutes had passed, she found herself again starting to doze, and soon fell into a heavy, chemically-induced sleep. Mr. Joyner scooped up her limp body and placed it onto a bench of straw. He indeed thought that all his dreams were about to come true. But after the grisly procedure, it became apparent that things were not going according to plan. Margaret had two tiny feet, and to their soft, fleshy undersides, Mr. Joyner, with a hammer and multiple inch-long wall-tacks, had brutally nailed two steel shoes into her delicate flesh. On one foot, he had botched it, and a nail was visibly protruding from out the side of the girl's heal; and on another, a spike had been driven straight through the underside of a little toe, and was seen protruding, blood-soaked, right out the top! Margaret laid unconscious for most of the week, a crimson gore staining the hay around her and the now-trembling hands of Mr. Joyner as he reenters the barn each day to see to her recovery, each day as she seems to be getting weaker and weaker.

Lou didn't dare inform his wife of the situation at hand; she, in fact, didn't know whether or not he had even performed the long-awaited "fitting of the shoes," as she so psychotically called it. Lou simply avoided conversation with her on the topic, and instead told her that she had been ridding and grazing with the others most of the week, and that he didn't want to disturb her when she seemed so naturalistic and happy; and so instead, he told her, for the last few days he had been sitting on a bench in the yard, facing the fields, polishing to a shine her new shoes, and further contemplating how he was to proceed on the challenge of successfully carrying out such a task—a falsehood that now, as Mr. Joyner stands in the stinking barn, gazing down at the mangled body of his daughter, squirming, wailing in pain on the table of hay, I'm sure he wished was true, and a thing he certainly should have done to begin with. Now, for his own sanity as well as his child's, he was going to have to continue to feed her painkillers and sleeping pills until she was recovered, as he had been doing for the past four days.

At this time, after almost a week of declining health, Mr. Joyner had no other choice but to remove the shoes, and bring in expert medical attention. At any day, at any hour, her pulsating wounds would turn infected, and gangrene was almost certain to occur. It had been by some unfathomable luck, it seemed, that she hadn't succumbed to infections already. However, a theory I have heard on the matter of Margaret's longevity, and the resilience of her body to fight off any deadly bacteria that should have by now festered in her punctured flesh, was that the continuous cleansing of her wounds by the tongues of the three horses had acted as a sort of sanitizer, and hindered the onset of disease. Their saliva, it is thought, quite literally saved her life.

With that said, it was by no means a cure, only an antiseptic—if anything!—and without real medical care she wouldn't likely live to see another week go by. This medical care, assumed Mr. Joyner, quite wisely, could not by any means come from some outside source, any doctor of humans; whatever treatments she got, it had to be carried out right there on the property, in the stable, by someone who would never speak of it to another person. "What a challenge!" Lou thought; and for an hour he stood there over his defecated child, thinking. Then from the fields he heard his named called. It wasn't his wife though, it was a man's voice, and at its sound, Lou soon hatched an idea—though not like the partially humane idea mentioned before, but one of sinister intentions—and an intrusive smirk appeared on his scruffy face. The caller of his name was none other than a hired field hand named Abimael Rafal, who was thirty-five, a native of Israel, and worked on

Lou's property from time to time to study the livestock of swine and chickens; he was a sort of zoologist, so to speak; and he was calling his name because it was currently ten o'clock, which is when he came in to do his biweekly inspections on the health of the farm animals. Abimael, in fact, was a recently certified veterinarian, and was just now beginning to practice his acquired profession. "But never could he be sympathetic towards our situation," said Mr. Joyner to himself. "He'd just as soon call the cops, I'm sure!" And he began to grow quite angry with his predicament. "You have no other options…" whispered a solemn voice in his head. Was it his voice of reason? It's hard to say, for most believe that he does not have one. But every so often, it seems, it tends to show itself, and make itself heard—though not exactly at the most urgent of moments, or when it is really truly needed, as we have seen.

Leaving Margaret on the damp hay, he made out towards the field to where Abimael stood, peering curiously at the stable from under the heavily fruited branches of a crabapple tree. Lou waved to him as he passed the threshold of the door and onto the rough grass. *Come, Abimael*, he thought, *I have quite the job for you today!*

"Make haste now," said Lou, feeling an urgency that needed to be expressed. "We haven't much time."

"What's the matter?" asked Abimael, now approaching the entrance of the stable.

Mr. Joyner, seeing his acquaintance's obvious obedience, and thus sparking within him a sense of superiority, stepped back inside the gruesome barn-house and sat there next to his unconscious child, with the bloody hay as her only layette, certain that Abimael would follow. Upon his awaited entrance, we find poor Abimael in sudden shock, and trembling, he drops a toolbox of various implements onto the dirt floor.

"Alarming, isn't it," Lou sighed. "You are the only man for the job."

At this, Abimael had become no longer surprised, he had become fearful. One thought passed through his mind, and that was to run. Run right out that open door, to his ride, and to protection. Then he thought, *protection from what?—I cannot be forced to stay here. I can't be forced against my will!*

Lou Joyner, on the other hand, had already perceived of Abimael's thoughts and his opposing will. He had already planned on him wanting to flee; but now, at this point, since he had already seen the child, and her horrid deformity, could not be trusted to leave on such terms, no matter what. It was far too late for that. He was going to be more involved in this sick plot than he could have possibly imagined. He held his life in his own hands, and Margaret's just as well.

Abimael, staring out at Lou, who sat there on the blood-soaked hay with Margaret's head in his lap, soon realized the situation for what it was. There beside him was the door to refuge. But there beside Lou, as he had only now realized, was a twelve gauge shotgun, and its barrel was being gently caressed by a calloused hand: the hand of a man willing to use it: the hand of Mr. Joyner.

Lou, with reddened eyes, heavy with tears, and with the gun in one hand and his child in the other, beckoned Abimael to his side. Abimael, captured like a rat in a trap, slowly made his way across the stable. "Lord!" he cried upon seeing her injured feet and her appalling appearance. Her teeth were brown and rotten; and though as small as they were, seemed to always protrude from her mouth like those of a horse. She had lesions on her knees and palms and fingers, though to Abimael he did not understand why, and supposed she had been beaten. In fact, it was the lack of clothing and footwear that caused the wounds, and the fact that she seemed to believe she had four feet, as opposed to two and a pair of arms.

"She's not well;" Lou started, "it was a mistake, for she was too young to have shoes put on her; but God, I was so anxious, I couldn't help it! You've got to save her, fix her, and remove these spikes, or she'll die!"

"I'll call a doctor!" he replied, when, as he turned to make an escape, was seized by the collar by Mr. Joyner, and felt the barrel of the shotgun poking into his back.

"Why don't you come and have a seat next to Margaret," said Lou, spinning him around so he was facing the bed of hay, where upon its filthy surface a motionless child lay bleeding, dying before him. "She'd sure appreciate your help…"

He stood gazing down at the horror of what was the Joyner's life. Abimael turned his head and vomited onto the wall beside him; then he dropped to his knees and started weeping.

"Enough, Abi" Lou said. "You are the only man who can help. But, I must state, if you choose to refuse, well— I think you and I both know I can't let you tell anyone about this. I'll have to do what I have to do; I'll do whatever it takes to ensure that *it* doesn't happen."

Abimael couldn't believe his ears, and he stood up and faced his deranged enforcer, his commander of hellish duties. "What am I to say to that?" he said. "I will save your daughter, and then what? What shall become of me then? Give me your word to let me go, and I will take those shoes off of Margaret."

"You have my word," said Lou. "Please, she hasn't much time. You must start at once!"

And so he did. He, with his veterinary instruments, removed the spikes, cleansed and bandaged the wounds on her swollen, purple feet. Abimael had pulled out twelve nails total, six for each foot. When he was finished, Mr. Joyner, tearful yet again, picked her up and allowed her to dangle in his arms. Beside them in his stall, Leroy was lying on his side, depressed, watching with sympathetic eyes the events that had unfolded before him. The other two horses were there as well, and all witnesses of unspeakable things, but Leroy was the closest to all the torture, and the closest to Margaret emotionally, too. It was on Leroy's sofa-like underbelly, which protruded outwards as he lied on his side, that Lou had propped her up against, after draping a clean sheet on the ground where she was to lay. There she remained, unconscious but at last peaceful. It was as if she knew she was with someone like Leroy whom she recognized and trusted, and felt the protection and love that his body emitted for her alone.

"Lemonade, Abi?" Lou asked, with blood staining his shirt, and red-tinted droplets of sweat running down the sides of his head. "Wife makes a mean batch; why don't ya come inside?—you've done a fine job today, a fine job!"

"I'd rather be on my way," he said.

"Nonsense!" Lou objected. "Nonsense! It's a beautiful day out! We can get you cleaned up in the stream, and then come back to the kitchen for a glass of lemonade. We'll toast to Margaret, and a second chance!"

"Second chance at what?" Abimael inquired.

"Why, a second chance to get it right, of course!"

"Lou, what are you saying? Get what right?" he pleaded to hear the answer, though he thought that he already knew what it would be.

"I've got a perfectly good pair of horse shoes there, shaped like her little feet! I've spent weeks on them, and I won't just let all that work be for nothing. Obviously, Abi, she's too young for them to be tacked in, and far too gentle. Once she heals up, I'll simply glue them on. It's such a clear answer, they do it to foals with broken or abnormally shaped hoofs all the time. I've just got to get some polyurethane, and I'm in business!"

"No, Lou, don't do this!" Abimael screamed. "You can't put glue-on horseshoes on your daughter, her feet will be in just as bad a shape as they are now within no time at all!"

"Abi," Lou sighed, "don't say such horrible things. Glue-on horse-shoes are a top of the line, ultramodern way to fit a horse's hoof. It's a definite solution. You're starting to make me kind of nervous, son. Should I need to worry about you?"

"But Lou, she doesn't have hoofs, can't you see!"

At this, Lou Joyner's brow stiffened, and a stern demeanor flushed across his face. He looked down at Abimael, who was seated on the ground next to the mound of hay, and covered up to his elbows in partially dried blood. Lou had changed personalities. He now saw right through Abimael as if he were nothing, and like the predator her was, identified him as prey. And, to Abi's misfortune, this beast was hungry and ready to feed.

"Well," said Mr. Joyner, proceeding to take Abimael by the arm and stand him up. "Well, let's get that mess off of you." Lou stood stiff, and, holding the weapon behind his back so Abimael couldn't see it, and hoping that he would suppose it had been left behind, watched as his expectant victim walked outside and onto the lawn.

Lou Joyner led him to the small stream that ran through his property not too far from where a fenced-off meadow of tall grass stood,
where Margaret and her brothers often grazed and spent the major-
ity of their time aimlessly roaming, and trotting around casually from
here to there. This was her kitchen and her toilet, her bedroom and
her pantry. Margaret ate the ants and the beetles; she lived on grass
and leaves, and various wild berries of which her siblings had turned
her on to. At a distant corner of the field, where the trees had begun
to disperse, the lot which Margaret often roamed would have been
visible to anyone passing on the street nearby. So far, to the Joyner's
good fortune, she had remained hidden, and never accidentally seen
from some passerby. Lou had scarcely given his luck a single thought,
and it had been a significant coincidence that she was not long ago
discovered. Even Abimael, with his ten months of employment on the
farm, was unaware of the feral child's living conditions until today.
But as he leaned over the bank of the rivulet and washed the blood
from his arms, Lou, from behind him, lifted his shotgun and aimed
it at the back of his head. From the peripherals of their surroundings, the sound of a freight train racing down the tracks a half a mile
down the road began to grow louder and louder. When it reached its
pinnacle point of volume, it's most strident rumble, Lou pulled the
trigger, and fired a rain of buckshot into Abimael's chest—for he had
just then stood up to face his attacker, and for that reason was hit in
the front, as opposed to the head, which was the ideal target. His eyes
were open wide as he flew backwards from the blast and into the creek.
A moment later the train had passed away, everything was silent, and
the trickling water continued on downstream, slightly tinted, like the
trickles of sweat that ran down the flesh of Lou Joyner's face—slightly
reddened was the water, rufescent with his evading life.

———

That night Mr. Joyner buried Abimael's body in a shallow grave beneath
the crabapple tree. By morning all was still, unaltered and mundane.
His poor blind wife hadn't the slightest idea of the week's abysmal

occurrences. Nor did she even know who Abimael was, for Lou had never introduced the two, and she was, after all, sightless and bound to the confines of her home.

After a few weeks, once Margaret's wounds had healed and she was back on her feet, Lou once again, after creeping into her room, drugged her unconscious, spread her out on the bed of hay, and commenced to glue the metal shoes to her soft flesh, leaving them there until they dried. When he had finished he stood over her grinning, faintly crying, and sipping a glass of purple wine out of a deep crystal cup. When Margaret came to, Lou was in the house with Mrs. Joyner, sitting on the sofa listening to the midday radio broadcast. From the stables they suddenly heard not only the cries of their daughter in pain, but the wails of the horses as well. She and Lou began to worry, and she insisted that he go check up on them, which, it so happened, he had already gotten up to do. When he reached the barn door and opened it, Margaret was prancing all around the hay floor, bucking and kicking, shrieking loudly, and strewing up clouds of dust and dirt into the air. Motley, Leroy, and Nebraska were calling out just the same, and shaking the walls of their stables. Lou, assuming that they were feeling cooped up, and in the excitement of Margaret's new shoes, wanted to be let out into the field, rallied them together in the middle of the barn and prepared them, by inspecting their hoofs and faces, to go outside. He walked them to the field—the three horses first, and then Margaret. She hopped and skipped on her two heavy feet, and with her other feet—which for most would have been referred to as hands—she clawed at the earth, and flung up clumps of soil that flew behind her as they made their way down the trail. He looked down at Margaret and saw her wide grin of protuberant teeth, and thought she must have been smiling out of joy, and pleased with her new footwear. But, it is sad to say, we can't know for sure what she truly felt, for even she didn't know. Margaret was oblivious to human sentiments, and was as empty-headed as the typical house dog. She had no conscience, and no self-awareness. She was not concerned with personal appearance nor the improvement of personal existence. All she felt was pain or neutrality. Suffering or nothingness. It is possible that the horses themselves had more intelligence and passion within them than she did, though of no fault of her own.

That day, as Margaret and her brothers roamed the grassy field, Lou took a nap in the shade, after having smoked his tobacco pipe and eaten his lunch of potato salad and bread. He dozed off, the hours passed, and he didn't wake up until well into the evening. The sun was beginning to set as he reopened his eyes to the twilit world around him, and peered over to where Margaret had fallen asleep in the grass as well, next to Leroy who had seated himself beside her. For Mr. Joyner, the day had been a peaceful one; and he rallied up his stallions and his foal and led them back to the barn-house with a sense of calm satisfaction playing out inside him. He ate dinner with his wife, and that night on the couch drifted off into a state of unorthodox dreams as the last lit candle in the room slowly fizzled into darkness, and left a subtle trail of blue smoke to linger away solemnly up towards the ceiling.

What an uneventful day, it seemed, and the excitement of Margaret's new shoes had been long ago exhausted, and endured only as a proud reminder to Mr. Joyner of all his hard work. However, for a certain Mr. Wimble, whom we have previously been acquainted with, the day was anything but ordinary; in fact, it was quite significant, and led to a change in thought within Dominic's good-natured yet sheltered, one-track mind.

For him, the day had started out like any other. He woke up in bed next to his wife, and then took a shower while she made coffee. They drank it together once he returned, with dripping wet hair and in his white bathrobe, seated quietly around a table with a bowl of fresh fruit as its centerpiece. Mrs. Wimble left for work an hour later; and at noon, Dominic went off to a client's home, where he was scheduled to lay some new flooring, and tear up the outdated carpeting that the client wanted away with. Still, it was a normal day, and remained so until that evening on the drive home, in which he was obligated to pass by the Joyner's farm. As he drove along the road, out of sheer curiosity, he slowed down and stared across at the field where he knew Lou's horses were often kept and left to wander. Inching along at fifteen miles an hour, Dominic, leaning from his car window to get a better view, saw, to the disbelief of his own eyes, Margaret grazing alongside three large beasts, a mouth full of grass, and waddling around the green land like an injured creature, leaving blood-streaked indentations on the ground behind her as she moved.

Mr. Wimble, fighting off the urge to vomit, slammed on the brakes, and steered the car onto the shoulder of the road. He was in awe, and more furious than sickened. He worked himself into such an irate frenzy that it would have been quite unsafe for him to get back behind the wheel. Realizing this, and after taking multiple deep breaths in the effort to calm down, he stepped out of the car, lit a cigarette, and leaned up against the hood. From within him dormant passions and a sense of moral duty arose, and he was determined to do something about the injustice he had witnessed, not only that day, but three years ago, too—after her celebrated birth, and his sudden expulsion from their home. A few minutes later, with the sun slowly creeping beneath the rolling hills and distant trees, Mr. Wimble set off again towards home, his mind racing with a plethora of ideas in which the objective was to put an end to Lou's reign of terror. As he approached the quiet town's meager business district, where the bars and local shops were, he decided to stop at a favorite watering hole before bed, in order to vent his anger to his friends about the Joyner's and their abusive, torturous ways, and perhaps to get drunk.

Inside the bar, a table of familiar faces in the corner welcomed Dominic as he came in through the door. They sat playing cards beneath a large, vintage metal sign advertising an extinct brand of motor oil. He pulled up a chair and, after buying a beer, embarked on a tirade of slander and disgust in regards to what he had seen earlier that day. The men around him couldn't believe what he was saying, and he soon had the attention of the entire room, bartenders included.

"She was out there in the field eating grass," he said, "walking on all fours, with fucking metal shoes on! They were bonded to her feet, and caused her skin to crack, leaving tiny pools of blood on the ground with every step!"

"Lou Joyner's kid?" asked a man at a table who was having a hard time believing the story. "Lou Joyner, the dairy farmer down the road?—He's the one you're talking about? I can't grasp it! Lord, what a horrible tale; how could it possibly be true!"

"Well," said a man behind the bar, the apparent owner of the establishment, "if it's true, it adds up. The girl must be three or four years old by now, and I haven't seen Lou since she's been born. If some devilish change in him has occurred, it makes sense that it'd be within that span of time. I've always thought he was a pretty strange guy myself. Plus, Dominic, this ain't the first time that you've come in here all hyped up about this fella."

"But a child abuser?" said the other man, the nonbeliever, from across the room. "I can't imagine such a thing happening in this town, let alone anywhere else!"

"It is happening," interrupted Mr. Wimble, rising to his feet and walking over to the man behind the counter. "It is happening, and we've got to stop it. This little girl will be dead before winter if we don't put an end to this. For Christ's sake, she lives in a stable, sleeping on a bed of hay and grimy cloths; she's probably sick, and tormented with fleas and lice bugs!"

"I believe you, Dom," said the bartender. "I've had suspicions for years that something like this was happening. In fact, just last May I ran into him at a hardware store, said he needed some scrap metal to make horseshoes out of. I asked if he had gotten a new mare; he simply told me that his wife had given birth, and that they were to be a gift for his child when the time came. I asked what he meant, and he ignored me, and left the store without looking back. So, if you're going to put an end to it—if there is in fact something to put an end to—count me in!"

"Great!" Dominic exclaimed. "Everyone who wants to help, we meet at my house tonight, twelve o'clock or so. There's some horrible things going on at Lou Joyner's ranch, and it has to be stopped."

"I'll get the sheriff," stated the man behind the counter, and he hurried out a back door and across the street to where the police station was.

A group of ten people made up the resistance. They all met in Mr. Wimble's kitchen a few hours later and a plan was developed on what was to be done. Jedidiah Turner, the noted man behind the counter, informed the assembly that he had a large trailer that could be used to transport and conceal Margaret once they had snatched her off the property, and had a cousin who worked at a children's hospital and would surely take her in as a patient. Thus the plan came into effect. They would sneak onto the ranch during the early morning hours when the sun had not yet risen, break into the stable, and, hopefully without a struggle, retrieve Margaret, and take her away to a rehabilitation facility down state.

Sheriff Malcolm Coolidge had brought four of his men along with him to help. The plan was a solid one, and with five men in uniform, with their combined skills and protection, Dominic had little doubt that all would be a success, and that by sunrise, Lou Joyner would be sitting in the city jail, awaiting charges of abuse and endangerment of a child, a child that was his own. And Dominic, with any luck at all, he suspected, might be labeled as a hero. At this thought he grew quite proud, but tried hard to conceal his self-righteous enthusiasm until a more appropriate time.

At two in the morning, after a few hours of debating the specifics of their plot, a caravan of four cars took off from Mr. Wimble's home, and soon thereafter arrived at the field accessible from the road in back of the Joyner's property. A small makeshift fence barred them from entering, and they thought for a moment on how to best proceed. Sheriff Malcolm, utilizing his superior powers, opted to drive his truck straight through the fence. With the promise to keep his headlights off and speed to a minimum, he did so, and left a large hole behind him through which the others followed.

Here, as the group of vigilantes stood in the darkness of the field, Mr. Wimble took charge, ordering half the men to remain with the vehicles to await their return, and then set off towards the barn-houses across the property with the five remaining participants, which included himself, as well as the sheriff, two cops, and Jedidiah Turner. Silently, at a quick but gentle pace, they traversed the grassy field populated with glowing insects who created eye-level comets and shooting stars as they passed by and twinkled from around the stalks of corn and wheat and rows of vegetable gardens on either side. At the crabapple tree they paused, and peered out ahead at the sealed door to the barn where Margaret was confined. Jedidiah retrieved a bolt cutter from his duffle bag, and proceeded to break the locks of the large wooden door. After a loud snapping sound, the chain that had been slung across the entry went limp and fell to the dirt; they slowly opened the door to the barn-house, and one by one, like mischievous children, stepped inside.

There, lying on piles of hay in a room in the back, they found Margaret, and witnessed firsthand the suffering that was her life. The Sheriff gasped, after inspecting the shoes cemented to her swollen, sensitive feet, and turned away, fighting off a sudden wave of nausea. "My God," he cried, "it's true, it's all true!"

While our heroes pondered over the scene before them, and with great effort tried to suppress their venting emotions, Lou Joyner was asleep on the couch; it was approaching three thirty in the morning, and the candles had long since died out. All was seemingly calm and seemingly still. But inside his head, within a world of dreams, a battle was being fought; all hope, faith in God, pride, and physical existence came to a final showdown. Whether it was to be the mind or the body that survived once the war was won, only time, or perhaps the interferences of involuntary and preternatural events, would tell.

Down the spiral, the rabbit hole of unending torment, we find ourselves in the mind of a lunatic. As the scenes play out before his unconscious eyes, a dimensional divide soon appears, and quickly shows its presence. Two men who look exactly like Lou Joyner suddenly make themselves known. It is the moral, conscience-spoken man, and it is the harebrained, unethical, cruel and bitter soul of a devil. They are separate but one, and occupy two small couches in front of him, while Lou, captivated like never before, watches from the front of the room seated in a chair of his own. But he soon falls to his knees and begins shouting, for he actually thought that he was on trial, and pleading for his life. "No!" he screams. "What have I done, my Lords? What have I done?"

The man of moral principles gave him a harsh glare, and put his hand across the leather of a small satchel that he had placed in his lap.

Beside him the man of sin mirrored the actions of Mr. Joyner. Since he was nervous, the evil man in the chair shook his limbs in a violent shiver; since he was ecstatic too, and filled with rapturous emotions, he let out sporadic calls of intense laughter, which the man in the chair soon mimicked. It was completely maddening; and for Lou, who by all standards was already quite deranged, for something to make him feel as if he were going crazy, even after he already had, would be quite a remarkable thing. His eyes twitched, and the bad man in the chair winked at him, smiled, and said, "You'll be in my dreams tonight, too." And Mr. Joyner screamed, and leapt to his feet, but this time the wraith did not follow. He remained seated, and grinned up at Lou, while he paced around the empty room and around his chair, searching for an exit.

"That is quite enough," said the other man, the one of virtues and human kindness. "You must make a choice—you can be a devil, or you can be with the golden souls, with the peace and passion of eternity, and walk with me in a place where all men and women truly belong. He, sitting in that chair, drooling with wickedness, nostrils flaring with the hatred of a thousand angry bulls, cannot hurt you. You can only hurt him, for he is you, and no one else."

"And who are you, if not I?" asked Lou.

"Who am I?" asked the wraith. "I am what you have the power to become, but as of today, you are not that person. No—I am only the person that God wants you to be, and that is all."

"Why, I just don't understand," said Mr. Joyner; "I long to be nobody but my current self. Am not crazy—in fact I am completely calm! Yes, I will admit I was a bit agitated a minute ago, but really I am okay! I just don't understand, my friend, why you come and speak to me tonight. Of all times, why now? Why now when everything in my life seems so perfect, and all are just as happy as I?"

"You are a fool!" shouted his now infuriated reflection as he rose up from the couch. His visage grew dimmer and dimmer with every passing second; it turned epicene, then blank, then overly chiseled, and soon the face hardly even resembled that of Lou Joyner's, for he was receding, and losing faith in the man he was trying to save, an unhealthy extension of himself. "Fool!—you have but one chance to correct your head, and that is now. Who do you chose to be—the man to your right, or I, the man to your left?" The choice was an obvious one, and the man to the left precipitously sprouted beautiful wings of ivory, and a pale white light began to glow around him, and would have lured even the most stubborn of souls; he had a small gold crown atop his head, and it was beautiful. However, as he slowly made his way towards this apparent angel, he glimpsed over to the man on his right. He still sat there grinning, drooling with madness, but in his hand he held a tiny horseshoe, and on his boots were two golden spurs that he kicked against the wooden legs of the chair like a child smashes roaches. They spun and spun, and gave off a gentle whine as the metal turned and slowed to a stop, and then was ignited again with another kick. It was all too much, and Lou's mind shattered; he cried out, and dove towards the man. He landed on his chest, but in a sudden puff, the man vanished, and Lou was left curled in a ball like a giant, well-dressed fetus on the couch.

When he turned his head, he saw the glowing man on his left approach him swiftly from where he had stood, and grasped him by the throat. His clothing transformed from what Lou was wearing into a long white robe, and from beside him in the satchel he retrieved a little mirror, and bid him look into it. Then from out his mouth he retrieved a two-edge sword, and forcefully thrust it into Lou Joyner's gut.

Suddenly his eyes shoot open, and he awakens in a fit of violent laughter. He falls off his couch onto the floor, and, as his laughter grows louder, and more and more vulgar, he looks down and sees that he is profusely bleeding from his abdomen; he cringes and strangles the blood-soaked rug in two tightened fistfuls, and continues howling wildly until his last breath passes from his icy lips, and then he is no more.

Not long before the Gates of Hell would welcome yet another citizen, outside in the barn-house the sounds of Mr. Joyner's demise frightens the men, and Dominic grabs Margaret in his arms and makes away with her towards the door. From beside him, three stalls with low, rickety doors serve as the only barrier between the tiny intruders and three massive animals. Leroy, always vigilant, sees Dominic sprinting towards the door with Margaret struggling in his arms. He is suddenly infuriated by this, and a primeval instinct, as well as a heightened sense of valor, drive him to ram the plywood gate and in one hit break free from his narrow room. He bucks and kicks at the men with his powerful legs, knocking them bloody and onto the ground. Motely and Nebraska, as agitated as Leroy, manage to break free as well, after kicking through the flimsy wall that divided their two stables, and leaped into action themselves. They called out to their appropriated sibling, and she sprung to life. With her shoe-heavy legs she struck Dominic in the chest and jumped from his sweaty arms. There was nothing the men could do, for one was now unconscious, and the rest were helplessly injured. The girl and the horses danced around the barn in a hay-strewn waltz, and neighed joyfully, and slammed their massive bodies against the ligneous walls, all hung up with rusted tools and whips, faded saddles and large brushes for grooming.

Limping along the dirt, Jedidiah, with a broken rib and blood leaking from his nose and quivering lips, slowly pushed opened the huge door. Outside it seemed that morning had come a bit sooner than expected, and a wholesome blue light filled the dusty stalls of the barn-house. Margaret and her brothers saw at once the grace of day, and rushed towards it in a revelry of spirit, trampling carelessly over the men lying in the path of their exit and one sure chance of salvation. With every powerful hoof hammered down and clambered across their broken bodies, the wounded men let out a chorus of tormented screams and operatic cries of anguish; but the immense pain and suffering of these good-natured men made no difference, and stopped them not, for Margaret and the horses continued on out the door, never to look back. All had been lost and at the same time won. The rescue team may not have thought so, but it is truly the case. Good had triumphed over evil, in some form or another; and the wild beasts were now left to roam freely throughout the endless countryside, as natured had intended. They dashed beneath the crabapple tree across the open field as they fled from their worthless home, a confined and earthen hell—and at a full gallop ran on, up over the flowered hills and into the sun.

In Search of Light

In the rural town of K—, a lonely suburb of northeastern Iowa, there is a large field of overgrown plants and bristly weeds that was once the spot of an abandoned farmhouse, long since demolished. Beside it there is an old growth forest that hardly anyone dares to enter, though from time to time some people do. Still, they do so not always with the best intentions, and quite often not with the best of outcomes, either; and sometimes one may never come out at all! But this is of no matter… There are gentle hills of floral that come and go like waves across the meadow, and the trees of the forest nearby are ecosystems in themselves; and if one looks closely, they will see hundreds of nests from hundreds of birds and squirrels stacked up like precious things on towering bookshelves. The branches are ornamented with blue eggs, and even if one falls, there is a nest beneath waiting to catch it. The birds, most perched in their nests so that someone standing below would only be able see their pileum or an occasional feather, thought it was no wonder that the humans didn't come to the forest—to them, to the birds, this wasn't Iowa, it was Shangri-La; and just as well, they were quick to pick out flaws in the characters of others. In regards to people, they believed that they were grumpy and ungrateful—hence the reason, it was assumed, that they didn't venture into the wilderness, for the birds felt that the humans would not be able to appreciate a place of such impeccable surroundings, and therefore neglected it.

Indeed the people did not come around very often; as was said, when they did it was usually not with the best intentions—thus was the situation, for one day it so happened that there was a dead man lying in the brush. He was a sad and lonely man whose wife had passed, and the rabid, ongoing self-seclusion brought upon by her absence had driven him to take his own life. So here his body lies, face-down in the damp earth; a red hole stands out on his otherwise black suede coat, visibly moist and festering between his slightly jutting scapulas, and is indeed an exit wound. He has a golden ring on his stiff finger, one protruding from a wide-open hand at the end of a long blue arm. It was his only extended limb, for his remaining ones were tucked tightly together, rigid, unresponsive, and inanimate; and to the creatures of the forest, he wass just another hill that rose up slightly in a field of high grasses. He cannot be seen from the distant road, and perhaps his body will never be discovered.

This man, it is safe to say, has little to do with our story; yet to get to the plot one must first set the scene. This man is but a platform, and for some he makes a perfect stage. Throughout this field many creeping creatures lived happily side by side, and within a society not unlike our own. A society made up of many different, colorful groups, and within these groups, one can always expect to find certain distinctive characters. In the society of insects, it was the distinguished praying mantis, who was hailed as a born chronicler and the Wordsworth of his time. He was a true romantic, a man of letters, and the poet laureate of his state. He had read up on all the great insectile literature, knew all the classics, and was an avid writer of dramatic plays. However, of his numerous skills and employments, his favorite was that of a raconteur, and his friends and neighbors, and most every creature of the forest, praised him for his many prolific tales.

Every Saturday night the mantis would hold large performances, and ensue to tell wondrous legends and stories to all the animals and insects of the nearby forest and field. On this day, the weekly congregation was to be held on the dead man's back, for the mantis had a flare for the extravagant, and a desire to thrill his audience as much as possible. He had also held spectacles in a tin soup can, which amplified his voice tenfold and was a huge success. He had spoken to half the forest one time from the highest branch of the highest tree; and, at the occasional dramas and theatrical performances, he could be found riding on the back of a chipmunk or a frog to portray to his viewers a knight on horseback or a sword-wielding soldier charging into battle on his white steed. But often times, when no such peculiar location could be found, and the chipmunks were too busy to act in a play, the tales were told beneath the massive trunk of a collapsed maple tree that had created a nook between the two hillsides over which it had fallen, way out deep in the heart of the forest. This spot was chosen as a regular stomping ground not only because of its auditorium-like atmosphere, but because of its extraordinary ceiling. On the log overhead, the exoskeletons of hundreds of ancient cicadas quietly hung like eerily beatific effigies, their glossy blind eyes remained frozen, gawking down from above, twinkling in turquoise moonlight and watching over those assembled below. They were as if made of dark glass, but one could not tell whether they were as fragile as it or as solid as stone, as the petrified log on which they hung. This was the amphitheater of the forest.

Today, however, the event was to be held on the body in the field, on his back, covered by his dark jacket with its rolled up sleeves. The tale was rumored to be an amusing one, and all the birds and squirrels and insects had been waiting anxiously the entire week just to hear it. They all arrived for the show—it was his biggest crowd yet!—and this is the tale they heard.

Once all in attendance had amassed around the corpse, the mantis stepped up onto the stage of the man's back and bowed proudly as the forest dissonantly erupted with applauding creatures. It came from the treetops, from the far-off shadow of the woods and tall bushes, and especially in the hordes of infatuated insects standing before him. They clapped and shouted for a respectable amount of time, and then quieted down in unison as the mantis began his story. Thousands of antennas and black, bulbous eyes peered impatiently at him.

'Welcome all,' he said, 'how wonderful that you could be here!' The crowd was overwhelming. He paused, and everywhere he looked he saw a creature looking back at him. From beside him, sitting on the curvature of the man's ear, an eager centipede urged him to resume by yelling for him to do so, and a current of constricting muscles rippled across his long body with its many little intensely kicking legs. The mantis was obliged. 'Tonight,' he continued, 'I have not only just a tale of great magnitude, but one of truth, if you desire it to be! It exists and takes place right here in our own backyard; and what it is, my friends, is a sign from God!—a light sent straight from heaven and down to earth for us to ascend. But that's not all! I believe it is a true light of rapture, and the gateway to unimaginable happiness!'

And the mantis continued to tell of the importance of the light.

'Yet to all of your misfortunes,' he then said, 'I heard of the light from a source who wishes to stay anonymous; but he made me a map, and I followed it to where he said it would be. It took me all day and well into the night. I was soon going to give up, but suddenly I saw orbing before me a bright blue light! I was frightened to begin with, and I observed it from afar. And what I saw, I must admit, was nothing short of a miracle! I saw many pious insects, moths and beetles, and even mosquitos, all fly into the light! They entered in an array of bright flourishes and never came out the other side!

'I thought, this can't be! It is too great, too fantastic; and I wept when I realized that you all wouldn't believe me, but that I wouldn't be able to stop myself from telling you. Because you must understand, good creatures—this isn't a fiction, this is a miracle!'

The crowd cheered; and there was, in fact, some truth to his words. This story was not like his others, it was much shorter, more like a news report, and he was acting as would a questioned witness testifying at a trial. It was bizarre and unordinary and exciting. Most of the insects sensed the change in the mantis's style of performance, for this was no performance at all! Though what was indeed his only hope in getting them to believe in his words and take him seriously, in the end only succeeded in heightening their interests and joy of having been thoroughly entertained. They all cheered for him as if it was another farfetched tale, as if it was a circus spectacle, and he was walking above them on a tightrope or swinging from a trapeze, the crowd below half cheering him on and half gazing in captivation.

'No, no!' the mantis cried, 'No—do not cheer, hear me out! This is a matter to be discussed, and listened carefully to, for we do not know just what this light may be, regardless of my prior enthusiasm. It could be, for all we know, an alien weapon! So I do not want souls wandering out of excitement in search of it; I could not handle having to know I caused someone's demise as a result of my careless display of words. But with that having been said, from having seen what I have, I'd say, with all my heart, that this was a light from God, or, as it seemed, a light straight to him!'

And the creatures,—the saxicolous, the green and winged, the brown and burrowing— from the high branches of black trees, to the haunting depths of the forest, to right up around the stinking body— all the creatures broke out in a chorus of praise and applause, so loud it could have been heard by folks in town, most peacefully asleep by now and in their beds. But this is not what the mantis desired; he wanted attention, not admiration. He wanted to inform the people on what he had seen, not merely amuse them. In that moment, he would have rather preferred dead silence. 'We must seek it,' he continued, 'but not all at once. We shall go in a small party at first, led by myself and a handful of others. This journey should be taken with the utmost caution, and with the complete dedication of its travelers. That is why I am to make the first trip, and with the help of some close colleagues. I'll set off in the morning, and we can meet back here at this time tomorrow night, where I shall report to all of you what I've seen. The truth, I say, shall be revealed!'

He, with his cane in hand, which was in itself the quill of a porcupine, and after waving thoroughly his long green arms to the creatures whose cheers shook the bloated corpse on which he stood, walked quickly down the man's back, across the extended arm, over the gleaming ring, and up into the semi-hollow shell of an old turtle who was his personal chauffeur. He slowly waddled off into the surrounding brush and disappeared in a field of roaming darkness.

Most went home that night enthralled and well entertained. Most knew not to take the mantis's tales too seriously, too literally; and all over the forest wise parents ensured their young that the light wasn't real, and that it was not in fact something one could seek. However, at the front of it all, standing the entire duration of the mantis's story on the dead man's hand, around his golden ring, were three flies by the names of Aniston, Langston, and Sebastian—three flies who were rather impressionable when it came to the words and beliefs of their idols, and had taken the story as absolute fact; suddenly they found themselves infatuated with it and the rapturing light of which it foretold. It seemed to awaken a longing inside of them, a Libertine-like mentality for freedom and knowledge and never-ending escapades, with underline touches of restlessness and angst. They were the youngest of sixty siblings, and the most neglected by a solemn mother who longed to be a larvae once again, in order to taste the forgotten sweetness of parasitic youth. She was almost a week old, and quickly drawing closer to being one with the dirt, as she had been as a childish grub. The three flies, now completely captivated by the mantis's words, were but twelve and a half hours old, which is about the same in terms of human years, for minutes are like months, and the seconds ticked by in a way that could never be imagined. A person could not fathom the scale of time on which lived the flies; it is comparable, I suppose, to fathoming the vastness of space, and where it is we stand in the heart of it all. And so these three flies, with little deliberation, prepared to set off in search of light.

Although quite boisterous about their plan to the creatures near them, they still lingered around the body until all had left the field, just to make sure that there was no one else with the same agenda. An hour passed, and finally the multitudes had cleared away, and nothing but trampled grasses and heavy nightfall stood around them. At this time they started on their journey, but quickly realized that they did not know the way, for the mantis had never revealed such important information, nor described the specifics of his acquired map; and they retreated back to the body in the field seemingly in defeat. They hovered there in deliberation, their three particolored bodies appearing like bits of green and blue and other metallic-colored crystals suspended in the night, bobbing in air below two shuttering translucent wings. From the leaves of a tall weed beside them, as they descended and perched in curiosity upon the heel of the dead man's shoe, they heard the sounds of someone beckoning, summoning them towards the shadows. 'Flies!' called the voice, 'Flies, over here!' And they quickly pursued it, giving not a thought to potential consequences, nor the dangers of interacting with those who creep in the night.

'Flies,' said the voice, 'I know what it is you seek!'

They buzzed around the leaf, and quickly discovered hiding behind it a coiled snake. His body was a deep shade of red and patterned with yellow spots, and his slender tongue quivered from his diamond-shaped head like a blade of grass in the wind. The flies saw him and quickly scattered, for they had been taught never to interact with snakes, otherwise they would surely be harmed, one way or another. But this snake ensued to beckon them once again, and assured them that they would not be hurt. Gullible as they were, although they for but a moment did in fact grow reluctant, the three flies eventually flew back over to the weed and perched themselves on the leaf below which the snake had curled.

'You've heard the mantis's story, I presume,' he continued. 'Well, my little friends, what would you say if I told you that I knew where the light was?'

'But how could you know?' asked Sebastian, the most assertive of the three.

'I know,' said the snake, 'because it was I who drew the map!'

'You…' murmured Aniston, the most reclusive of the three.

'Yes, I!' cried the snake, apparently basking in his own self-satisfaction.

'And so you've come to rub it in our faces, I suppose—and get our hopes up just so you can watch us wallow in our misery!' said Langston, the most distrustful of the three.

'Why, no. I wish to give it to you!' replied the snake, now fluttering his tongue quicker than he had before, and slowly uncoiling his body from the knot it was in. When he was straightened and no longer balled-up under the leaf, the three flies saw, lying in the grass where he had sat, a crumpled piece of paper.

The flies, having seen this, and rightfully assuming that it was the crucial map, quickly fell into a fit of despair, for, as they soon revealed to the snake, they did not know how to read. 'Not a problem,' said the snake, 'I shall read it for you. It is quite simple, and easily committed to memory. There is only one direction, and that is straight ahead, right down that distant road beyond the field. You'll travel it, and the first thing you will see, after what may have seemed like an endless journey, is a signpost. At the signpost take a right. After this you will see the light's glow, and it'll get bigger and bigger. It hangs above the steps of a human structure and simply cannot be missed!'

'Thank you,' they cried; and the snake slowly coiled himself, like a winding liana, up the trunk of a spruce tree and was lost to the branches. And as he slithered away, he chuckled quietly to himself, and flickered his tongue in the cool midnight air, tasting his surroundings and the first drops of dew that had started to grow over the grass in the field and on the leaves of the tree. What possible reason might the snake have that could honestly justify why he had decided to point the flies in the direction of that allusive and enchanting light? In this life, whom can one actually trust? The insects, so they had been taught, could only ever trust themselves, their quickness and their intuitions. That is all.

So, with the instructions in mind, and more driven now than ever before, the three flies set off across the meadow in the direction of the road. When they reached it, they stopped to catch their breath and hovered around the rotting pumpkins that amassed atop the vine-strewn soil beneath them. From within a hollowed gourd emerged a noise, and they were soon distracted by the chiming nocturne of a lone cricket. It played out for a while, and then came to a sudden stop.

'Hello!' said the cricket to the hovering flies above, 'what brings you to the patch at this hour? Couldn't say I thought you lived here.'

'We're going down the road,' Sebastian stated, 'but we don't have time to waste on crickets; we are in quite the hurry!'

'As you flies always are...' replied the cricket in a disappointed tone. 'All you flies ever do is buzz around aimlessly and annoy the other critters. I detest you.'

'Then why have you stopped to speak to us?' Sebastian asked. 'Why are you wasting our time, as well as your own?'

Seeming to have overlooked these questions, the cricket simply asked, 'So where is it you're going?'

The three insects glanced their many little eyes at each other indecisively. They did not know whether to tell the cricket or to keep it a secret. However, they figured that since they had already bragged about it to so many creatures in the field after the story, it couldn't hurt to brag to the cricket as well, at least just to get him off their backs. And they were all quick to inform him that they were in search of light.

'In search of light, or in search of *the* light?' asked the cricket.

'In search of *the* light!' the flies exclaimed, and buzzed excitedly all around the rotted gourd where the cricket was living.

'Oh, no, no!' said he, 'you mustn't seek it; you must go home!'

'Why, I can't believe what I'm hearing!' Sebastian said to the others derisively. 'The mantis tells us all that there is a heavenly light waiting to bring us to paradise, somewhere within reach. With that knowledge, how can we stop? How can we just go home now, while down this very road there is the gateway to eternity, the door to *real* life, to supreme existence! It would be a foolish thing to ignore and act as if it didn't concern us, as if it didn't concern us all!'

'You must listen to me,' started the cricket, 'for perhaps I can sway you in the opposite direction. You see, this is not a light to heaven, for it has taken from me all that I ever loved. Yes I know of the light, and have long before that crazy mantis fella started spewing the tale to everyone in the forest! Oh, I know of it quite well!'

'What has the light possibly done to you?' Langston asked, and they all perched themselves on a thick vine that snaked from the head of a large pumpkin beside the cricket's gourd. 'How could something so magical have caused you harm?'

'Ever since the light showed up,' said the cricket, 'all my friends and family set off to discover what it could be, for they too thought it was a miracle. They all set out to find it, and when they did, they vanished into the light and never returned. It gives off a beautiful humming melody, you see, but only we can hear it. Now, I'm afraid, I can't find anybody to play music with me in the evenings, and I'm so alone.

'We crickets, I must admit, aren't normally drawn to that kind of thing, like most other winged creatures; but we are rather more susceptible to hysteria, it seems, and tuneful melodies, and suffer from a tendency to commit rash actions in a time of provoked agitation or intense emotional confusion. But, I suppose, so do most of us. Yet there is no doubt, young flies, that if you seek this thing you shall all meet the same fates as those I once loved.'

But the story did not sway the flies, and they were still convinced that what they sought was truly worth seeking. They labeled the cricket a coward, and a sacrilegious, simple minded creature. Before they left, as the cricket practically begged and cried for them to return home, Sebastian invited him to join them on their journey, but he refused. Taking flight and soon ascending some ways off the vine, they said goodbye to the cricket, and, though they inwardly resented him, still wished him the best of luck in finding someone to make music with in the night, and said that they were sure he'd meet another of his kind soon enough. But the cricket paid no attention to their kind words of departure, and simply gazed at them in desperation. They were helpless, both he and the flies; and down the road they continued on, looking back only once to watch as the pumpkin patch faded away into horrible darkness.

The road ahead had as many hills in it as did the field, and one could never quite tell when or where it would end. Nevertheless, the flies strode on and made good time. They were rushing, for they knew that the light would be easier seen in the dark, and thus wanted to find it before the sun crept above the horizon. But soon they grew weary and weak, and stopped to perch upon a dandelion sprouting in the cool grass on the shoulder of the road that was starting to dampen with silvery drops of dew, of which spectacularly glistened from the myriads of blades and trickled slowly down them. Their moisture was enhanced by the moonlight, which is the most water-like of all the luminaires, and detailed every pebble of liquid under which its blue light cast. From the dampness and darkness of wet soil beneath, there arose a gentle tremor, and soon the blades of grass around the dande-lion began to shake, and out of the dirt appeared the probing head of an earthworm.

'You flies have awakened me!' he exclaimed.

'You don't even have a face,' Sebastian remarked, and buzzed around the worm tauntingly.

'Yes, but that doesn't mean I am senseless!' he replied. 'In fact, my senses are extraordinary! I was deep underground when I heard you three coming from down the road. I went even deeper as you all came nearer. I must have been far beneath the grass roots when the three of you landed on that plant; that's when I couldn't take it anymore! The buzzing was too much, it drove me mad. So here I am asking you to leave, for I have much sleep to catch up on, and much soil to move.'

'We apologize,' said Aniston, 'we are only here to rest and will be on our way shortly.'

'Indeed,' said Langston, 'we don't have time for worms.'

'And why is that?' asked the worm. 'Why, even the birds, who are always in a rush, have time for worms! Where is it you are going to in such a hurry?'

'To the heavenly light!' they cheered, and buzzed even more excit-edly and noisily around the head of the agitated creature.

'But you mustn't,' said the worm, 'you certainly mustn't go to the light.'

'What would you know about the light?—you, with no eyes!' said Sebastian. 'Together, my brothers and I have hundreds of eyes! And they desire to see wonderful things.'

'I don't need to see the light,' said the worm; 'it is not the sight of it I fear, no. What I fear is its heat. As should you, for it is not like any other heat. All day long I must stay underground otherwise the lights will stiffen me and dry my skin. Darkness, my friends, is what I must seek. For me heaven is under the earth.'

'No!' cried the flies, 'it's what's above! But we cannot fly high enough, we know this. But the light we seek is in our potential reach, and that is why it is so important that we find it, for it will take us to paradise.'

'Flies,' said the worm, 'it is not what you think!'

'If not heaven,' asked the flies, 'then what is it?'

"It is two things,' said the worm. 'It is the devastation of existence, and the existence of devastation! All lights are certainly wicked.'

But the worm understood that he could not sway the flies, and so he crept back beneath the dirt, and returned to his tunnels to sleep. The flies, even though they knew that the worm did not know about the light which they spoke of specifically, and as they had with the cricket, still thought that the worm was a coward and an unbeliever, set off down the road again, and this time without looking back at the dandelion they had left swaying gently in the wet grass, in the blue light; nor did they give anymore thought to the dangers of what it was they pursued.

The world may be a threatening place, and although to the birds the forest was a utopia, it was still a dangerous existence, especially for insects. And it is true here, as it had been true for the shepherds of old, that even in Arcadia there is death. And even if Poussin himself had been out painting a landscape background of the field that day, he too would not have been able to sway the flies. They were uncontrollable; some great and mysterious grasp had taken hold of their minds, and was never going to let them go. But aside from that, the mostly harmonious forest, much like our own world, was, and had always been, a somewhat peculiar place. Oh, how many bizarre happenings did secretly occur in those woods, though most not as strange as the mantis's performances. Yet, in regards to bizarre happenings, the flies had seen a few. For example, in the early days of Sebastian's life, which occurred within the first few minutes of his existence, he had witnessed a strange thing, the thought of which stuck with him always as a ponderous reel of memory replaying in the back of his mind, frequently throughout the day, before his many subconscious eyes. On the outskirts of the field, far from the little shrub where he lived with his family, he had seen an entire generation of ants, numbering into the tens of thousands, living solely off the nourishment of a splattered melon that someone had thrown out the window of a car and into the grass as they drove by on the dusty road. It was the image of those many, many beings all working together in a singular mass—scurrying, clicking, chiming with the sounds of their needle feet and chomping pinchers—that he replayed in his mind again and again. Sebastian's mother told him about the ants, and that they had been there since she was little, and thus believed that it would take a hundred years for them to fully consume the fruit, as they had already been working on it for several decades. And to this day, as our three flies make their way down the dark road, closer and closer to their certain fates, those ants are still there gnawing away slowly, mechanically, day and night, at the orange, rotting flesh of the melon.

Near the end of the dirt road there stood a street sign. It directed passing motorists towards the town, for at this sign the road split, and left one to choose between two paths. The sign was attached to a rough wooden pole. The pole was dark and old and very nearly a cactus, as it was spiked with protruding ends of rusty nails. They were all that was left of decades of lost dog posters, missing children posters, garage sale advertisements, and other flyers of the sort. As the three flies approached this signpost, they saw in the moonlight perched upon a nail the silhouette of a large moth. He was a Polyphemus moth to be exact, and the largest of the Saturniidae family in the United States. He had two dots at the end of each fuzzy, membranous wing, and they looked like gawking eyes. The moth referred to them as defense mechanisms. They were there to confuse predators. But it seems a futile trait, for whether you are bit in the ass or the face, if you happen to be an insect, you will die either way. Still, like a flounder camouflaged with the seabed, the eyes made the moth feel safe, but offered no physical form of protection.

Our three flies, coming up the road and seeing the moth upon the nail, flew up and hovered around him. This time, though they would not have admitted to it, they did in fact have time to spare on the moth. 'We do not know right from left;' said Aniston, 'would you tell us which way the light is?'

The moth, still crouched on the rusted spike, wiggled his antennas and peered up at the inquiring flies. 'The light?' said the moth. 'Is that what you seek? May I ask you why?'

'Why, it is heaven, ain't it!' said Langston, 'how could we not?'

'Heaven!' said the moth, 'Bunkum! It's just another six letter word. The only thing you'll find is darkness; go back the way you came.'

'You do not have to like us or treat us politely,' started Sebastian, 'but it would be decent enough if you pointed us in the direction called *the right.*

'I don't know about no lefts and rights,' said the moth, 'but town is just down this here road, that there road takes you to the bridge above the river.'

He had given the flies all the information they needed, and they would have soon been off again if the moth hadn't spoke up and kept them from going. The flies were detained for the moment, which only heightened their prior annoyance. Meddling bugs annoy us all. What is a moth but a pest? A person doesn't have to be a lepidopterists to know that. They will forever be overshadowed by the butterfly. But just because something is a pest, doesn't mean it cannot be wise. That's just what this moth was, a wise pest. Yes, wise, in the realm of insects, that is, but wise nonetheless. Although he was wise, he came off as a nuisance, and the flies had already barred him from their senses and ability to follow rational impressions like the ones many sympathetic creatures had been trying to instill in them all night—such as letting them be swayed into not seeking the light, and immediately returning to their home, et cetera, et cetera. The flies were forming grudges against those who halted them on their journey, those who challenged them, warned them to reconsider. They were so absorbed in their stride that any additional time wasted between them reaching the light and them interacting with unwelcome interlopers made them furious. The funny thing was, however, that the flies themselves were the true meddlers, and the source of much discomfort and frustration throughout the night.

Anyways, I have already told you that the moth was wise; he was, in fact, the only remaining chance the credulous flies had to live, the final potential savior of their souls, the last of three. 'Stay a minute,' he said, and they remained, hovering quietly above him.

Now, prior to hearing what the wise moth has to say, it should be addressed that it may not necessarily seem plausible to most people for insects to grasp the concept of God and religion and at the same time not be able to differentiate between what to many would seem to be an ordinary luminaire and a light of rapture. However, the insects were fairly accurate in their presumptions, for, though not exactly, what it happened to be was not too dissimilar. The fact is, every creature in the forest knew about God, or a god. From the time the forest had begun to grow, in centuries past, the critters within it had always been deeply devout, here more so than any other forests in the state. It could have been something in the vegetation, I suppose, or in the air. It could have been something in the soil, too. But with that said, it was most likely a union of the three, along with the fact that the townspeople nearby were all quite spiritual, or so they appeared.

The wilderness was only wild in the sense that great things were given the chance to grow and roam free. Every leaf, every worm in the dirt, all were free. They were subject to no government, prisoners of no war, sufferers of no fiscal crisis. They were a society of a million bodies that lived as one. The only laws they followed were the laws of instincts: one needed food, so one found a way to get food; one needed water, so one found a way to get water; one needed entertainment, so one sought entertainment; and most of all, one needed a home. Parents of the weaker creatures taught their young to survive among the stronger creatures; and the stronger creatures taught their young how to remain on top. They all lived as we see them living—as birds in trees, ants in hills, bees in flowers, and foxes on the hunt. One should not undermine them, or view them as if we are superior—we are not, it must be assured. Though they seem simple, it is only because you curious men and women, you bizarre children who observe them, are far too complex. You only disbelieve in their credence in God because you've never heard of such a thing, as they have no way of telling us. Nonetheless, they have faith, each and every one of them. Most of the time, these creatures, and bugs in particular, kept their religious beliefs to themselves. They were modest about it, for they all respected one another, understood one another, mammal and insect, reptile and bird. It is for this reason that our story is so intriguing, for things like this—like interpreting an ethereal light as a holy doorway—did not happen often to the creatures of this particular forest. We all must understand, however, that our woodland creatures are still evolving, and learning from their mistakes, as we have throughout our past, with examples such as human sacrifice and the religious purging of pagan communities. I can recall a time in our human history, and still to this day, where people practiced heliolatry, or believed that nature itself is a divine spirit. Nevertheless, these are not false philosophies, nor are they forgotten. These are all still quite compelling and practiced beliefs in the world as of the twenty-first century. So, with that said, it is again appropriate to state that though what they sought was not what they presumed it to be, it was fairly close, and their assumption was as good as any based upon the beliefs that they had grown up on and the wonderful forest they had grown up in.

The moth, too, was a devout soul. He had a love in God, but cared more for the wellbeing of others and of his world. He was actually quite the philanthropist, and had singlehandedly funded the preservation of hundreds of beloved cicada exoskeletons on the log that was their amphitheater. They were bonded firmly to the tree overhead; they were coated in a waterproof finish, comprised mostly of honey supplied in abundance by the bees, and a plaque was etched into a small green stone by a hummingbird to commemorate the heroic and bygone creatures that hung above them, as well as the present creatures' token of appreciation to the moth for his generous contributions. For this, the moth was admired, and he was also quite wealthy. He made his living painting eyeballs onto the wings of insects who had them not. One could say he was almost an armory dealer, or an instructor in the arts of whimsical preservation and self-defense. But of course, the moth was an ardent pacifist.

So the flies did what the moth had told them, and they stayed a minute. They hovered there above him and waited impatiently, but he said nothing, nor did he say anything a minute later. 'We have to go,' said Sebastian, 'we haven't the time for this.'

'Don't go,' said the moth. 'You can if you want, but I suggest you stay and listen to what I have to tell you.'

'Well,' started Sebastian, 'go on then, say it! We don't very much have time for invasive species.'

And so the moth said:

'Trust not in your eyes, my flies, nor your hearts. Though I know you have many, and of course we all have but one, I urge you still, do not finish what you have begun... Now, I mustn't rhyme any longer, this situation is far too serious. If the knowledge of your predicament is enough to stop a moth from rhyming, then surely you are in quite the predicament! The light, flies, is not a warm one. It is an icy light, for it glows blue, as blue as an oceanic glacier. There is no heat to be felt from it, it only glows and hums, and if you get too close, it'll snatch you away. I had friends, and I had children, all of whom, of no fault of their own, have been taken from me because of the light. We love the light—not the light you seek, but other, much safer lights. Simple bulbs, streetlights, that sort of thing. We love it because as caterpillars we were never able to get close to them with the exception of the sun. Though, even that was a difficult risk, for then we'd leave ourselves open to the birds. But never, my friends, have I seen a light that takes you away like one, like a bird to a caterpillar bathing in the sun. Never have I seen something that is so mysterious, yet so obvious in its actions.

'After leaving my host plant,' the moth continued, 'the first thing I decided to do was go find a light. And when I did, you can be sure I hovered round it the whole day. But this, this one is not like the others. I was there when my dearest friend, a gypsy moth named Ford, decided he'd fly right on in. He had been wondering about the light for days, dwelling on it, in fact, and driving himself crazy over it. So one morning we went there, and he flew in.'

'Then what?' asked the flies.

'Then nothing,' said the moth, 'that is just the problem! He never came back out, nothing happened. He flew in and then in a flash he was gone, and still has yet to return.'

'Well, that suits us fine,' Sebastian replied, 'because we don't plan on returning. Perhaps your friend didn't want to either, and that's why he never has.'

'What are the chances,' said the moth, 'that you are wrong and I am right, or that you are right and I am wrong? Would you say 50/50? Would you say 40/60? Well what I'd say is that it doesn't matter. I know what I've seen with my own eyes. You three, on the other hand, are only believing in what you have been told, and without proof. So, wouldn't it then by wiser to take my advice and go back to your home?'

'We are going home,' said the flies, 'though not to the one we have left behind.'

'I'm sorry,' Langston said, 'but we have to leave now, the sun will be up soon. Thank you for the directions.'

They had defeated him. And unable to get himself to look up again at the presence of the three flies, for he knew that the prolonging of their existence was futile, he sorrowfully spread his wings and took flight. He faded away into the dark sky above, and all that was left were the spikes in the pole, the vacant road, and the many stars. Langston then led the way, and they flew on into the night, in the direction the moth had indicated. The road was soon coming to an end, and in the distance they saw a pale glow suspended in air. They said nothing, but grew intensely eager, and flew faster than they ever had. Their tiny wings flapped so quickly that they became invisible, and the light grew larger and larger as they approached it.

At last, our three flies have made it! They knew it, and they buzzed with joy, and flew in whirling circles through the air. Oh, how captivated they were; their journey had not been in vain. The flies set off on their final stretch, their final stride. Yet it was to be, in fact, the finale of their lives. In their many eyes the light shone bright. Its hue was a shocking blue color, and it filled them with energy. They, without hesitation, without spending even just a second to reconsider, all flew into the brightness. Their entrance was followed by three tiny flares, and then the night grew still, and the light grew brighter, but only for a moment, then it dimmed and was once again restored to its natural orbing glow. The flies did not come out the other side, nor did they come out the way they had come in. Instead, as the moth had foretold, nothing happened, and all was still. Slowly from behind, another light began to creep itself into view. It was the sun, it was rising, and the surrounding world, the woodland, the houses, and the road, once again became visible.

It was around this time that a certain praying mantis, followed by a few of his cronies, had made their way down the trail and finally approached the pale light, much more pale than it had been just moments ago, for the sun had diluted its shine. The mantis and the others climbed their way up the wooden column of the build which the light suspended from. They made their way to the eve of the roof, and stood there on a shingle looking out at the light. They were confused, and the mantis grew solemn and quiet. What they witnessed was nothing divine, and surely nothing to be captivated over. What they saw, to their utmost shock and repulsion, was a steel tray that hung from a chain beneath the dim, pulsating light. In that tray the bodies of a hundred critters lay unmoving and deceased. Those who flew were left with wings that were slightly singed; and those who climbed the wood column to reach the light were left with crooked, charred legs and bent antennas. What they all had in common was the fact that they were dead.

The mantis cried out in agony and then collapsed. With his long, probing arms he clawed pitifully at the ground and in the light's direction. With some effort, his roach cronies picked him up, put him on their plated backs, and like a coffin on a litter during a funeral procession, carried him away down the gutter. He would never recover mentally from what he had seen, nor regain the hope he had lost. All lights were cursed to him now, and he never told another tale again whose undertones were not intensely morbid and filled with despair. He was depressed, and the heavenly light, in its falsified existence, had ruined him. But the creatures of the forest never lost their respect for the mantis, instead, the mantis lost respect for himself, and felt wholly responsible for the death of the flies and the many other creatures left to rot, alone and forgotten in the metal dish.

The ball of light was nothing more than a mere human invention. It was yet another cruel machine designed to shock the life out of unsuspecting insects, undeserving of such a fate, and most in search of their own salvation. This bug zapper, in all its cruelty, hung from the eve of a chapel; and in the belfry overhead, as the three lifeless bodies of the curious flies *slept* with dozens of others in the basin of the collective compartment which was attached to the light, the call of Sunday morning congregation rang out and sounded across the virgin land, through the fields of tall grass and wheat, and the hidden bowers in the brush where creeping things contemplated their own existence, and dreamed. Soon thereafter, down the way appeared the people of the town, the well-dressed churchgoers. They formed pyramids in the road, with the children at the peripherals holding onto the hands of mothers slightly taller, who walked beside stern men in plain, ironed clothing; each was taller than the last, except for the one uninteresting man in the middle, he was the pyramidion. They were all blank-faced, pale and child-like, oblivious to most everything around them; and as the preacher welcomed the congregants heartily from where he stood in the aisle between the many pews, the people of the town strutted happily up the wooden steps and into the chapel, they themselves in search of light.

The Restrictions of Consciousness

RANTS, PROSE & POETRY 2012-2014

My Flesh of Earth

This year I've sent for shovels, axes and picks, to move the land. I shall exhume my heart, for a night and a day. I must hear a beat, or else forget how to stand, stand up with my back straight. O bipedalism!—the first great achievement of man. I've grown bored beneath the sky's crystal glow. I've grown solemn with the droning of flies and retention pond toads, and the peacefulness of gossamers suspended across fields of verdant stems, burnished with golden sunset lights. I feel like the microbial soil, like the festering earth. I also have a sense that my flesh is your cloak, his smoke or her perfume; extract my coveted attar and make yourself smell lovely! But this earthly scent of mine, this earthly flesh, it makes me wonder… makes me wonder, what are the elements? I feel like one of those coquinas you find on coastal beaches, a stone that within it there are shells and fossils and treasures of the sea. Yes, just as the feces of owls contain the seeds of many berries and the skeletons of mice: we are conglomerates, combinations, accumulations of the land and sea.

Oh, and the next thing I knew it was dark out, and I was with a friend. My day was nearly done, and much work had been accomplished. We gazed at the sky, no longer a crystal blue; I was not bored, though I was contemplative. And so I confessed, "I wish I had been there on the day that God picked away the firmament at night with his nail and left the crescent moon." "What happened when it came to be full?" he asked in return. And so I told him, "That's when God stuck

his finger through the sky; stuck out his finger and pointed at us all!"
And so he sighed, with tired eyes, and looked up at it once more. Then
I thought to myself, now completely satisfied with my work, when day
breaks I shall rebury my heart, and my muscles again will become dirt
and cater to worms; my eyelids will shut on the frail shells of snails, and
the roots of spider plants will silently coil with my hair. I'll sense it not,
for I am not there. I am asleep. And the stone above my body will say:
Thank you. Please leave me to my imaginings.

A Distant Glimmer

No one is aware of your movements,
Only I.
From the low green hill upon which is built your home,
A far cry.
A distant glimmer from the partially hidden road:
The silvery wristband of a man with a hooked nose.
Go run and get your mother, get your sister, too!
Have them bake him sweets and golden pastries,
And pour him a glass of cider, or some other warm drink.
But wait, perhaps another time…
For now, show me no coyness, my love;
With drapes over every window, and the sun creeping low,
The gradual abstraction of our sartorial gear
Needs no longer to be so slow.
In her pupils a distant glimmer shines;
Not a tear has she to cry.
No one is aware of your movements, my love,
No one is aware, only I.
From on the slope of your lawn we lay, and in the approaching night.
From your lips comes the utterance of a promise;
From your eyes beams a distant light, and so we chat…

Brendon Kolodziej

Let us become Shramanas, my love, for our homes are stifling!
And in this dark orange dusk I smoke until my heart aches;
We mock ourselves until our faces turn blue!
You laugh the words of a silly song;
I hum the words I wish were true.
Then from a neighbor's hot oven, through their open window,
Comes the scent of baking bread.
Something garlic, or raised with shredded cheese, is being fed…
And you lean upon my chest.
Slowly, from the grass where we lay, with your soft white hand
You'll trace the markings in the sky,
Though slightly immured here by great plastic fortresses
Standing tall at our feet, and in our tiny, glassy eyes,
All safe within sprawling cornfields
Like ramparts around our city.
We've traversed along backroads, teeming with vacancies.
And in some old car we'll drive,
Or on foot gently wander, and find our way home
By the markings in the sky.
No one is aware of your movements, my love,
No one is aware, only I.
Together, we trace the glimmering dimples of intelligent design.
And together, you know, we crave the power to live forever high.

Paraclete

Of Patriarchs and mad men, somber acquaintances,
And cold air blowing in the night.
We meet in backyards, on doorsteps and in hallways;
We stare into mirrors, gaze upon the faces of strangers,
And act as if no one is there.
It is only you and I.
It is only you.
The future waits for no one,
Yet we all await the future.
So please, line my coffin with terra-cotta,
Lacquer my bones.
Dress my memory in satin gowns
And carve my name into the sandstone.
And be calm, while walls turn grey in the evening.
In the morning they are white and shinning,
And in the evenings they are always grey.
But it can be a good thing,
Grey is comfortable,
Especially when wrapped in seeping sunlight.
All we are is alive, and yet,
It seems no one can figure out
Whether or not that's an understatement.

Never Before Seen

O the great Midwest!
Through its many seasons fluctuates between life and death.
There the Color Blind Painter who willingly resides
In states of mostly nonexistent tides
Stood on the dew-fresh lawn,
Staring wide-eyed up at the sky.
Gawking beneath the veins of electrical wire,
Idle there until the stars poured vapor
And the clouds rained down on him with fire.
Simply waiting for some subtle change in movements
That he was so sure would come,
Through the prevailing winds, or the rattling of tins,
As men in their machines made their way to distant destinations.
The Color Blind Painter watched
As passing shadows and hues grew fainter.
Lonesome and solitude in the soggy yard
Allowing the surrounding world to discard
All the colors of which he has never before seen,
Though he knows them well, recognizing them most anywhere;
Distinguishing quite accurately between
The daily shades of yellow and red and blue and green,
All of which he has never before seen... never before seen.

A Caravan of Angels

A caravan of angels shall come and lift me up
And carry me back to my homeland.
There I'll wade through the shallows and
The riptides of the captured sea,
Across dunes of red sand as high as God himself,
And sumptuous valleys where deer roam and eat the land,
And cry softly into each other's breasts
Throughout the otherwise silent night.
Then I shall behold the faces of the young!
And the fanfares of burning youth,
Endless hours of unbroken thought,
Ceaseless wonder and careless days.
The silhouette of the lights of Heaven scour across the green land,
Over the chateaus of the royal and the cabins of the lowly,
And into the arms of Eternal Silence.
There I shall meet your cries for attention…

Decoy, Illinois

To live or to die, alone in some room
In a house in Illinois…
I'm always trying to avoid everything,
So won't you be my decoy?
Gaining the strength to ask,
But I know that you don't want to know me;
I can smell it in your hair.
I think I can tell when the time is running slow,
And I know I can tell that you don't care.
"Neither do I," I'd say,
But that would be unfair.
"So when will you die?" she'd say.
"I'll die on the day that you care."
A conversation that never occurred,
Another dead language, another dead word.
"A poem a day keeps the witch doctor away,"
A man once told me, in a booth, at a play.
I wish I could trade one day for another,
Kill your sister to save your brother.
Hey kids!
Who's a fan of proper grammar?
I want to prove to you that words can be just as cool as cigarettes.
At least until addiction drives you mad

Like a head full of crickets.
Strangled to death, and knowing no right from wrong—
Our society's hands have been wrapped around your throat
For far too long!
Born without a conscience, born without a care,
No worries in the world because to you nobody's there.
Now look at me and what do you see?
There is a flaw that sticks out in everybody.
Flaws with claws that tear through your flesh
Like nails into walls.
Hang a painting from my forehead;
Hammer it in tight so I can suspend from above your bed.
A decorative memory of chemicals and entities,
A colored portrait of someone's long-lost empathies.
In conclusion,
I'll live a life of delusion
Or dissolve in a solution of verbal pollution.
But you can have it your way
Because I don't long for restitution.

I. Elsewhere

I see you rise out of my ashes,
As if they were yours to hold.
You come and go like the flash of matches,
Come back again before I get too cold.
Suspend your disbelief,
Trade all your pain for grief.
True beauty lies in the eyes of the blind.
Just because I'm breathing air
Doesn't mean I'm really there;
Replace my blood with serotonin
And start seeing things the way
They were meant to be seen.
I guess I'm just lucky enough to be unlucky.
I'm waiting for my mistakes
To mist on down and take me.
When the air is dead,
And as dense as lead,
Like a humid and damp spring day,
Our lungs suffer water damage
For as long as the protracting heat
And moisture continues to stay.

II. But in the Winter

Every cold and wretched Sunday,
For as long as I can remember,
I'd walk on into the local funeral home
And ask to be cremated, but to no avail.
"We don't cremate the living," they'd say.
"I am not the living," I'd say.
"We're sorry, come back again when you're dead," they'd tell me.
"I guess I'll try my luck elsewhere."
So where is this elsewhere?
One might ask.
Chewing on diamonds and robbed from behind,
You've been fooled again by all of mankind!
For only in elsewhere do I wish to stay.
Sure, one day I will refer to today as being back in the day,
But by then I will be elsewhere,
In a place not too far away.
It is a place one can sense
Through the faint detections of a winter approaching:
My mini Bic lighters don't seem to work when left out in the cold.
You can only die once before you just get old.
Watching as the recall is continuously sold,
Here's to another somber tale of a tale never told.

The Diagnosis

Behind the door a fire is burning
And all your possessions crumble into air:
A mattress, a stereo, and a stack of books…
My heart is swollen;
My lungs are charred with the heat that emits from my chest,
My passion, my soul.
It is a conflagration.
Invisible, and more icy than molten.
Yet, hotter than the sun,
And hotter than the stars.
Oh, what great giants we are!
With minds of gods,
And hands, capable of unimaginable creation.
Still, I talk like an idiot,
For I know the root of my stupidity, my worldliness, my fire…
I am sick.
A little tether of infectious bacteria is lodged in a lobe of my brain,
Sprouting from a cavity in my tooth.
It will eat me alive.
I will die.
And water will hail from the sky
To land on the flesh of another,

Perhaps one in the same;
Perhaps we are all each other,
But known by a different name.
And the diagnosis, I'm afraid, is love.
But what is it?
Lately its presence is alternating.
And in the night,
While fires burn
The fields of grass and clover
And pale wild flowers around the corner,
A body weeps,
While another sleeps,
And still others pray.
But as for me,
I'll lie, smoking, searing with the flame,
While all your possessions crumble into air.

The Revival of Vivisepulture:
A Long-Forgotten Culture

Take us back to a time of bronze swords
And great religious conquests.
A time knotted with sadism, genocidal colonization,
And hikes to the top of Montmartre.
Ah, yes, it is a revival!
Let us recall the vivisepulture:
Odran of Iona, willingly buried alive
So that the walls of a chapel could rise.
Saint Columba, save his soul!
He sees *the truth,*
Which none shall know…

———

Now time has passed, and I lay here fighting off the alpha waves.
But they will soon mutate, attempt to defeat me,
And ultimately succeed.
And so in a slightly conscious dream I seem to emerge, and listen
As a young scholar portrays to me, quite eloquently,
The city of Ravenna.
But settings soon change from sweet to deranged

With vivid depictions of Cambodia killing fields
Of the Khmer Rouge regime,
Where genocide was anything but a hassle.
Then like a native's arrow I shoot through time,
Moving into H.H. Holmes's Chicago Murder Castle.

———

I startle myself awake, but I am?
No—I find myself suddenly drowning now in a dried-up lakebed,
With mollusks and coral reefs burrowing deep into my head.
I seem to be a looney!
I seem to be throwing away my dreams for education,
When education is the only way to reach my destination.
I seem to be drifting...
And the people I knew and the times we had
Soon trail off and out of my head
And into the past as I lay in my bed,
Trying desperately to force the onset of a more peaceful sleep
In the hopes on being able to start the new day
With some sort of optimism.
My head feels full from the knowledge I pull;
Droning on and on, lethargic and listless,
Adding yet another improbability to my never-ending wish list.
Right from wrong and wrong from right,
I'm growing weaker with all my might!
And blinded by the absence of light,
Not everybody sleeps in the middle of the night...

America

From the dark Chicago underground:
Locked inside the house of the Manic,
Who shall save the Widow's son?
Tempers fading to a calming panic,
Prisoners of war to an army of none.

Oh, how our society is like a priory!
So keep secret the pages of your diary,
Or else risk revealing your soul
To the socializing machine.

Oh, what pure beauty one can find through ancient folklores:
The deforestation dryads of your oak wood floors;
Mop them weekly, lock the doors
In the night or when there's no one home;
Seed the garden and thank the gnome.

Cold shoulders that reflect yesterday,
God plays favorites and I pay to play.
I'll forget before I forgive.
Assisted living, it's how we live.

So cover your skin with another's fur,
While living in a home made of poly-carbon fiber.
I'm the number one seed,
But so are you.

Label me a Judas in the City of Angels;
Stamp my name into the boulevard.
Brush away my strains and bothers,
We cannot escape the sins of our fathers.

I look up at the airplanes scaring the sky
With the gases they expel.
I was told to swear to never tell.
Is there death after life or life after death?
Or is it just regicide, regicide, another guilty, guilty suicide?
O Lady Macbeth!

Spread your wise words and melodies like Malaria.
Either I'm retarded or you're a genius—
What a perplexity, yes,
But only in America.

John Doe

A day in the life of John Doe, whose name it seems we do not know.
He's hidden away
Deep In the womb of his tomb, but paving his way down the pavement,
Stepping into my room.
He proceeds to rest his dejected head of gloom upon my bed,
Sinking into the cushions and sheets of red.
And in doing so, experiences a sensation
That one would expect to feel
While jumping into a pool where the water has been drained
And replaced with jagged spikes and electric eels.
"That's exactly how this feels!" he shouts.
"Ah, yes, for it was here, outside this window we would peer
Up at the near-earth objects and creatures in the air,
White in the city at the Chicago World's Fair!—
We're never getting out of here," he says to me.
"They'll never let us go; they'll never let us be!"
Then silence slowly refills the room,
And a frigid draft begins to chill my ankles.
I'm standing on the other end of the apartment now,
Fiddling with a broken pocket watch with a tool,
And observing as wobbly clock parts
Scatter across the dark wooden desk.

I turn around in responsiveness like so,
But once my body had completely rotated in his direction
There was no John Doe!
The window by the bed where he had sat stood wide open
With salmon-colored curtains hanging down the two sides of the frame
And fluttering subtly in the cool breeze,
Waving gently and eerily as if some phantom had just passed by.
I walk up to the open window, stick my head out and gawk down
At the congested city ground.
"1893 couldn't come to an end more quickly!—God, how this year has
Consumed me! I was on top of the world; I was where I needed to be;
But everyone else was so damn jealous! Everyone just wanted to
Take a piece of me, but they can't have any!" I scream,
Frozen like a stone effigy as I perch my body through the aperture.
And so the Overlord of the Bored
Stared down from his window at the cemetery city of the dead
Where he resides.
Staring down at the sidewalk watching as an old man limps
Miserably across the land of nymphs;
A pale blue fog lingers over the swampy bog
That is the city;
One rich with legend and legacy and knowledge for the few—
O Sappho! Where has history taken you?
A muse of such reputation,
But only through fragments can we see your affectionate hue.
The Greeks claimed the heart of Lord Byron.
Noah sailed the deific flood.
Prophecies of Apollo, valor of a lion;
Julius Caesar, blinded by his own blood.
And directly under the window,
Fifty feet down on the sidewalk he lay in shade,
Cringing, bloody and aborted, with valgus bones intorted,
But no one came to his aid.
And now, as we all know, poor nameless John Doe

Escaped from his confined mind
And out onto the white city below.
And so, I wondered
As I stood there distraught
And ogling down at the crime scene beneath me…
Will I soon follow?

O my heart

O my heart
Will you let me slip away?
Outside where the trees rise,
Will you lie in wait
For veins beneath flesh
To work its blood through you?
Outside where lights are alive
And sand dollars wash upon coral shores;
Where the sunlight
Meets the water from the sea
And vultures perch upon iron gates…
O my heart
Will you let me slip away
Into endless nights,
Into gemstone days?
Here I beckon the rulers of the world!
I summon the hands of Faith Eternal!
Of the word made flesh,
Of orgiastic tides foaming with liquid salts
And streaming banners of white across the spanning gulfs!
Outside where the trees rise
Will my heart survive
Until I can plant one of my own?

Brendon Kolodziej

No—it's all blown smoke and shimmering mirrors,
A protracting land of dark clouds above
For veins beneath flesh
To work its blood through you.

Upon Reaching the Turnpike

Upon reaching the turnpike, that goddamn tollway, I felt for my wallet that I knew should be quietly waiting its removal in my back pocket. My kakis had slowly turned a shade of dark brown as the rain gently fell from above. It was nighttime, and the cars on the highway beside me whooshed by in the distorted figure of shooting rockets. I stumbled around the neglected land that one always had the pleasure of seeing through car windows while passing by, thanking their lucky stars that they were not actually there standing on it. The aging cigarette butts seemed to outnumber the blades of grass, though hardly distinguishable now that the summer had long since departed, and with it, seized the lives of common roadside vegetation. It was hard to keep myself from falling over, curling into a ball, and giving up as would an animal after being hit by a truck, fatally wounded, yet still alive. Oh, the pleasantness of road-kill! I had just stepped over one with caution: the contorted remains of a possum. My vehicle was one in the same, now miles away in the black distance.

With my left hand in my pocket fingering through loose change, I extracted my wallet—empty. No license, no cash, no credit card— empty. Why have one? I thought as I grasped the icy rail that ran down the side of the road; my breath, drifting in visible clouds from my body, wandered away into the air. God, why couldn't I? The approaching exit sign said two miles. Isn't it strange the way one's mind always yearns for the easy way out, which is, quite often, nothing other than death?

I would have rather died right then, happily consenting the rest of my potential days on this earth to age and sink down into the soil with the cigarette butts and the flattened possum. I would have rather jumped in front of the speeding Pontiac approaching me from behind than have to endure another two miles of this painless torture. But all sad and irrational thoughts aside, I couldn't seem to shake the feeling that something about tonight that was a little bit more disturbing than the consequences of a dead battery or a shitty engine.

After walking on and leaving the informative sign in the past, I approached a sight unknown. Something bright, not with luminance, but with character, shape and design, stood only a few yards ahead, the presence of which made me shiver. It was a girl, she was pregnant, and her long summer dress, a sky blue, fluttered wildly in the cool midwinter gusts— the kinds that leave you with the sensation of a million little needles prodding at your skin when it hits you in the face. Lipstick was smeared across her frost-bitten cheeks. Her nose a bright shade of pink; her eyes glowing with emotion from some recent happening unbeknownst to me, but obviously traumatic; and with tousled locks of hair encircling, streaming across her face and around her neck like a scarf, I ran towards her, ready to offer any assistance needed. However, she took off running when she saw me coming up from behind. I yelled after her, "Let me help you!" But she only picked up pace.

It was no use; she ran faster than I could get the words out of my mouth; sprinting wildly, and holding her gut as if the infant within would fall right out. She was already twice the distance she was from me when I had first noticed her existence. At a loose jog I followed. I was too exhausted from the traumas of my own recent happenings to run. Eventually, as I knew would likely be the case, my smoker's lungs got the best of me; I bent over and pressed my hands to my knees, fighting for a breath. I spit the cold phlegm that had slowly made its way up my throat out into the snow, and when I looked up, I saw that the girl was doing to same. She had stopped and was sitting cross-legged in the mud, breathing heavily with her eyes closed.

"I'm not going to hurt you!" I yelled, now on my way again. I approached her with care and sympathy, body shivering in the dampness of my clothing. She, on the other hand, was amazingly still. The cold seemed to have no effect on her; the rain only doused her hair and clothes, but left her skin with an unexpected aridity. "Why are you out here on the road?" I asked, placing my coat over her shoulders. "You're bare foot!" I cried. "Who's left you like this?"

She never offered a response. After gazing into her pale eyes, however, I suppose I got the answer I was looking for. In a sense, her eyes told all that needed to be known. Her lips never moved, yet those eyes spoke to me in a way that words could have never succeeded in doing. Her entire being was a shocking perplexity. The blue dress that covered her naked figure, void of any patterns, style, or brand, drooped down to her ankles and casted a shadow over her unprotected feet. I was able to raise her up, and we strode on. Though as we moved, she began to struggle to keep her balance, more than once nearly falling into the roadway, now quiet and vacant of its usual traffic. I held her up with an arm around her waist; she bowed her head towards the ground, tears dripping from wilted lashes and onto my hand that was entwined with hers.

A sign, littered with bullet holes and graffiti, informed us that the exit was now only half a mile away. As we passed it, the girl fell to her knees. With all her weight dropping downward, I lost my grip, and she hit the dirt hard. After a failed attempt at standing, she rolled over onto her backside.

"What's wrong?" I asked, beginning to panic, feeling the tension of indecision swelling inside my chest. "Who are you? Where can I take you? You've got to talk to me, honey, you're not well!" But still, she said nothing.

I picked her up and held her in my arms. In one odd motion, she dangled her head back and tightly shut her eyes. I walked for as long as I could; I strove hard to get to the exit, trying only to save the life of this poor girl, even though she was a complete stranger. It didn't matter; she was a person, just like me, just like you. So young and beautiful, what a disgrace it would have been for her to fade away with the possum and the ends of cigarettes that were scattered all around it. What a shame it would have been for her to leave this earth!

I pressed on until I could no longer. A blast of pain suddenly shot its way up my spine, and I collapsed down to my knees, still cradling her in my arms. She moaned, like one does while in a deep sleep, and looked around once or twice with empty eyes. "Where have you come from?" I asked in a last-ditch effort to try and ignite some mutual communication. "Where have you come from?"

Moving aside the golden tresses of sopping hair that blocked her from seeing, she looked up and whispered in my ear the only words she would ever say to me: "I descended with the rain."

Thunder crackled overhead, and I looked down in amazement as her now-liquefied body seemed to seep through my fingers and pool in a sort of widespread mere on the grass beneath my feet. Before I could contain what so little was left of her being, she was gone. In a puddle of lifeless water I sat motionless with an unfilled dress strewn across my lap, a sleeping infant curled in my arms, gleaming and undisturbed, my palms shaking, breathless because of the cold. Overhead the clouds parted and gave light to the moon. I stared up at it with a sense of magnificent deception quarrelling within me: the surge of a hundred thousand thoughts indolently pervading through my tormented mind.

Some-Body

There is life with a drive that cannot be contained.
Given control of an entire planet we reigned,
And through our history most knowledge is gained.
You will never be more juvenescent than you are right now.
You will never be less intelligent than you were yesterday.
With the youth of our planet all reaching for the stars,
Most with ambitions much more significant than ours,
I'll tally up the things that make me the person
That I am at the end of each day.
You hate the way I feel.
I feel the hate you weigh.
I'll use this moment in time to write this line
Because I know that it won't be permanent
If it's only saved inside my mind.
I know some people who are just way too into being people.
I know some things that no one will ever get to know.
I can find out all there is to find out about!—
But where will it get me?
I retain nothing, now my mind is a drought.
Insulting me, consulting me,
Like helpless fish on a reel.
No matter how hard I try,
I know you hate the way I feel.

Nerves

I spent all last week inside my head,
If it wasn't for me then I'd be dead.
My nerves, my nerves, the herbs…
I'm a wreck. Shaking and twitching and stuttering,
No control, total control.
Every time I drive my car down a lonely road
Free Bird is playing like a scene in a fucking movie. Groovy.
Observing is what I do best;
Description is not my strong point,
But observation is true preservation.
No immunity without community.
I'm a ticket seller, sitting here in a booth all day.
Stuck like a tooth in a cob of corn,
Your first loose tooth, your fight to be born.
How did I win that fight?
It must have been luck. Damn luck.
I'm no fighter; I'm more of an oyster.
I can't describe it, you'll just have to observe.
Take some time, pinch a nerve.
Paint my skin your favorite colors.
On a day like today who could ask for anything more
Than the fog on the glass
And the heat in the air

That wraps itself around everything and everyone...
Holding it close.
I think I've had enough.
Turn on a fan and shoot the scene into the future,
It's no better.
Finger nails and floor boards,
Florescent lighting and mercury-soaked bed sheets,
Everything she finds, everyone she meets.
Cold isolation followed by a knock at the door,
The fear of what's to come
And the fear of what has come before.

In my Mind

In my Mind
Fathoming is different from understanding. I understand
Understanding is different from knowing. I know
Knowing is different from learning. I've learned
Learning is a lot like living.
Living is an occupation of trying to fathom
What we cannot know.
I've learned that
I think.

—Written by JP Murphy

The Little Shaman

Last night I slept in a drawer stuffed with old handkerchiefs and scattered silverware. The night before that I slept with a cup in the cupboard. But it is here, tonight, sleeping with the fleas on the neck of a dog, that I have been most comfortable, and most able to rest. And while awaiting the onset of consciousness-no-more, I fill my mind with the thoughts of things I'd like to dream, passionate fantasies enough to last me through the night.

O my heart!

O my desires!

Take me to the seventh heaven...

I want to go to the Holy Land and to Mecca. I want to walk the banks of Jordan and the Nile. I want to ascend the mighty steps of El Castillo, see firsthand the great pyramids of Egypt, and touch the golden sand of kings.

I want to go to Pere Lachaise and mingle with the bones of my idols; kiss the graves of Morrison and Wilde, and rest with Ernst in a forest of doves. While outside these stone walls the wars rage on, and only for a moment can I escape the truths of our day. When art is made from the loss of blood, not even Dada can save the sensitive souls from breaking their neutral ties and bearing arms with the masses.

Against all morality, religious reasoning, and false hopes of human unity—the working man will starve! The rich will cannibalize! and the poor will continue to wash the dishes of the dead and beg for scraps, until they are sent off to war and then forgotten.

But the dog rolls suddenly in its sleep, and I'm sent with my gang of fleas onto a wooden floor, next to a tail and a paw and a coiled leash. Beyond the window there is a rising sun, and with my life all but knocked right out of me, I watch the stars fade into another day.

We Can Drive

I spend my time as would a sponge,
Absorbing everything around me,
Only for it to be squeezed back out.
Earthquakes and volcanism,
The ground shakes, the victims shout.
Riding shot gun, dodging the gun shots,
Falling into sunspots, unaware as your youth rots.
We are the compost for the next generation,
Food for the ground consumed without hesitation.
I'm filled with anxiety by the time you arrive,
And caught up in the vibes that you can't deprive.
Come on baby, while we're still alive,
Let me take you on a drive.
Because soon another moment will be spent
Without even knowing where it went.
So how much more time can we spare
Trying to avoid this world like it's not really there?
Even though it lies right beneath our feet,
Whether the air is cool or you're dying in the heat,
You can't escape this world,
But you can live your life without defeat.
I'll absorb the things that I think are real.
And you can squeeze me dry like I don't feel,

But while I'm young I'll take the wheel.
We can drive around from meal to meal.
We share the one thing that time can't steal;
And it's because of you that I know my wounds will heal.
We share the one thing that time can't steal,
And we can drive.
To run from the pain or just to feel alive,
To our deaths or until our destinations we arrive.
We can drive,
Away from the world.
We can drive,
Away from the people that we hate.
We can drive,
Trying to avoid our fate.
We can drive,
I know it's not too late.

Time Deflected

Welcome to the 21ˢᵗ century.
Make yourself at home with the present day treachery.
Observe the perfidious actions of rival factions,
Arrogant nationalism and delayed reactions.
So I caught the red-eye to Madrid and I arrived in time to dine.
I ate my supper with an elegant Spanish woman,
And we were having and excellent night…
That was until she spoke of an incurable doubt.
The room began to spin and the next thing I knew I had blacked out.
Without even a moment to stop and think,
I suppose she had roofied my drink.
In a daze I felt the scrape of red gravel pressing against my cheek
As I awoke on the ground from an involuntary sleep.
And as my eyes adjusted and I came into awareness,
I suddenly realized I was no longer young.

I must have aged 100 years…
My entire life was gone, my youth had faded!
Aeschylus was the father of tragedy,
We must be related.
So what has come over me?
What happened to time?
What has happened to the 21ˢᵗ century?

Where do we draw the line?
Or has it already been drawn
And then erased and now it's gone?
And all this time deflected,
In my dreadful solitude I am neglected.
With an all-inclusive era come to pass, I awake resurrected.
The 21st century is so outdated
And all its treachery has been deflected.
How did I ever get so lucky?

Pottery

His name is Pottery, he lives in my house.
In my house there are two.
The first is Pottery, the second is a sleeping fiend.
He's the spawn of a womb,
Which is much like a kiln.
They are both as fragile as little mice,
And the first is as coarse as stone.

Yes, he is rough and rigid, but glossy just as well.
What we do not see in him we see in ourselves.
He is round and stout and comes with a lid.
He spends his days upon the shelves.

He's made of ceramic pottery and crumbles very easily—
Keep him out of the dishwasher and clumsy hands!
It is no secret: we marvel at his captivating stupidity.
It is no secret: we cast him off into the moorlands.

But today he sits on a shelf here,
Not unlike yourself, dear.
He sits and collects the dust in the air, as do you.
Yes, it would appear that you are flesh,
Though he is too—he is a protector!

He is but flesh of a different texture.
No—we still marvel at his captivating stupidity.
Keep him out of the dishwasher and clumsy hands.
He's made of ceramic pottery and crumbles very easily;
We cast him off into the moorlands.

Now there is something droning in the next room—
It is a machine!
It awakens my guts and stomach;
It awakens the cats and dogs and the sleeping fiend.
He is ill, and in response stumbles to his feet and into the hall,
But suddenly he falls right out of himself!
He's crippled now and immobile,
And he falls into the shelf.

The ceramic pottery tilts and totters,
But there is not much damage.
He's beached on the floor now,
A heap of flesh. He moans.
This paralytic is just as inanimate as he who sits above him,
The man of ceramic.

Either of them could shatter at any minute…
Oh, does it have to be so soon?
There is much to lose, even after you win it.
There is something droning in the next room.

Aunt Crisco's Egg

Aunt Crisco stared at the world with endless confusion.
Am I alive? Am I real?
What the fuck am I doing?
All questions she asked herself daily, hourly perhaps.
Alone in her kitchen dipping eggs into a
bowl of colorfully dyed water.
So many eggs, so many colors, but so little time!
There's a scavenger hunt in progress.
The kids of the town anxiously waited on the drive-
way outside her decaying home, desperately trying to
catch a glimpse of old Aunt Crisco in action.
After much deliberation, the front door of her house swings open.
Mischievous wonder fills the air.
Aunt Crisco emerges through the dilapidated doorway wearing her
Sunday best, and with a large wicker basket of eggs held at her side.
Parents nervously watch from their windows.
"Aunt Crisco is mad!" they say.
Fixed in a gaze, immovable and dazed as she tries to understand
why the fuck these kids have all congregated on her driveway.
Then suddenly she departs!
Down the street and across the tracks, the chil-
dren follow and struggle to keep pace.

Storming the gates of an abandoned factory, she hides
her eggs all around the industrial wasteland.
They're hidden by the thousands! behind leaking chemical tanks
and piles of rusting barb wire; and the kids sprint into action.
An egg hunt is on, an egg hunt to lead you to your death!
All the kids are frantically searching.
Jesus is here again!
Aunt Crisco rings the church bells in hysterical laughter.
The sound so loud it echoes throughout the town, cracking all the eggs, and bringing the day to an end.
The excitement slowly drains from the bodies of the chil
dren and sinks into the ground, leaving a trail of adventurous joy and colorful shadows down the road as the kids
walk back to their individual homes and into bed.
Aunt Crisco retires to her kitchen to get a head start on next year's
hunt; dipping and turning, flipping and dunking, it will be another
365 days before she will be seen again. With her basket of eggs and
a smile on her aging, sanity-ridden face, the Holy Spirit lives on.

The Looming Crow of My Disguise

An endless line of beggars extends from out of my head,
All waiting in line as I sell them crack under my bed.
Their shoes scuff my floor and my service brightens their day.
After all, it is my job to hold back the knife;
Life is to death what death is to life.
I have the power of the purse,
Just ask Congress, it's a curse.
And it is safe to say
That it's healthy to have at least four near death experiences
Each and every day.
Otherwise you may forget that you're alive,
And fatality might come and catch you by surprise.
One can't quite see with the sun in their eyes.
You have to learn to jump before you can dive.
Sirens stir up the night, racing around street corners,
The sound winding down all through the sleeping town…
What was once somebody's life now meets the ground.
I rest my head back and close my eyes,
Thinking of how you reveal yourself to my disguise.
I only feel safe when I am alone.
You hear my voice as a low and tired groan,
While others say I am happy and seem well-shown.
I live a couple different lives throughout the day,

Each one blends into the environment in which I lay.
As the perching owl outside my window,
All night long, holds a conversation with himself,
I become well informed, like the books upon my shelf.
Watching as the stains on the carpet begin to grow,
Eyesores looming and watching you like a crow!
The gods of man are looming and watching us like a crow.
Hanging from the streetlights, looming, and watching me was a crow.
Building nests in the vacancies of our lives,
Looming was the crow,
Watching you reveal yourself to my disguise.
Reminding me again that fatality
Can surely catch you by surprise.

The Tomato

Today is the last day of existence for countless tomatoes all around the world. This scenario to most people may seem dull and lacking in excitement, and both visually and descriptively unappealing. However, for one tomato the events of its final hours are alive with eloquent details that will paint a lasting impression on the minds of the reader.

The tomato sat still on a plate, approaching the final moments of its existence. It is a solid shade of red. One stem, half an inch high, protrudes out of its top and is curving slightly to the right. A blade is wielded and comes crashing through the air, down onto the wooden chopping block. The aggressor here is a relentless force and will never stop. Now sliced in two, we find the tomato trickling its liquids out onto the plate where it has been placed and presently resides. Dozens of moist seeds spill out from where the cut had been made, the tomato juice glistening in the light from the lamp above. The air in the room smells of ripe vegetation, though it is in fact a fruit. The smooth, clammy surface of the tomato is wet with its internal content and left there on the plate until its eventual consumption, and then it is no more. But let's not get ahead of ourselves.

Rewind time, two hours earlier. It is 9 a.m. on a Saturday. A young woman in a home somewhere in America rouses from her slumber. She rises to her feet and makes her way to a window. Staring out the glass and across the green lawn of her fenced-off backyard to where a small garden thrives, the woman spots a ruby-red tomato as ripe as can be, hanging from the plant on which it had been birthed and has lived for its entire life... until today, that is. She makes her way from the bedroom now, down the hall and out her back door. She approaches the tomato, still hanging from the blooming plant, and snips its bristly stem with a pair of gardening scissors. She holds the tomato in her palm and observes its flawlessness, feeling its smooth skin on her fingertips, and salivating at the thought of soon being able to taste the essences of acidity and sweetness that she knows is harbored within its liquescent mesh and glossy skin.

The woman walks up the stone steps of her patio, under the pergola, and into the kitchen. She takes a sharp right turn around the marble counter tops and places the tomato onto a paper towel. She walks with it to the large stainless steel sink and flips on the faucet. With warm water flowing, she proceeds to wash the tomato thoroughly. She observes the steam rising from its red flesh, shining with droplets of water yet to fall away. Finally, once her conscience tells her that the food is clean and safe to eat, she dries it off in the paper towel and leaves it there on the plate. "It is a near perfect circle, and a nearly perfect specimen of nature, if I had ever seen one," says the woman, still fantasizing about her meal to come. But for the tomato, this will be the last supper.

If fruits and vegetables could feel pain, it is at this point in its journey that the tomato should be glad that it doesn't. The woman has been standing there by the drawer for some time now, her back turned so that we can't quite tell just what she is doing. Then, ever so slowly, she turns herself around; there is a long steel knife in her hand, sharp as a razor. She makes her way towards the tomato at a hurried pace, her countenance is that of a lunatic, and her eyes and nostrils flare with perverse enjoyment. Then, suddenly, in one split second, and in the swiftest of motions, the tomato is chopped in two and the pieces fall apart and onto their backs. The two halves lie there on the plate with their insides gushing out of them like a slimy avalanche. Pinkish-red juices and pale yellow seeds spill out from their sides and are illuminated with moisture. Although bisected, the tomato had been plump and ripe, thus, when it was cut it did not squish or flatten, it held firm, and all was over in one clean slice. It is now that we get to see the tomato for one last time. The woman picks up the plate and scrapes the slices off into a wrap filled with chicken, cheese, and other vegetables of sorts. The final preparations have been made. Soon the tomato will be encased inside the tortilla and consumed by the woman. She had brought it into this world, and just as quickly she had taken it out. And yet, it is far from over. For years and years to come the woman in her garden remains, planting and picking, eating the ancestors and the offspring of the tomato consumed just moments before. She is like the Cyclops of the garden, she is like Saturn the Devourer, and she is feared. However, it is all okay, for it is but human nature, that is, to feed the hunger of one's desires. And the woman, she was now full... and she was satisfied.

Her garden continued to thrive as dozens of tomatoes still safe on their vines grew to perfection. And once they reach that pinnacle point, a woman lurking within the confines of her home will again spot from her window this masterpiece of nature that is the tomato. Desire takes control, and that fruit will be picked and consumed before the day is done. The woman cannot resist, for the pleasures that its flavors call to her are all too tempting for her to circumvent. One does not avoid desire, one chases it! And here, in this garden, the tomatoes have nowhere to run. Palatable thoughts of sweet yet faintly sour juices enhancing the savors of her diet, the flawlessness of its shape and boldness of color, are all factors that lead to this splendid fruit's eventual downfall. And for the woman, it is simply a delectable indulgence, and a divine compliment to her every meal.

Dwellings

My brain is cracking and shattering;
I can feel it crumbling apart like wet drywall,
With the faint indication that my consciousness
Is blowing away in the breeze.
I climb a tree to get a better view,
Attracted to the vibes coming off
Of the place in which our mindful awareness dwells.
Sexuality is a joke!
You all totter on the parapet of a burning building.
Crippled by my growing pains,
The hairs on my head grow one at a time,
And I'm left looking like an unfortunate cancer patient,
But without the sympathy.

Commanding Voices

Can anybody hear me?
She wonders.
Green iron statues.
She doesn't smile.
"Straight ahead!"
Commanding voices said,
Approaching the steps of an aging structure.
"They're laughing at your scars, you know."
She thinks about every person she's ever known:
Self-realization is but a thorn in my side.
Run back to your law firms and convenient stores,
Run back behind your walls and find a place to hide.
"The hole in my head doesn't hurt that bad," she said.
"Our way of life really isn't so sad."
The air around her smelled of changes:
Life-making or life-taking;
Waste Management cars are braking,
Stopping dead in the street,
Rising to their feet
And fleeing the scene,
Doors slamming behind them.
I'm just trying to get the hang of money
Before money gets the hang of me.

Starting in on an unknown future;
She walks down the steps
And past the green iron statues,
Across the courtyard
And into a cab…
"Take me home."

Once

Once, in the heart of a burgeoning city, two children—a boy, who was aphonic and slightly ill, and a girl, lively, beautiful and small—and an old, opulent man (their grandfather), lived together in the topmost rooms of a tall apartment building. Having retired many years before his time, the grandfather was well-off, for his career had been a prosperous one, but the apartment showed it not. Instead, all one saw was normalcy: half-empty tea cups sitting on desks and tables, an unexceptional antenna television, a dusty couch strewn with woven blankets, a sink full of dirty dishes below a taxidermy trout mounted to the wall above. It was quite unremarkable. The children shared a room together, as there were only two, and the other was occupied by the old man. Inside his room there was a small bed, and nothing much else. Behind his closet door however, hidden somewhat behind his hanging clothes, was a latched wooden door that opened up to ample skies, though not before obliging one to crawl up a rusty ladder and out a narrow, chimney-like tunnel.

It was in the early morning hours of a hot summer, when the grandfather awoke the children in their sleep and led them from their room and into the closet. Out the door and up the ladder they appeared, and stepped barefoot across the stone surface rooftop. Around them the city was crawling with moving lights across great spans of chrome, and beaming glares that danced off nearby high-rise windows. The sounds of morning traffic, the building's humming air ducts, and the calls of circling seagulls wrapped them in a funnel of competing noises. But then they saw laid out before them an enormous tarp. It was colorful, with triangular patterns of green, yellow, white, and red.

"Into the sky!" cried the old man, his pale mess of hair blowing sinuously around his grey face, and standing beside the children with wide eyes of great intensity, and glaring with an excited passion at the scene in front of them. For a time he had gone unnoticed, but was soon discovered by the little broods to be standing within a massive wicker basket. At its sides ran a tipi of steel frameworks, and a small, black, cylindrical apparatus was supported up top by the rods below.

The man waved for the children to follow, and they both excitedly climbed into the basket. Soon, as gentle morning sunlight and white clouds appeared in the sky, large flames and sounds of fiery propulsion erupted from the device above. Before them the large tarp expanded with hot air and rose up overhead. The children cried with delight, and wore large smiles that let their small, pearly teeth be shone. Then, as the basket began to jolt, and totter left and right, the old man held the kids by their hands and said again, "Into the sky!" With another explosion of fire, they rose up off the roof and into the air, and soon found themselves soaring high above the expansive metropolis. Yes, they rose up, out of the adulterated city, past the blimps, past the seagulls and the birds, into a hazy realm of silent clouds. And as they rose above those clouds, they came into a city all their own.

Sheboygan

So far from the world, never left my home;
Leave me for dead—without my arms or legs—
Sprawled out on barren land in Sheboygan, Wisconsin.
Every town is declared historic
For broken buildings
And aging graveyards.
But it is a land of unpretentious beauty,
Which lies vacant and unseen
During the winter so mundane.
And when the suns of summer finally do cast,
The once long dead come back to life at last,
And live amongst the living.
You'll seek not of weapons or a gun blast,
For their spirits exist now only for giving.
And then comes the change in seasons,
And with it a change in reasons.
The dead die off and are cast away,
Along with the suns of summer
That I can sense drifting farther with every day.
But they'll be back, so I'll be waiting
For that moment to come
When I finally sense
That this long, dark winter is fading.

Pursuit or Security?

I envy those who find enjoyment with the greatest of ease.
Tuberculosis is but a poet's disease,
Bringing versifiers to their knees,
As you please...
My heart echoes in my chest,
The percussive sounds of its beat
Keeps me up at night.
It drives me mad!
Am I not right?
Under a shingled roof:
A broken hoof,
And out of the race,
Another horse displaced.
Once great Roman highways
Are now cracks in the road.
To have to choose between pursuit or security,
One decision forever shaping my future.
Suture this wound,
A fate so finely tuned,
And I'm left so very unhappy.
Here's to the world's longest suicide note—
To continue milking the goat,
And once wrote, clear thy throat, dock thy boat, and go home.

Love

Love is a Rosary.
Love is having faith in things that are hard to believe.
Love is here one day and gone the next.
Love is the meaning in a secret text.
Love is a mallet and love is a lyre.
Love is a grin and love is a sneer.
Love is me and love is you.
Love is hate and love is true.
Love is pink and love is grey.
Love is night and love is day.
Love is a ring and love is a knife.
Love is death and love is life.
Love is earned and love is an heir.
Love is a cuss and love is a prayer.
Love is fuck and love is sex.
Love is the now and love is what's next...

Oh, Don't Mind Me, That's Just My Brain Speaking

I'll carve a line into my chest for every day I've ever lived
And for every bird who's left their nest.
On your wooden tables steaming, or above our head's flying
While you fry her children in a pan,
It's just more energy transferred to another man.
So would you be able to relate or school
When I confess to you that my intelligence
Makes me feel like a fool?
With that off my chest, my self-esteem cools
And returns to its normal liquid state.
Sensing everyone else's confidence begins to fuel my hate.
I am not angry though, far from it.
In fact, I seem to be utterly incapable of not remaining calm.
Is it a lack of interests or caring?
Or is it the fibers of my youth simply tearing?
It seems to me that I'll grow up and so will you,
There's nothing any of us can do!
We'll grow so old that we disremember the new;
Our minds will starve like indigenous bellies.
And as a child I was taught that all creation is Muslim—
Give alms, give alms!

Some say the Final Testament is inimitable,
But so is our depravity.
Oh, how all the prophets couldn't dispense the humor
I find stained across the face of human downfall.
And as our guts growl, we pretend we're chewing food.
We dream of eating slop, of eating whites and yokes;
We all call for help when a child chokes!
Incessantly, I try to decipher the tragedies from jokes,
But with no luck, a heavy darkness cloaks.
Oh, and I've since realized that the right side of my brain
Is more dominant than the left, how unfortunate!
He is constantly bullying my less governing half,
Belittling him and underestimating his contemplations.
It is with this behavior that I certainly do not approve.
I am left with the negative effects:
A lack of coordination, for the lack of a better explanation,
It seems my mind should take a vacation.
I am nothing but a bystander to my own mental abuse.
But my subjective well-being helps to keep me from fleeing;
A genetic depression is what I appear to be seeing.
I desperately do not want to perceive things the way they are.
I can sense a change in the prevailing winds.
Prescribe me your magical medicines
So I can deal with not being able to deal with anything.

Espionage

Everybody is mute, making me the talk of the town,
The center of attention for the blind.
What a story of success, what a mess!
I'm constantly mocked by the mockingbirds, giving me the bird flu.
On coming headlights make me feel lightheaded;
Steel Mill Bill walks the trails once treaded.
So useful it's almost useless, and I fall into obscurity.
Good old fashion nonverbal communication—
The writing is on the walls!
El tiene la cabeza de un leon.
Read the words, an unknown language.
The color of her eyes changed with the rising tides,
Washed away in the blink of an eye.
I begin to cry, drowning all the gilled creatures;
A failing grade to all the teachers, as squirming
Leaches upon leaches, suck up the blood from all the beaches.
He reaches… so close. Grab it! Grab it! Don't let go!
I've been dancing with my true love,
She's been dead for ten years.
Now I'm laughing with my new love,
But I still hear you, and I'm all ears.
Spying on the espionage; go turn my life into a collage
And hang it on the fridge!

Bury all the pictures and photo albums alive in the backyard.
There are still a few more things I need to work on
Before I can become a fully functional conformist.
Give me money, give me money,
Or give me shelter!
I've been spying on myself
And what I have found
I'd love to share with the whole world round.
But it's classified,
And the Man says that it's none of my goddamn business.

Like Shore and Tide

Oh, how strange times have come, we crash and collide,
Like day and night, like shore and tide.
A beloved fatherland is divorcing your mother tongue!
Another grandiose, elaborate plan,
In the corner of the room a wool coat hung.
Passed down from him to her to you to me,
Passed down like shells in the sea.
Admiring the thriving housing markets of the hermit crab,
Stranded on the sandbar, calling you a cab.
Alert the cowering grounds keepers,
Fearing the everyday Grim Reapers,
Awakening the heavy sleepers
And bringing solace to the grieving weepers.
Oh, how strange times have come, we crash and collide,
Like day and night, like shore and tide.
I do things without even thinking about it.
The events of my day are all involuntary.
Through the thin plaster wall I can hear the elders talk:
"When did your son first begin to walk?"
"MTV is fucking evil!"
"Why do kids still play with chalk?"
Watching us all with the eyes of a hawk,
I feel your retinas on my flesh.

The Mooch, the Thief, the Liar & the Manic

You whisk my life into a mesh.
You split my ends, I soon divide,
Until I take up all your room, until there's nowhere left to hide.
Oh, how strange times have come, we crash and collide,
Like day and night, like shore and tide.

Seasons

I'll use the sharpest knife to end my pointlessness,
Waste my turn then guess again.
Pick the flowers from the garden,
Can't wait until fall to be condemned.

Wrap me up in the words of strangers;
Lapsing nights can never be divided.
Swaying signs, and flags, and crooked branches display
Phantasmagoric scenes of momentary life ignited.

We ask for compassion,
To be kept warm in the winter, and to see the persistence,
As the royal hands reach out for assistance—and think,
What price must I pay for my own existence?

Then the seasons skip a beat.

Even if my life is on string, he says,
I can't hang for everything!
And with little children clawing at his coattails,
He passes through the mob, the festering horde of bodies,
And into the cathedral, where a man with faith
Shall lend a confidential ear.

The Mooch, the Thief, the Liar & the Manic

No harm will come from expelling guilt in a house of God, they say.
No flame shall be felt, no heads shall nod
In shock or dismay.
For he who confesses and sees his unfortunate fate,
His soft-spoken voice and errant slate,
Shall not be cast away!

So latch me down with the news of the world,
On every channel we'll watch it unravel.
Another season that we travel,
I watch the grass give way to gravel.

Pebbles once came from colossal mountain peaks,
And heroes have sprung from the sides of loving mothers.
If messianic crucifixion is what it takes
To cleanse the World's soul of sin,
Then a guilty confession
Means less than nothing.

Jaw Bone

Jaw bone, resting cold and alone,
Lying on the side of the road.
Mandible of a fox or a dog,
Long since dead,
Nothing left but the teeth inside its head.
As surrounding grasses begin to coil
Through seasonal rains and cars leaking oil:
A jaw bone is lying on the side of the road.
Squeezing in between raindrops,
Swerving from side to side
And back and forth,
Slowly forgetting all that you're worth.
A smile seen around the world!—
Put clean sheets on my death bed.
I'm done with your arms race,
I'm sick of giving in and feeling out of place.
I've reached the end of my rope,
Just like a jaw bone, the symbol of lost hope.
More inspirational than a pope;
Put your future in the past
And use your muse to help you cope.
One day, all I'm going to be is a jaw bone.

The Vengeful Hour

I always knew this day was approaching:
I'm yet another fallen victim to the vengeful times out poaching.
Eyewitness to the sight of consecutive circulation:
The ventilation of our infestation
Supporting the host of the lingering ghost
That lives in the walls and wants you the most.
In the middle of my room I sit idle,
Like I've done for each and every day without a title.
Even though I know the time I waste is finite and vital,
All it seems that I can do is try to keep from being suicidal.
I hit the light switch and open the door
To let sweet engulfing night into the room.
I lay in my bed as a thin sheet drapes my body like a membrane.
I shut my eyes, awaiting slumber in its reign.
And so a dream begins…

———

I came into some money.
I came into some wealth.
It freed up all my free time,
Extending my poor health.
Biding you adieu: Francisco Pizarro, the great conqueror!

In the city of Peru, solidifying his claim and watching money grow.
Diseased Cortés: landing on the shores of Mexico.
Moctezuma slayed!
Illnesses degrade!
Another fallen victim to the triangular trade!
Yet another victim of time, it seems.
Lost and distraught in the darkening woods,
Frightened by the wolves and howlers.
Francisco Pizarro: assassinated by Almagro's followers!

———

Ah, the poaching times arrive at last!
Revealing to thee thy greed and crass,
Revitalized by loots of silver and gold
That in the end will leave you decaying and cold.
I was never dreaming at all! I have never tasted a sight so sour:
The treacherous intentions that one might flower,
In order to conquer, gain money and power.
Ah, it seems that we have reached that pinnacle hour,
Where the approaching times out poaching arrive and scour
In the drastic winds of a thunderous shower,
Hanging and hailing above your cozy bower!
The tell-tale signs of vengeful times approaching,
Coming to claim your power.
Build up the strength to cower and surrender to the vengeful hour,
Moving through the thunderous shower as you
Climb the steps of your masonic tower, retreat into your cozy bower,
And rest your bones until the new day can flower…
Fleetingly escaping the wrath of the vengeful hour!

Meet me in REM

Making out with the Meth-Mouth,
When she asks if you wanted some dome.
"Well of course you do," she says,
"So make yourself at home."
"Looking for work?"
Said the man with a smirk.
"It's about time," I say,
"Or lock me in a freezer."
I don't have that mystique to me, I suppose.
I'm not interesting to anybody.
So who will be the one to win the race?
Who's going to be the first to meet their fate?

The N.R.A. sends me automatic weapons in the mail; I stockpile them.
Let's give a gun to everyone,
It's the perfect gift for a secret Santa.
Pure plutonium linoleum,
And he'll die there on the kitchen floor.
"Take my life but leave my money!" he cries,
But the choice is not up to him.

I find myself unamused, and I leave him to his fate.
The Meth-Mouth has gone to powder her nose,
And I recline back in an easy chair.
Ah, transcendence!
Now I am content, and walking inside myself,
Taking an internal stroll
Up and over disbanded bridges
Scattered across my soul.

Yet I can hear sounds all around me:
Her coughing up a lung in the bathroom,
And the man howling for his depleting life
On the glowing kitchen floor.
Then the girl emerges, and I'm content no more.
She's crazy and she's after me, but she's completely sane,
And she's completely fucking crazy!
And she's after you, too.
She turns the corner and glares at me wildly from across the room.

Okay, so being alive is pretty droll.
And I doubt that being dead could be much better,
Except if we all really do get halos and wings, that'd be swell!
Sorry, I seem to be getting off topic.
But when were we ever on it?
You have no clue what I'm talking about.
But how could you?
It is the restrictions of consciousness,
So meet me in REM.

The Room

Death rays and pathways that lead you to ashtrays,
And hidden behind bookshelves and magazines.
A secret doorway may take you to Norway,
Or right back where you started,
Back to what you have just begun.
I'm trapped in a room with just one door,
And behind that door is a room with one door…
The very door I have just opened.
There are no windows, no vents or drains,
Just one door… and two rooms… but only one door.
So who's the second room for?
And what should I do?
I don't know how I got here,
And I don't know where to go.
I'm stuck.

100,000 Oceans

100,000 oceans fill the land with eclectic potions.
Harboring life deep within their depths,
Along with corals and currents and gleaming waves like silky repps.
Teeming with halophiles and luminescent organic consciousness,
So beautiful and simple and free;
Everything that we are and everything that we have
Once came and shall again return to the sea.
Whether they be frozen or rising or choppy or calm—
100,000 oceans resting in my palm!
A vast and almighty presence that ensures
There is no such tether cut to divide the weather,
As there is no divide between shore and tide.
I find myself so gratefully lost
Amongst 100,000 oceans in which to hide.
I've crossed the roads, I've crossed the lands,
I've sank my toes into the sands.
I know the joys of solitude;
I know its despair as well.
But all my pains, in an anodyne of waves,
Are washed away, as foaming tides begin to swell.
Amongst the breakers I find my glee,

My peace of mind, my spirit free.
All that we are and everything we can be
Once came and shall again
Return to the sea.

Photophobia

Another fucking bright light hits my face like sulfuric acid,
Emitting from sources unknown, screaming to hide my face,
So that's what I did.
The emulating lights break down my door
And furiously storm into the room.
Shouts and insults directed towards me
Are heard from all sides, but to little affect.
I know I am correct—
This is because the one who asks the questions
Is the one who can surely find the answers;
And if there's anything I have a lot of, it's questions.
To state a few:
What am I?
Where do we go when we die?
Are ancient aliens real?
How about gods?
Souls?
Willie Hughes?
What is the truth, I ask, behind the death of the People's Princess?
Atlantis?
Reality?
Spontaneous Human Combustion?
Whatever, as I was saying…

The lights start to grow angrier
And become more and more hostile.
They criticized me and my future, saying things like:
"You're too used to doing
Whatever the fuck you want,
Whenever the fuck you want;
You'll be dead in six years!"
Cheers! Here's to being young and being able to do
Whatever the fuck you want
(It's good).
But will it last?
It's not likely.
So play it safe, I suppose,
And go to college for a triple major in making money,
Boredom, and committing suicide,
Or, run and hide, give up all faith and let the lights decide.
I hope I can stay along for the ride with you,
My friends, I'm going to try.
Now, kill the power and watch the lights die.

Made in the USA
Lexington, KY
17 September 2015